Grimbolt

Grimbolt

Hugh Pendexter III

authorHOUSE®

AuthorHouse™
1663 Liberty Drive
Bloomington, IN 47403
www.authorhouse.com
Phone: 1-800-839-8640

First published by AuthorHouse   01/12/2012

ISBN: 978-1-4634-4880-6 (sc)
ISBN: 978-1-4634-4879-0 (ebk)

To my beloved grandchildren

Elizabeth Ackerman

and

Peter Ackerman

I dedicate this new adventure

CONTENTS

I—Royal Mysteries

"Damn this thing!" Queen Regent Elsa flung the royal scepter across the room. It promptly proved its value as a weapon by smashing the statue of King Humber IV and returning gracefully to her hand. It was not a decorative implement: its head was a substantial spiked ball of fallen star metal which glowed softly in the afternoon twilight. Where this spiked ball was attached to its sturdy handle a platinum collar supported three huge blue diamonds which brilliantly refracted the light from the star metal.

"Your majesty knows that the scepter will communicate only with the rightful king." Lord Septimus, the High Steward, crossed to the bell pull on the north wall of the Royal Study and signaled for a servant.

"Blast it! I am the rightful ruler until we get young Humber back."

Lord Septimus waved the footman toward the wreckage. "I fear, Milady, that we cannot repair the statue." They waited patiently while the servant hauled the fragments of plaster away.

"You know, I always thought that thing was marble." Her Majesty settled into the desk chair and slammed the scepter on the battered desk."

"After you destroyed the bronze bust of Humber I, we took the precaution of removing all the valuables from this room, lest your majesty's experiments with the scepter seriously impoverish the realm. The weapon is very effective, and it seemed extravagant to smash the original art works. It costs enough to repair the walls and replace the copies. Even those lead reproductions of the Royal Seal cost 100 gold sovereigns to replace."

"You mean, I didn't shatter the original gold one?"

"No, your Majesty. The original seal is safe in the Royal Treasury."

"So the mace will work as a magical weapon for anybody?"

"Anyone of the blood royal. The High Priest explained everything when he first placed it in your hands after the death of His Majesty. You can wield the mace as Regent, but it will only communicate with the king and his heir who are bonded to the scepter at birth."

"But King Humber worked magic with it."

"When His Majesty was born, his father, King Humber VI placed it in his infant grasp even before he presented the prince to his subjects. No one except the king and the High Priest know the words which were spoken, but at the Moment of Impressment the scepter glows with magic fire and thereafter it imparts to its rightful wielder the secret of its use. Your majesty saw the same thing happen when Crown Prince Humber was born and his father introduced him to the scepter."

"I thought it was a lot of nonsense," she snapped. "The baby was screaming for his mother and they wouldn't give him to me until they'd gone through that silly ritual with the mace and then carried him out on the cold balcony to present him to the yelling mob." She glared at Lord Septimus. "It makes me furious even now. They tortured my baby with all that flummery while I waited to comfort him."

"Nevertheless," Lord Septimus patiently stationed himself across the desk from her, "it was by that flummery that the power of the scepter was keyed to the body of the prince. In that moment of magical flaming the scepter recognized the blood royal in the babe, and Prince Humber became the second person whose touch controlled the artifact."

"And because those witches in the Pythoness' tower killed my husband and spirited the boy away, the kingdom lies defenseless."

"Oh, I should hardly say 'defenseless,' your Majesty. The royal army is still very effective." Several servants entered to clean up the remainder of the dust and debris."

"Find a suitable replacement for the statue as soon as possible," Lord Septimus commanded. "I don't suppose you have another Humber IV?"

"I'll see what I can find," the head footman replied.

"The fact remains that the scepter is the only real defense we have against the Priestesses of the Pythoness. Every time they make demands, we have to knuckle under." She stood up and paced back and forth across the costly Draecian carpet. "And nobody has found any trace of young Humber?"

"Our best Mages and trackers are working without rest, your Majesty. We cannot prove that the poison administered to your royal husband originated in the Hegemony of the Pythoness, and we have found no trace of Prince Humber. Lord Slythers has placed the entire resources of the Thieves Guild at our disposal, and they assure us that the prince is not imprisoned in the Pythoness' Tower."

"King Roger of Quatch isn't going to wait forever. So far he has permitted Princess Catherine to remain as our guest, but he has made it clear he has no patience with long engagements. If she isn't married to Prince Humber within a couple of months, he's going to cancel the alliance and marry her off to some other prince. King Roger is not a patient man."

"We are doing everything in our power to keep his Majesty placated."

"And this damned thing won't cooperate. I'm sure its magical link with the prince could help us trace him if only it would tell us." She stamped back to the desk and seized the scepter. Lord Septimus took the liberty of placing his hand upon hers to restrain her from throwing it again.

"May I suggest, your Majesty, that you spare the rest of the furniture. The servants are beginning to gossip."

She turned on him with her fingers crooked for slashing, but at the last minute dropped them before his affectionate gaze. "And the High Priest still won't try to perform the ceremony with Prince William?"

"Prince Humber, so far as we can determine, is not dead. So long as he lives, he is the only rightful King of Arragor. Not even the High Priest has power to depose him and transfer the crown to his brother."

She flounced back into her chair and glared at her High Steward. "Incidentally, what brought you snooping around my study?"

"I came to remind you that King Peter's emissary has been waiting in the Throne Room vestibule for half an hour. I presume you do not wish to alienate Zharkovia."

"Can't you take care of these people" she demanded. "You know all the slimy language of diplomacy. I have a kingdom to govern."

"The Zharkovian emissary is entitled to an audience with the Queen Regent if he requests it. If you hope to keep the good will of your neighbors in your quarrel with the Hegemony of the Pythoness, you have to be pleasant to their emissaries. Your Majesty knows this. I am not King and Prince William is too young to be taken seriously." Lord Septimus heard the threat of impatience in his voice and paused to control it."

"Oh, dear Septimus, I must be a trial to you." She smiled gently up at him. "While he was alive, Humber always took care of these things, and I could be pretty on the sidelines." She stood up and straightened her gown. "Do I look presentable?"

"Always, your Majesty." He allowed himself to relax slightly as he pulled open the door.

As they strode along the corridor toward the Throne Room, Elsa slowed her pace to a more stately tread and lifted her chin to a more authoritative attitude. By the time they reached the Bronze double doors she was able to sweep down the long aisle and up the steps to the throne. Lord Septimus readjusted her crown to keep it from drooping over her ears and signaled the page to admit the emissary.

Lord Nicholas strode up the aisle, knelt on one knee at exactly five paces from the steps to the throne for exactly five seconds, and approached with face depressed. When he spoke, his voice rang beautifully clear, but pitched two octaves above what the queen expected: When he lifted his face to address her, Queen Elsa gasped at its beardless innocense. "I regret the need to trouble your Majesty on a day when you do not customarily receive, but his Majesty King Peter has entrusted me with an urgent letter to which he requests an early reply." He handed an ornate packet to the page, who carried it up the steps to his sovereign.

"Let a chair be provided for Lord Nicholas. I shall peruse his Majesty's letter immediately."

She handed the packet to Lord Septimus, who carefully slit the seal, opened the document, and returned it to her hand.

> From: Peter, Rex Zharkovia
> To: Elsa, Regina et Regent Arragor
>
> Be it known that the Mages assigned to investigate the death our brother monarch Humber VII have reported to us that the circumstances of his demise are, indeed, suspicious in the extreme. The presence of oil of bitter almonds in the contents of his stomach and the evidence of a magical assault upon his son suggest the blackest of crimes.
>
> It is to be regretted that there seems to be no direct evidence connecting these circumstances with any particular culprit, The assumption that because Priestesses of the Pythoness were present at the time of his Majesty's demise, therefore they were responsible for it lacks physical corroboration.
>
> This letter introduces our emissary, Lord Nicholas Cantorus, of our Intelligence Service. His instructions are to assist your Majesty's officers in determining those responsible for the crime. You will find him discreet, intelligent, and incorruptible. If it is determined that the death of our

lamented brother was indeed caused by international agents, it will be necessary for Zharkovia to act swiftly in accordance with our treaty of alliance with Arragor. If, however it is determined that King Humber's murder was a domestic affair, we must refrain from interfering.

Lord Nicholas is a faithful servant who has authority to negotiate for us in this and other important matters. We request that he be treated with consideration, for he has irreplaceable talents.

Your affectionate brother in authority,
Peter, Rex Zharkovia

The queen's wrath faded as she looked down into Lord Nicholas' violet eyes framed by long jet lashes. His boyish smile was irresistible, and she smiled in return. "We are deeply disappointed that your royal master doubts our word about the murder of Kung Humber and the abduction of the Crown Prince," she began sternly, "but we shall not allow that disappointment to mar our hospitality. Lord Steward, see that King Peter's emissary is suitably quartered. We shall receive him in our study tomorrow at the fourth hour. You shall also attend us at that meeting."

Lord Septimus bowed and descended to escort Lord Nicholas from the Throne Room.

"Lord Steward!" she called after him, "attend us in our study when you have seen to Lord Nicholas' needs."

Lord Septimus bowed in reply. Queen Elsa strode from the Room, calling over her shoulder to the footmen who panted after her, "Have supper for two served in our study. We shall not dine in state tonight."

The desk received several new scars as she tapped the scepter impatiently. She knew King Peter was suspicious of everything. Perhaps that accounted for his long reign. Nevertheless she was infuriated that he questioned her account of the murder of her husband. Then she thought again of his strangely disarming emissary. He moved with the grace and precision of an expert swordsman, yet his face and voice suggested a woman in disguise.

"But he doesn't feel like a woman." she protested. "He's more like my William before his whiskers began to sprout. He has that same damned innocent grin."

The arrival of footmen with a small table and the appurtenances of supper interrupted her thoughts, and she tapped the scepter on the desk as she watched them lay places for two. Before the food arrived, Lord Septimus joined her. "The emissary is supping in his chamber, your Majesty. Everything is in order."

"Sit down. Over supper, I want you to tell me everything you know about this Lord Nicholas. He seems to have a man's body and a woman's voice."

The Steward sank into a comfortable chair at the table, and the Queen took the other. The servants brought in the raw oysters with poignant sauce and withdrew. Septimus inhaled an oyster, smiled appreciatively, and reported: "King Peter obviously takes King Humber's murder very seriously. My guess is that he is as suspicious of the Priestesses as you are. This Lord Nicholas is a great favorite of his. About five years ago the Empress Dowager of Draecia gave King Peter a castrato slave boy with a peculiarly beautiful soprano voice to serve as soloist in King Peter's court choir, which is internationally famous."

"Ah, that accounts for it. How old is Lord Nicholas?"

"Young, but well past the age when puberty usually sets in. The whole purpose of the castrato operation is to prevent the growth of the boy's voice box which normally accompanies puberty and deepens his voice. Lord Nicholas has grown into full physical maturity—with a man's powerful lungs, but with a boy's vocal instrument. The result is a childlike tone coupled with adult power and training. Those who have heard him sing report that Lord Nicholas voice is sublimely beautiful."

"So Peter is sending me a singing eunuch to check up on my story?" Elsa leaped to her feet and grabbed the scepter."

Lord Septimus stood up. "Your Majesty, will you please let me finish my report before you go racing down the corridors baying for blood? King Peter has not insulted you. This man is truly remarkable, and his Majesty has sent you a very shrewd advisor."

"Damned choir boy!" She slammed back into her chair and almost choked herself on an oyster.

"My spies report that the King called young Nicholas into his chambers to congratulate him on his singing and discovered that the young man had a mind. That first interview apparently lasted three hours, and Nicholas was assigned a private tutor. He still sang in the choir, but he was at the same time trained in etiquette, dance, swordsmanship, and literature. King Peter personally supervised his education. There were rumors that the boy had become the King's catamite, but royal mistresses continued to produce bastards.

"Two years ago the boy tracked down a thief who had made off with a one of the royal concubines' jewels. As a result he was given a place in the royal council and the title of Lord Nicholas. During the next month he was challenged three times to duels, and each time he killed his challenger with his sword. In each case he demonstrated to the King's satisfaction that the challenger was involved in treasonous plots. Since then he has enjoyed the king's favor without challenge. The interesting thing is that he still performs vocally both in public recitals and privately for the court. So you see, my dear, King Peter is taking our problem very seriously."

The footmen brought in the creamed leek soup and departed with the soiled dishes.

"And just what am I supposed to do with this deballed hero?"

"I should wait and see what he suggests in the morning," replied Lord Septimus. "It should be very interesting to see what happens when you introduce intelligence into our court."

"That slur is un-called-for."

"You're probably right, my dear, but you must admit we have some very stupid courtiers."

"Pea-brained peacocks!" she agreed, "but supporting them at court is the only way I can keep an eye on them."

The next morning Queen Elsa and Lord Septimus met in the royal study a few minutes before the fourth hour. Punctually, as the servant was turning the hour glass, a footman tapped on the study door and announced, "Lord Nicholas of Zharkovia."

He entered with an impeccable genuflexion and stood with eyes averted at precisely the correct distance from the desk.

"We do not stand on ceremony in this room," the queen announced. "Please sit down. I wish to see your face while we talk."

Septimus pushed a chair toward him, and he sat gracefully, but still at attention.

"Confound it! At ease!" she barked.

He gave her a startled fawn look, but settled back slightly and flashed his boyish grin.

"Lord Septimus insists that your arrival is not a calculated insult on the part of your master. He assures me that you are both intelligent and capable—that you are a trusted confidante of King Peter and not a mere court butterfly."

"Lord Septimus is well informed, your Majesty. I was given to his Majesty as a pet canary, but his Majesty has since promoted me to Royal Bloodhound. His Majesty is deeply concerned about the death of your royal husband and sent me because I have some skill in tracing the threads of cause and effect."

"King Peter does not accept our word that the murder of King Humber and the disappearance of the Crown Prince are the first steps in an attack upon our realm by the Priestesses of the Pythoness? We wrote him to invoke the implementation of a defensive treaty between Zharkovia and Arragor."

"His Majesty does not accept words until he finds the facts behind them. He is suspicious of the behavior of the Priestesses and sent his Bloodhound to nose out the facts."

"We are not sure we want his bloody gelding sniffing around our court."

"Nicholas stiffened on his chair and glared frozen-faced at the carpet."

"Your Majesty!" Lord Septimus leaped to his feet.

"Oh, sit down." Her eyes daggered him. "We will not be bullied."

He sat, and she looked back at Lord Nicholas. "Didn't King Peter's spies tell you the Queen-Regent has a sharp tongue?"

He raised his violet eyes to bore back into hers. "Oh yes, but they said nothing of its venom."

The silent confrontation lasted a full minute, but he never wavered. At last she settled back in her chair. "You are both right. The remark was unjustified and unkind. The Queen extends her apology."

He paused, still alert. Then he drooped his long eyelashes and eased slightly the rigidity of his back. "King Peter's Emissary accepts."

Another long pause allowed all three to begin breathing again.

"Have you a plan of action?" Lord Septimus asked.

"I should like to study the place where His Majesty fell. Then I should question everybody who was near at the time. After that I will need her Majesty's permission to 'sniff around.' I have a good nose and a logical mind. Mysteries often yield to that combination."

The Queen shrugged. "I suppose it has to be, though I dislike opening my court to a foreign spy. I need Peter's help if I'm going to keep the Pythoness out." She gestured dismissal. "Take him where he needs to go."

She sighed as the old man and the young emissary left the room.

"Is she always this prickly?" Nicholas asked as they paced the long carpeted corridor.

"The last two years have been difficult. King Humber was a conventional monarch, and his Queen had the scepter thrust n her hands with no warning."

"May I examine the place where the murder took place?"

"Certainly. Her Majesty has authorized full run of the palace and grounds."

The boy looked sharply at the Lord Steward. "You take my bloodhound metaphor quite literally." he observed.

"Would you prefer the phrase 'free flight'?"

Lord Nicholas stopped and glared at Lord Septimus. "Am I never to be taken seriously?"

"Seriously enough for me to jest with you."

"You hope I have a sense of humor to match my wits?"

"Precisely, my Lord. Without humor this court can be unbearable." Septimus led the way through a heavy door into the garden. "A jest can restrain her Majesty from violence." They walked to a deserted summer house, heavily overgrown with vines. "Her Majesty never uses this bower now." He pushed a tangle aside to allow Lord Nicholas to enter. "The place has hardly been touched since the tragedy."

"It happened out here?"

"Yes. Their majesties were entertaining a Priestess from the Tower and the Ambassador from Quatch. Lord Harper the Seneschal, General Plotz, and Lady Madelain Harper, her Majesty's senior Lady in Waiting were also present."

"You were not?"

"I was busy belaboring the palace staff to avoid a blunder in protocol. The Lord Steward's position is not a sinecure."

"And the Crown Prince?"

"His Highness, I am told, arrived just after the footmen who brought the tea and pastries. He had found a number of ripe peaches in the orchard and rushed in to present them to his parents. His Majesty did not normally trust Prince Humber to behave with decorum on state occasions, so that the prince was not included in the conference. Nevertheless the prince was so delighted at his find that he rushed in unannounced."

Nicholas looked at the furniture scattered around the floor. "Am I right in assuming nobody bothered to straighten the place after the murder?"

"There was no time for neatness on that day, and after the crown Prince's disappearance, her Majesty forbade anyone to enter this place again. Of course, it has been visited by investigating Mages and by representatives of the Thieves Guild, looking for information, but as you see, no servants have set it in order." Septimus wearily righted a chair and sat on it.

Nicholas darted about examining the upset chairs and tables. He sniffed at fragments of broken china and at the moldy peach pits.

"Interesting." He righted a chair and sat facing Septimus. Even after two years, a scent of bitter almonds lingers around the rotted peaches. Of course there is a trace of oil of bitter almonds in peach pits, but this intensity is unnatural. I wonder whether the aroma of a peach could have masked the smell Furthermore there is no lingering odor about the broken cups." He bounced to his feet and examined again the wreckage around the most ornate of the fallen chairs. "I assume this was his Majesty's seat."

Septimus nodded. "You think the poison was in the peaches rather than in the tea or the pastries? Everyone assumes it would be easier to hide in a pastry."

"I must question the seneschal and his lady, as well as the general. I need to know exactly who did what and in what order."

"That won't be easy. General Plotz was slain last year in an engagement with the wild Pigborn, and Lord and Lady Harper have retired to the warmth of their Draecian estate. I fear you will have to disturb her Majesty if you need a first hand account."

"That should be entertaining." Lord Nicolas shuddered. "How soon after his father's death did the Crown Prince disappear?"

"It was only a few days—two, I think. His Highness was convinced that he knew who poisoned his father. He told me he was going to defy his mother's order to stay out of the bower because he thought he could find something that would prove that the Priestess of the Pythoness was the one who did it. The prince was almost hysterical over his father's death."

"Was anything belonging to the prince discovered in the bower after he disappeared?"

"Nothing was reported. Of course, when the Thieve's Guild inspected the place, anything valuable would have gone with them."

"One of my gifts is sensitivity to psychic memories of inanimate things. I'm going to try to feel whether the decayed peach that remains here by the royal chair might still have some emotional echoes of the King's death. If he had it in his hand when he died, echoes of his agony might still haunt the remnant." He sank down beside the royal chair and placed his nose close to the fallen peach pits and his hands upon the chair. After a long pause he looked up sharply. "Did someone try magically to bring the King back after he was poisoned?"

"I think not. Nobody mentioned magic in connection with the King's death. I'm sure her Majesty would have mentioned any such attempt."

Nicholas straightened up. "I can assure her Majesty that King Humber's death agony is associated with the peach. I would guess that he was eating it when he died and that it killed him. The memory of his death still lingers in the fruit and in the wood of the chair. But there is also a very strong scent of necromancy clinging to the chair. Some one cast a very powerful necromantic spell here within the last five years. There is also on the chair a very intense memory of emotional distress besides the death agony. I would surmise that the Crown Prince was investigating his father's chair when he suffered a violent necromantic attack."

"You think one of the Priestesses caught the Prince out here and killed him?"

"That distress is not a death agony. I do not believe the Prince was killed here, but something else happened which led to his disappearance. They may have killed him subsequently, but not here."

"Her Majesty and I have concluded, from the peculiar behavior of the royal scepter," said Lord Septimus, "that Prince Humber is still alive, and the scepter is still tuned to his blood."

Lord Nicholas continued prowling around the bower sniffing and feeling. At last he sank back into a chair and sighed. "Someone suffered the aging effect of casting a powerful necromantic spell in that dense clump of rhododendrons on the far side of the summer house. Even the plants were aged by the intensity of the spell. I fear I must trouble her majesty with a report and with some rather intrusive questions." He looked appealingly at the Steward. "Would it be asking too much to request that you accompany me when I face her. You seem to have a calming effect on her temper."

"Her Majesty will be so glad to learn something specific that she will probably embrace you," laughed Septimus. "Of course I shall be there if you need help."

"Who's there?" demanded a voice.

"Septimus, Lord Steward of the realm."

"Come out and be recognized."

Lord Septimus extricated himself from the tangle of vines and emerged on the lawn. "Ah Crabhook, what brings you to this deserted end of the garden?"

"We heard that a foreign spy was snooping around the old summer house." Lord Crabhook and the two soldiers accompanying him saluted the Steward.

"As a matter of fact, her Majesty sent me with Lord Nicholas, Emissary of King Peter."

Crabhook drew his long sword and dagger. "We heard her Majesty had been duped into allowing . . ."

"Her Majesty authorized an investigation. Who is this 'We' who presume to call her Majesty a dupe?" Septimus stiffened his back and glared down the blades."

"A number of her Majesty's loyal subjects have agreed to protect her from foreign influences. I am here to confront this so-called emissary."

Nicholas—with rapier at salute—slipped easily out on the lawn. "Then by all means confront him." His bell-like soprano rang ominously. "I, Lord Nicholas, servant of his Majesty, King Peter of Zharkovia, Emissary to Queen-Regent Elsa of Arragor, salute you."

Crabhook took a step backward. "You are guilty of defiling the forbidden shrine of the death of King Humber VII."

"Nonsense!" sputtered Lord Septimus. "The queen forbid admission to the summer house in order to preserve any evidence which might lead us to his Majesty's murderer. Lord Nicholas is pursuing a remarkably successful royal investigation."

"King Peter's eunuch catamite has defiled the place of King Humber's demise."

Nicholas swept past Lord Septimus and pressed his rapier point against Crabhook's throat. "Retract the foul insult you have uttered against his sacred Majesty."

Crabhook retreated three steps, but the unwavering point still pressed. "Retract or die." The voice was now a deep contralto chest tone, yet it retained its pure clarity.

Crabhook batted the rapier aside with his long sword while his dagger thrust toward Lord Nicholas' breast. With three swift thrusts his rapier punctuated the Zharkovian's challenge: one slashed open Crabhook's codpiece, one rendered his sword arm inoperative, and one drew a blossom of blood from his throat. The voice leaped an octave at each word, "Retract or die."

Struggling to clutch his testicles and his throat with his left hand, Crabhook dropped his weapons and croaked, "I retract," as he curled up on the grass. The soldiers rushed to his side.

Lord Nicholas turned to Lord Septimus and gently suggested, "I believe her Majesty expects a report."

Septimus nodded, then turned to Crabhook. "I'd suggest you see a surgeon about that arm." They walked slowly back toward the palace. "There's no danger of his bleeding to death, is there?"

Nicholas shrugged. "I didn't stab very deep except his arm. He should be able to walk back to the palace once he gets over the fright."

II—Recruits

The Barque *Alicia* proudly rode the incoming tide, smartly lowered her sails, and dropped anchor within inches of her assigned spot in Quatchport harbor. The Harbor Master's skiff pulled alongside and the Port Inspector scrambled up the boarding ladder to check the cargo. Alsenius, Grimbolt, and Njal made arrangements for delivery of their chests to the King's Arms Inn and dropped into the skiff for transport to the pier. Njal and Alsenius sat near the stern with their cloaks wrapped close about them against the autumn chill, but Grimbolt, crouching in the bow flaunted his furry pelt.

"Southerners I see," remarked the Inspector to the cloaked pair. "It must seem a mite chill to you."

"I haven't been warm for a month," Alsenius growled.

"I hail from Frostport on the east coast," said Njal. "We have it cold, too. Do you have trouble keeping the port open all winter?"

"Nah! There's a warm current that washes along the coast and keeps the ice out, but it brings heavy fogs in the winter. Sometimes ships have to wait for days before they can see their way into the harbor, unless they have the courage to come in using the lead lines. My Coxswain has a demon's own time smelling them out for me." He looked forward at Grimbolt. "He your friend or your pet?"

"He won't take kindly to that slur," Alsenius snapped. "He's as much of a man as you, and a whole lot more dangerous as a Fighter."

"No offense intended." The Inspector coughed nervously. "But most folks don't grow their own cloaks."

Grimbolt shook the spray from his fur and turned aft. "Nothing familiar," he called past the oarsmen. "Not a ghost of a memory." He felt his rowing muscles moving in harmony with the oarsmen's stroke. "A lot easier than the *Golden Crab*."

Alsenius shuddered at the memory of his brief stint as a bargeman. He turned back to the Inspector. "Do you know of anyone who has need of a couple of swordsmen?" He patted his ornate long sword.

"If you're good enough, there's always a need in the City Watch. I don't know how the Watch Captain would take to your hairy friend, but it takes a lot of men to keep order in the port." He scanned Njal's delicate frame. "I don't suppose you're a mercenary, too."

"No, I'm by way of being an entertainer." The Illusionist twiddled his fingers and pulled a large gold coin out of the Inspector's helmet. "Don't try to spend it," he chuckled as it thudded in the Inspector's palm.

The Inspector bit it suspiciously and thrust it into his belt pouch. "You might find a job at one of the taverns. Can you make music?"

"Music to charm the last feather off a fan dancer." Njal gestured casually and produced a mahogany block flute. Carefully shielding it from the wind, he coaxed a serpentine melody from his instrument. Suddenly both oarsmen leaped to their feet as a hooded snake reared itself from beneath the rowing bench. The oars splashed overboard and the men were prepared to follow them when the snake's head dissolved into a crimson amaryllis bloom waving on a sturdy stem.

Laughing, Grimbolt reached to port and Alsenius to starboard to rescue the oars. "Do you think he's employable." Alsenius demanded.

The flower disappeared, and the oarsmen tentatively settled themselves and their oars in place. The Inspector reached into his pouch and pulled out a crumpled scrap f parchment upon which appeared the word "Gold." He sidled to place as much distance as possible between himself and Njal. "I wouldn't hire him if he paid me wages."

Njal sheathed his instrument and Grimbolt returned to his place in the bow. The oarsmen made record time to the pier.

"I wish you'd stop scaring people," Alsenius grumbled at Njal. "We'll have a hard enough time finding jobs for a black warrior and a hairy bastard without advertising a crazy Illusionist."

"I'll try to confine myself to song and dance," laughed Njal, "but that Inspector was so full of himself he needed a puncture."

"The trouble is, you're always finding people who need a puncture. Now behave yourself or we'll cast you loose."

"But you can never tell when you might need a good illusion at your back."

"And you can never tell when you might need a set of hairy fingers around your neck." Grimbolt growled. "We don't need to call any more attention to ourselves."

"Pax," said Njal, and conjured the illusion of a white dove hurling itself out of his cod piece.

The Inspector had given them directions to the King's Arms, and they checked with the landlord to reserve a room and make arrangements for their luggage. The landlord looked skeptically at Grimbolt's pelt and Alsenius' dark skin, but accepted their silver for lodging. The Fighters decided to visit the headquarters of the City Guard. Njal investigated the local taverns in quest of casual employment.

When they met for supper, Grimbolt and Alsenius reported no success with the City Guard. Citizens will reluctantly accept law enforcement from men who resemble themselves, but will rise in fury when a stranger tries to make them toe the line.

"Unfortunately the stupid Guard Captain is right," Alsenius complained. "With my dark hide, I'd have to knock down every citizen I caught pissing in the street."

"And the uniform would drive me mad," Grimbolt added. "I'm all right with a kilt—even a loose shirt—but those tight uniform trousers, ugh!"

"I could take you around the country as part of a traveling circus," Njal suggested. "See the Pluvian blackamoor decapitate a pig with one stroke! Wrestle the Draecian bear-man for one gold piece; win a crown of figs if you throw him!"

"Mop the floor with the Frostport Illusionist," Alsenius snapped.

"The fact is, you would be a lot less conspicuous if we advertised you as freaks," Njal insisted. "I could make up exhibits of two-headed snakes and island dancing girls. We could hire a couple of wagons and a barker and go anywhere in the northern kingdoms."

"Stuff it!" Grimbolt growled ominously.

"I'm performing at the Wanton Wench tonight, and I could probably get a lead on a couple of acts . . ."

"Stuff it!"

"We're going upriver tomorrow to High Koronal," Alsenius announced. "Once we show off our skills, we'll have no trouble signing up with the army."

"They won't trust you," Njal warned, "And army uniforms are worse than Guard uniforms."

The Fighters gnawed their roasted ribs and glared at him. Presently Njal slipped away to disguise himself for his performance. It was after midnight when he returned with a sack full of coppers and a surprising number of silver coins.

In the morning Njal quizzed Grimbolt, "This may be your native country. Do you remember anything at all?"

Grimbolt shook his head sadly. "I would swear I had never seen this city. We took a long walk yesterday afternoon, and I remember nothing."

"Oh well, it may be the wrong kingdom. You may be from Arragor or Zharkovia. You may even be from the capital here. Perhaps the glories of High Koronal may stir a twinge. But be alert. If anything twitches in the back of your mind, stop and examine it. Memory may sneak back in tiny flashes."

Grimbolt nodded despondently. "I beat my head till it aches, and I can't get back before that moment on the gangway of *Golden Crab*. I knew I had to go aboard and get a job—nothing else. I don't even think Grimbolt is my true name. I think somebody suggested it to me, but I can't remember who."

"Don't struggle with it," Njal urged. "Just let it happen. But keep alert. If this is the region of your birth, you may remember something."

"You know, I just thought of something. You notice that the people around here respond to a friendly greeting by striking the right fist against the left breast? Well, I found myself doing the same thing without thinking about it. It feels natural."

"You're probably right. It's a memory too deep in the body's reflexes to be erased. Watch for other customs." Njal eyed him closely. "You know, I think we're going to find you here. You're outrageously alien, yet you somehow belong here."

"This doesn't feel like home, but you're right, it's closer to home than Draecia." Grimbolt flung himself down on the mattress and was unconscious in a moment. Njal brooded for a while, then settled back and let himself drop asleep.

Early in the morning Alsenius routed them out and hurried them through breakfast. They decided not to commit themselves to the expense of horses until they had a dependable source of income, so they set off afoot along River Road. There was still a trace of fog over the harbor and a nip in the air as they strode along. They reached the city gates too late in the afternoon to enter the city. Even so the guards questioned them closely, suspicious of their alien appearance.

"I could create an illusion to make us less noticeable," Njal suggested as they turned back.

"Damn your illusions," Grimbolt snapped. "I realize they're your life's work, even though I can't see any of them, but they cause more problems than they solve."

"You also realize I can make a very respectable Fireball."

"Look" Alsenius stopped and looked him in the eye. "I know you're a formidable Mage and a good man in a crisis, but you don't have to show off. I can kill most of the people we meet, but I don't keep reminding them of the fact."

Njal grinned, shrugged, and offered Alsenius a small white rose.

"Damn you!" Alsenius smiled in spite of himself and fastened the bloom to his breastplate.

That night they found a room at the Wayfarer's Inn outside the walls of High Koronal. They found the fare tolerable, and Njal quickly arranged to earn his keep by singing for the patrons in the evening. This time he confined himself to playing and singing without illusions, and Grimbolt and Alsenius found themselves applauding the performance along with the other guests.

In the morning they joined the stream of merchants, farmers, and travelers who filed between the guards at the city gates. When the Fighters asked for directions to the recruiting center, the guard referred them to the Corporal, who gazed at them searchingly. "You look fit enough," he observed, "but I don't know how you'd do at Parade Maneuvers. You're both tall enough, but I don't know how the Sergeant-Major would fit you in." He signaled his messenger. "Take these men to the Sergeant-Major's office." He looked at Njal, "You're definitely too small for a soldier."

Njal curbed the temptation to stand tall in illusion and meekly said, "I'm not as helpless as I look."

"Well, good luck to you. I hope the Sergeant-Major is in a good mood."

They followed the messenger along the broad boulevard that led toward the palace complex. "You must be from far away," the messenger commented.

"Almost diagonally across the continent," said Alsenius. "I hail from distant Pluvia, where you'd be a curiosity with your pale face."

The messenger dropped his eyes and continued along the away till they came to am imposing brick building standing well back from the boulevard. He led them up a brick walkway and held one of the heavy doors for them to enter. He saluted the guard on duty and led them across the granite foyer and opened a dark wood door on the far side. "I bring candidates from the Corporal of the Guard at the River Gate," he announced to the corporal at the great desk.

The corporal dismissed the messenger with a nod and turned to Alsenius. "You wish to volunteer for his Majesty's service?"

"We are mercenaries from afar who would place our swords at the service of his Majesty. I am Alsenius of Pluvia; this is Grimbolt of Draecia, and Njal of Frostport." Grimbolt struck his fist over his heart, while Njal made a careful minimum bow.

"Can you read and write?"

"Enough to handle military information," Alsenius answered. "Grimbolt, how about you?"

"I have the skill, but my hand blurs the tablet."

Njal bit his tongue, clenched his fists and confined himself to a nod.

The corporal produced three waxed tablets and waved them toward stools at the side of the room. "When you have finished answering the questions, bring them to me." He turned to the man who had entered behind them.

"I need to talk with Captain Barrett," the man said. He waited while the corporal passed through the door behind his desk. Presently he returned and escorted the man through. Before they had completed their wax tablets the man emerged and hurried away.

Alsenius gave the tablets to the corporal, who looked them over and gestured for them to follow him through the door behind his desk. Here they found a sergeant behind a desk piled with tablets. He looked up, took their documents, and glanced over them. "A blackamoor, and bear, and a lightweight. Why can't someone bring me some soldiers?"

Alsenius performed an elaborate sword salute during which his weapon seemed to fly of its own volition. It ended with the point a half inch from the sergeant's nose.

"Oh I'm sure you can fight. I can see that without the flourishes. As a matter of fact I wouldn't challenge you for a thousand gold pieces. But what would his Majesty say if I marched you three past a reviewing stand. Soldiers are supposed to come out of a mint like coins. You're not supposed to be able to tell one from the next."

"But what good are they in battle?" Alsenius demanded.

"Who fights battles? The kings strut and shake their swords at each other; then they march their armies up and down along the borders and hold complicated maneuvers. Then their chief ministers get together and yell at each other for a couple of weeks, and we all go home."

"We're offering you a mercenary team unmatched in the area," Njal protested, "and you intend to ignore us because we won't look good in parade. You don't even plan to test us?"

The sergeant shrugged.

"Then at least take us to somebody who can evaluate our skills," Njal demanded.

The sergeant signaled a messenger, murmured in his ear for a moment—while Njal gave two twiddles—and sat back while the boy dashed off through a small door to the left of the desk.

"You told him to ask the Sergeant Major if he'd see us." Njal announced.

"So you guessed."

"You called us a mouthy midget, a fur-ball, and great brute of a nigger."

The sergeant had the grace to blush. "All right, how did you do it?"

"The same way I can hear your messenger telling the Sergeant-Major's guard that you have three odd fish you don't dare throw back."

"That little bastard!" The sergeant leaped to his feet, then suddenly sat down again. "I'll have him peeling onions for a week. 'Don't dare throw back!' I'll . . ."

"You leave that boy alone or I'll make you kiss my arse." Njal started twiddling again.

"Stop it!" Alsenius commanded. "We came here for a job, not a fight. If you cast that Charm spell, I'll break your neck"

"You'll have to reach it first." Njal scuttled suddenly on the other side of Grimbolt, who began to guffaw. When he recovered his breath, he warned, "This really isn't the time for jokes."

"Why not?" demanded Njal, "this whole army is a joke. They're so crotch-bound in their uniforms, they couldn't fight a battle if they fell into it."

The sergeant watched them with mouth agape. "You are talking abut the mightiest army in the Great Northwest."

"Well so far I haven't seen any three of you that I couldn't tie up with my bare hands." Grimbolt grabbed a poker from the fire place in his hairy

20

hands, bent it into an overhand knot, and tossed it with a clang on the desk. "Njal's right. You have neither the strength nor the brains of a flock of chickens."

The sergeant was still staring at the poker when the messenger came back to say that his excellency the Sergeant Major would see the recruits in half an hour.

Njal sniggered suggestively and gestured.

"We have to wait while he finishes with his whore." snarled Alsenius, whose patience had become frayed. "Tell his excellency that we are coming now."

The messenger dashed off.

Grimbolt turned back to the sergeant. "You really need to learn the difference between a mercenary and a recruit." He marched after the messenger, followed by Alsenius and Njal, who left an explosive stench behind him as he slammed the door.

They followed the messenger into the guard room. The guard stood to challenge them, but Alsenius brushed him aside, knocked peremptorily in the bronze door, and flung it open. The Sergeant-Major, who was in fact engaged with a woman, sprang to his feet and adjusted his clothes behind his massive desk. "Who in the seven hells let you in?" he demanded as the woman scrambled out a small door in the back of the office.

"Alsenius of Pluvia, Fighter 13th level."

"Grimbolt of Draecia, Warrior par excellence."

"Njal of Frostport, Mage extraordinary. We have come to demonstrate our prowess that we may serve his Majesty as mercenaries supreme." He set off a small tangle of sparklers in the air over the Sergeant-Major's desk.

The Sergeant-major finished fastening his attire: "I set you an appointment for thirty minutes hence."

"We regret that we do not have thirty minutes to waste in your anteroom." Grimbolt slammed his fist against his breast, thus forcing the officer to respond.

"If you will provide your most skillful swordsman, I will endeavor not to kill him in my demonstration of skill." Alsenius went through his sword salute to which the Sergeant-Major responded in kind.

"You are an impertinent dog, but an apparent master. I will accept your challenge. Since I am not wearing my armor, I suggest you take off yours so that we may duel in our shirts for first blood."

"Agreed." Grimbolt and Njal helped him to unlace his armor. "If you will lend me a weapon, I will lay aside the advantage of my magical sword."

The Sergeant-Major slammed the gong behind his desk and commanded his guard: "Two rapiers on the double, and bring Captain Blyte and Lieutenant Cameron as witnesses."

Both witnesses and rapiers appeared quickly. The two stripped to their shirts and kilts, saluted and began cautiously jabbing and parrying. It was immediately clear that both were master swordsmen. The Sergeant-Major was burlier, but Alsenius' supple muscles gave him a slight edge on dexterity. The dark Fighter gave ground at first, feeling out the rapier, which was a much lighter weapon than his long sword, and testing his opponent's skill. Then, as the wall began to crowd him, he pressed his attack, slashing and thrusting rapidly. When he cut the Sergeant-Major's shirt, Captain Blyte barked, "Pause!"

Both men snapped to attention while the captain examined the Sergeant-Major's chest. "This match is for first blood?"

Both me nodded.

"No blood visible. Match to continue."

"Perhaps we should shed our shirts," Alsenius suggested.

Both men stripped off their shirts and returned to the bout. After ten minutes of furious swordplay, the captain again called, "Pause!"

They halted and looked to him. "It is time for a breather."

Alsenius protested, "On the battle field the man with the stronger wind wins." It was obvious that he was breathing easily, while his opponent had begun to puff."

"But we are gentlemen at a match." Meanwhile the Lieutenant Cameron massaged the Sergeant-Major with a towel and produced a flask of water with two tumblers. "We do normally break every ten minutes."

"You might at least give me a towel," growled Grimbolt. "Alsenius has a right to a rub-down too."

A towel appeared, and both men sipped sparingly.

Through the second round Alsenius forced the officer to pursue him, intending to take advantage of his greater endurance. Both men now realized how evenly matched they were, so that their motion became increasingly dancelike. There was no evidence that the Sergeant-Major was hampered by his slight shortness of breath, but Alsenius still looked ready to battle all day. The third and fourth rounds were an increasingly intricate play of mind and blade as the contestants employed ever more complex patterns of motion, striving to out-think each other. The witnesses watched with awe as the duel continued.

During the next break, the floor had become slippery so that they pulled off their boots after the witnesses had removed as much of the sweat as they could with towels. "Perhaps the gentlemen would prefer to consider the match a draw?" Captain Blyte suggested, but by then both men lusted for triumph.

In the fifth round both men began to try more risky ploys. Twice the Captain had to call a pause to determine whether an apparent touch had drawn blood. Suddenly Alsenius backed up a step and slashed with a stroke which the weight of a long sword would have made irresistible. The comparatively light rapier could not drive through the Sergeant-Major's parry, and the officer's blade slid along Alsenius' to nick him slightly in the shoulder."

"First Blood!" declared the captain.

Both men stopped, came to attention, and saluted. "Bravo!" cried the Sergeant-Major. "I have never faced such a swordsman—not even my mentor."

"You are no slouch yourself," Alsenius replied.

The officer grabbed a towel and turned to the captain. "You realize this man normally fights with a heavy long sword." He gestured toward Alsenius' jeweled blade. "The rapiers gave me an edge. I couldn't have beat him with a heavier sword." He grasped Alsenius' forearm, then smote his own chest with his right fist.

"Does that mean we can negotiate a place for us in the army?"

"It means we talk with the general, and perhaps his Majesty. There is still no place in our regular battalions for a man with your complection or for a hairy brute like your companion, but we cannot afford to let anybody else snap you up. Is the hairy one as good as you with the sword?"

"I prefer to take a man hand to hand or with a staff." Grimbolt grounded his staff. "If I have to use a sword, I want one I can't break."

The Sergeant-Major grunted. "I don't know anybody who would want to wrestle with you. Perhaps we can take your strength on faith." Then he turned to Njal. "I can't see what possible good you can be, though my corporal tells me you have a mean tongue."

"I'll take on the four of you at once, and not one of you can lay a finger on me before I slit all your throats." Njal pulled out his block flute and made an obscene gesture with it.

"Surely you jest," Lieutenant Cameron sniggered.

"You, the captain, the giggling lieutenant, and your guardsman! Put on your armor, draw your swords, and drop dead."

"I'm afraid he's deadly serious," said Grimbolt. "He'll make you look silly."

The Sergeant-Major pulled on his shirt and prepared to resume his uniform. "He's no match for that girl I was enjoying when you so rudely interrupted me. Shall I give her a dagger to chase him?"

Njal stamped his feet in frustration and suddenly appeared to be seven feet tall and muscled to match his stature. Then he pointed his little finger at the lieutenant's cod-piece so that it burst into flame. "Surely I jest," his giant voice boomed. "Kiss . . ."

Grimbolt grabbed him and interrupted his next spell. "That's enough! Settle down!"

Njal dwindled to size and gestured a stream of water to extinguish the lieutenant's flames. "I like to make jokes because it's fun, but you'd better take me seriously. I repeat my challenge. Set four of your best men on me with swords and armor, and they won't be able to touch me."

"Excuse me, sir." Lieutenant Cameron saluted with his right fist while covering himself with his left.

"Excused!"

"Move out there on the parade ground," Njal demanded, "and give me my trial."

"You ask what use he is," Alsenius urged. "Why not give him a test."

"All right. But don't complain to me if he gets hurt."

Half an hour later four fully armed soldiers stood at one end of the parade ground with Njal at the other. The Sergeant-Major had ordered everybody away from the area except himself, Captain Blyte, Alsenius, and Grimbolt. When I lower my sword, you are to charge," the Sergeant-Major commanded.

"The four of us charge him?" One of the men protested.

"You are to charge and knock him down. The one who drops him gets promoted to corporal. The rest will peel onions for a week. Do you understand?"

"Yessir!"

He raised his sword, then swiftly brought it down. Before the men ad reached the midpoint of the field, Njal had become a line of eight Illusionists grimly waving their fingers. The men hesitated, bewildered, then resumed the charge. Suddenly two of them froze in mid stride as Njal's **HOLD** spell took effect. The other two continued charging until they could swing. The eight Njals leaped aside, avoiding the blades, and the dashing soldiers rushed by. By the time they had turned around, Njal had produced the illusion of a huge foaming wolf between his selves and the attackers. While the two men were fighting off the wolf, Njal mimed the slitting of the throats of the held soldiers, adding gruesome illusory details. By the time the men had overcome the wolf they were both bleeding and terrified. While they slaughtered two of the multiples, only to have them pop out of existence, Njal created a complex shadow image of an enormous ogre with huge clubs in both hands.

The terrified men turned to flee, only to be confronted with a wall of fire. One of them dived through the wall and dropped unconscious on the far side, while the other simply dropped his sword and collapsed into fetal position on the ground. The illusions vanished, and Njal mimed the slitting of two more throats.

The Sergeant-Major looked in horror at the bodies of his four soldiers.

"Don't worry," Alsenius consoled him. "It's all illusion. The damage isn't real. They just got so scared they dropped unconscious."

Njal waved a hand, and the damage vanished. "The two I **HELD** will have to stand there till the spell wears off," he explained. "Of course I could have thrown a real **FIREBALL** and incinerated all four of them, but that wouldn't have been kind. The real **FIREBALL** would have prepared anyone who saw it to believe in illusions. Then my illusions would have made dozens more drop because they would think they were burnt. I could have defeated a whole platoon."

"My men aren't dead?"

"Oh no, this was just a test for me."

"I give up. You're more dangerous even than the Fighters. I will put you up in an officers' barracks, where you will find the quarters quite comfortable. You will sup with me at the senior officers mess, and I will arrange for you to meet the General. I believe his Majesty has been looking for someone to undertake a secret mission abroad, and you may be just the men to undertake it. Please consider yourselves on the payroll. I don't want you wandering around where somebody else might snap you up."

"But you haven't tested me," Grimbolt protested.

"I would not like to risk that hairy embrace, and I'll not order any man to face a challenge I won't accept myself." The Sergeant-Major marched off the field, leaving Captain Blyte to escort the three to a messenger, who led them to a spacious suite upstairs in the main building.

"Can you have our luggage fetched from the Wayfarers Inn? The Sergeant-Major seems to want to keep us under his eye until we've signed a contract."

"Yessir!"

Alsenius handed him a handful of silver. "You'll have to pay the reckoning out of these."

"Sir, I can't accept money . . ."

"It's not a tip, it's money for expenses."

The boy looked suspiciously at the coins in his hand.

"Look, boy," said Grimbolt, "you'll need to pay our bill at the inn to get our luggage. Whatever is left, you may use to pay for your food on the way back or to pay a porter—whatever you judge to be necessary."

"Anything?"

Alsenius nodded. "Anything you decide is necessary."

He gave a snappy fist salute, turned smartly on his heel, and marched out.

"You are corrupting the King's army," Njal accused.

"It's high time he learned about bending regulations."

They spent the rest of the afternoon exploring the complex, watching parade maneuvers and prowling any open rooms along the corridors. Everywhere they saw evidence of the over-regulated inefficiency typical of military operations everywhere. "If it's not spelled out in the handbook, it can't be done," Njal summarized as they returned to their quarters to change into their best kilts and shirts.

Promptly at beginning of first watch, the messenger appeared in full dress to escort them to the Sergeant-Major's quarters. Soldiers, who had never handled a weapon more dangerous than a table knife, served deftly at table under the supervision of a corporal, whose elegance should have graced a castle.

"I have arranged an interview with General Blyte," the Sergeant-Major informed them over the soup course. "There is a mission which requires the utmost discretion and delicacy, which seems beyond the skill of our military officers. I believe you might qualify, if you can convince the general that you are as discreet as you are powerful."

"You mean the general has to be handled with padded gloves?" asked Njal.

"He is very conscious of his rank."

"And would resent a saucy Illusionist," Alsenius put in.

"Or a challenging subordinate," the Sergeant-Major added.

"But we are not subordinates until he hires us," Grimbolt protested.

"A distinction the general will not accept. If you want employment, you will treat the general with the deference you would offer a Guardian. He will require respect and"—He glared at Njal—"he will neither recognize nor tolerate humor."

"I will practice up on my groveling," Njal grinned.

"And just what is this mission which demands more them military prowess?" demanded Grimbolt.

"It involves protecting a member of the royal family without appearing to be there at all. I cannot tell you more, but the dangers are very real and the diplomatic tangles are very complex and fragile."

"And your general admits he lacks the skill to deal with it?" asked Alsenius.

"His Majesty has made clear his doubts of the general's intelligence."

"Which makes the general even more touchy?" Njal added.

"You don't happen to have a nice open battle that requires expert mercenaries instead?" asked Alsenius. "We are a lot better at fighting than groveling."

"Your little friend's skill at magic makes you ideal for this job. You have a very good balance of military skill, close-in fighting, and concealment. If you can avoid offending the general, you will serve his Majesty's purposes very well. I have arranged for an interview with General Blyte promptly at the fourth hour tomorrow."

"Incidentally, is your captain related to the general?"

"Younger son. The general wants to keep him out of the field. He's his mother's favorite, and the general has sensitive ears."

"And how does the captain take to his mother's protection?" asked Grimbolt.

"Fury. He wastes more time applying for dangerous missions than most men do bucking for promotions. He keeps the general in a constant temper."

For their appointment with General Blyte Njal decided to wear his Invisibility ring and watch the ante-room unseen. Alsenius approved of the idea because it would require the Illusionist to keep quiet.

"You don't really think he's going to stay out of mischief, do you?" Grimbolt protested.

"No, but he's certain to make the General angry if he comes with us."

When the Fighters joined the Sergeant-Major at his office, he asked, "What happened to your magical friend?"

"We thought perhaps the General might not enjoy his comments," said Alsenius.

"He is a bit free-spoken." the officer agreed. "I can vouch for his effectiveness as a Mage without having him demonstrate." They marched across the parade ground to a smaller brick building set in a fenced garden. As they walked up the path, he added, "It might be as well for you to let the General do most of the talking. You can answer questions, but he enjoys his own voice."

The guard at the door asked for their names and led them across a broad reception room to an ornate mahogany door bearing a crest of crossed swords. He tapped twice with the handle of his sword, paused for the count of eight, and stepped inside: "The Sergeant-Major of his Majesty's ceremonial forces; Fighter, 13th level Alsenius; Fighter 10th level Grimbolt." He smote his breast with his sword fist, bowed 45°, and allowed the three to pass before him. He was making his ceremonial exit when he stumbled against the invisible Njal, recovered, and stared for a moment at empty space before he carefully stalked out and closed the door.

The General's office was a large oak-paneled square room with a polished parquet floor. A broad strip of crimson carpet led to the center of the room and divided, leading to two oak doors which flanked the General's massive desk. The Sergeant-Major marched to the parting of the carpet, saluted with his fist, and bowed 45°. Alsenius and Grimbolt flanked him—one step behind—and copied his salute. The General, from a low dias, looked over the desk and gestured to three small chairs placed geometrically at floor level before the desk. The three marched smartly to the chairs and sat at attention.

"We have received your communication about the mercenaries, two of whom you have brought with you. We approve your judgment in leaving the non-military agent in quarters. Your report indicates that you have examined these three and find them qualified for the rescue mission."

"I have personally matched rapiers with the Fighter Alsenius and find him very well qualified. I matched the Mage against four competent Fighters, and he defeated them without suffering a hit. The Fighter

Grimbolt uses methods unsuited for military personnel; therefore I have accepted Alsenius' evaluation of his prowess."

The General stared at Grimbolt. "What unconventional methods do you employ?"

"I am competent with a two-handed sword, but my weapons of choice are the staff and my bare hands."

"We have no one who can examine him in staff and wrestling? None of the peasant footmen?"

"Order number 5,278 of the Manual of Procedure specifies that members of his Majesty's army shall be proficient in long sword, short sword, bastard sword, dagger, pike, and halberd. Members of the auxiliary shall be proficient in pike, long bow, short, bow, cross bow, and such siege weapons a catapult and arquebus, as well as the normal mechanisms of siege warfare. There is no provision for the claymore, which is unsuited for close order marching, nor for staff or bare hands, which are suitable only for brawling. His Majesty's soldiers are forbidden to brawl."

"Yet you recommend employing this Fighter in spite of his limitations?"

"I recommend both him and the Mage because they are singularly equipped to deal with the unconventional problems which challenge the mission."

At this point the door facing the desk swung violently suddenly open, revealing a little dark figure kneeling with a listening device to his ear.

The General stood and roared, "Marston!"

The little one scuttled away and disappeared. The guard presently appeared, saluted, and bowed.

"Marston, approach!"

The guard marched to the divide in the carpet, saluted, bowed and saluted again.

"Marston, who was that man listening at the door?"

"Man, sir?"

"Man! Why were you not at the door yourself?"

"I was summoned to the side door to deal with an intruder, sir."

"How long were you absent from your post?"

"Perhaps ten minutes, sir. She was a most importunate intruder,. sir."

"Your post is to guard my door."

"Sir, I was summoned to deal with a problem beyond the authority of the outer door guard."

"What of the Corporal of the Guard?"

"Sir, she had disabled the guard and severely injured the corporal."

"She what?"

"Sir, she kicked the guard where no lady would kick, and she raked the corporal's face so that he had to retire to the infirmary."

"She disabled two of my men?"

"Yes sir. I was compelled to leave my post and knock her down. I had to find two men to guard her; then I heard you call. And I came."

"You didn't see anyone running away from the door?"

"No, sir."

"Who opened the door?"

"I do not know, sir."

"Damnation!"

"Yes, sir."

At this point a messenger appeared in the doorway. "Marston, sir, the bitch got away," he shouted. Then he said, "Oh guardians!" as he saw the General and dashed away." Marston froze, uncertain whether to continue his report or deal with the emergency. The General bellowed, "Dismissed!"

Marston fled.

The General shouted "Shut the damned door!"

Njal invisibly shut the door, leaving the General with his mouth open.

"Is there a problem with security, sir?" Grimbolt asked innocently.

General Blyte gulped. "Sergeant-Major Benbow, investigate that commotion and report."

Benbow performed a perfect about face and marched toward the door, which opened before him to reveal the confusion in the ante-room. He marched through as if nothing unusual had occurred, but hissed as he want by, "Stop that, you blaggard."

Njal invisibly shut th door before he could turn.

Benbow grabbed where he thought Njal might be, but the Illusionist suddenly appeared in a dark corner of the room. "You called?"

"Was that you listening at the door?"

"You saw through my disguise?"

"No, but I suspect you on principle."

"Not a bad principle." Njal smiled amiably.

"You opened the damned door so the General would see you?"

"He seemed very sure of himself. I thought he might need a little uncertainty in his life."

"And I suppose you had nothing to do with the woman who produced this chaos," Benbow gestured at the soldiers running back and forth through the room while Marston swore at them.

"The woman was a carefully programmed illusion, if that's what you suspect."

"Damn! Damn! Damn!"

"Should I go in and explain?"

"Great Guardians, no! The General would have a stroke."

"Perhaps . . ."

"Perhaps you should go back to your room and read a book. Whatever you do, don't cast any more illusions. Your friends were making a very favorable impression on the General, so just leave them to complete the interview."

"But . . ."

"Just go away and keep out of mischief." The Sergeant-Major paused to return Marston's salute.

"The woman seems to have slipped out of her bonds and run away from my soldiers." Marston reported. "The corporal's face mysteriously healed before he got to the infirmary, but he and several of the men swear she scratched him like a bear. I don't know what you can tell the General. They are usually very dependable men."

"I'm sure they are, Marston. I advise you to return to your post and make sure we have no more disturbances. I will try to prevent major disciplinary action." The Sergeant-Major turned on his heel and strode back into the General's office."

"Well?!" There was a deep, ominous tremolo in the General's voice.

"Sir, I propose that we use this breech of security as a test for our candidates. Let them examine the testimony of the soldiers and explain how that man succeeded in listening at your door. If they succeed, we can recommend them to his Majesty."

"You have no explanation for this gross breech of security? No guards to be placed on report? No negligence to be punished?" His voice dropped even lower.

"Sir, I am reluctant to punish the wrong men. Good men are hard to recruit, and these men are the best we have."

General Blyte scowled at Alsenius and Grimbolt. "You will report to the Corporal of the Guard and wait until you are summoned." As soon as they had left, he turned back to Benbow. "Sergeant-Major, men under your command have failed in their duty. There should be floggings at the least. Probably bodies should hang on the parade ground as a warning."

"Sir, successful discipline must rest on justice. I cannot command the loyalty of my men if I flog a man who has done his duty. The fault may lie in a weakness of the system, not in disobedience or negligence of an individual. If a catapult misses, the fault may lie in the machine, not the operator."

"You are a part of this system."

"Sir, if you believe I am at fault, I will submit my resigna-tion forthwith. I am convinced that we face outside plotting. Ordinary military methods are not designed to cope with foreign intrigues. I suggest that we use these strangers as a special fact-finding force. If I am wrong, please replace me."

General Blyte leaned back in his chair and glared at his subordinate. "This rebellious attitude is not like you, Sergeant-Major."

"My apologies, sir. I cannot conscientiously punish men who face a problem they are untrained to meet. If your Excellency rejects the Sergeant-Major's best judgment, it would be best to appoint a new Sergeant-Major."

"You would desert me in this emergency?"

"I have submitted my best judgment as to how we should proceed. Please dismiss me and seek other judgment."

"Dammit, stop bullying me!"

"The Sergeant-Major has no authority to bully the General."

"You know damned well it's your level head that keeps this army running efficiently. I need you in charge of the men."

"Then sir, I must protect the men from unjust punishment."

"Damn you! Bring back those mercenaries and see what they have to say."

The Sergeant-Major opened the door and signaled Alsenius. "Can you find that wretched Mage? The General wants any information you can supply about this intrusion."

"We'll find him," Alsenius answered, and he and Grimbolt stepped outside. "Njal," he called.

The Illusionist removed his ring and popped into view.

32

"The General wants answers."

"And you want me to give him some?"

"Look, this mischief of yours has just about queered our chances for a job." Grimbolt snarled.

"And you want me to straighten it out." Njal grinned up at him. "All we have to do is blame it on the Pythoness." He straightened his blouse and brushed off his kilt. "Let me do the lying, and I'll trust the fighting to you." He led the way back into the building.

"My Sergeant-Major has suggested that you investigate this invasion of our privacy as a proof of your usefulness," the General grumbled.

"As I understand it," Njal stepped forward, "your men faced a female intruder at the outer door who injured two of your guards in order to draw the guards away from the door to your office. After that, a small figure was seen apparently listening at your office door."

"The door to this office was opened without authorization, and we saw a dark little man—no bigger than you are—kneeling in the doorway." The General corrected.

"Are you certain that it was a man you saw and not a woman in man's clothing?"

"I didn't feel for his balls, but he looked like a man."

"At any rate, we can assume that the woman outside and the figure by your door were confederates."

The General nodded assent.

"Now in thwarting a recent attempt to assassinate the Draecian Emperor, we incurred the displeasure of the Temple of the Pythoness. We came to this region because we suspect that your local Temple of the Pythoness is engaged in some form of skullduggery in this region, and the priestesses will undoubtedly try to keep us from consulting with the local governments. Have you heard of any mysterious deaths or disappearances within the last two or three years?"

"What about the death of King Humber of Arragor and the disappearance of the Crown Prince?" suggested the Sergeant Major.

"That was over two years ago. What can it have to do . . ."

"Ah-ha!," Njal interrupted. "That's just the sort of thing we have been investigating. The Pythoness' Priestesses had infiltrated the Draecian court—they even had operatives working in the Emperor's harem. We were instrumental in uncovering their activities there, and in the process discovered information which led us to suspect they were up to mischief in this region."

"You admit to being spies?" General Blyte reached for his dagger and looked up at his gong.

"We prefer the title of investigators," Grimbolt interposed.

"Lord Ambloq, Priest of Alfather, is leading an investigation of the Pythoness' activities continent-wide."

Njal seized the reigns of the conversation again. "He had to remain in Draecia to clean up the tangle her Priestesses had woven there, but he dispatched us to find out what is going on in the North."

"And you think the local Priestesses recognized you?" asked Benbow.

"My complexion and my friend's pelt are, unfortunately, rather conspicuous." Alsenius put in. "Even Njal is easy to recognize."

"I should say you are," the General snorted. "Whatever made you think you could fit into our army?"

"We thought you would welcome expert Fighters regardless of appearance," snapped Grimbolt. "No competent recruiter would turn Alsenius and me away."

"Which is why I brought them to you," the Sergeant-Major interrupted. "The regulations require a physical resemblance among our men, which prohibited me from signing them on. I did not want to lose such skills as these men have demonstrated. I was sure your sagacity would recognize and correct the weakness in our regulations."

His flattery took the sting out of Grimbolt's remark. Instead of striking the gong with his dagger, the General laid it back on his desk. "It is true that I perceived the danger of letting such capable Fighters move to some other service, but this intrusion reveals new hazards."

"Which hazards," the Sergeant-Major added, "these man are singularly qualified to confront."

Before the General could muster a reply, Grimbolt pressed on, "Njal's guess as to the cause of the intrusion is still only a guess. It needs confirmation. Your question ought to be, 'Are these men the best qualified to investigate the facts and to deal with what you recognize as a hazard?'"

The General cleared his throat, coughed gently into his hand and looked hopefully at his subordinate. Sergeant-Major Benbow took the hint. "Might it be appropriate to appoint the 13th level Fighter, Alsenius, to the temporary rank of Major and place him in charge of a special unit whose assignment is to deal with the possible threat of infiltration by units of the pythoness' temple? You could appoint Njal and Grimbolt as Lieutenants and the I could assign appropriate enlisted personnel to assist them."

General Blyte looked especially wise and important as he considered this advice. He cleared his throat again and tapped his dagger meditatively on the desk. "The Sergeant-Major's suggestion agrees with the solution we were contemplating." He looked directly at the Sergeant-Major. "Make it so, Sergeant-Major, even as you have outlined the action. Dismissed!" He struck the gong decisively, and the guards escorted everyone from his presence."

"Major Alsenius, will you bring your detail to my office." Sergeant-Major Benbow spoke loudly enough to be heard by everyone in the anteroom. "We must arrange for your commissions and for specific secret orders to be drafted."

As they closed the general's door behind them, Alsenius turned to Marston who was still guarding the entrance making sure everyone heard him. "Soldier, your conduct in this emergency is to be commended. I shall speak to your superior for the record." He turned smartly and followed the Sergeant-Major out of the building.

It took the rest of the day to produce official commissions for the new officers. Alsenius was also armed with a parchment authorizing him to draw whatever supplies he needed and to reassign any personnel to his project.

"I want that soldier, Marston, assigned to us," said Alsenius. "He knows his way around the army and he acts intelligently in an emergency."

"I agree," said Grimbolt, "and he should be promoted to corporal in case we need to put him in charge of other enlisted men."

"I will have him report to your quarters as soon as he has been relieved of his present duties and promoted." Benbow looked quizzically at Njal. "That surmise of yours was an ingenious piece of fiction. You confessed that the woman was an illusion, and I was not fooled by the invisible listener."

Njal grinned impishly and slipped on his ring. After a moment he reappeared in his disguise as the eavesdropper."

"Why?" demanded Benbow.

"Your general has the mind of a guppy. The only way to get him to hire us was to create a problem he couldn't solve."

"But . . ."

"Why involve the Pythoness?" Njal interrupted. "Because we know she is planning a continent-wide coup. Her Priestesses are recruiting girls everywhere. In Draecia they had infiltrated both the Emperor's harem and the brothel that serviced the Palace Guards. Just before we left Megalopolis, they attempted a palace coup and succeeded in murdering the Empress Dowager. We were sent here to try to thwart whatever mischief she is plotting in the Northwest. By making your general suspicious, we have provided ourselves with a base from which to work and at the same time justified an investigation of her activities."

"And the first place we need to investigate is the recreation haunts of your army." Alsenius brought the discussion to a focus. "Priestesses of the Pythoness are trained in the art of enslaving men. They use spells of Attraction and charm, and they practice the professional arts of the prostitute. If they can run the brothels which your men use, the army will have no secrets, and they can even subvert the obedience of the soldiers."

The Sergeant-Major gulped.

"Do you provide recreation for you men, or do you just turn them loose on the towns where they are billeted?"

"We provide mess halls and limited recreational activities, but we have always discouraged fraternization with women."

"You know soldiers don't 'fraternize,'" Grimbolt snapped. "They go to whore houses, they seduce, and if no other way is open to them, they rape. The question is, how much control do you have over the brothels?"

"Officially, none. We pretend they aren't there. If too many of the men get diseased or if the places get too rowdy, we march in and close them up. The Standing Orders prohibit the men to frequent such places, but . . ."

"You ignore the orders because they are impossible to enforce."

"As a matter of fact, the threat of raids keeps most of the places in line. Most of the men would rather go to a well-run place, if the prices aren't too high."

"And I suppose that there's a special place reserved for bachelor officers," Njal suggested

"There are a couple of places which send 'hostesses' to visit the officers' barracks. The officers always reserve 'guest suites' for that purpose. We discourage women in the men's quarters."

"In short," Njal summarized, "your hypocrisy permits gross lapses in security, deliberate undermining of discipline, and a serious corruption of health and morale."

"Now wait a minute!"

"He's right," Grimbolt declared, "and you know it."

Benbow gulped again.

"I assume you have a list of all these establishments." Alsenius intervened. "You keep a covert eye on everything?"

"Of course. The General may be obtuse, but I am a realist."

"And we shall have access to your information?"

"Certainly. I will provide a private room at Headquarters for you and a full-time clerk."

"Can you lend us a chaplain who can help us detect and neutralize CHARM spells?" Njal demanded. "I can DISPEL, but we need someone with special skill in detection."

"I can introduce you to someone who might be more help than a chaplain. A few years ago the Draecian Temple of Aphrodite sent a cleric up here to convert the heathen. He hasn't been very successful—his shrine only attracts a few silly girls and an occasional lonely man—but he is quite an adept in the lore of passion, and I have heard him condemn the Pythoness for perverting the rites of his Guardian. He goes by the name of Brother Lambent. I sent him private who got into trouble trying to seduce some of his comrades. The men were going to tear him apart. I had to toss him out of the army in spite of the fact he was a good soldier.

"Lambent took him in and taught him a spell for recognizing other men with the same tastes. He came back with the suggestion that I form a special platoon for queers. Brother Lambent had apparently been helping a lot of soldiers stay hidden in the ranks."

"Did you do anything about it?"

"As a matter of fact, I did. I set up a special unit and gave them a barracks all to themselves. Lambent helped with the details, and the new unit is one of our fiercest fighting units. They're absolutely devoted to one another, and they discipline themselves. They leave the regulars alone and the regulars have gotten used to having them around. So whenever I run into a sexual troublemaker, I turn him over to Company 96."

"Where is this shrine of Aphrodite?" Alsenius asked.

"About three miles down Port Road, you'll see a side path that leads up to the top of a little hill. I think there's a sign at the crossroad."

They set out early in the afternoon and soon came to the path marked by a small arrow bearing the symbol of Aphrodite.

"She chose a hill of appropriate shape for her temple," Njal remarked as they started up the gentle incline. As they proceeded they noticed that the fields were increasingly dotted with wild roses, creeping jenny, daisies, dandelions, buttercups, thistles, and heather. Soon they saw a low domed shelter standing in the middle of a garden of cockscomb, amaryllis, roses, lilies and other showy flowers. The sides of the shrine were open so that they could see the altar with its sacred symbol. When they came up, they realized that what they thought was an altar was in fact a broad raised couch upon which lay the most beautiful man they had ever seen.

Their arrival triggered an **ALARM** spell which played an amorous tune upon a flute. The figure on the altar stirred, sat up, and smiled with gentle dignity. He stretched and stood, revealing a body like the masterpiece of an inspired sculptor embodying the ideal masculine form. When he spoke, his voice was like the deep caress of a golden horn played by a master.

"Welcome," he said, "welcome in the name of Love." He gestured toward a cluster of padded stools, embroidered with flowers. "I am Brother Lambent, Priest and consort of the laughter-loving Aphrodite."

As they sat, Alsenius introduced himself and companions.

"You are far from home," Brother Lambent remarked. "Is the laughter-loving one adored in your homelands?"

"Grimbolt and I are men of war and labor, yet all men must yield to Love if their line is to continue."

"I serve the Lord of Mischief, Loki," Njal added, "yet I also dance to Aphrodite's tune."

"You are mercenaries?"

"Njal and I are in the service of Ambloq, Priest of Alfather. Grimbolt is my henchman."

"And it is for Grimbolt that you seek my aid?" Brother Lambent looked searchingly at him.

"One object of our quest is to find out who I am. I have been deprived of both my natural form and my memory."

"I wonder at your ability to make beauty out of your affliction."

"Beauty?"

"You have come to terms with your unusual appearance. The grace of your psyche has tuned your body into harmony with itself." His smile blessed them all. "You all express amazing harmony, which is the essence of true beauty." He settled back on his couch and gestured gracefully. Immediately a stir manifested itself in the air. Lambent addressed the invisible servant. "Our guests need refreshment." Almost immediately small tables appeared beside each of them bearing crystal goblets of a golden beverage and plates dotted with small cakes.

The Priest raised his goblet. "I trust you will find the juice of amaranth to your liking. Let us pledge to love and beauty."

"To love and beauty."

"Now, my friends, we have shared food and drink. Now let me hear how I may serve you."

"I assume that Aphrodite has not allied herself to the Pythoness," Alsenius began.

Brother Lambent almost choked on a cake. "Allied to that demon? That perversion of all that is beautiful? That desecration of the act of love?"

"That's what we thought." Alsenius sipped and peered over his goblet. "You may have heard that the Pythoness is plotting to overthrow the balance of the Guardians and establish her own dominion. Lord Ambloq is in service to Alfather and the Guardians who have allied themselves to thwart her. We believe that Grimbolt's ensorcelment is in some way the work of the Pythoness, and we suspect that the key to his identity lies here in the northwestern region of the continent."

"If the Pythoness has become aggressive in this region, she is using subversion rather than force." Lambent gestured languidly, and a gentle breeze stirred through the garden. "The Hegemony of the Pythoness has a small army of Amazons, but they would be no match for King Peter's Grand Army of Zharkovia. I doubt that they would be able to defeat even our Army of Quatch."

"We suspect that the Pythoness has infiltrated the brothels that serve the armies," said Njal. "If she can charm enough of the officers, she will know all their plans and might be able to upset discipline."

"And you think Aphrodite has some connection with the brothels?"

"Well, she is the guardian of love and beauty."

"And you connect love and beauty with a brothel?" The scorn in Brother Lambent's voice would peel an elephant.

"Oh, I see what you mean." Njal dropped his eyes, abashed.

"Yet the Lady is intimately associated with the act," Alsenius protested.

"At its best the act is associated with the Lady, but divorced from unselfish affection and beauty of thought, the act is both bestial and ridiculous."

"But if that beautiful body of yours is a true human animal," Grimbolt urged, "you must know that the appetite can be overwhelming."

"But like all appetites it must be governed so that it harms no one. A woman compelled by poverty is raped just as surely as a woman compelled by weakness." Lambent's dark eyes bored into Grimbolt.

"And does not the Lady compel?"

"Aphrodite may use a man's corruption against him, but she never corrupts."

"Then," said Njal. "I offer the Lady my apology and my continued service, for I have shared bodies only with women whose desire was as great as mine, and if I gave money to some, it was not to compel but gratefully to relieve poverty."

Brother Lambent smiled. "I acknowledge the innocense of your mischief, for self-interested though you are, you have never been a tyrant. My Lady has smiled on you." His smile broadened to include them all. "Brother Alsenius, you have the beauty of a predator—strength and grace—yet I see in you no cruelty. Even while I shudder at your destructive power, I honor its purity. Brother Grimbolt, you have the brutal innocense of a giant infant. I wince at your pain and marvel at your forbearance. You have suffered a terrible wrong, and it has not corrupted you. My Lady weeps, yet smiles on you."

"We're grateful for any smiles we can get." Alsenius pursued his purpose. "But the main question is, 'Will you help us defeat the temple whores who are probably corrupting the army's brothels?'"

"How?" Brother Lambent was suddenly all business.

"We need be able to explore these places without being enslaved by **ATTRACTION** and **CHARM** spells. Njal might be able to clean things up with his **DISPEL MAGIC**, but even he is in danger from the repetitious and powerful magic of the Pythoness."

"Your purpose is to make these places less corrupt—less enslaving. I believe My Lady would approve. If the women were to serve out of genuine love of the Male and the men could achieve an honest appreciation of the Female, the places would be less abominable." He clapped his hands and the invisible servants cleared the refreshments. "I suggest that you enjoy my Lady's gardens for the rest of the afternoon. We will share supper in the shrine, and you may hope for blessed dreams through the night. I shall commune with my Lady, and in the morning I will know how best to help you." Brother Lambent faded out of their sight.

"Do you think he'll help?" Grimbolt asked.

"I think he'll try." Alsenius studied the couch-altar. "He's not at all what I expected a Priest of Aphrodite to be."

"She's apparently not the lusty old tramp I expected," Njal remarked. "I always thought she was a lot like the Pythoness."

"Ambloq would like her," Alsenius added. "He's lusty as a stallion, but it's always tied to his devotion to Krimhild."

"At least a priest of the love Guardian ought to be versed in anti-love charms."

"I felt him searching my consciousness," Grimbolt mused. "He was a warm presence. I think he knows more about me than I do. I hope he'll tell me something more." He stood up and wandered out among the flowers. "It's peaceful here. Somehow I feel I could lie here and forget all about my troubles." He settled in a patch of daisies and stared blankly out over the river valley. Presently his head drooped upon his knees.

"It must be lonely rattling around in an empty memory," sighed Njal. "And I can't even give him an illusion to cheer him up."

"You noticed that he accepted this place the same way we did." Alsenius continued to stare at the altar-couch. "Apparently there's no illusion about our naked Brother Lambent. That beautiful body must be real."

"He must cause a riot if he strolls around the streets that way. I wonder where he went when he disappeared."

"He seems to have calmed Grimbolt down. Look at him. He's gone to sleep."

Njal spent the afternoon studying the flowers and imitating them in illusions; Alsenius strode restlessly across the fields, occasionally decapitating one of Njal's illusions. As the sun set, the covering of the shrine began to glow softly, so that the couch-altar was constantly illumined. Presently Brother Lambent appeared and the invisible servants provided a candle-lit supper. Grimbolt awoke and joined them.

"I regret the tedium of your afternoon," Brother Lambent apologized to Alsenius.

"Not boredom," he answered. "I think better in action. You gave me plenty to think about."

"I believe," said the Priest, "that you are right about the Pythoness, and I am sure that, if you expose yourself to one of her servants, you will be battered with suggestions, charms, and subtle appeals to the senses. My Lady's enchantments are no substitutes for alertness and self-control, but these little amulets will significantly enhance your resistence to such impositions. He presented Njal and Alsenius with small golden amulets of Aphrodite's symbol: ♀. These will adhere to your skin and should be applied where they cannot be seen. If the slaves of the Pythoness see them, they will know you are protected."

He handed Grimbolt a larger ♀. "My Lady has assured me that the Pythoness is partially responsible for your plight. She finds the ineptitude of your ensorcelment singularly amusing, though she empathizes with your pain. The slaves of the Pythoness have demonstrated ludicrous incompetence which will, in the long run, frustrate her purposes."

Grimbolt bristled at the Lady's amusement, but kept silent.

"I must ask you to uncover your chest." As Grimbolt parted his shirt, Brother Lambent stretched his left little finger and touched a spot just to the right of his left nipple. A tiny spark snapped from the finger and burned away a patch of hair; the priest pressed the amulet against the seared skin, and Grimbolt felt it fasten itself.

"The Pythoness' slaves will not be able to see your amulet. Others may wonder at it, but you can explain it as a gift from our Lady. Your symbol will act like those of your friends to increase your resistence to charm and suggestion, but it will also prevent those associated with your affliction from recognizing you as its victim. It will also render you immune to any further magic from that source."

Grimbolt fingered the image and found it firmly imbedded in his skin. "You cannot undo the magic, but you have prevented them from making it worse."

"Exactly. In their bungling way, they have cast potent magic—one might say they have miscast a powerful spell. I hope that you may some time meet a Priest of sufficient potency to neutralize its effects. I can but shield you from further persecution."

Grimbolt dropped to his knees. "I believe I have always loved the Lady without knowing her. Now through this symbol on my breast, I feel the laughter of her blessing. I think I must always have been a man of peace, for her symbol on my heart gives me great comfort. I have strange memories of a great Goddess. Perhaps I worshiped her before I was changed. She teaches me that it is natural to kill for food, but that I must always ask forgiveness of the beast I eat and I must waste nothing of its body."

Brother Lambent placed his hands on Grimbolt's head in silent blessing. "The Lady Aphrodite is a Guardian dedicated to the pleasures of love. In my visions of her, I have felt the presence of a higher power, a deeper presence of Nature herself. I once saw an ancient scroll which mentioned a great Triple Goddess Gaea. She was described as Nymph, Mother, and Crone—Love, Fertility, and Death. It may be that you remember her worship from before your enchantment. Perhaps my worship of the Lady Aphrodite is but a part of the worship you remember. That is why you take joy in the Lady's symbol."

"Could it be a sign that I'm getting my memory back?"

"Possibly, but more likely your devotion to Gaea lies too deep for magic to interfere. Cling to what you remember, and perhaps it will lead you. Somewhere, far from the distractions of civilization, you may find what you dimly recall."

Grimbolt stood and bowed deeply to Brother Lambent and to the shrine. Then he joined Njal and Alsenius and walked quietly away.

III—Choral Incantation

Queen-Regent Elsa and Princess Catherine of Quatch were having tea in the palace rose garden when Lords Nicholas and Septimus strode up the path preceded by a soldier.

"You were not summoned," Her Majesty glared at the soldier, who snapped his salute and stiffened. "My—your Majesty—Lord Crabhook said—that is Lord Crabhook . . ."

"Majesty!" Lord Septimus swept a bow. "Lord Crabhook ordered our arrest and sent us in this man's charge. Lord Crabhook objected in rather offensive language to our investigation of the summer house where his Majesty died. Lord Nicholas interpreted his words as a slur upon King Peter's morals, and Lord Crabhook has retired to the infirmary."

The soldier tried to shrivel into invisibility while standing at attention. Her Majesty decided he had already observed too much. "Dismissed!"

He saluted and vanished.

"Men! Can't you children learn to play without getting into fights?" Queen Elsa stormed. "Can't we even have a quiet cup of tea without being interrupted by a brawl?"

Lord Nicholas flourished to one knee. As Princess Catherine saw his deep violet eyes looking up through his tousled ringlets, she felt her breath constrict. When she stood up involuntarily, he shifted his bow and grinned artlessly up at her, then lowered his gaze. The Princess caught her breath, and carefully subsided to her chair, but could not take her eyes from him.

He deepened his voice as far as he could. "Lord Crabhook is a foul-minded, incompetent slanderer. I was forced to chastise his lewd insinuations. Your Majesty will, I beg, forgive my fervor in defending the name of my royal master."

"His defense was most dextrous," Lord Septimus put in, "and aside from bandages to crotch, sword arm, and throat almost harmless."

The queen noted that Nicholas was unmarked and unruffled. "I should have thought your operation might have tamed your aggressive masculinity."

"If need be, I can rise to any occasion." He rose gracefully to his feet and bowed, then met Princess Catherine's eyes and bowed specifically to her.

The beauty of his voice sent small mice up and down her spine as she rose to curtsey. She lowered her gaze.

Queen Elsa broke in with irritation, "As King Peter's ambassador you will, of course, claim diplomatic immunity, but we should be grateful if you wold refrain from injuring more of my courtiers and exposing yourself to harm." She turned to Lord Septimus. "You will convey to Lord Crabhook my condolences on his injury."

His Lordship bowed.

"I suppose you might as well sit down and have some tea." Her Majesty gestured to a hidden servant, and additional cups, seed-cake, and chairs appeared. "Have you found anything at the summer house besides cause for squabbling?"

"I shall report to my royal master that there are strong indications that the Priestesses of the Pythoness had a hand both in the murder of his Majesty and the disappearance of his Royal Highness. How the poison got into the peach which his Majesty was eating when he died, I cannot prove, but the presence of Priestesses at his death and the evidence of high-level necromancy involved in the disappearance of the Crown Prince indicate major clerical involvement."

"You say 'disappearance'?" Princess Catherine moved to the edge of her chair. "You believe the prince to be alive?"

"There are still psychic echoes of King Humber's death, and the odor of oil of bitter almonds remains, but there are no echoes of death associated with the evidence of necromancy. I would suspect that the Crown Prince returned to the scene of his father's death a few days afterwards and that he was necromantically attacked and probably abducted at that time." He turned his eyes back to the Queen. "How closely guarded has the summer house been since his Majesty's death?"

"Not at all until after the Crown Prince disappeared. That was when I forbade anyone to disturb the place except those involved in the investigation."

"But you felt no echoes of a second death?" Princess Catherine interrupted.

"No, your Highness." His eyes almost met hers and his clear voice throbbed.

"So, you see, my dear," Queen Elsa interrupted, "that nothing has changed." She sipped her tea, found it cool, and flung the contents of her cup on the grass. Before she could place her cup on the little table beside her, a servant had filled it with fresh steaming brew.

Septimus drained his cup and gestured to Nicholas. "I shall have to see how Lord Crabhook is faring." He rose to his feet and bowed to the ladies. "Shall you accompany me Lord Nicholas?"

Nicholas looked up in surprise, emptied his cup, stood, and bowed. "It seems that duty calls," he said. "My apologies if my zeal disturbed your Majesty's household."

The Queen extended her hand, over which he bowed. The Princess almost extended her hand, then stopped and curtseyed. He turned and followed Septimus down the garden path.

Queen Elsa signaled a messenger. "Summon the Royal Physician," she said, then turned back to the princess. "So you see I was right in telling your father that nothing has changed." Queen Elsa took another seed cake.

"Yes, I am still a wayfarer in your Majesty's court, engaged to an absent prince with no prospect of change. My father is rightfully concerned that my value as a marriageable princess diminishes daily as I age on the vine."

"You are only fourteen years old; your value is still in the bud. Don't you love my son?"

"Madam, I saw him perhaps a dozen times at court functions. I found in him nothing to object to, though I rather wonder that he hankered so little for military glory. My royal brothers are both seasoned warriors, yet Prince Humber remained safely at court."

"Lord Septimus says he is already an skillful diplomat. He is an accomplished musician, a master of eight languages, and a champion wrestler. He was—is—neither a coward nor a fool. Did you not find him attractive?"

"Oh, he was pleasant enough. I'm sure I could have lived with him as a husband and presented him with enough heirs to satisfy the realm. I was perfectly willing to do my duty as a wife, but now he is gone, perhaps I could make better use of my youth than mildewing in a foreign court."

"But is there no warmth of feeling, no longing to have him back?"

"Your Majesty, I am a princess. I have been taught since childhood that my purpose in life is to marry some royal male and give him heirs. After we have done our duty, we will both be free to satisfy our desires so long as I avoid scandal. Of course his mistresses won't matter so long as

I don't make a fuss, but my lovers must be discrete. I do not know what profitable arrangements were made between my father and King Humber, but I was delivered here in expectation of a contract. If either the Crown Prince or I had found the other revolting, the contract might have been voided; detestation might not produce issue. Apparently when we were presented to each other Prince Humber felt sufficient lust to approve me, and I found his body comely."

"You talk like a woman of thirty. When I was engaged, I trembled with excitement at the thought of my wedding night."

"My mother taught me to face facts, ma'am. She took me with her when the mare was led to the stallion. She explained about royal bloodlines and the need to keep them pure. Like the mare I would submit to my lord and hope that he would be both adequate and gentle."

"And she told you nothing of love?"

"She told me that my father was a very considerate and capable stud and that I could be grateful if I was given to as good a man."

"So you have had not wild dreams of passionate love? No sudden pallor such as I observed when you first noticed the elegant Lord Nicholas?"

Catherine ignored the hint. "I have read the old stories, but the Crown Prince was hardly a knight on a charger—though he sat a horse very respectably. Any dreams of passion would have to wait."

"And you are prepared to go back to your father to be auctioned off again?"

The princess hesitated.

"You wouldn't be better off living comfortably with us while we try to recover the prince? Perhaps toy safely with a harmless diplomat?"

"Are you suggesting I might do worse?"

"Your father might choose from several eligible males in the neighborhood." She began ticking them off on her fingers. "There's King Severus of Brieland. His last Queen was executed for high treason—she took a lover—and he is still trying for a male heir at sixty. He has six legitimate daughters and eleven documented bastards."

"But Brieland is practically frozen in for six months of the year."

"And you would have a fat old king to keep your bed warm, if he wasn't busy elsewhere."

"Ugh! I had forgotten about old Severus. I remember Mother arguing with Father that Arragor was closer to Quatch and would make a better ally."

"And there is Prince Schlarr of Grand Isle. His father is very anxious to get an heir out of him before he dies of the wasting sickness. Then there's Count Draco . . ."

"Please don't mention him. He hangs around the court in hopes my brothers will get killed in battle and he can claim the throne." Catherine looked ill at the thought of him "He likes to hurt people."

"Yes." The queen rubbed her nose in it. "I remember hearing some scandal about your father having to pension off one of Draco's mistresses because of the count's lovemaking technique. Of course there are some younger candidates your father might pick for you, but are you sure you wouldn't be better off waiting for my absent son?"

"I see what you mean. Prince Humber may be almost unbearably tame, but I could do a lot worse."

"Furthermore, my dear, he is now of age. The regency ends when he returns, so that you will become queen when you marry. If you are very good to him, you can probably have your own way most of the time. Now, dear, are you sure you want to send that letter to your father?"

Catherine's face drooped. "I'm afraid, your Majesty, I've already sent it." Suddenly she stiffened. "How did you know?"

"My dear, it's my business to know everything. That's what it means to be queen. Now are you sure you want that letter to leave Arragor?"

"You mean you have not only read but stolen my letter?"

"The Queen does not steal, she intercepts. It is in the interest of Arragor to have the Kingdom of Quatch as an ally. Your letter might disturb the alliance. Therefore it will not be delivered until everything has been done to prevent that disturbance. You are more than a pawn in this game of international relations—perhaps even a rook—but you are neither King nor Queen. I am consulting you as a major piece. Are you sure the letter I am holding is exactly what you wish to say to your royal father?" She extracted from an ornamental pouch at her side a folded and sealed sheet of papyrus and extended it to the Princess.

"How did you read this without breaking the seal?"

"That comes under the heading of state secrets." Elsa smiled grimly.

Catherine shattered the brittle wax and read her rather imperious letter to her father demanding that he bring her home and arrange a proper marriage for her.

"Your letter implies unkind treatment at our court and a strong preference for a husband other than my son. Are you certain, in view of the alternate candidates for your hand, that it accurately expresses your wish. I had thought our hospitality was more cordial than you imply, and perhaps our court has charms you had not noticed before."

The Princess flushed a little. "I resent bitterly your 'interception' of my letter."

"If it will soothe your anger, I regret the necessity for the interception. The question remains, 'Is this exactly the letter which would best express your feelings and wishes?'"

"Oh damn! I think, perhaps, since it has not been sent, I might change a few phrases."

"Would you be willing to write a letter less likely to arouse your royal father's displeasure toward the court of Arragor?"

Princess Catherine rose with careful dignity and curtseyed. "I believe there has been more than enough delay in answering my father's last letter." She folded her letter, gathered her dignity, and stalked back toward the palace.

Her Majesty again emptied her cup on the grass and found it promptly filled with steaming tea. She gazed after the Princess and sipped, then reached for another tea cake as she spied Lord Septimus ambling across the lawn.

"I have moved the feathered hound to quarters less accessible to Assassins." He settled with a bow into a chair, accepted a cup and took a little pastry. "I fear we are running out of metaphors since, to mix another, he has blossomed into a formidable wasp. I have never seen a rapier wielded with more devilish skill. He is a rare bird, and King Peter has had him very well trained."

"It's too bad he can have no children." Queen Elsa savored the steam from her cup. "The way Princess Catherine looks at him he would make a dangerous game piece if he were complete."

"He's already bubbling with plans for a reception to entertain some of the Priestesses of the Pythoness. He says they might let some information leak if we could get them relaxed. Does your Majesty think it might be possible to schedule a recital by Lord Nicholas of Zharkovia to which a few senior Priestesses would be invited?"

"Perhaps it might be diplomatic to invite the Pythoness' temple choir to sing with him. It would be a musical coup, and it would insure good attendance. Can you see to the arrangements?"

"It will be my pleasure." He finished his tea, wiped his fingers on a napkin, and headed toward the palace.

She was preparing to rise, when she noted the approach of the Royal Physician. "Ah, Sir Grendal." She extended her hand to be kissed. "You have recently attended Lord Crabhook?" He bowed. "Would you describe his injuries as serious?"

"For a week or so, I would not recommend that he sing, employ his right arm, or attempt to pleasure his mistress, but these disabilities are of a temporary nature."

"Then you would not describe these wounds as of murderous intent?"

"Oh, dear no. Anyone intending his death would have aimed for the heart or slashed more deeply at the throat, where the thrust was very carefully controlled. His assailant was most skillfully restrained."

"Tell me, Sir Grendal, would it be possible to arrange for a disabling, but not life-threatening fever to strike an individual?"

"Fevers are very tricky, your Majesty. They are not to be trusted."

"And sleeping droughts?"

"Are normally of short duration, Ma'am. An induced sleep of more than 24 hours would be very suspicious and might be deleterious."

"Nevertheless you may extend to Lord Crabhook our sincere condolences," her Majesty cooed, "and encourage him to prolong his rest as long as is necessary for complete recovery. We make no demands upon his service or his presence until he is fully recevered." She extended her hand for the parting kiss, and watched the physician crunch along the path.

She sat pondering for a few minutes, hoping that the Grendal would take her hint and somehow keep Lord Crabhook out of circulation. Then she noticed Lady Mabel, who had been standing outside of hearing range, but within the royal sight. She nodded. Lady Mabel curtseyed and, at a gesture sank into a chair and received a cup.

"Your Majesty, a document has fallen into my hands which I believe your Majesty would want to peruse."

"Another letter from Princess Catherine?"

"Yes, your Majesty."

"You have opened and will be able to reseal it?"

"Yes, your Majesty." She extended the open letter. The Queen swiftly read it and nodded. "This should go off immediately. The little minx has complained about my tampering with her letters, but that will convince her father that I didn't force her to write. Make sure it's perfectly resealed. I should like him to think she succeeded in sneaking it off."

Lady Mabel rose and curtsied. "Mabel, my dear, you have handled this whole business with great skill. We are very grateful."

Lady Mabel blushed prettily. "The senior page, Rupert Morley, has been most ingenious about the seals, your Majesty."

"And is there anything else we ought to know about Master Morley?"

"I have heard that he was praised very highly for his performance with sword and buckler. I believe he hopes to win permission to appear in the next Royal Games."

"That permission must be won from the Master of the Games. If he is diligent, his sword master will recommend him." She looked archly at Lady Mabel. "Our question was of a more personal nature. Do we detect some desire on the part of a Maid in Waiting to become a Matron in Waiting?"

"Master Morley has made no improper advances, Ma'am."

"And he doesn't dare make proper ones until he is Sir Rupert. That is understood, but have you given him hope that proper advances would be welcome?"

Lady Mabel's face made answer unnecessary.

"We are not displeased," Queen Elsa smiled. "Your talents for discreet snooping might be even more valuable if linked with a talented husband. We will watch Master Rupert Morley's performance with interest at the next Royal Games."

Lady Mabel curtseyed and turned to depart. "You might both remember that the wax used with our royal seal is especially brittle and will not tolerate tampering."

Lady Mabel knew better than to reply.

Her Majesty thoughtfully drained her cup and gestured for the tea things to be taken away.

Meanwhile Lord Nicholas wrote a careful report to his king.

> There are disquieting indications that the Priestesses of the Pythoness were involved in the murder of King Humber and in the disappearance of the Crown Prince. I would counsel that my mission continue until I have made certain whether the Priestesses assisted a local regicide or plotted the act. I believe your Majesty's best interests would be served if I could help recover the abducted prince. Instability in Arragor could threaten our own realm.

I might add that the Queen-Regent is very comely and very capable. She might well satisfy your Majesty's desire for a consort after the Arragor succession has been settled. In the meanwhile, your Majesty might profitably observe Zharkovia.s court to see whether there is undue influence from abroad. It might be especially profitable to inquire about the loyalties of recently acquired court mistresses—even your own.

My projected recital with the choir of the Temple of the Pythoness will give me an excellent opportunity to test the protective magic Father Ambrose cast on me. I shall also be able to question many of the temple novices about temple espionage."

Instead of sealing his report and sending for a messenger, Lord Nicholas sprinkled it with powder from an unlabeled shaker box. Then he tossed it into the fire, from which it promptly vanished without burning.

Plans for the recital proceeded with remarkable speed. The Temple of the Pythoness not only approved their choir's performance in the Arragor Palace but also extended an invitation for Lord Nicholas to sing with the choir in a performance at the Pythoness' temple. Arrangements went forward for rehearsals in the Grand Ballroom where the first performance would take place and for practice in the Pythoness' temple. The choir mistress took special interest in Lord Nicholas.

"It is most strange to hear from a man such glorious soprano singing." She moved a trifle closer to him. "One hears that your voice was preserved at an exorbitant personal cost."

"Indeed," he answered, "I was deprived of the possibility of fatherhood. I shall never be able to pass on my voice to my heirs."

"That indeed was a ruinous price—to be robbed of the highest pleasure."

"Yet all pleasure is not lost." He smiled innocently as he dropped his gaze to her revealing vestments.

"But surely . . ."

"Surely I can get no heirs, but it is the act, not the begetting, that provides the pleasure."

"It is true you have a magnificent voice, but to lack . . ."

"Not everything is lost." He noticed that her hands were busy under the cover of her clerical apron. "But it is of the voice that we speak. It seems to me that your choir must be limited to music not dependent upon a bass line. Are you not required to use an orchestra to provide a foundation."

"On the contrary, we have enticed a number of tenors and basses who willingly serve us. For pleasure to be complete, there must be men to fulfill the women."

"Then my place must be to soar above and around the blended voices. The instrument for which I paid the price has extreme range, virtuoso dexterity, and great power." He demonstrated first with a four octave scale, then with a tangle of trills, arpeggios, and leaps, and last with a pianissimo high C which slowly swelled to fortissimo, and finished with a four octave glissando followed by and ascending series of trills before it leaped again to a climactic sustained G above where it began. "I believe that few singers can sustain a longer phrase over a greater range."

She stared at him open mouthed. "Such range, such purity of tone, such power and breath, combined with unbelievable flexibility—it is indeed a voice to worship. I see now how a single voice can balance an entire choir. We shall indeed have an unprecedented performance."

"Some time we should attempt a duet for no audience but ourselves," he murmured suggestively, hoping that she would assume her spell had taken effect. "But you have priestly duties to perform, and I must return to my diplomatic labors."

As he turned to leave, the Choir Mistress muttered a few words under her breath and gestured as if sweeping him toward her. He felt a momentary twinge in his gut and thanked Father Ambrose for the protective magic he had cast before Lord Nicholas left King Peter's court. He paused and gazed suggestively at the Priestess, then strode purposefully out. She gestured imperiously at his back and uttered a sharp command. He broke stride momentarily, looked back as if in longing, but exited with only a momentary pause.

She cursed softly under her breath. "His operation has removed what is most affected by our magic," she mused. "Yet he spoke as if there still remained some masculinity under that soprano voice. How much did his body change before they cut him? He has no beard, yet I would swear he was flirting with me." She stiffened and began collecting her music scores. "Damn you, Lord Cutpurse, I'll strip off your little mysteries before I'm through with you."

Meanwhile Nicholas strolled back to the wing of the palace where his quarters were, and he was mildly surprised to find his thoughts straying back to the intense face of Princess Catherine. "Strange," he thought, "I have never been so stirred by a woman. Surely, when they cut away my manhood they must have taken the urge as well. I must contrive to speak with her Majesty's physician, for what is left of my body is certainly behaving strangely."

Rehearsals kept Nicholas busy as he and the choir learned to balance and blend their tones in the sacred anthems and folk songs of the program. One song which the Priestesses insisted on singing presented great difficulties, since the words were in tongue he had never heard. They coached him carefully, but he found the mouthing of what seemed like random syllables unsettling.

"Can you at least translate for me? How can I match tone to word if I don't know whether I am wooing or cursing."

"There is no translation," the choir mistress replied. "Think of it as a prayer or invocation."

"But what am I praying for or invoking?"

"You are invoking the spirit of the sound. You are not singing words, only sounds, and these exact syllables on these exact pitches will stir the very psyche of the audience with delight. Do you not feel your heart uplifted as you sing?"

"Singing always uplifts me, bit this piece only baffles. The harmonies include dissonances that do not resolve. The words are no words. There is no melody. It is virtually unsingable."

"Yet we of the choir can sing it. Are the musicians of Zharkovia so limited in their scope?"

He shook his head. "This recurring phrase—'Ut mianio min nim oinam tu'—what is it invoking that requires such random leaps?"

"Just sing it the way it is written, and it will have its effect."

"And how can one utter 'shchkhypf' on a high C? How can one sustain a tone on a mouthful of consonants?"

The choir mistress produced a gargled choking screech which disgusted Nicholas. He imitated her voice with such scorn and power that a large vase of hydrangeas shattered, spewing shards and flower fragments over the choir.

"Perhaps," the choir mistress suggested, raking a large purple mess from her hair, "it would be better if you did not attempt 'shchkhypf.' At least not at full volume. We can alter the music to give that passage to the soprano section while you perform a trill on 'Ah.'"

A squadron of footmen rushed on the Grand Ballroom floor and began sweeping up the debris.

Still unsatisfied, Nicholas continued studying his score until, on the afternoon of the performance, he finally grabbed a quill and began scribbling notes on his score. Presently he hastened from his quarters to the Grand Ballroom and began riffling through the conductor's scores until he found the offending piece. He stuffed a copy into his pouch and then set to work altering the conductor's master score, to match his revisions.

"I hope these changes are enough," he murmured to himself. "I can't change the choir's parts, but these alterations in mine should draw the poison." From there he sought Lord Septimus, finding him in his quarters dictating letters to a scribe.

"Oh, hello Nicholas. Why aren't you at the Grand Ballroom?"

"Emergency, sir. I've found some more evidence that the Pythoness is up to no good."

"Oh?"

"One of the pieces I'm singing with the choir is very suspicious. The music is so discordant that no audience will put up with it, and the words are in some language I've never heard. They are almost unpronounceable. I have finally decided that the whole piece is an elaborate spell designed to enchant the entire audience. My guess is that it is some sort of CHARM spell."

"You think they're going to CHARM all of us at once?"

"You don't have a Wizard who might be able to analyze the combination of syllables and tones to figure out what it is supposed to do?" He handed the old man his stolen copy of the piece.

"We don't do a whole lot of magic around here," Septimus confessed. "There's a lot of prejudice against it."

"Well, I've altered my part so that I think I've upset the spell, but I can't be sure what the changed spell might do."

"There isn't time before the performance to fetch Wizard Quackenthorp from his tower, but I'll get High Priest Farsyte to stand by ready to DISPEL any mass effects. I'll show him this copy of the score. Since the Priestesses wrote it, the spell is probably clerical. Do you have a copy of your alterations?"

"Only the one I am to sing from."

"Can you manage from memory?"

"You think it's important for Lord Farsyte to see what I'm going to sing?"

"I'm sure it would help."

Nicholas bit his lip and stared a long time at his score. "All right, I'll chance it. Make sure the High Priest realizes that I may not remember exactly what I wrote. There may be variations on the variations."

"Leave it to me. Farsyte and I will do everything we can. At least we're forewarned."

"I need to assemble with the choir." Nicholas started for the door.

"You realize that this is proof that the priestesses are working against Arragor," Lord Septimus urged, "that they almost certainly had a hand in King Humber's death."

Nicholas gestured an affirmative as he dashed out.

"Lord Nicholas, we feared you had succumbed to stage fright." The choir mistress' chill soprano quivered with disapproval as she watched Nicholas take his place at the end of the line. "We have delayed our entrance by a minute and a half."

"I marvel at the accuracy of your measurement. My sundial stops working with the sun."

"Choir, you may file in now that the prima donna has arrived."

"I am still 'don,'" Nicholas corrected, "though my voice denies it."

She stifled a snarl as she led the line of choristers into the hall and up on the risers arranged at the end of the room. As soloist, Nicholas entered next to last, directly in front of the conductor, who bowed to accept the applause while her chorus settled themselves in position. She turned and tapped her baton to produce the absolute hush which must precede the singing. She gestured, and Nicholas' voice emerged barely audible and very high from the silence. Gradually the volume increased until it seemed no human lungs could prolong it any longer; then it trilled upward as the chorus built a chord structure beneath it and commenced the melody of the first anthem. Not a cough, not even an audible breath distracted as the voices wove the magic of devotion in the hymn of praise to the Guardians. As the voices faded into silence, the audience sat for a count of ten before the first applauding thud of a foot struck the floor. No one had heard such singing before.

A series of foot-stamping folk songs followed, and the audience roared its approval. Then the choir turned to the piece which Nicholas feared. The conductor stared at her altered score and shook her head. She started to gesture toward the choir mistress, then stopped and examined the score to evaluate its musicality. She looked up inquiringly at Nicholas, who stood empty handed a few feet from her. She silently mouthed a question at him, and he smiled his most innocent smile and hinted at the ghost of a bow. Finally she tapped her baton, lifted it, and pointed to the tenors to begin.

The dissonance of the music jolted the audience, and for the first time the hall rustled with wriggling and rasped with quiet throat clearing. The sopranos, then the basses and the altos, made their entrance, and the restlessness of the audience increased. Suddenly Nicholas' soprano cut across the pattern of sound and wove a haunting melodic thread into the texture. The audience quieted somewhat as their ears found repose from the tension. The choir mistress felt with fury the changes Nicholas was making and she strove to lead her sopranos into singing louder to overbalance his melodies.

At the back of the audience the High Priest, Lord Farsyte, began mumbling his prayers, striving to adjust them to what Nicholas was singing. As the music marched through the third repetition of 'Ut mianio min nim oinam tu,' Nicholas broke the pattern of nonsense syllables with a phrase from a familiar hymn 'Grant us, O grant us peace!' Desperately the Choir Mistress rushed her sopranos up the jagged approach to her climactic 'shchkhypf!' which tore at their throats. Suddenly Nicholas' clear voice rang a third above them the single word, 'Peace!'

At the same moment Lord Farsyte finished his mumbled chant as his clear baritone rang out "Dispel!"

The word wiped the jangled chaos of the singing from the audience's mind, protecting them from the effects of the musical spell, but the singers were unprotected. Absorbed in the harmony of his own voice, Nicholas felt only the quiet inspiration of his single word, "Peace!" The conductor and the male members of the chorus were stunned by the clash between the choral chant and the solo. Some stood frozen to their spots and some collapsed into unconsciousness. The women singers were driven into fury and ferociously attacked whoever was nearest to their claws. The High Priestess, who had been leading the alto section of the choir shrieked into an incantation—Transform—and climaxed by pointing at Nicholas and shouting "Down Dog."

The Choir Mistress at the same time produced a pair of daggers from her bodice and launched herself at Nicholas just as the spell took effect and he became a massive rust-colored bloodhound. One of the Choir mistress' daggers ripped into the bass standing behind Nicholas and the other embedded itself in a riser. She lost her balance and fell upon the dog just as his bell-like howl completed the tone he had begun as a human.

Stunned by the shock of his transformation, Nicholas clamped his teeth on the arm nearest him. Meanwhile the members of the choir, frenzied by the effect of their distorted spell-chant, fought violently against each other. The risers, designed to hold stationary singers, swayed perilously under the struggling mob. The High Priestess lost her footing and stumbled against another alto who immediately turned from pummeling the woman next to her and twined her fingers n the High Priestess' hair. As a result, both pitched forward into a tangle of tenors and thence to the main floor. At this point the upper level of risers collapsed, pitching singers into the melee below, so that the lower risers also collapsed.

Out of the chaos the bloodhound instinctively wriggled. As he realized what had happened to him, Nicholas nosed among the fallen looking for the woman who had enchanted him. He reached her just as she was struggling to cast another spell. Nicholas felt an ominous rumble in the back of his throat as he flung himself upon her, intent on fastening his teeth in her. Her staff struck him on the side of the head as she darted away, and the smell of her identity overwhelmed him as he collapsed on the floor. As soon as she found herself free of the crowd, the High Priestess TELEPORTED back to her temple.

By the time Nicholas regained consciousness, the audience had fled and the guards had rescued the singers from the wreckage. Concerned with human casualties, the guards had dragged his body out of the way and continued their labors on behalf of the injured people. Long before he opened his eyes, Nicholas became conscious of a vast confusion on smells: fear, blood, rage, sweat. He shook his head and let the odors sort themselves out in his head. As his impression of the room cleared, his ears began to register the shouts and clatter of the rescue operation. Finally, his human consciousness asserted itself and recognized the speech patterns of men working near him. They were sweaty men, working hard, but not angry or particularly afraid. They must be footmen cleaning up after the disaster.

Nicholas was relieved to find he could still understand language. When he attempted to speak to the men, he realized that his mouth and throat could no longer produce speech, but at least his mind was unchanged by the spell.

"Good dog," one of the men said. "You'd better run along and get out of the way." He reached down and scratched behind Nicholas' ears, patted him on the head, and gestured toward a doorway. By this time Nicholas had opened his eyes and realized that, while he could see the man and his gesture, his vision was strangely unfocused. His eyes caught flashes of motion indicating excellent peripheral vision, but he could not make out individual faces, and the shapes of objects were shadowy. He scrambled to his feet, shook himself, scattering saliva in all directions, and wobbled uncertainly toward the door.

"Good boy," the man encouraged, "You must have taken quite a knock."

He sniffed the air and recognized no individual scents. He was grateful to have four solid paws under him as he staggered toward the door. He wandered vaguely along the corridor, stopping frequently to lift his leg and mark his way. Suddenly he recognized the familiar scent of his own human body and realized that he had found the track of his progress to the Great Hall. After that, it was a simple matter to follow himself through the maze of halls and staircases to his room. The door latch defied his attempts to bat it up with his paw, but finally he managed to place his nose under the handle and lift his head until the door swung open. Once inside, he reared against the door to close it, shook himself vigorously and leaped into the center of his bed. He was asleep before his muscles stopped twitching.

IV—Checking

The first step for Alsenius, Grimbolt, and Njal was to get billeted in Officers Dormitory. They requested rooms near each other and were assigned to adjacent rooms 305 and 307 with Njal across the hall in 310. They ate supper at different tables so that each had a chance to talk with different men about recreation. They learned that the twelve rooms on the sixth floor were permanently unassigned and therefore available for 'guests' at two gold pieces per night. Most officers had 'cousins' for whom they reserved rooms on a regular schedule.

Recreation Ensign Bottomly, who shared a table with Alsenius, explained that it was necessary to reserve rooms at least a week in advance because the guest quarters were in heavy demand. Room 612—the Guest Suite—was sometimes available on short notice, but it cost eight gold pieces because it had four capacious beds.

"Some times a group of officers want to entertain their cousins by playing party games, and the Guest Suite has thick walls. Of course if all the rooms are taken and some officers have emergencies, they can share the suite if they can do without privacy. Last Saturday, for example, five officers entertained their 'cousins' together in 612."

"And what about officers who don't happen to have local 'cousins'?" Alsenius asked.

"There are some public 'hotels' down by the river where a man can meet people, but they aren't as comfortable as our guest rooms. Sometimes the Sergeant Major's Emergency Patrol investigate the hotels and even make arrests, since His Majesty's officers are supposed to be available even on off-duty hours."

"Am I right in assuming that you have charge of renting out the guest rooms?"

"Yes sir. I pay the Sergeant-Major a monthly rent for the sixth floor, and then I rent the rooms out to the officers."

"And do you sometimes provide 'cousins' for a fee?"

"I sometimes can find a friend to whom I can introduce an officer."

Alsenius leaned close to the Ensign and muttered, "As you can see from my complexion, I have no cousins in this part of the world, and it is sometimes hard to find a pleasant companion."

Ensign Bottomly murmured. "I suppose that both you and Lieutenant Grimbolt are far from family. I don't know if any of my friends would like to be introduced to foreigners from so far away."

"If you could find a 'cousin' for Lieutenant Grimbolt as well as for me, we could even take Suite 612 on short notice. I believe Lieutenant Njal can find a relative for himself. We understand that it might cost money to finance a search for such relatives."

"It might take a day or two—and about ten gold pieces."

"Could we, perhaps, reserve Suite 612 to entertain 'cousins' next Wednesday?"

"Major, I will do my best."

Alsenius reached into his pouch belt and pulled out a bag of coins. "I trust this will be enough to finance the enterprise, including the women's fees."

The Ensign balanced the bag in his hand and smiled.

When Njal escorted Tanya to Suite 612 on Wednesday, he also brought several servants from the local cook's shop, who swiftly set up a table in the center of the lounge and arranged a comfortable supper for six. As they left, they met Ensign Bottomly escorting two 'cousins'—Vara and Natalie. Njal greeted them warmly and waved toward the supper table.

"The women have been warned that their cousins are unusual men?" Njal asked the ensign.

"Oh yes, they know they are to entertain foreign gentlemen."

"You warned them exactly how foreign?"

"Not in detail."

Njal cursed gently under his breath, then turned to the 'cousins.' "Vara and Natalie, you have been warned that my fellow officers are very unusual?"

"Ensign Bottomly said one was dark and the other was hairy."

"Did he tell you how dark and how hairy?"

They shrugged.

"I should be getting back to my office." The ensign coughed, and headed out the door, closing it discretely behind him.

Njal twiddled his fingers as he turned to the women. "I think you should know what the men look like. At that moment his illusions of Alsenius and Grimbolt clad only n the briefest breech clouts appeared. Vara screamed and Natalie dropped into a chair.

"They are very different." said Natalie. "The Ensign said 'dark,' but this man is . . . ." She paused to examine Alsenius' muscular figure and generous bulge. "He is very dark, but very much a man." She examined the image of Grimbolt and extended a tentative finger. "How real is he?"

"Only an image. You'll have to wait till he gets here before you can feel him. I can assure you he's very well put together."

"He has almost a man's face and a man's hands." Vara commented, "No snout and no claws, but what about . . ."

"Oh that's human," Njal reassured them. "Of course normally you can't see anything because of the hair."

"You have seen him?"

"No, but Alsenius, who traveled many miles with him, says women find him very satisfactory." Njal gestured, and the images vanished. "Now that you have seen everything, are you willing to stick by your bargain?"

"The black man is very beautiful," Natalie sounded excited. "I could enjoy that body no matter what color it was."

Vara shuddered slightly and shank into herself. "All that hair rubbing against me. I thought he would just have a lot if hair on his chest and legs but . . ."

"Nonsense!" Tanya suddenly interrupted. "He had beautiful hands and a wonderful face behind that beard. I think he'll be exciting." She turned to Njal. "You don't mind swapping, do you?"

"I did pick you out for myself." Njal exaggerated slightly his reluctance, then crossed the room to Vara and stuffed a curried shrimp gently into her mouth. He looked mischievously into her eyes and said, "I think we ought to manage."

They had just started on supper when Alsenius and Grimbolt burst in. "I think we have a lead," said Alsenius. "The woman in 601 stopped us at the top of the stairs because her 'cousin' just passed out and she wanted us to carry him down to her wagon."

"And there was no question about it, she cast some sort of spell on both of us when we went into the room to get him." Grimbolt interrupted.

Njal tried to hush them, but they were too excited to notice.

"She was screaming furious when we carried her victim down to Bottomly's office instead," Alsenius went on. "She started casting spells without even trying to hide what she was doing."

"We tied her up and gagged her, and Bottomly called the Emergency Patrol. They'll take the officer to the infirmary, and keep the woman locked up till we get around to questioning her." He stopped and looked at the 'cousins.' "Oh hello, I'm sorry we're late."

The women clutched each other and seemed ready to run.

At this point, Njal cast a detection spell and found no evidence that the women were magically enhanced or that they had been casting spells in the room. "I think, while we're eating, we ought to tell you a little about ourselves," he said. "As far as I can tell, you three are honest women of pleasure."

"And you're some kind of cops." Vara stood up and started for the door.

"And we're on your side." Njal moved swiftly between her and the door. "Please sit down and listen. We need your help in catching some very nasty people who are trying to ruin your business and at the same time mess up the army."

"That woman we caught this evening," Alsenius urged, "was not an honest 'cousin' entertaining a young officer. I'm sure we'll find she is an evil priestess whose job was to CHARM the officer so he would answer all her questions and remain her slave for as long as she had a use for him. She tried to CHARM Grimbolt and me, but we have some protection against spells."

"And you want us to keep a lookout for priestesses who slip into our hotels and start casting spells. That's why you brought us here." Natalie seemed more curious than frightened.

"We hoped you were honest so we could have a proper party," Grimbolt hastened to reassure them. "If we found you were priestesses, we would have to deal with you, but since you aren't, this is just a regular job."

"But you're going to try to rope us into your spying game." Vara brought the discussion back to the issue. "You want us to stick our necks out and spy for priestesses."

"Njal quietly twiddled his fingers, then extended his hands toward the three and commanded, "Forget!"

The women looked blankly at the men, and Tanya announced, "This is a great supper you've ordered for us. We're going to make sure you have a good time, especially the hairy one. I'm dying to see what's under that kilt."

Njal took Alsenius aside. "I've blanked out their memory of everything since you came in. All they will remember is that you're unusual customers. I suggest that we talk to Natalie in the morning. I think she might be willing to help."

"I agree," Alsenius nodded. "Vara and Tanya are honest whores, but Natalie has more brains."

They returned to the table, and the party proceeded as the woman had expected. After breakfast Njal signaled Natalie to linger after Tanya and Vara left.

"Would you mind answering a few questions before you go?" Alsenius asked.

"You're all good lays, and we'd be glad of a repeat invitation," she countered. "Tanya actually got excited over Grimbolt. I think she'd give him a discount for another night."

"I want to talk about more important business," Njal interrupted. He reversed the spell and waited for her to adjust. "I apologize for meddling with your memories, but we are involved in a secret investigation for the army. The woman Alsenius and Grimbolt captured last night was a priestess of the Pythoness who enrolled in one of the 'hotels' on the waterfront to spy on the army. She cast spells to enslave the young officer so that he would tell everything he knew and perhaps even betray his trust. We are convinced she is one of several. The Sergeant-Major has asked us to investigate. Do you know of any newcomers who cast spells on customers or on other women?"

"There's no new women at our hotel, but they have quite a turnover at Sailors' Rest. I haven't heard of any trouble, but I heard you say last night that you had to rescue an officer."

"You're very observant."

"The more you know about a man, the better you can please him, and it's a lot more pleasant with regular customers."

"And you're pretty sure all the women at your place are honest?"
She nodded.

"One more thing," said Njal, "would you be willing to send us a note if you hear anything about spell-casting women at any of the hotels? We'd be willing to pay for any expense, and you would be helping to keep your profession honest."

"We're not trying to stir up trouble," Alsenius added. "It's the outsiders who are going to spoil everything if we fail."

"I've heard that the priestesses of the Pythoness have power to enslave men, but I thought they all live at the local temple or up north in the Hegemony of the Pythoness."

"Unfortunately we believe they're trying to expand," said Grimbolt. "I am convinced that they were the cause of my problem." He spread his arms to show his hairy torso.

She dropped upon a stool and stared into space for a full minute. Then she lifted her head and met Njal's gaze. "All right," she agreed. "I'll let you know if I learn anything." She dropped her eyes demurely. "And if you need me professionally, I'll be glad to serve you."

Alsenius slipped a jingling pouch into her hand. "For expenses," he said. "Send for us if you have any trouble."

She giggled nervously and slipped out.

"Sailors' Rest," Njal mused. "Not a place the army would be expected to use. I wonder if our prisoner came from there."

Ensign Bottomly reported that Lieutenant Briggs had been returned to duty and that the woman was dead.

"How?" Alsenius demanded. "I told you to keep her restrained."

"She was tied to a chair and gagged as you instructed, sir, but when the guard went in to give her breakfast, she had ceased to breathe and there was no heartbeat."

"Ambloq warned me about that," Alsenius grumbled. "I should have questioned her immediately."

"And she would have died immediately," Njal answered him. "The only way to prevent precast spells from acting is to **DISPEL** them before they can take effect. I cast **DISPEL** on her as soon as she was tied up, but the death spell was done by someone much more powerful then I. And that probably means a High Priestess." He extended his hands palms up in a gesture of surrender. "We can do only what we have power to do. We have neglected one thing, however. We need to take Briggs to visit Brother Lambent. Just because he behaves normally doesn't mean he isn't still under a spell. I've done what I can, but I'd like to have a cleric look at him before I turn him loose on the army."

"I agree," said Alsenius. "I suppose our immediate order of business is to visit Sailor's Rest."

"I'd rather wait and see what Natalie reports," Grimbolt objected. "As soon as we go down there we announce that we're suspicious."

"Furthermore, we're probably going to be ordered for an interview with the King," said Njal. "And he's going to send us on some mission that will take precedence over our investigation."

"At least we have enough evidence to convince everybody that the priestesses aren't to be trusted." Alsenius stuck his head out of the room and called a messenger. "Go find Lieutenant Briggs and ask him to report to me as soon as possible." The messenger dashed off.

Grimbolt sighed and put on his kilt and jacket. "I suppose I have to dress if we're going out."

"You're shocking enough even with your clothes on," Njal jibed. "Of course you can take it all off when we get to Brother Lambent's."

When he reported to Alsenius, Briggs protested. "I'm all right now. The medical officer said I could return to duty."

"He says you're physically all right, but I want to be sure that woman didn't cast a mind-affecting spell on you." Briggs opened his mouth to object, but Alsenius overrode him. "I'm sorry, Mister, but I outrank you and I order you to accompany us."

Briggs looked at the major's insignia and glared. "Yes, sir." He slammed his fist against his breast. He marched obediently, but refused conversation beyond punctilious brief answers to his senior's questions. When they arrived at the shrine and he saw Brother Lambent get up from the altar in response to the musical alarm, Briggs staggered back in horror. "That guy's bloody naked." he gasped.

"Of course I am," Brother Lambent casually replied. "What good is beauty if you cover it up?"

"I'm not going to let that queer check on me."

"He's not queer, he's just naked." Grimbolt explained patiently as he pulled off his own clothes and stacked them neatly on the ground. "There's a difference."

"But . . ."

"Look," Njal snapped, "a soldier has to keep his head no matter what the emergency. You are an officer and a leader of men. A naked priest is not such a serious emergency as to make an officer in his Majesty's army panic."

"I haven't panicked. I'm just shocked to see my superior hob-nobbing with queers."

Brother Lambent collapsed on a stool, laughing. "I'm sorry my body offends you. I have always believed it was a thing of beauty." He gestured, and his nakedness faded into a cloud of golden fog. "Please sit down and have something to nibble on." He gestured again and his invisible servant produced padded stools together with small tables on which were tumblers of cool beverage and mounds of fresh cherries.

Briggs sank to a stool and stared.

"I'm sorry to disturb your rest." Alsenius sat and popped a large cherry into his mouth. "I didn't realize our army was so narrow minded." He spat out the seed. "Briggs, here slept with a whore last night, and she put him into a trance. When he came to, the medical officer sent him back to duty, but we suspect she did more than put him to sleep. I don't know anybody else around here who can tell what happened."

"Did you eat of drink anything while you were with her?" The priest straightened up and scrutinized Lieutenant Briggs.

"She gave me a tiny cup of dark stuff. It was very sweet and very butter at the same time. She told me to sip it very slowly, and it would make me very hard for a long time."

"And did it?"

"Ooooh yes! The taste was wonderful after the surprise of the first sip, and she was right. It really stiffened me up."

"It didn't put you to sleep right away?"

"No. She did amazing things to me, and we kept on doing it for hours. Then, all of a sudden I must have passed out, because I woke up in the infirmary."

Brother Lambent knelt in front of him and stared into his eyes. Briggs could not look away. He sat motionless and stared blankly for about three minutes. Then his eyes closed.

"It's a good thing you brought him here." Brother Lambent turned to Alsenius. "The drink knocked him out at the first sip. Then she planted memories of all sorts of impossible pleasures. She also implanted some commands of which he has no memory."

"What commands?"

"I can't read them. I can just feel that they are there."

"Can you wipe them out?"

"Yes. The spells are relatively elementary, but unfortunately he'll lose the whole night. I hate to take away the high point of his life."

"It's got to be done. Otherwise he's a threat to the whole army."

"Will he know how much he's lost?" asked Njal.

"No. All the suggestions will cease, and he'll know he was cheated by the drink."

"I wonder whether that's what happened to me," Grimbolt sighed.

"He'll lose nothing real. Please get to it," said Alsenius.

Brother Lambent turned back to Briggs and murmured a few words. The lieutenant opened his eyes and stared blankly. The priest retained unblinking eye contact as he crooned softly for several minutes. At last he closed his eyes, releasing Briggs, who shook his head and looked around him in bewilderment. "What did he do to me?" he demanded.

"He took away an illusion." Grimbolt patted him on the shoulder. "What do you remember about last night?"

"I had a woman up from Sailors' Rest and . . ." For a moment he felt the ghost of a lost memory. He groped in his mind for something he was sure he remembered, but all he found was the bitter taste of the drink. "She drugged me. The dirty whore cheated me." Fury almost choked him. "I paid her fifty gold pieces and she doped me."

"She did worse than that," said Grimbolt sadly. "She gave you a false memory and crammed you full of hypnotic commands. Brother Lambent has freed you from both."

"I'll have the Emergency Patrol on her. She can't cheat his Majesty's officers and get away with it. Back to the city!" He lurched toward the path.

"Hold on!" Grimbolt grabbed him. "Don't mess things up by racketing around brainlessly. There's nothing you can do about her. She's dead; a SUICIDE spell killed her as soon as she was tied up for interrogation. But she probably wasn't working alone. There may be others, and you don't want to scare them off. Think, man!"

"May I suggest a cup of tea and a pastry," suggested Brother Lambent. "Your friends need to plan."

"Plan, hell! All I want is to call the Patrol and lop heads."

"Well first you have to find the heads." Alsenius interrupted. "If whoever sent her learns you've been freed, they'll either send somebody to kill you or wrap you up in spells again, or they'll panic and rush back to their temple. Then we'll have to start over again from scratch. If you let them think you still remember that impossible night she planted in your mind and that the hidden commands are still in place, they'll continue with whatever they're plotting. Work with us, and we have a good chance bagging the whole crew. My guess is that Sailors' Rest has a nest of Priestesses working together." He emptied his cup and got up to pace back and forth.

"Fifty gold pieces! She fleeced me out of three months' pay," Briggs fumed.

"Look, we'll get the money back from her corpse," Grimbolt promised. "If Bottomly has pinched it, we'll get it out of his hide."

"Serve the little pimp right if you cut it out of his crotch."

"We should check Ensign Bottomly to see whether he's been CHARMED. If he's free, we should protect him, because he runs the whole operation for the bachelor officers. Then we'd better check as many officers as we can—especially the Emergency Patrol."

"We need to find out whether the mistress of Sailors' Rest is a priestess," Njal urged. "If the Pythoness is running the whole place, the Sergeant Major should just close it down and lock everybody up. If, as I suspect, there are two or three priestesses working under cover, we don't want to destroy the business, because we can be sure it will be replaced by something worse."

Alsenius turned to the priest. "Brother Lambent, is there any chance you could be persuaded to disguise yourself as an officer and come with us. We need to test everyone we can catch, and we need protection against spells."

"I'm sorry. I should really like to help you, but I must stick to my post here and serve my Lady."

"Codswallop!" Grimbolt exclaimed. "Serve my foot. All you do is lie around here admiring yourself and conjuring up wet dreams. If you want to serve your Lady, you'll get off your beautiful arse and fight her enemies. How many new worshipers have you recruited in the last month?"

"Well, I can't really be sure. I've had several visitors to the shrine."

"Several visitors? No converts. Your Lady has got nothing out of you but sleepy admiration. Meanwhile her rival the Pythoness has sent priestesses all over the continent casting spells on innocent victims and herding in the worshipers by the cartload. You're no priest. You're nothing but a freeloading, self-admiring, male prostitute. If you were my priest, I'd turn you into a toad."

"But . . ."

"But! But! Get off your butt and get down on your knees and ask your Lady what she wants." Grimbolt grabbed him by the shoulders and forced him down. "Now shut up and pray."

Brother Lambent inched toward the comfort of his altar couch.

"No you don't. You're not going to lie down all comfy and hope for a dream. You're going to bruise your knees until they peel, but you're going to find out there's more to service than being a dream stud." He stood menacingly over him.

Briggs stared in amusement; Alsenius nodded his approval, and Njal laughed gleefully. The priest tried to shift his knees off an inconvenient twig; Then he tried to find a comfortable way to kneel. Then he silently cursed Grimbolt's bullying, but Grimbolt kept an uncompromising hand on his shoulder and held him down. After ten minutes of increasing discomfort, he attempted a half-hearted prayer. By another ten minutes, his fervor increased, and soon after that, he found himself pleading for some sign that would convince his persecutor that he had prayed.

To his dismay he thought he heard Aphrodite's shimmering laughter. His back ached and his knees were killing him, and the laughter-loving Aphrodite laughed. Knowing that his Lady was capricious and often cruel, he dared not interrupt. Then he discovered that his companions heard the laughter and were sharing her amusement. "Damn it, it's not funny."

"Oh, but it is." Her musical voice cut through his protests, and he felt her fingers gently tickling him in embarrassing places, adding lust to pain. "The hairy one is right. You have never served me; you've served yourself while putting me off with words. You haven't even worshiped me—just that beautiful body I gave you."

He tried to shift his knees again, but her hands weighed him painfully down. "Hear me! You will cover up that body before I cover it with warts and wrinkles. You will follow these men and do their bidding, and you will have no pleasure until you have converted twelve followers of the Pythoness to my worship." He felt a cutting sting across his back, and the welt of a whip cut appeared across his satin skin.

"Ouch!" He leaped to his feet as another welt appeared across this buttocks and Aphrodite's laughter echoed audibly through the shrine.

A swift gesture produced a kaftan, which he flung over himself as a third whip cut marked the back of his thighs. "All right, I'll go. I'll go."

The laughter of Aphrodite almost prostrated his visitors as Brother Lambent conjured a cloak and sandals and started off down the path toward the city.

"He did something to my memory," Lieutenant Briggs complained to Grimbolt. "When I came up here, I remembered something that happened last night. Now it's gone, and all I remember is drinking that bitter stuff and passing out."

"She wanted you to think she earned her fee, so she planted a false memory along with some sneaky commands. Brother Lambent erased the commands, and the false memory went with them."

"So she really did cheat me. Why don't I feel horny, then, if nothing happened?"

"I'm the last man to ask about memories," Grimbolt sighed. "I've had most of my life taken away from me."

With Aphrodite's mocking laughter driving Brother Lambent, they made remarkable speed back to the barracks. Alsenius provided Brother Lambent with a Lieutenant's uniform and sent him to Ensign Bottomly for room assignment. While they were arranging his housing, the new Lieutenant stared into the Ensign's mind for hidden trash. Aside from a CHARM spell, he found nothing to erase. Then, while Bottomly was logging the room assignment, he cast an IMMUNE spell to provide what protection he could against further enchantment.

That evening, Alsenius received an official message commanding him and his two assistants to appear in the presence of the King at the seventh hour in the royal office. He took Brother Lambent aside. "I'm sorry to dump this investigation on you with so little notice," he said, "but we're going to be sent of a royal mission. Briggs is too dumb to trust and Bottomly's too slick, so you're going to have to keep up this investigation. I've asked Natalie, the woman we've trusted to find out what she can, to come to you as soon as possible. That should give you a chance to inspect her for hidden spells and cast your IMMUNE on her. She might have learned something more about Sailors' Rest. You'll have to use your own judgment about how to act on any information you get. If you use her professionally, make sure you pay her. She has dues to pay to her 'hotel' and somebody will notice if she works for free. I'll tell the Sergeant-Major about you. If you need help or advice, go to him."

Brother Lambent started to protest, but felt his Lady's squeezing hand and nodded. Apparently she meant what she said about converts.

The next morning Alsenius, Njal, and Grimbolt put on their dress uniforms and reported to Sergeant-Major Benbow. He escorted them to the royal waiting room. To their amazement, a footman appeared promptly on the seventh hour to escort them into the presence.

King Roger sat behind a massive desk. He received their homage with a courteous nod and gestured them to seats. "We have received favorable reports of your skill, and we have approved General Blyte's decision to give you commissions in our army. We understand that you are inquiring into the provisions for maintaining morale in our army."

"We believe that alien agents have infiltrated the brothels which supply women for the entertainment of your Majesty's bachelor officers."

"You imply that our officers frequent houses of ill repute?"

"Oh come," Njal interrupted, "Your Majesty cannot believe that bachelor officers have sworn celibacy."

The royal spine stiffened. "We are aware of the facts of life, though one does not usually introduce them into serious conversation."

"An army may march on it's stomach," Njal retorted., "But it sleeps on its . . ."

"We are aware of the army's anatomy." Icicles hung from his words.

"The fact remains, your Majesty," Grimbolt interposed, "we have proof that prostitutes are casting mind-affecting spells on some of your officers, and that military secrecy has, therefore, become a myth."

His Majesty blinked twice and drummed his fingers on his desk. Sergeant-Major Benbow ignored his sovereign's wrath and pursued the issue. "Your Majesty, General Blyte has authorized a thorough study of the problem. A serious threat to military security has been uncovered, and the Army has the courage to recognize its peril and to deal with it."

"Blyte is a pompous imbecile. If he has done anything intelligent it is because you tricked him into it." The icicles showed signs of melting.

"If your Majesty will trust those of us who influence military policy, we have already taken important steps to correct the problem. We are reforming the system to thwart the foreign influence on our junior officers and our troops. We are designing more suitable recreational facilities and plan to employ trustworthy experts to provide appropriate leisure activities for our glorious troops."

The uplifting rhetoric warmed the royal mood, and his Majesty turned to the real purpose of the meeting. From the drawer of his desk he drew a plain, but impressive, dagger. "Would you say that this is an unusual weapon?' he asked.

"Only in the hands of your Majesty," Benbow responded. "A royal dagger should bear suitable adornment."

"And yet, your Majesty," Alsenius interrupted, "its workmanship is excellent." He reached for the weapon and tested its edge. "This is no ordinary iron dagger, nor was its blade fashioned by an ordinary weapon smith. What is it made of." He examined the satiny silver finish of the blade and tested its edge by dropping a hair upon it. The hair parted and the pieces dropped to the floor.

"Lord President of the Thieves Guild presented it to us, saying only that it was a master weapon fashioned of 'star metal.'"

"Metal extracted from a fallen star? That is indeed a rare weapon."

"Do you know of any local legends of a fallen star?" Njal asked. "It would have made quite a spectacular landing."

"That is part of your mission. A fallen star was observed about sixty years ago in northern Arragor, near the Zharkovian border. This dagger was stolen from one of the Pythoness' Amazons. If the female warriors of the Hegemony of the Pythoness have access to weapons of this quality, the neighbors of the Hegemony have serious problems. Under cover of a mission to rescue my daughter, Princess Catherine, from the court of Arragor, you are to seek out the site of the star fall and learn whether star metal can be extracted from the site.

"You may be aware that our royal daughter, Princess Catherine, was betrothed to Crown Prince Humber of Arragor. Our purpose was to strengthen our alliance with King Humber VII with intimate family ties. Regrettably, King Humber was assassinated about two years ago, and the Crown Prince disappeared shortly afterwards."

"The assassins were apprehended?" Alsenius ventured to ask.

"They were not. Two years have passed, and Queen-Regent Elsa still detains Princess Catherine while her counselors dither ineffectually. We have requested the return of the Princess so that we may negotiate a favorable treaty with another of our neighbors, but the Queen-Regent insists that Prince Humber is still alive and will soon return to his duties. For the last two months we have received no communications from Princess Catherine. We conclude that she is no longer at liberty, or at least that her letters have been intercepted."

"And your Majesty wishes us to investigate?" suggested Alsenius.

"My Majesty commands that you rescue Princess Catherine and deliver her safely to her father's care without causing a war between Quatch and Arragor." Suddenly everybody knew the interview was over.

The Sergeant-Major rose from his chair and bowed. "May we request permission to withdraw and consult about the details of the mission?"

His Majesty nodded. "You will report directly to us as soon as the rescue party has set out, and the party will keep us informed of all progress. The Princess should grace our court within three months so that she may greet her new fiancé."

V—Sniffing Around

Nicholas awoke to the sound of someone entering the room He quickly recognized the scent of the serving maid who did for him, and he rolled over to look at her. She almost dropped the tea tray when she saw a hound lying in Lord Nicholas' bed. "Shoo," she shouted. "Get out of here." She set the tray on a table and flapped her apron at the beast. "Shoo! Get out of here! Shoo!" The apron upset his vision, but he saw her reach for the poker from beside the fireplace.

He had rather enjoyed her cheery chatter when she brought him his morning tea, so that he had no desire to bite her. He tried to speak soothingly, but could only bark. Since the poker looked very threatening as it approached, he decided to scramble off the bed and allow her to drive him out the door. The pressure on his bladder convinced him that he should seek the garden. He was still disoriented by the limitations on his vision, and especially his drastically lowered point of view. Still, he could clearly smell a fresh draft from the outside, and he quickly found a door. Since he found it difficult to manage the handle, he resorted to howling. He was relieved to hear that his voice was still clear and accurate of pitch, though he could not force his mouth into articulation. He tried howling a scale, but found a canine glissando more comfortable.

A footman dashed along the corridor and hastened to let him out. He headed for a tree and managed to balance on three legs long enough to relieve himself. "I have to let the dog do these things—mustn't think about them." Then the overwhelming volume of odors demanded his attention. It took him a long time to trace the tangled patterns of servants dashing about their jobs. He sniffed out the scent record of several assignations in the Gazebo. Then he caught the trail of a young rabbit and followed it eagerly to a hole in the garden. He soon found that his feet were not especially adapted to digging, but he made enough progress to scare a victim out of a hole a few yards to the right of his excavation. Swiftly he pounced and soon enjoyed the succulent crunch of breakfast.

He was still uncomfortably covered with debris from the crash of the night before, so he sought out a quincunx pool with a lot of vague statues spouting into it. Without thinking he lunged over the side and landed with a splash about a foot below ground level. He found his swimming skills completely adequate, and he enjoyed paddling around. He tried to remember what the pool looked like to human vision, but soon gave up. When he tired of swimming, he discovered that he could touch the muddy bottom with his hind legs and keep his head above water by splashing. Then he looked up at the ornamental wall which surrounded the pool. It wouldn't have bothered him when he was human, but it was certainly too high for him to reach it with his front paws. He tried hopping on his hind legs to hook his front ones over the edge of the barrier, but his body was too heavy and his legs too short.

He paddled to one of the points of the star, hoping he wedge his way up with the rough stone to support him on both sides, but he had no fingers to grab with. He was in no danger of drowning, but imprisonment threatened him with panic. "It's damned embarrassing to get trapped in a silly place like this," he thought, "but I've got to get out and about my business." He settled back into the water and braced his back feet. Then he lifted his head and filled the neighborhood with his howls. Presently he heard the beagles in the hunter's kennels mimicking his voice. After that the dalmations from the carriage house joined in. Even the ornamental pekes and spaniels began yapping.

"Oh damn, now everybody knows what a fool I've made of myself." He flung himself against the acute angle of the star point again, and this time his paws found purchase on a rough spot. Painfully the dragged himself upwards, cursing at the way his body gained weight as he emerged. Then he found a low-hanging branch of an ornamental shrub and clamped his teeth upon it to hold his weight while he scrabbled for a higher purchase with his paws. At last he got his right rear claw caught in a crack. Inch by inch he shoved upward until he found a niche for his left rear foot and drove himself up to hook his neck over the edge of the wall. By the time the gardener finally came to investigate the noise, he needed only to grab the loose hide around Nicholas' neck and drag him out.

Unthinking, he drenched his rescuer as he instinctively shook himself and sprayed the entire area.

"Damned fool hound," grumbled the gardener. "You'd think he'd have more sense." He shook his head and chuckled at the dog's stupidity, then beat a hasty retreat as the bloodhound launched into a second convulsive shake.

Nicholas slunk into the bushes, pausing for a couple more shakes, then lifted his leg with *savoir faire* against an oak.

"I need to tell somebody what happened. The trouble is, I can't talk. Maybe if I go back into the palace I can find somebody I know." He thought for a moment about knowing. "My eyes are pretty good for seeing around, but I can't focus them well enough to recognize faces. I can recognize anybody by smell, but when I was a human I never smelled of anybody. I haven't the ghost of an idea what Septimus smells like. I could identify the queen's perfume, but half the women at court wear the same stuff. Damn it, what does Septimus smell like?"

He realized that finding his way around the palace presented the same problem. He had always recognized corridors by sight. He wandered back to the palace, but the door handles were too high and badly arranged for his height and paws. When he tried to sneak in past a footman coming through, he tripped his doorkeeper and got chased away. Finally he overbore a little housemaid and dashed down a corridor before she could right herself and see where he went. He could distinguish hundreds of scent trails of people who had gone this way, but could not guess where the hallway led. He suppressed the temptation to lift his leg and mark the trail. If anyone caught him doing that, he'd be thrown out. As a matter of fact about ten minutes later a young footman caught him by the loose hide on his back and dragged him, protesting, out through a door.

He sniffed his way to the kennels and growled a dalmation away from a grim looking pile of mush. It didn't taste bad. In fact, it went down so fast he didn't really taste it at all. The dalmation started yapping about a damned gelding that stole his meal, so he bolted and sniffed his way around the garden looking for something familiar. When he nosed his way into the vicinity of the overgrown summer house, he remembered his mission. "I learned a lot using my sensitivity to psychic impressions. I'll bet I can nose out a whole lot of stuff out here now," he thought. "I smelled the prussic acid, and I identified the necromantic magic. Maybe I could even identify old Septimus' scent." He nosed around the area. "Ahha! Here's the place where Lord Crabhook and the soldier arrested Septimus and me." He inhaled deeply and let the scents flow across his nasal passages. "I'm pretty sure that footprint is my human scent. So this one right beside mine must be old Septimus." He sneezed on a heavy scent of perfume. "Ah, that stench is Lord Crabhook. I remember I thought he used too much perfume." He sniffed cautiously. "There, underneath all that stink-water, I can just make out old Crabhook's natural scent. That means these others are soldiers." He dashed a few yards back-trailing Lord Septimus; then he stopped. I can follow this trail any time. Maybe I had better learn all I can about this place."

He headed for the bushes outside the summer house until he found the place where the necromantic spell had aged the priestess who cast it. "Now I'll recognize the old bat wherever I scent her." He stopped and pondered all the information his nose was giving him. "She's very old and doesn't bother to wear any perfume, so she probably looks like last year's bouquet and doesn't care. She's pretty dried up, and she doesn't get around too easily. Her trail starts and stops very abruptly, so I assume she TELEPORTED in and out. Her trail leads into the summer house. Ah! Here her smell merges with that of the young man who was hit by her spell. She must have grabbed him while he was still stunned and TELEPORTED both of them. So that must be the scent of the missing crown prince. He smells good. I think I could like him. There's no meanness about his scent, and surprisingly little fear, considering what just happened to him."

Nicholas settled his rump on the deck and scratched his left ear with his hind foot. "You know a dog really has a lot going for him in this investigation game. I've learned more in this visit than all the mages and thieves found out over the months. Unfortunately I only snuffed the surface when I was human." He was turning to check out King Humber's chair when his nose detected something else. "Hey, wait a minute! Here's a track of the prince heading northward. Maybe the priestess didn't take him with her when she TELEPORTED away." As suddenly as he had spotted it, he lost the track. "Damn those courtiers and servants. They've tramped their scent all over everything. I can't tell whether the prince got carried away or escaped."

Discouraged, he turned back to the throne chair. "Yes, the poison was definitely in the peach, and the king knew it before he died. I can smell his fear even after two years." He went to the chairs on the other side of the enclosure. "These must have been the chairs of the general, of the old seneschal and his wife, and of the High Priestess." He checked them carefully. "It wasn't the same priestess who made off with the prince. But this is her scent over here. There have been too many people tramping around here. I can't be sure whether she went near the king, She could have got a peach from the prince and poisoned it, then tricked him into giving it to his father." Suddenly a new idea struck him. "I have to find the orchard where the prince found the peaches. It was the wrong time of year for peaches; that's why the prince made such a fuss over finding them. What if the priestess sneaked into the orchard and enchanted the peaches. She could have poisoned one of them and then hypnotized the prince to make sure he gave his father the poisoned one." Then he paused again. "What if it wasn't that priestess who did the poisoning. What if the one I smelled in the bushes went to the orchard and hypnotized the prince to give his father the right peach. I must find the orchard and see if I can smell some remaining trace of her." He felt his tail wagging furiously as he thought.

"Maybe now is the time to track old Septimus back to his chambers. Heaven knows how I'm going to get back into the palace, but I need his help to follow this through." He picked up Septimus' trail and trotted along it, while trying to sort all the information his nose had given him. Suddenly he discovered that he was in full pursuit of a rabbit trail, slavering hungrily as he went. "Oops! Belly before head, eh? I forgot I'm a dog. Oh well, a rabbit would taste good, and Septimus won't mind waiting."

After crunching the rabbit he slurped in a decorative pond, watered a few trees, and wandered back in quest of Septimus' trail. He came upon the remains of a dead bird. "Too ripe to eat," he thought, "but just right for a good roll." He flung himself on his back, and maneuvered himself until he could spread the mess all over his back as he wriggled, rolled, and stretched. Finally he righted himself, shook vigorously, and turned his attention back to the trail.

Even though the scent was old, he had no trouble following it, except that he found himself easily distracted by tracks more interesting to a dog. Finally he reached a large ornate portal and set himself to watch. As soon as he saw the door begin to move, he gathered himself for a rush. Two footmen started out the door carrying a heavy table. Carefully timing his dash, he scooted past the outer footman and between the legs of the table. Unfortunately the second footman's legs blocked the space between the table legs. There was nothing for it but to slam his skull against the man's shins, scattering himself, the footman, and the end of the table half way back into the corridor. There was considerable cursing, but the dog was up and running down the corridor before the men could disentangle themselves from the table. A rapid search pattern located a fresher scent of Septimus which he followed rapidly.

Unfortunately the track led him, not to Septimus' quarters, but to the infirmary, where Lord Septimus had gone the day before. When he reached the door, the place smelled dreadfully wrong. "Drat! I followed him the wrong way, and I don't dare go back for fear I'll run into those footmen again." He sniffed the traffic patterns around the door. "Ah, there he goes down that hallway. I hope he's heading back to his rooms."

Just then the infirmary door opened and Lord Crabhook eased himself cautiously out, using a cane in his left hand and still carrying his right arm in a sling. Without thinking, his Lordship swung the cane and clouted the dog across his nose. The dog's bite reflex sent his Lordship clattering to the floor before Nicholas had time to think. He released the thigh he was chewing and hurtled blindly down the hall, barely managing to dodge an incoming stretcher. Fearing imprisonment if he was caught, he slunk along a side hallway and up a narrow back stairway, only to find his way blocked by a door.

He braced his front paws n the door and examined the latch mechanism as well as he could in the semi-dark. More by luck than skill he raised the latch lever with his nose, and the door creaked open. He slithered through and leaned on the door to close it again. "This must be servants' quarters," he decided. "Maybe I can hide somewhere till night time. It would be easier to follow a scent if there weren't so many people dashing around. He was cautiously prowling the hallway, testing for unlatched doors, when he heard a woman's voice behind him. "Oh, Myrtle, look at that poor dog. He must be lost."

"He's certainly a mess," said Myrtle. "He's got blood all over his face, and it looks like somebody's whacked him across the nose."

Nicholas settled back on his haunches and tried his 'lost boy' look—hoping his bloodhound face would look appropriately sad and innocent. The sagging flesh and drooping ears of the bloodhound, combined with Nicholas' large violet eyes melted Myrtle's heart. "Oh, Flossie, look at him. Did you ever see such a heartbreaker."

Myrtle extended a hand to pat him, but drew back at the mixed rabbit blood and slobber which had accumulated. "He looks so sad, and he's so dirty. If anybody finds him in here, they'll beat him and throw him out. What do you say we give him a bath and find something for him to eat."

"Nobody would bother him in our room if we can keep him quiet. He looks gentle, even if his is so ugly."

Nicholas decided it was time to look harmless, so he flung himself down and rolled helplessly over on his back.

"Oh, the poor dear," Myrtle crooned. "Somebody's cut off his balls, so the poor thing can't have any fun at all."

Nicholas tried to shrink through the floor, and in the process looked even more harmless and miserable.

"Quick, let's get him in our room before somebody comes along." Flossie trotted down a few doors and opened one. In one swift twist, Nicholas flipped to his feet and slithered into the room before his hostesses could change their minds. By the time Myrtle closed the door behind her, he was well under one of the small cots that served the maids for beds.

"I'll go down to the laundry and get one of those big tubs and some soap," said Myrtle. "You can start hauling up some water. Once he doesn't small so bad, we can keep him as a pet."

Nicholas sniffed critically and could find nothing unpleasant about his scent, but obviously the women had their own standards. The idea of a bath under their supervision made his flesh crawl, but he desperately needed a safe refuge inside the palace. Finally he forced himself to yield to their coaxing and crawled out from under the cot. He was too heavy for them to lift easily, so that he had to cooperate with their attempts to tip him into the hot water nose first. There was considerable splashing while he righted himself. Then they knelt by the side of the tub and applied the laundry soap. It was harsh, and it stung, especially when they tried to get the dried blood and slobber off his face. Myrtle crumpled his left ear like a wash cloth, so that he had to shake vigorously to protect it. That splashed soap in his eyes and occasioned a lot more head shaking. Flossie wanted to tip him over and soap his belly, but he made it clear that no one was to mess with his private parts but himself. The women finally yielded this point and began pouring the rinse water over his head and shoulders. By this time he had had enough, so he scrambled to his feet, shook himself violently, and—placing his front paws on the edge of the tub—sprang out, spewing most of the bath on the floor. The women tried to dry him with cloths, but he sprayed them thoroughly as he shook them off.

At this point he tried to make it clear he needed to go outside. He scratched at the door and whimpered in the approved fashion, but they were preoccupied with sopping up the water on the floor. Finally he jolted them with a sonorous bark, and Myrtle said, "Oh, he wants to go outside."

Nicholas put on a vigorous show of scratching and woofing.

"How can we let him out without being seen?" Flossie worried.

"I think we'd better try before we have more to clean up." Flossie opened the door and the bloodhound bolted through the door and down the stairs, shaking water all over the carpets as he went. Fortunately the outside door was ajar, and his weight burst it open. He dashed outside and flung himself on the grass for a good roll. There wasn't anything much to roll in, but at least the grass rubbed his hair the right way. Then he bounced to his feet and shook some more before he headed for a bush and lifted his leg. A footman strolled to the door as Flossie opened it for the dog. Nicholas knocked the man aside and streaked trough the opening.

"What was that?" The footman righted himself and walked in while Flossie held the door.

"That's our new dog," she said. "We found him wandering in the halls and decided to adopt him. He must belong to somebody because he's house broken."

The footman debated whether it would be more profitable to raise a fuss and get praise from the Head Footman or to cock his eye at the two women in hopes of making time. Sex won out, so he stroked Flossie's leg, ogled Myrtle and day-dreamed of blackmailing them over the dog. Nicholas, meanwhile was shaking himself outside their door. The footman held the door for them all, but was not invited in. He decided it was too early to insist, but noted carefully the location of the room.

The women soon left the room to be about their duties. Nicholas slept much of the afternoon and marveled at his capacity for sleep. He studied the door latch and labored over ways to open it. Since it opened inward, leaning his front paws on the door defeated his purpose. After an hour of experimentation, he managed to balance himself on his hind legs and lift his nose under the latch, but that left him with an unlatched, but closed, door. When he extended his paw to hook a toenail between door and casing, he fell forward and had to start over. He was once again balanced at the latch when his mistresses arrived bearing a great plate of table scraps from supper. They were delighted to find him 'begging' and quickly set them in the corner. He wolfed them down, marveling again at how little he tasted. Remembering delicious meals of his human life brought floods of saliva coursing from his jowls, and he shook them off impatiently, much to the disgust of the women.

They dashed off about their evening chores, and he resumed his practice until he mastered the complex maneuvers necessary for escape. When they returned, they were exhausted and fell with little ceremony to their cots. Soon their snores freed Nicholas to attempt his stealthy exit. He reared up, lifted the latch, and stretched to hook a toenail in the door crack. The squeak of the hinges silenced the snorers, but didn't fully waken them. Nicholas managed to slip out into the corridor. "I hope nobody finds the open door," he worried. "That footman looked very closely at their door, but I doubt if he'll dare come around tonight. He needs to make sure of his welcome first. Nicholas shook himself and trotted along the corridor searching for an open stairway.

The dim corridors were a labyrinth of unfamiliar scents, but he trotted confidently to the nearest exit. Here he identified his own trail and those of Myrtle, Flossie, and the footman. He chose a hallway and pursued it to its end at another door, sniffing for anyone familiar. Then he followed another, wider, corridor and sniffed his way to a more imposing entrance. He found more perfumed trails, which he assumed belonged either to women or to more self-important men. Suddenly he sniffed a trail which screamed of fear. "Someone—he thought it was a woman—was moving stealthily from the door to his right along the hall.

"She's not running—no sign of pursuit from the door. Maybe a thief who got in through a window and found her escape route blocked." He tested the door, but found no easy way of opening it. The trail was quite fresh, and it hugged the side of the hall, speeding up when it came to a torch and slowing as the way became darker. "She must be an amateur because a thief with experience would stalk down the center of the hall pretending to have serious business. She's small, and she's not carrying anything very heavy. She must have broken in with something specific in mind. I wonder whether she has it." He sniffed carefully. "Her fear covers all other scents. She's terrified of getting caught. I wonder if she's a spy." As the trail approached a monumental doorway into some kind if state chamber, the fear scent intensified The little thief must have frozen here in the dark behind a great pillar while someone passed. Nicholas examined the tracks going the opposite direction and found one that smelled very self-satisfied which emerged from the grand entrance way.

Suddenly the bloodhound melted into the shadows as important sounding footsteps thudded along the heavy carpeting. As the man opened the great double doors, Nicholas remembered the faint musty odor of the Throne Room. "Surely," he thought. "Septimus must have passed through this entry hundreds of times. I'll just prowl here until I can find his tracks."

The important man lighted a torch in a throne room sconce and strode inside. Nicholas was tempted to follow him inside to see what he was up to, but decided the dangers of being locked into the room were too great. Instead, he slid along the corridor wall following the thief's track, which apparently sprinted along to the great portals that led outside. The fear faded from the trail as the thief apparently sneaked outside undetected. The bloodhound, sniffed the locked and barred portals. Then he picked up Septimus' scent exiting through the same door. He was so delighted at this discovery that he momentarily forgot the important personage in the Throne room. He was back-tracking Septimus' trail when he almost ran into the armored shins.

"Hello, what's this?" The man looked down in surprise.

The bloodhound said "Yipe!" on a very high note, reversed himself into a ball, and then straightened out into a rust-colored streak following his own back trail. The man started to clank in pursuit, but quickly gave up, and Nicholas decided he had searched enough for the night. He had almost reached the stairway to 'his' room when he heard heavy footsteps approaching from ahead. The shadows seemed inadequate for hiding, so he reversed himself and returned to an intersection with what seemed a lessor hall. He retreated along it and hid in the shadow of an opening. Unfortunately the footsteps turned into his hallway. Nicholas backed farther into the shadows and felt empty space under his hind legs. He grouped himself, turned, and plunged down into the dank darkness.

A voice at the head of the stairs challenged, "Come up here immediately!" He heard the man fumbling with his flint lighter, and a few moments later a torch at the top of the staircase smoked alight. The dog's eyes were not sharp enough to identify the man, but his ears carefully recorded the voice, "Who's down there? Advance and be recognized!." Nicholas padded noiselessly away from the stairs while his nose struggled to analyze what lay ahead of him.

As he moved into the darkness his nose warned him of something unidentified, but unpleasant. He felt the hair on the back of his neck rising into a hackle. The place stank of magic, and only the hostile presence at the top of the stairs kept him from bolting.

"Damn it, what's going on down there?" the voice was nearer, but an edge of fear obscured its authority.

Nicholas hesitated between fear of the man behind and apprehension about what lay ahead. He crushed a rising temptation to panic and struggled to think. "There's certainly magic at work. It affects both the man and me. I desperately want to turn tail and run, and he sounds as if fear was nagging him. Perhaps somebody has cast a **FEAR** or **AVOIDANCE** spell down here to keep everybody away from something."

"All right, stay down there and get eaten. See if I care." By this time there was stark terror in the man's voice, and Nicholas heard him turn and retreat.

"He's obviously a brave man, or he would have run," Nicholas reasoned. "I'm a dog, and I'm scared but not panicked; therefore the spell is tuned to humans. Probably the only reason I'm scared is my human consciousness; so let's stop thinking and start sniffing." His hackle still bristled as he prowled into the darkness, but his nose kept feeding him information. Suddenly bells of recognition went off in his mind. "There's almost no recent traffic down here, only three tracks of two women, and I've smelled both of them before. The older scent goes only one way—it's about a month old. I've had a whiff of her somewhere." He stopped and focused his nose on that track. "The second track is only a couple of days old. She went somewhere along here and then returned." He blanked his mind and concentrated on the familiar smells. Suddenly his hackle raised all the way down to the root of his tail. "The older scent is the choir mistress, the priestess who led the alto section in the recital and transformed me when the music came apart. She's up to something down here in the darkness, and she doesn't want to be disturbed." Fear crept up on him as he inched farther down the corridor, and he felt an almost uncontrollable urge to howl and bolt for the staircase. "If only I had a torch," he gasped. "Then he remembered that the need for light was the human dependance on sight. "Use your nose, you fool." His heart slowed a little. He sniffed carefully at the second trail. "There's very little fear in this scent, yet the witch must have cast the Avoidance spell as soon as she got here. It was a man who chased me down here and got scared off. I'm a man—or most of a man—who's been transformed into a dog. This trail is a woman, and she doesn't seem to be affected; therefore the spell must in some way be keyed to masculinity. I can fight it off, perhaps because of my operation, perhaps because I'm a dog, perhaps both."

Then suddenly he recognized the second scent. It was the smell of the thief in the upstairs corridor. He had missed it at first, because upstairs the identity had been masked by the smell of fear. "Does that mean the witch has been working on the thief? Whatever the case, I need to follow my nose a little farther."

Mustering all his will-power and concentrating upon his nose, he inched his way along the long narrow corridor. The scent trails led him on against what had become a screaming mental resistence. He was panting with the effort by the time the trails turned abruptly to the right and ended at a door, which radiated menace and revolting disgust. It was several moments before he could force himself to touch it tentatively with his paw. Nothing happened; so he brought his sensitive nose close enough study it. It seemed to be an ordinary solid wooden door. The nauseating scent of magic made him glad his 'mistresses' had not given him any more table scraps. He forced himself to rise on his hind legs and lean his forepaws against the door while he explored it with his nose. He could find no latch mechanism, but there was what felt like a metal plate near the right-hand edge. He pressed it with his paw, and a painful jolt shot up his leg. He yelped and backed off, nursing his paw. He could smell no blood, but it ached deep into the bone.

"I don't think I'll smell that plate," he thought as he sniffed the floor around the doorway. "This is as far as the trails lead. That would suggest that the choir mistress came from outside, sneaked down here, and set up housekeeping. But that doesn't make sense. She might want to use this place for mischief, but she certainly didn't move in. She came to rehearsals and she was at the performance to **TRANSFORM** me."

He scratched his left ear and shook the saliva off his jowls. "I really ought to go out and spray the garden for a while." His mind wandered to the rabbits he had enjoyed yesterday, and he found himself starting back along the hall. The pain of putting his front paw down brought him up sharply. "Wait! I was thinking something out. What was it." He forced himself back to the door. "Ah! **TELEPORTATION**!" The thought flashed across his mind and cleared the whole picture. "She must have come here and set up a base. Then she memorized the room and **TELEPORTED** out to do her other mischief. Once she had studied the room carefully, she could **TELEPORT** back whenever she wanted to without any danger of being detected. And the last time she came back, she summoned the little thief." Pain and fear pressed more vehemently against his will, and he decided to retreat, holding his front paw crooked in the air.

Relief came quickly as he turned his back on the door and followed his own trail back to the staircase. He found he could use his hurt paw to ascend the stairs, and the distress from the **AVOIDANCE** spell faded as he poked his nose into the hallway above. As he followed his track back toward his room, he found it difficult to think of the place he had just visited. "Apparently the spell affects the memory. That means I had better concentrate on the problem before I lose it."

He came to an outside door with a guard standing watch, and felt a strong urge to wander in the gardens. The guard looked bored, and when he saw the bloodhound ambling toward him, he stooped to scratch behind the dog's ears and ruffle his loose hide. Nicholas tried his most endearing lost boy look, and found it translated into a very respectable lost puppy expression, which melted the soldier. He stooped down and stroked the dog's face and ears. "Do you belong in here?" he asked. Nicholas ventured a nod, then turned and scratched at the door. "Oh, you're housebroken and somebody was too lazy to come down and open the door for you. OK. I'll be your doorkeeper for tonight. Scratch when you want in again." He straightened up and swung the door as if for a nobleman. Nicholas took his cue and strutted out as if he owned the palace.

Once outside he headed for a massive oak, then swaggered across the green. "Now, let's see, I came out here to think something through. Something about a room—a room in the basement. Oh, yes, it had an **AVOIDANCE** spell on it. The Pythoness' witch is using it to come and go. It repels men, but doesn't bother women. A woman, not too long ago, went into the room and came out—probably the same day." The song of a nightingale distracted him, and he found himself dreaming of rabbit. He shook the saliva from his face and forced himself back to thinking. "What if the witch attracted the woman somehow to come down to her. She must have wanted to cast some spells on her to make her do something for the Pythoness. Then she sent her back into the palace to work some mischief."

The strain of concentrating started a buzzing in his head, and his mind wandered back to the taste of fresh rabbit. He found he had actually started hunting for rabbit tracks when he forced himself back to his puzzle. "Of course! She sent the thief to steal something. I need to talk to the Queen and Lord Septimus to see if anything important is missing." He shook himself again to get rid of the buzzing in his head. "I can't do this any more. My dog's brain just won't take this human abuse any longer. I just hope I can remember all this in the morning."

The thought of his 'mistresses' beckoned him irresistibly, so he trotted back to the palace. He scratched softly at the door and uttered a gentle high pitched sound which might have been his own voice shining through his doggy vocal chords. The guardsman opened the door wide enough for him to slip through, and he hurried back to the women's room. He nudged the door shut and curled up under the tiny window. Within moments his legs were twitching as he chased the rabbit of his dreams.

VI—Where is Lord Nicholas?

Queen Elsa was nibbling on a kipper in her dressing room when her maid burst in. "Your Majesty, Lord Septimus is at the door and he insists on seeing you. Says it's an emergency."

"Oh, bother! Emergencies are suppose to wait till I'm dressed." She was on the point of sending Therese away but changed her mind. "Oh send the old fart in. He doesn't usually make a fuss over nothing." She wrapped her robe more securely around her and sat up straight.

"Have you seen Lord Nicholas?" Septimus blurted out while he was kissing her hand.

"At this hour? In my robe?"

"The maid came screaming to my room about an hour ago, saying that she found a dirty red dog sprawled on his Lordship's bed. She chased the beast out, but could find no sign of Lord Nicholas. You know, I was so busy cleaning up after the fiasco at the choir concert that I had no chance to check on individuals. The last time I saw Nicholas was just as the risers collapsed and everybody got dumped. Incidentally we were lucky the accident didn't kill somebody, but we have an infirmary full of injured singers. I saw the Choir Mistress go after Lord Nicholas with her daggers just as everything went smash. After that we were very busy dragging the injured out of danger, but there was no sign of either Lord Nicholas or his assailant among the victims."

"My guards rushed me out of the hall at the first sign something was going wrong," said Elsa. "It was right when they all started to sing off key and Nicholas began that remarkable phrase about peace. I gather the choir was up to something."

"High Priest Farsyte thinks they were trying to cast some sort of mind-control spell with their singing, and Nicholas spoiled it for them by singing something different from what was written. I know he was upset about the music, but I didn't understand what was bothering him. What I fear is that the priestesses somehow got hold of him and spirited him away in the confusion. The only trouble is that I can account for all the priestesses through the infirmary, and nobody saw Lord Nicholas with any of them. In fact, as far as I can determine, I was the last person to see him. But what are we going to say to King Peter if his pet canary is missing?"

"I suppose we'll have to tell him the truth. You will write to King Peter explaining the situation. I will sign your letter tomorrow if we haven't found him by then. Could he have disappeared on his own?"

"He liked to snoop without interference, but I should think he would let us know if he planned to fade out."

"Well, keep me informed." she popped the rest of the kipper into her mouth and washed it down with a swig of tea.

Lord Septimus bowed his way out. He headed out to the summer house, thinking that Nicholas might have returned there. Then he went to the Great Hall where footmen had already removed most of the evidence of the disaster. The fallen risers were gone, and the floors were slippery with fresh polish. He checked with the Head Footman to find out who cleaned up after the collapse. Afterwards individual footman after footman reported to Lord Septimus' office and answered questions about anyone seen entering or leaving the ballroom.

When one of the men hesitated, Septimus prodded, "I'm trying tp find out anything unusual that happened. Even if it seems to have nothing to do with the collapse of the risers, I want to know anything out of the ordinary."

"Well, sir, there was a big rusty bloodhound wandering around, and I wondered how he got in for the concert. He looked kind of groggy, but he went quietly when I sent him out."

"Did he look as if he'd been in the wreck?"

"He was pretty well messed up. As I said he walked like he was groggy. But I patted him and told him to get out of the way, and he went."

Finally, late in the afternoon Lord Septimus went to the Queen's study. "There's not much doubt that the choir were singing some kind of incantation, which Nicholas spoiled by singing about peace. Farsyte was praying to protect the audience, but Lord Nicholas' interference with the singing spell must have rebounded on the choir, because they all started fighting among themselves. That's what caused the risers to collapse. I saw Nicholas with a priestess going at him just as things fell apart. One of the footmen on the clean-up crew said he saw a bloodhound wandering around the Great Hall as if he was dazed. The only other lead we have is the dog the maid chased out of his bed. I suppose we could assume that they are the same dog, and that suggests a strong possibility that the priestesses turned Lord Nicholas into a dog. I plan to check with everybody to find out where the dog went."

"You think one of the priestesses turned him into a dog because he messed up the spell?"

"It's the only lead we have. I'll talk to all the guards who had door duty this morning to see where the dog went out when the maid chased him."

"Maybe some of the maids saw him wandering around. Most likely they would chase him outdoors. I'll get Therese to question the women."

"Thank you, your Majesty. I shall have my hands full with the guards."

It was about an hour later that her Majesty strode into her study and settled at her desk. She automatically reached where the scepter normally lay, and her fingers grasped nothing. Startled, she looked about and saw it lying on the floor.

"Must have been a novice cleaning my study last night." She stooped to pick up the scepter and noticed that one of the desk drawers was not closed tightly. "Damn! I've told Therese to make sure the cleaning maid leaves my desk alone. That stupid girl must have picked up the scepter, and it jolted her so she dropped it on the floor." She glared at the desk. "But how did she open my drawer? They're all trapped." She slammed the scepter on the desk, producing yet another scar in the finish, and savagely yanked the bell pull.

"Therese, who in blazes did you send in here to clean my study?"

"Why, Miriam always does your room, your Majesty."

"Fetch her immediately."

"Is there something amiss, your Majesty?"

"Amiss? That girl knows she's not to touch my desk, and I found my scepter on the floor and one of my drawers half open."

"But your Majesty told me no one could open any of the drawers without your signet ring."

"Fetch that damned girl!" The Queen reached for her scepter, and Therese fled. Queen Elsa yanked open the offending drawer and uttered a yowl of fury. This time the bell pull came down and tangled her in golden cord. The guard came in first and ducked as the scepter crashed against the door frame, then returned gracefully to its mistress' waiting hand. "Fetch Lord Septimus," she roared, winding up for another throw.

The guard scuttled out, slamming the door behind him to protect his rear. Elsa returned to the drawer and pawed furiously through it, flinging its contents around the room. Therese rushed in, prepared for evasive action. "Your Majesty rang." An ornamental ink pot flew by and spattered the tapestry.

"Where is that damned girl?"

"I sent one of the messengers to call her, your Majesty. It will take her a few minutes to dress."

"She's stolen King Humber's signet. Get her down here immediately. I don't care if she's naked; get here down here now!" Therese fled.

Elsa picked up the scepter again, preparing to demolish another statue, when Lord Septimus pelted in. "Oh, put that damned thing down. What's the matter now?" The anger in his voice stopped her, and she glared at him. "Whatever has set you off, you won't solve it by having a fit. Remember you're the queen; sit down; and think." His eyes took in the fallen bell pull and the spattered tapestry as well as the clutter on the floor. "What's missing?"

She dropped into her chair. "How did you know . . ."

"Because you were having a tantrum and were obviously searching for something in your desk. Now calm down and tell me what's wrong."

"King Humber's signet. I keep it locked in my desk. That blasted maid stole it."

"Step by step, please. Your desk drawers only open to someone wearing your signet. Have you taken it off?"

"Of course not, stupid. I don't even take it off in my bath. The desk also opens to the other royal signets."

"Call Prince William and see whether anything has happened to his." He got up and opened the door to call the guard. When he returned he was still pondering. "King Humber's ring was inside the desk, so that could not have been what the thief used. Was Prince Humber wearing his ring when he disappeared?"

"He always wore it. Furthermore it wasn't in his rooms when we searched them."

Therese rushed in hauling Miriam by the wrist. The maid had been asleep after a long night of cleaning, and she wore only the negligee she had seized when routed out of bed.

"Where is the ring?" Queen Elsa demanded.

"R-Ring, your Majesty?" Miriam tried to curtsey.

"Ring, you idiot! You broke into my desk and stole my ring."

"Oh, no. your Majesty!" This time her curtsey was a disaster.

Septimus cleared his throat suggestively. "Would you permit me, your Majesty?"

She reached for the scepter, but sat down and nodded.

"You are the maid who regularly cleans her Majesty's study?" he asked.

Miriam looked gratefully up at him. "Yessir."

"You cleaned the study last night as usual?"

"Yessir." her voice steadied a little.

"Did you find anything unusual when you cleaned it last night?"

"No, sir. There weren't even no broken stuff to throw out, sir." She looked horrified at the condition of the room. "Everything was neat and clean when I left, sir. Honest, I wouldn't leave a mess like this."

Lord Septimus gestured toward the desk, "You're sure you cleaned the desk thoroughly?"

"Oh no, sir. Miss Therese always tells me not to touch the desk. She says there's magic in there that could kill me if I touched it."

"You didn't even try to polish out some of the scratches on the top?"

"Oh no, sir. I dassn't touch it at all, sir."

Lord Septimus turned quietly to his Queen. "Your Majesty, may I suggest that we send this young person back to her room? We know where we can find her if we have any other questions."

When the Queen nodded, Miriam fell to her knees in gratitude so that Therese had to half drag her out.

"Now, before we stir up any further crisis in the household," Lord Septimus suggested, "shall we settle down to thinking this through?"

"Damn you!" She leaned back in her chair and slammed the scepter back on the desk.

Thee came a tap at the door, and Lord Septimus called, "Enter."

A messenger stepped cautiously in and announced, "Prince William, your Majesty." He stepped quickly back outside and shoved the young prince in.

"You sent for me, Mother?" There was a quiver of fear behind his courtly bow. Then he cautiously approached and knelt to kiss his mother's hand. "I really have been good," he volunteered.

She embraced him hastily. "I'm sure you have, William. Your tutors tell me you have done well with your lessons, and Captain Fiers tells me you are handling your sword like a true soldier." At this praise the apprehension faded somewhat from his manner, yet the tension in the room still kept him wary. "She looked down at his left hand. "I see you are wearing your signet."

"Oh yes, Mother. Just as you commanded me, I never take it off."

"Never? It didn't disappear for an hour or so last night?"

"Oh no, Mother. It fits so tight, I would have to soap it if I wanted to take it off, and I wouldn't ever do that." The boy's eyes searched for a possible threat in his mother's face, but she hugged him and smiled.

"I'm glad you are doing so well in your studies. You realize that with your father and brother away, you have to be the man in the family."

He straightened up conscientiously. "Oh yes, Mother. I am ready to defend you from all enemies." His eyes, still wary, searched her face.

She felt tears starting, and swept him up in a mother's embrace. "I do love you, son; I really do love you, but we have so little time for love."

He melted. "I love you, too, Mother, and I'm always ready to protect you."

"Thank you, my son." Formality crept back, but love still glowed through her tears. "I think it's time for your lessons, isn't it."

"Yes, Mother." He snapped to attention, knelt to kiss her hand, retreated to the door, and bowed before he went.

"That leaves only Prince Humber's signet." Septimus summed up the case. "If the Pythoness' servants abducted him, they must have taken his ring. Now the question arises, "Why, if they already have the Prince's ring, do they need the King's?"

"The King's Treasury." Elsa reached for the scepter again. "They must think they can raid his secret treasury with his ring. That means they don't realize the treasury entrance is keyed to the blood Only when the king himself is wearing the signet will it open the door."

"Exactly!" Septimus stood up and paced. "I'll wager they have already tried to get into the magic treasure using the Prince's ring and failed. Now they're going to try the King's signet."

"That doesn't speak very well for palace security," she worried.

"The priestesses apparently have spies everywhere." He sat again and suggested, "It would be very much in character for you to order tea and something tasty if we're going to stay n conference for long."

She looked ruefully back at the tangled bell pull. "I suppose you'll have to send a messenger. And you'd better get this mess cleaned up." She gestured at the contents of the desk drawer and the ink-spattered tapestry. "I don't suppose they can clean the hanging."

"We'll find out." He opened the door and issued a stream of instructions. Then he sat down. "You realize that you have assumed the priestesses know about the King's Treasury."

"I'm prepared to assume they know everything. They must have mice in the court, the army, and the navy. The servants are all suspect. The nobles haven't the brains to be spies, but they leak gossip by the nauseating bargeful."

"Let's ask the real question. Whom do we trust?" Septimus looked her squarely in the eyes. "Before you commit yourself, have you answered the question. 'Is Septimus to be trusted?'"

"My lord Septimus, I trust you better than I trust myself. You are not only faithful, but wise. Unfortunately I am only faithful. Since there are spies everywhere, I have probably let all sorts of things slip."

"You are shrewder than you give yourself credit for. I would trust you to let nothing slip now that we are warned." He presumed to take her hand and stroke it consolingly. "On the same basis, I would trust Prince William, but not his tutors, servants, and playmates. I believe, if we explain the need for secrecy, he might be a very useful ally."

"But he's only a boy."

"He's a precocious boy who is devoted to his brother and his mother. If we want to plant misinformation, he may even be a good enough actor to seem irresponsible."

She looked at him quizzically.

"I've watched him read your moods, and he's one of the few people who can get his own way with you. He's very unsure of his place, and he has learned both to observe and to hold his tongue. I'll wager he can tell us which of his tutors and servants are to be trusted."

She smiled ruefully. "I suppose I have given him reason to fear my temper. You're right that he plays me very carefully. I think I have underrated my son—perhaps both my sons."

"What about Therese?"

"Oh dear! I hadn't thought about her. I take her for granted; she's so competent nobody notices her. She probably knows all there is to know."

"Can you doubt her without destroying her usefulness?"

"You mean still trust her to serve me well, but keep quiet about our plans?" She tapped her teeth with her index finger nail. "I can try. I really believe she loves me, but she might be misled into thinking a limited betrayal is for my own good."

"I will sift the Guard Captain," Septimus volunteered. "I believe he is loyal, but he may not be bright. We need to be very careful who guards your doors, and if we assign special guards to the King's Treasury, we need to be sure of them. Therese would be the ideal one to check on the maids. Perhaps you can question her about them and see how she responds."

A tap at the door preceded the footmen bearing tea and seed cake. The Queen and her Lord Steward sat for over an hour comparing notes on servants and courtiers. It was agreed that they would accuse no one and confide in no one until they had examined those closest to power. "I shall move into the King's Suite," Elsa decided. "It isn't as comfortable as mine, but that's where the King's Treasury is. I moved out after the king's injury, and when we realized that the boar had unmanned him, I never moved back." She sighed, and Lord Septimus squirmed uncomfortably in his chair. "I was pregnant with William at the time, and it seemed silly to disturb Humber's sleep when I was so restless. Afterwards the king thought it was too frustrating to share his bed when he couldn't do anything about it. But if I move back now, it will be more difficult for thieves and spies."

"I would sleep with a couple of daggers at my side," Septimus suggested. "You might even post a couple of guards inside the royal dressing room. At least you must lock yourself inside the bedroom. But it would be better for intruders to have to wade through armed men."

"It's too bad I don't have a heroic lover," she laughed ruefully as her gaze rested on her Lord Steward.

"If Prince William were a couple of years older, I would suggest having him sleep in the dressing room."

"Oh, but the scandal. As a matter if fact, I'd put you there except for the gossip."

The Queen prepared for a day of questioning servants while Lord Septimus returned to the search for the mysterious bloodhound. About noon he caught up with the guard who had let the dog out and in during the night.

"Yessir, he was quite the gentleman," he confided. "Obviously housebroken and used to being talked to. He wasn't your regular kennel dog. He's used to people."

"And you let him in a couple of hours later?"

"Yessir. He scratched at the door. Even nodded to me when he came in; then trotted off down the hall."

"Which way?"

The guard pointed. "Did I do something wrong, sir? I was that bored, and he was so sure what he wanted. I thought he must belong to somebody important."

"Nothing wrong," Septimus sighed, "but if you see him again, tell him Lord Septimus wants to see him and point the way to my quarters. I think I know him, and he may be lost."

"Oh., yes sir." The guard saluted. "I just tell him, like he could understand?"

"What's your name, young man."

"Smedley, sir."

"Well, Smedley, this is rather confidential business. I'd be grateful if you said nothing about the dog or about my questions. We have lost a very highly trained animal, and we'd like to get him back without making a stir. I would even suggest that, if you see him again, you call your relief and bring the dog personally to me. But we would rather this didn't get talked about." Lord Septimus strode out into the garden and sought, once more, the summer house of the murder.

Very early the next morning, Nicholas awoke to the sound of his 'mistresses' dressing. Flossie took him down to a side door and let him out for his morning run. "Come back for supper," she called after him. He turned and made the best bow a dog could make, then set off to sniff the morning news. The most urgent was a mole trail, which he followed stealthily to breakfast. After that he had a good roll in the grass and a refreshing splash in a pond whose side sloped gradually enough to provide an easy exit. Having rid himself of the disgusting smell of soap, he stopped for a good scratch, which reminded him that he was supposed to be thinking. After a good deal of effort he recalled his human business and decided to try the orchard to test his theory that the priestess who worked necromancy on the Crown Prince had tinkered with the orchard fruit and probably bespelled the prince to give the poisoned peach to his father.

"She would first have to enchant the peaches to make them ripen early. Then she would have to poison at least one, and CHARM Prince Humber into wandering in the orchard, picking the fruit, and giving the right peach to his father."

He stopped to mark a tree and promptly forgot his errand while he casually trailed a squirrel to its tree. Since he couldn't climb after it, and he was already full of mole, he watered that tree and wandered off until his human thoughts brought him up sharp. "They say that people who are TRANSFORMED into animals begin to lose their human identity if they stay changed too long. Being a dog is a lot simpler and more pleasant than being human, but I have to fight this, or those damned priestesses will get away with everything."

He shook himself vigorously and began sniffing a patterned search for a two-year-old scent of either the Prince or the 'Witch.' Fortunately few people had tramped through the orchard to obscure the old trail, but the task took long and tedious concentration on one purpose. He found himself again and again distracted by fascinating smells, some of which instinct identified for him, but others had to be thought out. He found a little cottage which had been boarded up for a long time. It disquieted him because its lingering scent reminded him of King Humber. There was also the scent of a woman, but it was definitely not the old priestess.

"The whole area stinks of magic," he grumbled as he prowled around the building. Investigating further the lingering smell of magic finally attracted him to an old peach tree. Someone had stood for a considerable time casting spells. At last beneath the magical stench he thought he identified the 'Witch.' She had apparently **TELEPORTED** to that spot and stayed there, for he found no trail either to or from the tree. He ran to the brook that watered the orchard and took a long drink. Then he took a long breath of fresh air while he shook himself dry. Then he went back to the tree and tried to ignore the magic smell and concentrate on the caster. "Yes," he concluded. "It's the 'Witch' all right. She must have summoned the prince here, because his trail moves directly to her side. She must have enchanted fallen peaches, because there's no smell of him climbing the tree. He wandered under this tree picking up fruit, and then his trail starts off at a trot in the direction of the summer house. Now, all I have to do is follow his trail back to the scene of the crime."

He had almost finished his trailing, when a shift in the wind brought him a fresh scent of Lord Septimus. Instantly he raised his head and pointed into the breeze. His dog mind took over: "I've found my human. Septimus will solved everything. Everything is all right! Without thinking he lifted his muzzle and bayed, then he flung himself toward the strengthening scent, and before he realized it he and Lord Septimus were entangled on the grass. Whimpering gleefully, he licked his Lordship's face.

After the first shock of collision, Lord Septimus struggled to escape the slobbering jowls. His terror at being overthrown yielded to a realization that he was not being devoured, but caressed. He lurched unsteadily to his knees and gave the dog a sharp rap on the nose. "Down boy!" He grabbed the loose hide and forced the enthusiastic face from his own so that he could stare into the intense violet eyes. "Down boy! Don't smother me."

Human intelligence returned to Nicholas, and he backed sheepishly away.

"It is Nicholas, aren't you?" Grammar fled as Lord Septimus labored to kneel upright and study the dog's face. "Nicholas nodded vigorously, tottered to rise on his hind legs, and managed a sloppy bow.

"You can't talk?" Septimus extended his hand to scratch the dog's ears. Nicholas shook his head into a shower of saliva.

"Can you still think?" Nicholas nodded. "A priestess transformed you while the risers were collapsing?"

Nicholas nodded, relieved that some communication was beginning.

"But she didn't take your mind away?"

The nod was accompanied by a dubious shrug.

"You keep forgetting you're not a dog?"

Nicholas wandered off and watered a bush; then he dashed back and began tugging at Septimus' sleeve.

"You've kept on investigating?"

Nicholas almost turned himself inside out and dashed about miming his search; then he began tugging again.

"You want me to come and see? You've smelt something out?"

Nicholas tugged again.

"All right, all right, don't rush me." He struggled to his feet, mopped his face with his sleeve, and attempted to order his attire. "You are even more unsettling as a dog than you were as a canary. But this is really carrying a metaphor too far." His Lordship straightened up and tested his confused joints. "All right, lead on—and not too fast."

Nicholas darted toward the summer house, then lunged back again, then darted off, covering three times as much ground as Septimus. He darted to water, then came crashing back to jolt his companion. "Easy, boy, while I'm not particularly fragile, I'm an old man."

VII—Nikky and the Prince

When they reached the summer house, Nicholas dashed to the spot where the Priestess had worked her magic, striving to pantomime spell-casting.

"All right, I understand something important was hidden in those bushes, but I can't guess what." He sank into the king's chair and puffed in relief. The dog sat staring in front of him, willing him to understand. "Is it still there?" Septimus asked. The dog slobbered a negative.

"Thing or person?"

Nicholas pawed the ground encouragingly.

"Thing?"

More slobber.

"Person?"

A galvanic "yes."

"When?" Then he realized that he was frustrating the dog. "All right, I must guess and you will nod or spatter me."

"Recently?"

A shake.

"More than once?"

A gleeful yes.

"When prince Humber disappeared?"

Nicholas nodded, then jerked his head repeatedly back over his shoulder.

"He was there when the Prince disappeared, but he was also there before—maybe during the murder?"

A triumphant dithyramb of affirmation. Then Nicholas shook his head slightly.

"I'm right, but there's something I've missed." A nod. "Some one else was there?" A negative shake.

"There was only on man there, but I need to guess who he was?"

Nicholas grabbed Septimus' knee and mimed the act of a dog mounting a bitch. Then he shook his head vigorously."

"It was not a rape? I didn't think it was." Nicholas flung himself on his back and strove to look as amorously enticing as he could.

"Not a rape but a seduction?" A vigorous shake-off. Nicholas dashed to a bush and lifted his leg, shaking his head vigorously; then he squatted like a bitch and urinated."

"Oh! Not a dog, but a bitch. Not 'he' but 'she?'"

Another fandango of triumph.

"And she was priestess?"

Nicholas focused his voice and his clear soprano piped a grandiose march of the priestesses.

"More than one priestess?"

"What's going on here?" The voice of Lord Crabhook cut across the conversation.

Before Nicholas could spring and bite the intruder, Lord Septimus commanded, "Down, boy!" and grabbed the loose hide of his neck. "That's just Lord Crabhook protecting the 'sacred shrine'." He turned to Crabhook, "Sorry if we're out of place, but this seemed a quiet place to do some dog training."

"This is still forbidden territory." Lord Crabhook was not amused.

"Yes, I suppose you're right, but I'm trying to train this dog where nobody can see me." Inspiration struck. "You see, the Queen wants to surprise Prince William. The boy keeps begging for a dog, and her Majesty asked me to try to find one that would make a safe pet. Nikky here seemed intelligent enough to train for the prince." He gestured toward Nicholas. "Nikky, sit up."

Nicholas struggled to his haunches and flexed his paws in the traditional begging position.

"Now sing for your supper." Nicholas piped the tune of the military mess call.

"You see, he's quite intelligent." He noticed that Nicholas was swaying. "Down, boy!" Nicholas flopped gratefully into an inert heap. "And surprisingly obedient. I've only been training him for a few days, but I think he's ready to be given to the prince."

"Well I wish, Lord Steward, that you would find some other place for your training sessions. This is a spot sacred to the memory of our late King, and dog-training—even the prince's dog—is hardly a respectful and reverent activity."

"Nikky, sit!" The dog promptly sat up. "You are right as usual, Milord. I think it's time I showed him to the Queen. If she approves, we shall present the dog to the young prince this afternoon." He started along the path back to the palace. "Nikky, come!"

The dog tried to pull Septimus with him to the orchard, but the old man was determined to report to the queen. "I understand yo have something else to show me," he conceded, "but we must get you established in the palace before somebody steals you. It's going to be hard enough to explain to King Peter that you've been transformed. I don't want to have to tell him you're missing."

After a couple more abortive tugs at Septimus' sleeve, Nikky resigned himself to canine obedience. They entered the palace and strode quickly to the study. At the door, Nicholas began furiously sniffing about as he recognized the place where he had found the trail of the thief's flight. Finally he yielded to the Steward's insistence that he enter. As soon as they were alone with the queen, he bowed deeply: "Your Majesty, may I present Lord Nicholas of Zharkovia, Personal Emissary of his Majesty, King Peter."

Nicholas confirmed the introduction by piping an elaborate cadenza and looking woefully up at her with his deep violet eyes.

Queen Elsa blinked, then stared again. "You are Lord Nicholas of Zharkovia?"

Nikky nodded vigorously and reprised his solo with variations.

"You have found a coloratura pooch and conclude that it's Lord Nicholas?"

"A Priestess transformed him after the concert. He spoiled a plot to charm us all with one of the choruses, and I think she lost her temper. It was a thoughtless transformation, but very embarrassing for us."

"What are we going to do with him? How can we explain him to King Peter?"

Lord Septimus shrugged broadly with outstretched hands. "Until we find a spell caster we can trust, I suggest we give him to Prince William. As a royal pet he will have easy access to the family and safe lodging in the Prince's quarters."

"Can he fool William?"

"We agreed that his Royal Highness is one of the few people we can trust. I propose to tell him the secret and use him to protect Lord

Nicholas. Playing in the garden with the Prince will provide cover for whatever investigations the bloodhound wants to undertake."

"He's still investigating?"

Nikky promptly sniffed around the room and demanded to go out.

"He apparently found something outside your door. He is determined to investigate further."

Nikky scratched at the desk and the ran back and forth to the door.

"I think he must have smelled your thief." Septimus interpreted. "He turned to the dog and said. "Someone has stolen the king's signet ring from her Majesty's locked desk."

Nikky nodded furiously and raced over the thief's track again.

"He's already discovered a lot of things we only suspected. That dog's nose sniffs out secrets we cannot see. The only trouble is communication. Until we find a spell caster we can trust to do Speak with Animals, we're going to have to get along with questions and answers. I'm hoping young William and Nikky will work out ways to communicate."

"I suppose you're right. We can't be sure the priestesses haven't charmed even Lord Farsyte, and I wouldn't trust anybody in the Mages' Guild. They may all have sold out to the Pythoness. It's a great burden to put on my William."

"He's fourteen. He would be a father and landholder if her were a peasant. It's hard for a mother to realize how grown up a boy is at that age."

She tugged gently at the new bell pull. "Fetch Prince William."

"And tell him he's not in trouble." Lord Septimus interposed.

Nikky growled deep in his throat.

"I'm sorry, boy, but you've got to put up with human bossiness." Septimus scratched his ears. "You can't tell us what you want to do, so we have to do our best for you. You'll be freer as young William's pet than with any other arrangement I can think of."

The dog shook the saliva from his dewlaps, spotting everything in range.

The queen turned back to her Steward. "I think we're going to have to trust Therese in most things. She already knows everything about my way of life—even about how I think."

"I would agree that she is loyal, but her tongue is loose. I would prefer to keep Nicholas' identity from her."

Her Majesty nodded. "I'm afraid you're right about her tongue. The way she gossips about the maids! There's an old country saying: 'Them that will fetch will carry.' And she certainly fetches."

"Prince William, your Majesty," Therese announced from the doorway.

"Ah, William my dear, I hope we didn't interrupt anything important?"

"Only a geography lesson, and I already know practically everything about geography." His eyes fastened on the bloodhound and began to glow covetously. "That's an awesome dog." He risked offending protocol to cross the room and kneel down beside Nikky.

"Subject to certain conditions, he is yours," his mother announced.

The word conditions made mo impression. He flung himself upon the bloodhound with both arms around his neck. Nikky responded as a dog before his human dignity could assert itself. He swiped his great tongue completely across the boy's face and collapsed blissfully in the embrace."

"Therese," her Majesty overrode the emotion of the moment. "Please see to it that his Highness' attendants know about the royal pet. They need to provide a comfortable place in the Prince's quarters: bedding, food, provision for access to the garden. You know what is necessary. Go make sure the boy enjoys his dog."

Therese curtseyed and closed the door behind her.

"Now, William, pay close attention. I told you there are conditions."

He looked up suspiciously. "You mean he isn't mine after all?"

"I mean—Oh, dear, how do I explain this."

Lord Septimus cleared his throat, and the queen looked hopefully toward him.

"What your mother means is that this is a very special dog—if you can really call him a dog. We desperately need your help with a problem related to your brother's disappearance. The same enemies who killed your father and kidnapped your brother have transformed Lord Nicholas—you remember Lord Nicholas, don't you (the man with the high voice who is investigating for us)"—The boy nodded—"have transformed Lord Nicholas into this bloodhound."

Prince William started backward in dismay.

"It's all right. That's why we need you. Nikky—that's what we call him now he's a dog—needs somebody to take care of him. No one must know he isn't a real dog, and the best place to hide a dog is with a boy. But we need a very special boy—a boy with good sense, who can figure out the best way to enjoy a dog without insulting him as a man."

Prince William looked longingly at the dog. "He can understand me, just like another person?"

Nikky sat up and nodded.

"But he's a real dog, too?" Nikky nodded again and anointed his face with saliva.

"And we need to play together so that nobody knows he's not a dog?" His tone brightened. "Really play?" Nikky responded by shoving the prince to the floor and cuffing him gently in the face with his paw. William grabbed Nikky's loose hide and struggled to throw him off. Suddenly there was a rough-house that endangered the furniture.

"I think that's enough for now," his Lordship admonished. "We are trusting you with a state secret which nobody else knows. You are to assist Lord Nicholas whenever he wants to investigate, but you must fool everybody."

Prince William turned to his dog. "You agree?" Nikky nodded. "You'll wear a collar?" Nikky shook his head furiously. "But you have to mind me." Nikky nodded. "You'll be smart enough to keep out of trouble without a collar?" Nikky pawed the rug disdainfully. "OK, I keep forgetting you have a man's mind. You look like just a dog." The dog sprayed slobber.

William looked up at his mother. "You really have given me a man's job."

"Lord Septimus just reminded me that you would be of age if you were not a prince. If it turns out that something terrible has happened to your brother, you are King." She looked at him wistfully.

"And I've got to do a man's job by being a boy with my dog,"

Nikky stood up, bowed as best he could, and howled the royal anthem.

"Good!" William leaped to his feet and dashed toward the door, "Come on, Nikky, let's go out in the gardens and play." The two made a cyclone exit and rioted down the hall and out the door.

Nicholas was amazed at his delight in pure physical activity. He raced in circles, challenging his new master to catch him, and play filled his entire being. He allowed himself to be caught briefly, only to revel in the struggle to escape. When William grabbed a stick and flung it, paradise became the possibility of catching it in the air. He raced heedless across the grass, ignoring obstacles, with eyes only for the stick. Timing his every motion to the missile, he launched himself—mouth agape—to crunch his jaws upon the wood at exactly the right second. He felt his body plunging earthward and instinctively curled up to land with a jolt on his shoulder, rolled two or three times across the turf, and spring up, triumphantly clutching his trophy. He strutted around the boy, daring him to try to take it back.

When William finally got a hand on the stick they struggled in a slimy tug-of-war. When Nikky won, and his playmate made no further attempt to grab the stick, the dog dropped the trophy at his feet and backed off, eager to have it thrown again. At last the boy remembered his instructions and, panting, paused. "Nikky, are we supposed to be investigating?"

The dog looked at him blankly, then bounced back to receive another throw. The Prince dropped the wet stick and looked earnestly at his pet. "Lord Septimus said your enchantment might make you forget you're a man. Should we be doing something important?"

Nicholas shook himself and realized he had completely forgotten everything but the joy of play. He sat down and scratched his left ear, then strode aside and watered a bush. What he most desperately needed was a way to communicate. He had discovered things his friends needed to know before he forgot them. It was getting harder to remember his human purposes—even his human identity. They had to work out some way to talk. There was no way he could force his throat and tongue into human speech. He found a patch of bare ground and tried to scratch a message with a claw. The effort was a miserable failure, but he had William's attention. He rubbed out the scratches with his paw and tried to force his muscles to produce a single 'A.'

"Oh, I see, you're trying to write." Nikky nodded vehemently.

"You can't make your paw work like a hand?" Nikky nodded. "And you can't make your tongue talk?" Nikky ululated dismally.

"But you can still sing? I heard you do the royal anthem."

Nikky lifted his muzzle and performed a dazzling cadenza.

"Well, that gives us seven letters." The boy sang A, B, C, D, E, F, G, A.

Nikky sang the pitches 'FACE,' and William promptly answered 'face.' "Yes, that ought to work, if only we had more letters."

Nikky paused and scratched. Suddenly he sang a high A followed by E,A,D. Then he shook his head vigorously, splaying drool in all directions.

"Aead?" Nikky rushed over to him and slapped the back if his skull with his paw.

William put his hand to his head, and Nikky nodded so ferociously that he almost lost his balance. William stared at him and Nikky began slapping his own head, then shaking it."

"Head?" Nikky repeated his song; High A, E, low A, D. "Oh, I see. If you sing high A, that means "H." Nikky pushed him over and gave him a slobbery kiss. The he sang High A, High B, G, High A.

William translated, "H, High B—Oh, that would be *I*, so you sang *H,I,G,H.* Oh Nikky, we have an alphabet." He wrapped his arms around the dog's neck and hugged him. Then he stopped. "That means you've got to be able to sing four octaves."

At that point Nikky strutted around him singing a scale that began with a deep almost baritone chest tone A and ascending stepwise to the peak of his soprano F above high C. Then he carefully fluted C, A—two octaves up—F—up two, E, and grabbed the boy's wrist with his teeth and almost dragging him along.

As he puffed along, William struggled to spell out "Come." The Bloodhound streaked off to the summer house and wriggled inside. He attempted a bird dog's point at the throne chair and chanted "Father—Dead."

"My father was sitting here when he died?" Nikky nodded. Then he dashed out to the hiding place in the bushes and pointed. "PRIESTESS, SPELL."

"There was a priestess hiding out here and she killed him with a spell."

Nikky nodded and then shook his head.

"Priestess hiding here?"

Nikky nodded

"She cast a spell?"

Nikky fluted "More,"

'She cast a lot of spells?"

A nod.

"But that's not what killed Father?"

A nod.

"She cast them on Brother?"

They finally worked out that the Priestess had cast spells on Prince Humber a few days after the king's death. Then Nikky dragged the boy to the orchard and showed him the old peach tree beside the boarded-up cottage. "Priestess enchant peaches ripe. charm brother. TELEPORT away."

After a few false starts William was able to summarize. "So she made some peaches ripe, poisoned one, and cast a spell on my brother to make him give that one to Father. She came back a couple of days later and caught my brother checking out the summer house. So she carried him away on a **TELEPORT**."

Nikky nodded, then shook his head to indicate uncertainty about the carrying off.

"How much have you been able to show Lord Septimus?"

Nikky tugged at his wrist and started back toward the palace. At the door of Lord Septimus' office, the guard tried to brush them off. Nikky began a deep-chested growl, but Prince William silenced him with a gesture. Then the boy straightened up to his full five-foot height, glared in his best imitation of his mother's imperious gaze, deepened his uncertain treble to its most resonant, and commanded, "Prince William of Arragor, son of King Humber VII, Heir Presumptive to the throne of Arragor, demands immediate admittance to the presence of his loyal Steward, Lord Septimus."

The guard wilted aside and opened the door, announcing, "His Royal Highness, Prince William of Arragor."

The Lord Steward looked up from a parchment he was studying, and rose to greet the prince as Nikky slipped unobtrusively past the guard. "Welcome William. I see you've brought Nikky. That will be all." He motioned for the guard to leave. "You will exclude all others while I am in conference with the Prince." He settled back in his chair and shoved a plate with a couple of pastries on it toward the boy, who promptly grabbed both. "Tea?"

William nodded around the first pastry. As soon as his mouth was clear, he added, "Lord Septimus, Nikky and I have figured out how to talk." Lord Septimus almost dropped the teapot, slopping the steaming liquid into his lap and cursing roundly as he mopped himself off. "You've what?"

"We've worked out an alphabet." He cautiously held out his cup as the Lord Steward steadied the pot and poured. "Nikky, spell *head*."

Nikky: "A⇑, E, A, D."

"Ingenious! Pitch alphabet. The octave is 'H.'"

"He can sing four octaves, so we can do the whole alphabet."

"Sort of hard on his voice to do Z," Septimus observed. "Why don't you add sharps and flats to make it easier—Low C=A; C#=B etc. You could get your alphabet within easy range and save his throat." Nikky trilled gleefully.

William reported on the information he had already gleaned. "It's pretty slow, but it does work," he half apologized.

"It's brilliant. You've accomplished more in an afternoon than your mother and I did in days. You shall have a medal. If I could find a place to pin it, Nikky should have a medal." He stood up and looked at his lap. "I'll have to go change, but we must report this to the Queen."

Nikky tugged at Septimus sleeve, and William promptly interpreted, "He wants to show you something important."

"It will wait . . ."

Nikky's tugs indicated that it would not wait.

"But . . ."

The tugs got more insistent, and the dog began scratching at the door.

"Take him out quickly and I'll join you as soon as I change."

Nikky came back and tugged Septimus. Then he raised his head and started intoning. William and Septimus counted notes on their fingers, and his Lordship grabbed a pen.

"Emergency find. Come now."

Reluctantly Lord Septimus followed the dog, trying to cover his crotch with a fluttering handkerchief. Nikky led them past the queen's office to the staircase he had explored the previous night. By the time they had half descended, Lord Septimus and William were almost paralyzed with fear and loathing.

"Magic!" Nikky intoned.

His Lordship retreated to the top of the stair and puffed. "Whose?"

"Witch—Priestess. Headquarters below."

"Oh dear, how did you manage to go down?"

"Dog! Women not affected. Dog, less."

"Let's go see her Majesty. She may want to call on Lord Farsyte to try to DISPEL the magic, or she may want to send Therese or even investigate herself. This is very serious." He headed back along the hallway to the royal office door. "Her Majesty will want to see us at once," he told the guard.

The guard raised no question. He opened the door and announced, "Lord Septimus and Prince William—an emergency."

"Well, send them in," she barked.

Nikky shoved in first to make sure he was included.

"Your Majesty, you have a brilliant son. He and the dog have uncovered a Pythoness retreat in the basement of your palace. It is protected by some sort of **AVOIDANCE** spell, which neither William nor I can fight. I think we need the High Priest to try to **Dispel** it immediately. It is certainly connected with the theft of King Humber's seal ring."

Without hesitation Queen Elsa sent a messenger for the High Priest, then turned back for explanation.

"I think we may need Wizard Quackenthorp—much as I dislike trusting him with secrets." Septimus saw her sharp glance at his lap. "I slopped a pot of tea," he explained. "I didn't dare take time to change."

She sent one messenger for Wizard Quackenthorp and another for a fresh robe for his Lordship. "I assume we will say nothing to either of them of Nikky's identity," she said. "Now, exactly what have you discovered?"

"William and Nikky have figured out how to communicate, using the notes of the scale. Nikky told us that the High Priestess has set up a **TELEPORT** room in the basement of the palace. She has cast an **AVOIDANCE** spell on the approach. Nikky says believes that women are not affected by the spell. I gather that Nikky found track of one of our women whom the Priestess apparently summoned."

Nikky interrupted with a series of tones, and William translated a brief summary of his tracking of the female thief and subsequent flight down the stairs to the 'Witch's' spell-protected basement room.

"And you think she can **TELEPORT** in and out of our palace at will?"

Nikky says that she went in once only and never went out. That means either there is a secret passage, or she's still in there without any food, or she's **TELEPORTING**. He says there's only one other recent trail, and that's the thief he followed."

Septimus' robe and the High Priest arrived at the same time. After Septimus had withdrawn briefly into her Majesty's dressing room to change, they were ready to confront the **AVOIDANCE** spell.

"As far as I can remember, this staircase leads down to storage chambers," Elsa remarked as they started down the stairs.

"It certainly has an unpleasant odor," the High Priest commented. "Are you sure someone hasn't died down here?"

"I confess, this isn't a place I would choose to go, but it doesn't repel me." said the Queen.

"I feel the spell as a threat of nameless dread, even here on the stairs," Septimus confessed. "If I didn't realize I have to go forward, I would never go to the bottom of the stairs."

William looked ill as he forced himself down another step. "Something about this place makes my flesh crawl. I think I'm going to sick up."

"And you say it gets worse until you come to a particular door?" Lord Farsyte asked. "I protected myself with IMMUNITY before I came, and even so, I doubt my ability to pass down a long corridor." He and the Queen proceeded to the bottom of the stairs while the others paused in the middle. "What I intended was to place a brazier of incense as close to the center of the spell as possible, but I fear I shall have to perform the ceremony here."

"Will that neutralize the spell?" Queen Elsa asked.

"Probably not. It will clear a circle of about thirty feet, but it will not affect whatever symbol lies at the heart of the spell."

"So it seems your Queen is going to have to rescue all of you heroic men," her Majesty chuckled. "Give me your brazier and your flint lighter, and I will brave the horrors for you."

"But your Majesty . . ." Lord Farsyte started to object, but had to pause as a queasy impulse hit him."

She picked up the brazier and started down the dark corridor. Lord Farsyte was forced to surrender the brazier and wait. Nikky plunged forward, sniffing the trail. "Stupid dog, didn't you count the number of doors?" She muttered. The dog spattered her dress with his head shake and plodded reluctantly ahead. By the time she had counted the fifth door, even she felt a distinct aversion from her quest, but nothing compared to the quivering dread that shook the dog as he struggled to point at the opening. She quickly placed the brazier and lighted the incense, then called back to the Priest, who advanced as far as he could and chanted his prayers with as full voice as he could muster.

It was Nikky who first felt the effects of the counter-spell. The smoke of the incense dulled his sense of smell and quieted his stomach. Then, gradually his terrors eased and he was able to sniff the corridor beyond. The Queen examined the door, being careful not to touch the metal plate. "You are right, this door has been changed. All the others have normal latches, but this one has only a metal plate where the latch belongs."

Nikky mimed a hurt paw to warn her away from the plate. Presently the others approached and stood before the door.

"Clearly one must press this plate to open it," Lord Farsyte observed and extended his palm. Nikky jostled him back, and Septimus warned, "We have reason to believe it's trapped."

The priest lifted his staff near the plate. "You're right. Thank you for warning me. My staff says this plate is trapped."

"Can you open it?" The Queen tapped her foot impatiently.

"This kind of trap can be very tricky. I heard you mention Quackenthorp. Have you called him in for consultation?"

"I should prefer not to share information about state problems with an outsider."

"I agree that the Wizards Guild is not to be trusted, but a Mage can open almost any door with a **KNOCK** spell. If I experiment, we could have very unpleasant side effects." His gesture indicated considerable violence. "I gather that your Majesty only recently learned about this door."

She looked hopelessly at Septimus, who nodded. "I think, your Majesty, that we must brief his Grace about the intrusion." He turned back to Lord Farsyte. "Prince William's dog stumbled on the **AVOIDANCE** spell and dragged his master to explore. As you know the Priestesses of the Pythoness have behaved with overt hostility at the concert, and we have reason to suspect they may have been involved in the death of King Humber. If this mystery represents another hostile intrusion, we shall have to regard ourselves as no longer at peace with the Hegemony of the Pythoness. This is a delicate situation, and no one outside our little group must know about it, lest the Pythoness' spies learn of our plans."

"I can, perhaps, be of some assistance in detecting spies," Lord Farsyte volunteered. "I can examine individuals in a **DETECT TRUTH** zone in which a talisman changes color if it detects an intent to deceive. Do you wish me to go to the Temple and fetch the sacred pearl?"

"It could greatly facilitate our labors," the Lord Steward agreed. "Meanwhile, I suspect we might as well return to your Majesty's office while we await the Mage. I feel rather conspicuous standing around in a basement corridor. That **AVOIDANCE** spell isn't going to come back its it?"

"Not unless she casts it again. I will leave my brazier in your office in case we need it again and bring a fresh supply of incense from the temple." The priest parted from them at the office door.

"I notice you were very selective about the information you shared." Elsa remarked to Septimus.

"He already knows we're having trouble with the Pythoness. Incidentally, his DETECT TRUTH zone will allow us to test Therese and some of the crucial guardsmen. I should like to be able to trust at least your First Maid in Waiting."

Nikky piped in. "Crabhook."

"I don't need a spell to distrust him," Septimus grunted, "though I suppose it would be good to have our suspicions confirmed."

When Wizard Quackenthorp arrived, her Majesty told him only that she had learned of a magically sealed door in the basement of the palace which she need help in opening. The Mage quickly agreed upon a price for his assistance, and Lord Septimus led him to the place. Quackenthorp scrutinized the door with its metal plate. Then he placed a small heap of purple powder in his palm and blew it against the metal. The plate glowed brightly and coruscated with blue and yellow sparks where the grains of powder adhered to it. "Hmm! I would suggest that you withdraw to the end of the hallway. There may be a considerable reaction. Lord Septimus withdrew and the Wizard crouched on the floor as he chanted his incantation. At last he blew a puff of red powder at the door and curled up in a tight ball as the plate shot a bolt of lightning across the hall. The bolt rebounded from the opposite wall and crashed back against the door, then rebounded several more times. Meanwhile the door crashed open, and Septimus brought his lantern up to examine the room.

"Fascinating!" the Mage exclaimed. "Somebody has established a TELEPORT station right here in the basement of the palace. It has been used quite extensively, too."

"How do you know it's a TELEPORT station?" Septimus demanded.

"Oh, it reeks of magic to one with a trained nose. And that platform over there in the corner is a perfect spot to memorize for an arrival." He blew some yellow powder upon the platform. It formed into a vague wispy figure before it scattered across the floor and fizzed and popped vigorously. "Ah-ha! You're having trouble with the Pythoness, I should guess. That looks like the Supreme Priestess' spell-casting. You need to warn the Queen she lies in extreme danger. That woman is the most potent spell-caster in the whole Northwest, and if she has taken this much trouble to meddle in Arragor's affairs, she is planning important mischief. See, she has moved a desk in and had a platform built. This is magically expensive." He paused for a moment to rearrange some memories. "Magic was involved in the disappearance of the Crown Prince. Even the death of King Humber was suspicious, though everybody has made a secret of it." He paused again. "And the concert with the male soprano. That ended in a display of magic. And nobody has seen the singer since. Oh, yes, the Queen-Regent should be warned that she has great trouble." He dashed out of the room and led the way back to the royal office, full of his warnings.

It took considerable time for Quackenthorp to disburden himself to the Queen, and everyone listened silently. Nikky began to snore from his corner of the office. Presently Lord Farsyte returned, and Septimus interrupted the flow of information from the Wizard: "Sir, you are warning us of a crisis of which we are already aware What you have learned is extremely important, but the threat from the Pythoness is so acute that we dare to trust no one. We are reasonably sure that we can trust her Majesty, Prince William, myself, and the High Priest, Lord Farsyte. Everyone else is suspect. We desperately need your assistance, but we must ask you to submit to the test of Lord Farsyte's Zone of Truth. When he has established the zone, we wish to question you to make sure you intend no harm to the realm and no assistance to the Pythoness. Will you agree to such a test?"

"This is highly irregular. I am Senior Wizard if the Mages' Guild."

"And the Mages' Guild may be in the pay to the Pythoness," Queen Elsa interrupted. "We cannot share vital information with you unless we can be sure you are not one of our enemies."

"We expect to pay for your services," Septimus continued, "but only if we are sure the Pythoness has not already enlisted you."

"I detest the Pythoness. It is true that a Mage must charge for his services if he is to prosper, but . . ."

"Then you can have no objection to our invoking the law of the Mercenary," Lord Farsyte put in. "I have now established a **ZONE OF TRUTH** in this room. If anyone speaks with the intent to deceive, this pearl will darken. It does not detect the absolute truth of any statement, only that the speaker believes in its truth."

Lord Septimus stood and faced the pearl. "I affirm my loyalty to the royal house of Arragor, specifically to the Queen-Regent, to the missing Crown Prince Humber, and to the welfare of the realm which they govern. I pledge my best efforts on behalf of the struggle to restore the Crown Prince to his proper place, condition, and authority." He sat. The pearl remained white. He turned to the Wizard. "Will you affirm your loyalty to the Queen-regent and your willingness to reveal nothing of what you have learned or shall learn of this crisis. And will you affirm your willingness to do all that you can to restore the authority of the realm to its proper ruler?"

Quackenthorp stood and bowed to the Queen. "I affirm my loyalty to the realm of Arragor, to the reigning Queen-Regent, and to the missing Crown Prince and King-Designate. I pledge that I have not served and shall not serve the priestesses of the Pythoness or any other individual or agency which plots the overthrow of the rightful monarchy." The pearl remained white.

The Queen promptly summoned Therese and bade her repeat her oath of fealty. Once again the pearl remained white. The guard captain and those men who served regularly as personal guards of the family were then duly sworn again. When the lords of court entered, everyone assumed that Lord Crabhook would either refuse to reaffirm his oath or would be identified as untruthful. To the queen's amazement when he affirmed his loyalty to the King, to the Queen-Regent, to the royal house and to the realm, the pearl remained brilliant white. Lord Farsyte cast a quick Dispel Magic on Crabhook and asked him to repeat his pledge. Impatiently the old lord rattled off the oath again, and the pearl remained white.

Suddenly, Nikky scrambled to his feet, raised his muzzle, and sounded the pitches which affirmed his loyalty to his master, King Peter and his devotion to his assignment to assist Arragor in accordance with the treaty which allied the two realms. Prince William translated, and the pearl remained white.

"What does this mean?" Quackenthorp demanded. "What is this dog doing?"

Prince William spoke up, "This is Nikky, my dog, only he's not a dog because he's Lord Nicholas. King Peter of Zharkovia sent him to help us investigate Dad's murder and my brother's disappearance, only a Priestess turned him into a dog."

"And you can understand his howling?"

"Actually, he's singing, and I understand which letter each tone means."

"That's a clumsy way to do it. All you need is a **TALK WITH ANIMALS** spell," Quackenthorp interrupted.

"Well, it works, and we don't have to cast spells." He hugged his dog defensively, and Nikky lifted a lip to show a gleaming canine tooth.

"We are very proud of William for working it out." Elsa's tone had frosted.

Quackenthorp realized he had offended. "Don't get me wrong," he apologized, "your system is amazingly ingenious, and makes for a wonderful relationship with—" he bowed respectfully toward prince and dog—"with Lord Nicholas, but we could learn much more much faster if you would let me cast a spell that would temporarily make me a master of the dog language."

William looked possessively at Nikky, and his mother rightly read his face. "Could you cast the spell on Prince William? There is a special relationship between them."

Quackenthorp coughed a couple of times and admitted, "The spell could be cast on someone else, but I am better qualified to question the beast." Nikky promptly raised his hackle, growled, and showed both canines.

"You may not be so well qualified to question this particular dog," Lord Septimus suggested. "You are, after all, dealing with a human personality in canine form."

"Oh, I see what you mean. This dog doesn't think like a dog, so, perhaps he doesn't communicate like a dog." He looked down at Nikky, "How well do you communicate with other dogs?"

Nikky piped back—and William translated "I don't."

"Oh, dear, this is most irregular. He may not speak *DOG* at all." He turned away from them and muttered a few words as he sprinkled some white powder on his own head. Then he got down on all fours and barked at Nikky while imitating a rhumba with his posterior. Nikky backed away and growled under his breath. Quackenthorp pawed the floor and whined while cocking his head to the left and wiggling his right ear. Nikky piped and William triumphantly translated, "Stop making an ass of yourself and talk common. You may think you're talking *DOG* to me, but I can't understand your mongrel dialect."

Quackenthorp tried again, but Nikky merely turned his back and farted.

Septimus commented, "That was clearly human speech. No dog I know has that kind of body control."

"I do not believe we should be expected to pay for that spell." The Queen, while amused, had no intention of wasting her treasury on failures.

"Madame, this is a most unconventional animal."

Nikky pulled at William's sleeve and headed for the door. The Prince looked at his mother, and Nikky scratched the door authoritatively.

"That's not exactly *DOG*," said Quackenthorp, "but it is the way most dogs talk to humans. I fear he either cannot or will not speak in the language of his body."

NIkky lifted his leg threateningly, and William hastened to open the door and follow him out.

"That beast still has information," grumbled the Wizard, "and he is going to waste a lot of time communicating it in that clumsy code."

"Lord Nicholas has done things his own way ever since he came here," said the Queen. "I fear it is a way of asserting his own importance."

"And we still face the problem of what to do with the priestess' **TELEPORT** station." Lord Septimus forced them back to the problem at hand. "I would suggest that we have the room packed tightly with crates of something not too solid—perhaps large pine cones. Then, when the priestess Teleports in, her body will try to occupy the same space as the cones, and the result will be lethal, but not explosive enough to damage the palace."

"Surely she will scry the room before she **TELEPORTS** in," Quackenthorp countered.

"But at least it will keep her out," said the Queen. She tugged the bell-pull and commanded, "Send a platoon of men to the north pine grove and have them collect three hundred crates of the largest pine cones they can find. Then stack the crates in the basement store room we just opened. Don't bother t take any of the furniture out—just stuff in the crates."

"It would be more subtle if we strung the room with fine wires," Quackenthorp suggested. "She might not see the wires, and they would provide a very uncomfortable welcome if she Teleported in."

"I'm not sure I want to be subtle," snapped Queen Elsa. "What I really want is a big bang. Those priestesses have ruined my life long enough." She looked on the brink of tears.

Septimus went to her and patted her hand. "Prince William is getting the rest of Nikky's information; the soldiers are collecting the pine cones; what else can we do?"

"Perhaps, if your Majesty would authorize it, I could go over the entire palace detecting for magic to see whether there have been any other intrusions." the wizard stood up and bowed. "I realize that would mean trusting me with much information about your home, but . . ."

"You are right. We have checked your motives and found nothing hostile to our cause. I will instruct the Guard Captain to assign a man to guide you. You will, of course, not enter the private chambers of the royal family." She went again to the bell-pull and gave instructions. "You will join us for supper in my boudoir. By evening we should have notes to compare."

VIII—Mission to Arragor

The morning after their interview with King Roger, Alsenius, Grimbolt, and Njal set off on horseback with credentials to the court of Arragor. They were instructed first to wait on Queen Elsa and present her with a letter from the King requesting the return of his daughter. They were then to request permission to proceed northward on a side mission to Zharkovia which they were to accomplish while the Princess was making herself ready for her homeward journey. Alsenius was to return alone to serve as escort and guard while the other two were to disappear in search of the fallen star. It was understood that the Queen would probably protest the removal of Princess Catherine and that Alsenius would probably be delayed at court. While he was there, he was to learn everything he could about the disappearance of the Crown Prince.

"I suppose it's better for you to represent us at court," Grimbolt agreed, "but I'm going to be very conspicuous on the star metal search."

"Perhaps not," said Benbow "Your speech is very like that of Arragor. Cover up some of that hair, and you might pass as a native. At any rate, his Majesty has authorized money for expenses, and he will reward success most generously."

Brother Lambent, squirming in his officer's uniform, wished them success and gloomily watched their departure.

The road, while primitive compared with the engineered roads of the Augustian Empire, was well packed down and carefully maintained, so that there was little danger from pot holes of deep ruts. As a result they made good time through the farms and villages of Quatch. At the Arragor border they were required to open their packs for inspection. The border guard questioned Alsenius' sword, but backed down when the dark man demonstrated his lightning control of the blade.

It was already twilight two days later when they reached the capital, so they put up for the night at the Silver Tabard, within easy walking distance of the palace. Njal quickly struck up an acquaintance with the musicians who entertained in the public room. He was not invited to show off, but he improved their morale—and their take—with the illusion of an enthusiastic rain of silver which stimulated generosity from the audience.

"All the gossip is about queer doings in the palace," he reported to his companions later in the evening. "There was some sort of concert with a visiting boy soprano from Zharkovia and the Temple Choir from the Hegemony of the Pythoness. There was a magical disturbance which ended in a riot. Broke up furniture and put a lot of the choir in the infirmary. Apparently the Zharkovian soprano disappeared in the confusion, and everybody's making a fuss about looking for him."

"The Pythoness is stirring things up all over the continent," Alsenius put in. "I guess Ambloq is right about her preparations for an offensive."

"I wonder if this temple is mixed up with my problem." Grimbolt looked wistfully out over the dark streets of the city. "Somehow this place feels familiar. The people sound like home."

"Benbow is right, you do talk the same way these people do. Nobody asks you to repeat anything."

"But if this is my home, why can't I remember anything?" He slammed himself into a chair and drummed on the arm.

"Maybe we should march into the local Temple of the Pythoness and start asking questions." Alsenius started to pace.

"They are probably a lot more powerful than we are, especially in their own temple," Njal warned. "We've beaten off some attacks, but every time they just back off and strike somewhere else. Suicide is not my idea of fun."

"Ambloq usually sticks to fighting off attacks and gathering information. Of course we did succeed pretty well in Megalopolis." said Alsenius.

"But that took the Draecian army," Njal reminded him. "We helped, but Sokos used not only the whole Palace Guard, but major units of regulars. And again, we caught them off guard when they struck at us."

Grimbolt shook his head sadly: "I'm sick of gathering information. It never helps me."

"Let's wait and see what happens when we show up at the palace demanding to carry off the Princess," Alsenius decided. "That ought to stir things up."

Early the next morning they dressed in their finest and approached the palace. At the main gate the guard sent them with a messenger to a large reception room in the palace. There an official examined their credentials and sent off a messenger on the run. "Milords, it may take time to arrange for the appropriate appointment. Perhaps you might enjoy a cup of tea?" He gestured to a large table in the corner of the room where several people were standing around, sipping and nibbling, and turned from them to a group of new arrivals. About half an hour later a messenger came to them. "I will escort you to the office of the Lord Steward."

When they entered his office, Lord Septimus stood behind his desk and gestured them to chairs. "I regret that her Majesty is not free to welcome King Roger's envoys, but I am empowered to act for her in the matter of Princess Catherine.

Alsenius leaned forward. "His Majesty is most anxious for his daughter's return; since her betrothed has deserted her, he wishes to see her safely married elsewhere."

"It is my understanding that the Princess has written to her father urging patience." Septimus smiled. "Perhaps you should talk with her before you officially present King Roger's letter demanding her return to Quatch."

"His Majesty was most urgent in his instructions," Njal seconded his comrade.

"Her Majesty's instructions to me were quite explicit. She will permit an interview with Princess Catherine, but she will not endanger the treaty of friendship between Quatch and Arragor. There is every expectation of Prince Humber's return, but if our search for him ends in tragedy, Prince William will then become king, and Princess Catherine could still become Queen of Arragor by marrying him."

"We should be grateful to converse with Princess Catherine and to deliver her father's words to her," Alsenius replied. "We are aware that it will take time for the princess to prepare for her journey; we desire, therefore, an audience with the Queen-Dowager as soon as possible so that we may proceed with our diplomatic mission to Zharkovia while the princess is packing. His Majesty's instructions are that we should bring her royal Highness home within three weeks."

Lord Septimus rose from his chair. "I will arrange an audience with the Princess at her earliest convenience, for I am sure she will be delighted to hear kind words from her royal father. As to her departure, I will leave her to communicate her decision for herself. She informed us that she has recently written to her royal father of her desire to remain in the house of her betrothed until he returns for the wedding. There has apparently been a delay or miscarriage of her letter, and further correspondence may be necessary to clarify the desires and intentions of all parties. I will inform you of Princess Catherine's will as to your audience with her."

Grimbolt, whose concealing clothing itched unbearably, interrupted, "Well it had better be damned soon. We are representatives of his Majesty, King Roger, and his Majesty's patience is finite."

"Your concern for his Majesty's patience will be conveyed to her royal Highness." Lord Septimus bowed slightly. "No one dictates to the Princess who is destined to be our queen." His gesture marked the end of the interview, and a guard appeared to escort the envoys to their quarters. "My messenger will escort you to the chambers prepared for your comfort, and palace servants will fetch your baggage from the inn. We dine promptly at eighth hour and would enjoy your company. The gardens and the library are pleasant places to while away the interval. If you are indisposed after your journey, you have but to instruct the servants and they will provide dinner in your room." He bowed more deeply and resumed his seat in preparation for the next appointment.

"Damned brush-off," Grimbolt growled as he opened his shirt while following the guard along the corridor.

"But very politely brushed," said Njal. "I shall avail myself of the library. There may be records of the fallen star."

They had scarcely reached the door of their suite when a guard—messenger overtook them. "Her Royal Highness, Princess Catherine of Quatch, has instructed me to conduct her royal father's messengers to her suite."

"Oh damn!" growled Grimbolt, undoing the scarf which hid his neck hair and flinging off his shirt. "These clothes are a torment: I itch all over. I'll be no use to you with the princess. Leave me here and I'll scratch a bit and explore the guard barracks."

Njal quickly cast CLEAN cantrips on his and Alsenius' clothes, and they turned about to follow the guard.

Alsenius asked their escort, "Could you tell me where I might go to find someone willing to work out with me? I am a soldier by trade, and diplomacy rusts the fighting skills."

"I'd be glad to take you to the Arena. The men will fight for a chance to spar with a stranger. It's the best way to sharpen their skills. I'll wait for you outside the Princess' suite."

He tapped on the door before flinging it wide to admit them. Princess Catherine sat at the far end of the room on an ornate chair. The whole atmosphere conveyed the impression of a monarch receiving homage in her throne room. She waited for them to do obeisance and approach before she extended her hand to Alsenius and allowed him to kiss it. "Lord Septimus informed us that messengers from our royal father had arrived at court. We are always glad to hear news of his Majesty."

Since no chairs were offered, Alsenius stood at ease and presented King Roger's scroll. She ignored them while she read, then looked up. "Regrettably our last letter has been delayed, or our father would not have sent you." She stared at them with slight disapproval. "He usually sends messengers of appropriate rank."

"He sent us because we are powerful enough to protect your Royal Highness on the journey home." Alsenius bowed slightly. "I am a Fighter of the thirteenth rank; Njal," he gestured toward the Illusionist, "is a Mage of the ninth; and Grimbolt our third man, though unranked, is a puissant and dependable guard."

"But we have no intention of leaving the court of our future husband." She glared momentarily at Njal, who was studying the wall hangings, then turned back to Alsenius, who was more impressive. "By this time our father will have received my letter and sent you new instructions. He writes that you have diplomatic business in Zharkovia which you are to transact while we are preparing to depart. Perhaps, when you return from that mission, your new instructions will have arrived."

"Perhaps," Alsenius agreed, "but it might be well for you to pack, since his Majesty instructed us to "rescue" you from the court of Arragor."

"And his verbal instructions left no room for counter instructions from your Royal Highness," Njal interposed.

"We have no need of rescue by mercenaries." The royal foot tapped slightly and the floor and the royal back stiffened.

"Perhaps," Alsenius added, "Your Royal Highness would dismiss us to be about our other duties while we all await further word from his Majesty."

"We give you leave to depart." The frost in her voice was almost visible.

Alsenius and Njal made obeisance and backed away, hoping some servant would open the door behind them. Their guard led them back to their room where they found Grimbolt waiting. He had stripped to his kilt and was still scratching enthusiastically. The guard gawked at his hairy muscles.

"Can you find somebody who's good at hand-to-hand combat?" he grumbled, "I need a good wrestle to get this court air out of my lungs."

"Sergeant Scrubbs is a Handkrieger, and he's always looking for somebody to take him on hand-to-hand. He can't match you for hair, but he has a good thatch on his chest."

The messenger waited for Alsenius to strip down to kilt and soft shoes. On their way to the Arena, they left Njal at the library with a promise that some one would guide him back to the rooms in time to change for dinner.

Their guard introduced them to Sergeant Scrubbs and Lieutenant Wilder, who eagerly welcomed a workout with the newcomers.

Alsenius worked his way up the ladder of Guards officers until he had defeated the local champion. This, of course, led to an invitation to dine at the officers' mess, which he accepted.

Grimbolt found a booth to leave his kilt and emerged clad only in his breechclout and pelt. He watched warily as the Handkrieger sergeant stripped to his baggy trousers and gesticulated through his preparatory exercises. Scrubbs was much lighter and quicker, so that Grimbolt knew he must quickly close with him or be battered by a humiliating rain of deft blows. As the sergeant advanced, Grimbolt threw lightning punch to the mid-section, which he knew would be dodged. Then, as Scrubbs' hands started their sweep, Grimbolt flung himself to the ground and seized the leg on which he pivoted. When Scrubbs paused to regain his poise, Grimbolt stood and grabbed him in a bear hug. Hands beat upon his back and feet reached out to trip him. When he finally lost his balance, he made sure that his weight landed squarely on top of his opponent, and he clung fiercely, squeezing the supple body and driving his fingers into the muscles of his back.

Scrubbs went limp, but Grimbolt, knowing the explosion of action which was to follow, hugged him tighter and wound his legs around the sergeant's thighs to prevent his deadly kicks. After two flurries of Handkrieger skill, Sergeant Scrubbs yielded. As he swung gracefully to his feet, he stared unbelievingly at Grimbolt. "There is only one man who ever subdued me with a bear hug like that." He stared searchingly into Grimbolt's eyes. "Who in blazes are you?"

Grimbolt extended his hairy arm, and the sergeant clasped it. "My Lord, Prince?" he gasped. Then he backed off and shook his head. "You cannot be, for he has not those massive muscles and his body is almost boyish. Yet I swear I know any man by his style of combat." Still he clutched Grimbolt's forearm. "Who are you, man, that fights so like my Lord."

Grimbolt's eyes drooped as he allowed the other still to clutch his arm. "My name is Grimbolt, and I am what you see—a man accursed, no man at all. Grimbolt the Bear."

Scrubbs steered him to a bench and they sat. "Prince Humber used to train with me. I tried to teach him the art of the Handkrieger, but he was too much of the body for that mental discipline; yet he preferred hand combat to the sword, so that we developed a wrestling style which suited his physique and mind. Once in a while, he bested me with that clutch. You are much stronger, much heavier, but . . ."

"I remember only serving as an bargeman on Clear River in upper Draecia. I have no other past. I have no kin, no lineage, no memory. Alsenius took me from my barge, and I follow him as henchman. But I have no self." He studied his hairy toes. "Alsenius won commissions for us in the army of Quatch, and the King assigned us to escort the Princess Catherine home from Arragor. I serve Alsenius while I seek for something that will bring back memory."

"You talk like one of us." The sergeant searched his eyes again. "You do not have the Prince's look—not even about the eyes, where the hair cannot hide you. Yet my body still tells me you are my Prince. He is missing, you know. We think the priestesses of the Pythoness killed his father and kidnaped him. I must believe you are my Prince." He lurched off the bench and started to kneel, but Grimbolt prevented him.

"Don't. You have no proof. You give me hope beyond all hoping, but we cannot know."

"There was a strange half man half boy, a singer from Zharkovia, who came snooping around here trying to find some trace of your Highness, but he has vanished, and we hear rumors that the Pythoness stole him to keep him from finding out. Those women are very powerful. I would urge you to stay out of their sight."

"We must talk with Alsenius and Njal. They know more abut these priestesses than I. Alsenius escorted a woman who escaped from them across the continent from Megalopolis to Augustia. He picked me up me on the way. We tangled with a recruiting party of the priestesses in the back country." He chuckled maliciously. "One of them put love spell on me, and I lost control and raped her."

"Raped by a magical bear!" Scrubbs looked again at Grimbolt's massive body. "So I must keep silence?"

"I think so. I have not made myself popular since I came here, and your feeling is not proof. You must talk with Njal and Alsenius."

"I heard Alsenius accept an invitation to the Officers' Mess for dinner. Perhaps you would dine with me at the non-coms' mess. I think you should not dine at court where the priestesses might see you. Furthermore your appearance will not please the Queen."

"Unfortunately it doesn't please most people. Except for Alsenius and his friends, I have led a lonely life."

"Let us have one more bout, and then we'll dress for mess."

Scrubbs took care to avoid Grimbolt's bear hug, and when they ended their exercise, Grimbolt's pelt concealed a number of large bruises where the sergeant's strokes and kicks pounded him.

Njal, meanwhile, had found a volume dealing with the fallen star whose crater scarred the northern plains and he remained in the library until a servant summoned him to dinner.

As the footman was escorting Njal to a long table at the far side of the Dining Room from the royal dias, a second servant intercepted him. "Lord Septimus bids you join him at his table." He followed this footman the length of the room to a place at a small table just below the dias. Lord Septimus sat alone at the head of this table, and Njal was seated at his right hand. "A few courtiers will arrive late, and I expect that Prince William will desert the royal table for mine. I am particularly anxious for you to meet his dog."

Njal blinked. "His dog?"

"Yes, you are a mage, are you not?"

"An Illusionist, actually."

"But you do understand magic?"

"Yes, but I specialize in illusions." With a flirt of his fingers Njal produced a tiny Pekingese which nestled in his palm and barked sharply.

The Lord Steward hesitated, then extended his hand to examine the dog. "Amazing! This is an illusion? It looks, sounds, and feels real. It is even warm to the touch." He took it into his hand and stroked its silky fur.

Njal gestured again, and the Peke became a small golden snake which deftly coiled around Lord Septimus' arm above the elbow and constricted.

"Most remarkable! I could swear it was squeezing my arm. And it feels dry and cool like a real serpent."

"And would feel slimy to someone who knew less about snakes," Njal remarked. "Successful illusions adapt themselves to the mind of the recipient. I could even cast an illusion which would confront you with the thing you most fear, but that is a more serious spell."

"You can read my mind?"

"Oh no, the spell simply triggers a fear in your thought and your mind creates the image. Since I produced this illusion only for you, no one else can see it. If I had cast the spell on a wider audience, it could upset the whole hall." He noticed Lord Crabhook approaching the table and flickered his fingers again.

"May I join you my Lord?" Without waiting for an answer, Lord Crabhook seated himself. "I see you have finally taken to jewelry," he remarked. "That is a handsome arm ring." He extended a finger to touch the ring. "If I did not know it was gold, I should swear you were wearing a live serpent."

"Milord Crabhook, may I introduce Lieutenant Njal, an emissary of King Roger. He was just demonstrating the art of an Illusionist." They nodded in response to the introduction.

Njal gestured, and Lord Crabhook twitched in surprise as the serpent disappeared.

"Your ring was an illusion?"

Njal twiddled again and handed Crabhook a large gold coin stamped with the image of an upreared python. As his Lordship accepted the coin, the serpent emerged from the metal, hissed, and struck. Lord Crabhook clutched his wrist and screamed in pain. Njal twiddled again, and the coin vanished, the pain ceased. The injured man scrutinized his wrist and could find no mark. "That was an illusion?"

Two footmen rushed to the table, prepared to assist, but Lord Crabhook waved them off. "I am all right—just passing twinge." The another footman approached. "Milord Septimus, Prince William requests your attendance at the royal table."

Septimus looked up as the prince gestured toward the empty table on the dais where he sat. Septimus gestured for the prince to join them—pointing to Njal. Then he said to the footman, "Please ask his Highness to join us, as my guest has not yet been presented to her Majesty."

The prince nodded and rose from his chair. Nikky, who was settled beside him, promptly scrambled to his feet and followed. Lord Crabhook spoke loudly, "I shall not dine with that slobbering hound."

Prince William stooped and spoke a few words. Immediately the bloodhound turned aside, shook himself, and stalked away from the table. As he approached the double door, two footmen opened it before nim, and he stalked out like a prince of the blood.

"You will meet Nikky later," Septimus muttered. "He has no love for Lord Crabhook."

"No love!" Lord Crabhook shook his fist at the closing door. "That damned dog pissed on my ankle."

Prince William joined them as the servants began to present the first course. At first conversation languished, but the royal curiosity soon overcame his irritation at Nikky's banishment. "I understand you're one of the emissaries who's going to try to take Kate away from Mother," he said. "You won't find it easy, you know. Mother usually gets her own way."

"Your mother is the Queen-Regent," Lord Crabhook asserted. "It is proper that her decisions should prevail."

"Mother has convinced Kate that King Roger plans to marry her off to an old goat who's worse than Brother, so you won't have much luck with Kate either. Kate says Brother's a bore, but she can put up with him. Of course, what she's really hoping for is a chance to marry me."

Lord Crabhook bristled. "Your Highness speaks irresponsibly."

The prince obviously enjoyed his mother's absence and his freedom to bait his elder. "I'm only the spare heir; nobody minds what I say."

"Her Majesty has enjoined respectful and circumspect language upon your Highness."

"But my *Royal* Highness is too young for responsibility."

"Your Royal Highness is now of an age face consequences," Lord Septimus reproved, though his amused expression took much of the sting from the rebuke.

"Forgive me, Lord Septimus." The young man lowered his gaze. "I spoke without thinking."

"And that in an heir to the throne is most reprehensible." Lord Crabhook continued to bore in. "Your Queen-mother would not approve."

"And I suppose you'll tattle," snapped the prince.

Lord Septimus intervened. "I was about to introduce you to Lieutenant Njal. You will find his illusions very interesting."

Njal looked up from his soup and allowed the ghost of a wink to afflict his eye. "I admired the dignity of your bloodhound," he murmured. "His exit had the elegance of a royal dog. Does he really slobber?"

"I'm afraid he does, if he doesn't think. But he is very intelligent."

"I shall be honored to meet him when I'm not dressed for dinner."

"Were you casting illusions when I saw you earlier?"

Njal gestured, and a green frog poked his head out of the prince's soup. William dropped his spoon and nearly upset his chair. Then he saw Njal's grin and settled back to examine the frog, which opened its mouth and said, "Yes, I am an illusion"; then it turned into a rather dubious dumpling. The prince glared at Njal for a moment, then scooped with his spoon, popped the dumpling into his mouth, and crunched viciously. Njal quickly twiddled, and the dumpling suddenly exuded the richest and most savory flavor William had ever experienced—an impossible blend of all his ambrosial dreams. Stunned, he sat silently enjoying the illusion until it faded from his tongue. "Wow!" he exclaimed.

"Your Royal Highness has observed something?" asked Lord Septimus ironically.

"Yes," William reposted, "that Lieutenant Njal is a very good illusionist. I believe that Nikky would be most pleased to meet him."

"That dog is a scandal to the court," growled Crabhook. "He should be banished to the kennels."

"Your Lordship forgets that he is the gift of my royal Mother," snapped the prince.

His Lordship spoke nothing, but his opinion of the Queen's taste was clear.

The herring fillets in a tangy cream sauce arrived, and they busied themselves appreciating the chef's skill, but Lord Crabhook could not resist another thrust, "His Majesty, your father, maintained such an ordered court. He would never have countenanced such lapses of protocol."

"You question my mother's authority?"

"Not at all. She is the Dowager Queen-Regent, and her authority is unquestioned until young King Humber returns. Yet one looks back with regret on the old ordered days before the realm was turned upside down. Your own education, your Royal Highness has been sadly neglected since the murder of your father."

"The Prince's tutors report that he is progressing very satisfactorily," Lord Septimus put in, "and the guard Captain reports that he has graduated to the long sword."

"I was referring to training in decorum. Since the retirement of Lord Smothers, his Royal Highness has been allowed to run wild."

"Smothers was a pompous ostrich—all feathers and neck but no brain." Prince William was not sure how much farther he could go, but he was determined press on to the limit.

"The education of the Prince is the Queen-Regent's responsibility," said Lord Septimus, "and our authority to guide is limited."

Njal watched with amusement as they sparred through the rest of the delicious meal. He learned much about currents and counter-currents at court, And he decided that Prince William was an intelligence to be reckoned with. When the marzipan frigate had been devoured, he expressed his eagerness to meet the royal pet, and Lord Crabhook parted from them at the door of the dining hall.

"My rooms are pretty boyish," the Prince apologized. "I think I'd rather we met in the garden."

"I suggest that we meet at the forbidden summer house," said Lord Septimus. "I want Njal's opinion about the magical traces there. Nikky's nose is very good, but he doesn't understand spell craft."

"I'll go leave a note for my colleagues to join us there," said Njal. "I assume that the servants can direct them." He found a footman to guide him to their rooms and discovered Alsenius already napping on his bed.

"I think Grimbolt dined with the sergeant who was sparring with him. They seem to have hit it off very well." Alsenius grabbed the footman before he could leave and asked him to lead them to the summerhouse."

"But Lord Crabhook has ordered that nobody should disturb the place where his Majesty was murdered," the man protested.

"Lord Septimus and Prince William requested us to meet them there. Does not their authority exceed that of Lord Crabhook?"

At first the servant balked, but Njal twiddled his fingers and muttered a dozen words under his breath. Presently he decided that Alsenius' argument was correct. "I won't be responsible if his Lordship has you driven off," he said, "but I will guide you to where you can see the summerhouse."

He led them to a narrow path which led through the orchard. "If you follow this path through the trees, it will take you to the summerhouse. I daren't go any closer." He turned about and dashed back to the palace.

"I hope Grimbolt doesn't have any trouble finding a guide," Alsenius said. "He's not as convincing as you are."

"If he doesn't make it, we can tell him all we learn." Njal strode briskly among the trees.

They found Lord Septimus with Prince William and his dog waiting for them. Njal followed the bloodhound to the royal chair where King Humber died and Prince Humber met the Necromantic attack. Then they went to the bushes where the high priestess had hidden and experienced the aging effects of her spells. The Illusionist's detection spells confirmed what had already been learned, but added nothing. "The whole thing is too far in the past for magic to discover much. I am amazed at Nikky's nose."

Njal sat down on the throne chair and pondered. "Necromancy is a field of which I know almost nothing," he commented. "It is primarily concerned with death—with killing, talking with the dead, even bringing them back. Perhaps the old Priestess cast a DEATH spell on the prince."

"But the Scepter's behavior indicates that he is still alive. If he were dead, the Scepter would respond either to the Queen-Regent or to Prince William, the next in line for the throne. Furthermore, the King's signet refused to open the King's Treasury for either of them. This would indicate that the ring is still tuned to Prince Humber's life force."

"Was the Crown Prince magically protected?"

"He was certainly wearing his signet ring which provides limited protection."

"And the evidence of necromancy is strong, even after two years?"

"All the evidence points to an extremely powerful spell—one which aged not only the caster but the vegetation around her. High Priest Farsyte thought there was some possibility of a miscast spell." Septimus struggled to recall everything that had been reported to him.

"Could that evidence be interpreted as the result of two major spells?"

"I should think so. We'd have to ask Quackenthorp or Farsyte. Two spells ought to leave a bigger trace than one."

"I'm still surprised that the evidence is detectable so long after the casting." Njal persisted. "If she cast a Death spell and it failed to kill the Crown Prince, might it have knocked him unconscious. I know that a COMMAND spell to die produces unconsciousness of varying length, depending on the strength of the caster. It produces death only when the caster is of Arch-Priest strength and the victim is of very low rank.

What if the Prince's protection magic saved him from death, but left him unconscious? If her intention had been to kill him and then bring him back a few hours later, what would be the effect of a **RAISE DEAD** or even a **REINCARNATE** spell on a live man? Could she have intended to **REINCARNATE** the prince as—say—a frog?

"But if he was only unconscious, the spell might behave wildly." Septimus strode back and forth in excitement. "We know that miscast spells produce unpredictable results. You know, that might account both for the long lasting traces of Necromancy and the failure of the priestesses to demand ransom for the prince. It certainly would account for his being alive."

"Here comes Grimbolt and his sergeant," Alsenius interrupted. "Perhaps they might . . ."

Nikky suddenly leaped to his feet and pointed his nose into the breeze which was blowing from the approaching pair. For ten full seconds he froze at point; then he lifted his head and howled, rushing toward them like an oncoming cyclone. Before anyone could react he had planted his front paws on Grimbolt's shoulders, bearing him to the ground. The dog's nose buried itself in Grimbolt's neck; then he lifted his head and howled again."

Prince William followed as fast as he could and strove to pull the dog away, but Nikky held his victim pinned and began piping rapid scales and vocal leaps.

"He's what?!" William dropped Nikky's loose hide and stared down at Grimbolt, who struggled vainly to break the dog's pin.

Nikky piped again.

"Well get off him then," William exclaimed, yanking at Nikky's neck hide again, and dragging him off.

"Oh, ye Guardians protect us!" Lord Septimus exclaimed as he deciphered Nikky's message and dashed down the path.

Grimbolt struggled to his feet and glared at the dog, who continued his excited piping.

William stared at him for a shocked minute, then knelt. "My lord Brother—your Majesty!" He looked up appealingly. "I had no idea."

Lord Septimus puffed, "Are you sure, Nikky? This can't be the Crown Prince."

Nikky took another sniff and piped back. "I swear by my nose, this is the man that the priestess cast he spells on. There is no doubt abut the scent."

His Lordship sank to one knee, "Forgive me, your Majesty, but your disguise deceived me completely."

Grimbolt nervously scratched his chest and stared stupidly at the kneeling pair. "I don't understand. Get up! Get up!"

Septimus staggered to his feet. "It is all very confusing, Sire. Nikky is actually Lord Nicholas of Zharkovia, but a Priestess of the Pythoness has transformed him into a bloodhound. He swears that your scent is identical to that of the Crown Prince."

Alsenius ran to the summerhouse and fetched a chair for the Lord Steward, who gratefully sank into it. Prince William still knelt before his brother.

Meanwhile Queen Elsa, who had dined in her suite, finally finished dictating the day's correspondence to her secretaries and sent for Lord Septimus. When her messenger returned to tell her that his Lordship was meeting the envoys from King Roger at the summerhouse, she decided to stretch her legs and seek him out. She approached the summer house just in time to see a great hairy bear of a man grab Prince William and lift him into the air. Before she had time to think, she had hurled the royal scepter at the head of the monster with the command, "Kill!"

Her cry attracted all eyes to her, and everyone watched dismayed as the deadly missile streaked toward its target. Grimbolt, whose mind had ceased functioning, stared blankly and dropped Prince William to the ground. Then at the last moment he thrust his hand up to ward off the blow. Abruptly the scepter slowed, turned in the air, and forced its handle into his grasp. An overwhelming burst of thought exploded in his mind, and he recognized the scepter and its powers. He felt its recognition of his kingship. It forced the knowledge of its power as a weapon and of its magical abilities into the blankness of his memory. Stunned, he dropped to the ground beside his still unrecognized brother.

They all froze in place, staring at each other, but Nikky followed his dog instinct and rushed to lick Grimbolt's face.

"Ugh! Get away!" The new king shoved the dog aside and sat up to stare at the scepter in his hand. The artifact frantically searched the emptiness of his memory seeking the proper place in his thought to anchor its recognition spells. The resulting inner tumult left him oblivious of what went on around him.

The queen rushed to Prince William and dragged him to his feet. "Are you all right?" she demanded, "Did that brute hurt you." She turned sharply on Nikky, who was crouched at Grimbolt's side. "What good are you if you can't even protect your master from that beast?" She made a grab for the scepter and was startled to find it still clutched in the stranger's grip. "Give me the damned thing," she demanded.

Grimbolt sat blankly. The scepter still held his fist to its frozen grip.

"Septimus, what is gong on?"

"Your Royal Highness, he's the King." Even in the crisis he found her correct title.

"Who's the king? What are you talking about."

Lord Septimus pointed to Grimbolt. "The scepter has recognized him. He is the king."

"That hairy oaf? That's not my son."

Nikky began explaining, and Prince William automatically interpreted: "I recognized the King's scent as soon as he came near me. His body many look different, but his scent is the King's."

At the same time Alsenius was shaking Grimbolt, trying to pry an explanation from him.

"Your Royal Highness, I am Njal, one of King Roger's emissaries. May I suggest that you get this mob into your office where we can explain privately?"

"William, take that damned dog into my study." the Queen-Regent reasserted herself. "Septimus get this gang inside before everybody in the palace hears us." She glared down at Grimbolt. "Damn you, give me my scepter." She grabbed it and yanked. It responded with a violent electric shock which almost knocked her down.

Grimbolt stared at her in confusion. "Madam, it seems to think I belong to it. It won't let go." He reached out to steady her. "Perhaps we should go inside too."

She stifled the impulse to pull out his hair, brushed his hand away from her arm, and tottered off after her Lord Steward. Grimbolt looked down at the scepter. "Do you know the way?" The scepter tugged in his hand and guided him after the crowd, and in a surprisingly short time the Queen was seated at her desk and the others had distributed themselves on chairs—including Nikky, who had claimed the largest armchair for his nest.

Septimus introduced the emissaries to the Queen, ending with Grimbolt. "And here, your Royal Highness, is Grimbolt who is also your son and sovereign, King Humber VIII." He flourished a proper bow.

"This monstrosity is my son?" She glared at him.

"Let me see what I can do." Njal gestured at his friend, trying to create an illusion of what he would look like without his pelt and facial hair. "I would hope the magic which has changed him did not alter his bone structure." He ran his hands over Grimbolt's cheek bones and jaw line.

Grimbolt cursed under his breath. "You keep making those illusions. I wish I could see what you're up to."

Immediately the scepter flared brilliantly. When his eyes recovered from the shock, he cringed to see his figure stripped of its fur and clad only in the briefest of breech clouts."

"He does resemble the Crown Prince," Septimus observed, "if you disregard the slightly darkened nose and the hint of a snout. Of course the physique is far more athletic."

"I have been working as an oarsman," Grimbolt put in. "Your scepter believes I am your King, but I still remember nothing." He waved the scepter at the illusion. "Apparently this scepter lets me see your illusions. Would you mind covering that thing. It's indecent."

Njal gestured at his illusion and clothed it with white hose, a golden blouse, and a crimson jacket. He even placed a golden coronet on the head. "What sort of hair did the Prince have?" he asked, "I assumed the color would be unchanged."

"It was inclined to curl slightly over his forehead," said Queen Elsa.

Njal adjusted the image, and the Queen nodded sadly, "I see what you mean. I suppose the scepter must be right."

"My best guess," Njal continued, "is that the Priestess tried to kill him with a spell, intending to reincarnate him as a bear. Because of some protective magic, her **DEATH** spell merely rendered him unconscious. As a result, the **REINCARNATE** spell—which is designed to bring back the dead—misfired when applied to a living victim. It produced only superficial changes in his appearance—a slightly elongated muzzle and displaced ears as well as a stooped carriage . . ."

"And worst of all, it wiped my memory," Grimbolt interrupted. "Even if I am the Crown Prince, I still don't remember anything. All that has happened is that your dog recognizes my scent, Sergeant Scrubbs remembers my fighting style, and your scepter recognizes my blood. It's the mind that makes the man, and I'm mentally no more Prince Humber than anybody else. I can't rule a kingdom without a memory."

"That does pose problems," Lord Septimus agreed.

"Not the least of which is our mission for King Roger," interrupted Alsenius. "We may have found Princess Catherine's betrothed, but I'm afraid she won't swoon in his arms when they meet."

Queen Elsa strode to the bell pull and tugged it. "Fetch Princess Catherine immediately," she ordered the guard. She returned to her chair. "You say she has not met . . ." she gulped, "my son in his present form?"

"I wonder whether King Roger would want his daughter to marry the King of Arragor even if he is a bear." Alsenius brought the conversation back to his mission.

"Considering some of the oafs he has thought about marrying her to, perhaps he would not balk at a snout and pelt," Queen Elsa sniffed.

"If Grimbolt doesn't feel up to taking over the realm," Njal suggested, "then perhaps it would be wise to leave things as they are for a while. I spent a very profitable day in the library learning about the fallen star, and I suspect that King Roger's concern in that direction deserves our attention."

"You are suggesting that I leave my—ah—mother to rule while I go off with you and Alsenius to investigate."

Njal nodded.

"What is all this about a fallen star?" Septimus demanded.

"King Roger has a very beautiful dagger which he believes was fashioned from metal smelted from the remains of the fallen star that ploughed a large crater in the northern tundra." Njal leaned back in his chair. "I spent most of today studying what I could find in your Majesty's library about the crater. Apparently King Peter has authorized an exploration of the site, claiming it is on Zharkovian territory. There is also a report of a mission dispatched by the Hegemony of the Pythoness to study remains of the fallen star."

"But the crater is on our soil," protested Lord Septimus.

"I doubt that anyone has taken the trouble to fix boundaries in the far north," said Njal. "Your library indicates considerable ambiguity up there."

"Well, if it has value, we'd better make our right to it clear." Queen Elsa—in the absence of the scepter—drummed with her fist on the scarred desk.

"I suspect that one of King Roger's vital reasons for wanting the alliance with Arragor is his interest in the special properties of metal extracted from the fallen star. His dagger is of a metal far tougher and less brittle than iron. The blade was so sharp it could cut a hair dropped upon its edge. A sword of such metal would break an ordinary weapon and would cleave through normal armor. Supposing the Pythoness were able to equip even a small band of her Amazons with such weapons?"

"Supposing King Roger had such weapons—or King Peter?" Lord Septimus stood up and began to pace. "The whole balance of power could change."

"Then I certainly must go with my comrades to study this crater," Grimbolt exploded. He pointed at his mother. "You must continue to rule here, and we must keep my identity an absolute secret."

"But what about the scepter? You said it would not leave you," the Queen objected.

Grimbolt lapsed into silent communion with his scepter. "You are right. The scepter must go with me because most of its magic will work only for the true King. It will change its form into whatever weapon I am most proficient with—in my case a staff—and it will grant me protection from many spells. Furthermore it will throw a lightning bolt for me and perform other services I am not yet sure about. Perhaps Lord Septimus could have a fake scepter fashioned for you."

"As a matter of fact there is a very good facsimile in the Royal Treasury," Lord Septimus volunteered. "I hasn't been used for a couple hundred years, but I could have it polished."

"Then that's settled," Grimbolt declared. "You are still Queen-Regent, and nobody must know about me. We shall set out on King Roger's mission to the north in the morning."

Nikky sat up in his chair and piped urgently at them. William translated, "You'll need my nose on this venture." Then he added on his own count, "And I shall go with you, too."

Both the Queen and Grimbolt barked, "No!" Elsa added, "It's too dangerous."

Grimbolt grabbed his brother's shoulders and looked him squarely in the eye. "Until I marry and beget a son you are the heir presumptive to the throne. It is as unthinkable to send us both on a dangerous mission as it would be to send both the captain of a warship and his second in command upon the same landing party. I must go because it is my mission. You must stay for the safety of the realm. This is a sacrifice you must make."

William's eyes drooped. Then he straightened himself. "I shall be worthy of the crown by the time you return."

Nikky stood and piped again: "As King Peter's representative, I demand the right to explore what may well belong to him. William, my friend, I shall miss you, but my duty is as clear as yours. I must go."

The Guard tapped at the door, then opened it to announce, "The Princess Royal, Catherine of Quatch."

Njal gestured at his illusion and it vanished.

"She mustn't know who I am," Grimbolt warned.

Queen Elsa hesitated a second and then nodded her understanding. Her Royal Highness Princess Catherine of Quatch swept in.

The Queen had just time to signal the others to keep silence; then she rose graciously and gestured the Princess to a seat. "Your Royal Highness, we have just received an important communication from your royal father which concerns your betrothal to Prince Humber." Then she amazed the company with her swift improvisation. "He has agreed to confirm the treaty of alliance between his realm and ours in spite of the Prince's absence. We shall in future negotiate a suitable marital arrangement to cement our friendship. In the meantime, he wishes me to inform you that you are now engaged to his Royal Highness, Prince Grimbolt of Draecia, third heir to Emperor Alexis and King in his own right to the province of Attica. May I introduce you to your new affianced, Prince Grimbolt."

Princess Catherine stared blankly as Grimbolt rose and bowed. Suddenly the vision of her wedding night with this man rose before her and she gagged, turned, and fled the room.

IX—The Great Forest

After Princess Catherine's exit, Grimbolt shriveled down into his chair. Queen Elsa turned back to the group as Septimus observed, "Clearly, regardless of the evidence, the announcement that the Crown Prince has returned and will shortly wed the Princess of Quatch would be ill timed. I believe Alsenius and Njal are right that we must turn to the investigation of this fallen star immediately." He turned to Grimbolt. "I assume that you will represent the interests of your fatherland in this matter, despite any previous commitment to King Roger."

Grimbolt stared at the scepter in his hand. "I suppose I must be the missing Prince, though I still have no memory of my family or my homeland. But my first commitment is still to find myself."

Alsenius placed his arm over his friend's shoulder. "Come with us," he urged. "Your mother's High Priest and the Wizard can sift through the magic clues and figure out how to cancel the spells on your mind and body while we're gone. If you head north, there's less chance the priestesses will capture you again, and we can add information by exploring."

"You certainly cannot carry on a courtship." Queen Elsa gestured toward the door, "and I doubt if your subjects would willingly crown you."

"Oh no, I can't stay here and reign. You must remain Regent."

Nikky piped, "I have solved the mystery here, and I can't go back to King Peter looking like this. I am sure I will be more useful exploring. I suggest that William and I teach Grimbolt to understand my musical speech. Then we should leave as soon as possible."

"I shall take Sergeant Scrubbs with me," Grimbolt declared. "He recognized me by my style of wrestling, and somehow I feel comfortable with him." He asked his brother, "How long will it take you to teach me Nikky's speech?"

"It depends on how good your ear is. Can you recognized notes of the scale?"

Grimbolt rather hoarsely sang two octaves.

William turned to his mother, "Let us go into another room with Nikky, and we'll see how he does." He led them into his mother's dressing room and closed the door.

"I like the idea of taking Scrubbs along." Alsenius said. "He's the only other person besides you, Septimus, and William that knows who Grimbolt is."

"I think we should bring in another bloodhound for William to train and play with," Septimus put in.

"I agree," said the queen. "He won't have Nikky's intelligence, but a dog is a good body guard, and the Priestesses will be suspicious if the dog suddenly disappears."

"Incidentally, I suggest that you comment on the way young William is growing up," Lord Septimus urged. "He deserves praise, and at his age he needs it. Tell him how much you expect to depend on him now that he's proved himself."

Her Majesty frowned at what she felt as meddling, but she realized his advice was sound.

"We should have mounts for everybody and at least one pack animal." Alsenius brought the discussion back to practical matters. "I suggest that you explain our departure as a continuation of our diplomatic mission to Arragor and Zharkovia. That way you can explain Scrubbs as your special envoy to explain to King Peter that Lord Nicholas' disappearance is the result of foreign interference, not negligence on our part."

At this point the guard announced the arrival of Lord Farsyte. When the Queen told him the news, he immediately put his finger on the problem. "What about his memory? Grimbolt complains that he has no recollection of his background."

"That's why he is going to investigate the fallen star," Elsa explained. "He doesn't feel up to governing, and he is leaving me as Regent while he looks for restoration."

"He needs to struggle with his memory," the High Priest urged. "This discovery has given his mind a horrible jolt. If he really searches, he may discover memories shaken loose by the shock." He looked across at Alsenius. "While you were traveling with him, did you ever notice anything that might have been an unconscious memory?"

"Well, he told some farm people a rather convincing story about being reared by his grandfather, but he later told Clarissa and me that he just made the story up to avoid having to explain that he had lost his memory."

"We ought to question him about that. The story might indicate a memory that surfaced without his recognizing it. Anything else?"

"Well somebody taught him the worship of the Goddess. I remember the night he explained why he so carefully stretched the rabbit skins after we had eaten the meat. He said the Goddess didn't mind his killing the rabbits for food so long as he apologized to their spirits and made sure nothing of their bodies went to waste. Was that a worship he could have learned from you?"

"Good heavens no!" the Queen exclaimed. "We serve Lord Odin and Lady Frygge, not some nature Guardian. Lord Farsyte makes our sacrifices for us, but nobody taught Prince Humber to apologize to rabbits even if he wasted his time killing them."

"The Great Forest is the place where someone might pick up a notion like that. Do you remember any time Prince Humber visited the Great Forest?" Lord Farsyte asked.

"No, he was never much of a hunter," said the Queen. "Furthermore our hunting parties stayed clear of the Great Forest because the Great Druid wouldn't put up with hunting for sport."

"The Druid worships the Goddess Gaea," said Lord Farsyte, "and I don't know anybody else who could have taught Prince Humber her service."

"Well, Grimbolt had it all worked out," said Alsenius, "He gave Clarissa and me quite lesson one night."

They had still come to no conclusion when a footman appeared to ask whether he was to escort her Majesty to supper or serve it in the office. She ordered supper for everyone in the office. Shortly afterwards William, Grimbolt, and Nikky emerged from the dressing room and announced that the bear could now understand the dog.

Lord Farsyte took Grimbolt and Alsenius aside and began probing for memories. "Your friend tells me that you once told a story of being reared by your grandfather. Was it he who taught you the lore of the Goddess?"

"I don't know why I told that story about my grandfather. It just popped out. I have no memory of a grandfather." Grimbolt wandered aimlessly around the room.

"Hold the scepter very tightly and search your mind for an old man—any old man—who might have taught you the lore of the

Goddess." The priest grabbed him and shoved him into a chair. "This is important. The scepter has shaken your mind up, and random memories might surface without warning. I want you to grab anything that comes and try to tie it together. You didn't learn the lore of the Goddess here at court. Your grandfather died before he could have taught you anything as sophisticated as the Goddess' worship. Therefore you must have been exposed to an old man with the lore after you were transformed. Now think of the Goddess and an old man."

Grimbolt closed his eyes and scowled ferociously at nothing for some time.

"Try explaining the lore of the Goddess to me and at the same time pretend to be listening to someone explaining it to you," suggested Farsyte.

"You remember explaining to me why you were preserving the rabbit skins, even when we were traveling light." Alsenius suggested.

"Well, it's obvious, isn't it. If the rabbits give me their bodies for food, then I owe it to them not to waste anything they have given." His voice took on a solid certainty as he expounded what he felt as absolute truth. "The weak must participate in the power of the strong by submitting, and in return the strong must give back love and gratitude for the weak who feed. All participate in the strength of the Goddess, and her law fits everything in the universe into one harmonious whole. All receive what they need and all give what they are able to." Suddenly he stiffened. "I am hearing this in a beautiful orchard under a huge apple tree. I am a child and I'm very scared, and a beautiful grey-haired man is holding me in his arms and telling me about where I fit in the balance of nature."

He suddenly dropped to the floor and curled himself up into a ball. "She's tearing my mind apart. Make it stop! Make it stop!" His body convulsed into itself with a despairing howl. Then suddenly he relaxed and dropped into unconsciousness.

Farsyte grabbed his wrist. "It's all right. His pulse is regular. His memory just gave him too much of a jolt. He should be able to handle it when he wakes up." He stood and settled back into a chair. "He broke through to a bearable memory of the man teaching him. Then he remembered an older memory which tortured him." He shook his head sadly. "I fear we dare not probe farther for the present."

"Was it the Druid he was remembering?" asked Alsenius.

"I think so. I have never seen Leander the Druid, but those who have met him describe him either as 'a beautiful old man,' or 'a terrible old man.' I suspect that both descriptions are accurate."

"A beautiful old man, terrible in power," Queen Elsa mused. "I can understand such terrible beauty. It seems to describe the Goddess Grimbolt was talking of. The beauty of the she-lion protecting her cubs. I have seen such beauty."

"Could it be the Goddess who was tearing his mind apart?" Alsenius wondered.

"I think not," Njal put in, "It was the Priestess of the Pythoness who enchanted him. If she mangled the **REGENERATION** or **TRANSFORMATION** spell and then attempted to manipulate his mind to control it, he would have felt it as torture. I wouldn't be surprised if the old man stepped in and at least blunted his tormented mind to give him some peace."

"And then, perhaps **TELEPORTED** him to the boat landing where the Priestesses could not find him," Alsenius added, "and planted in his mind a name and a laborious occupation that would keep him from thinking."

"Then you think, maybe, he escaped from the Priestess?" William asked.

Suddenly Nikky burst into song, and William concentrated on interpreting.

"That explains it! That explains why the prince's trail starts off to the north. I forgot about that when I was telling you. He must have lashed out at the priestess and run away northward. She was so shaken by the aging from the spells that she couldn't chase him, so she must **TELEPORTED** out and let him run."

"Yes!" Elsa agreed. "I'll bet he knocked the old Priestess out of the way and ran due north until he came to the Great Forest. That's why the Priestesses haven't made any demands on Arragor. They don't have anything to bargain with. They don't even know where the Crown Prince is."

"Then if he goes back to Leander and asks for his memory back, the Druid might be able to restore him." Septimus drummed his fingers on the table beside him. "The question is, 'Has Grimbolt gained enough strength of mind to stand remembering the whole experience?'"

"He'd damned well better stand it," snorted the Queen. "He won't be worth diddledy-squat as a king if he can't handle his past."

"Let's face it, your Majesty, Prince Humber was a very pleasant young man, but he was no hero," sighed Lord Septimus. "He was really a very ordinary young man who happened o be heir to the throne."

"How dare you call my son 'an ordinary young man?'"

"But Mother, you know he was. I'm ever so much brighter at school work, and I've already graduated to long sword," William jolted the queen. "Brother will be a good king just because he's not too heroic. He'll follow good advice and let the army do his fighting for him, and everybody will love him because he makes them feel comfortable."

His Mother made a half-hearted gesture to box his ear, which he ducked and grinned impudently up at her.

"But don't forget that Grimbolt has led a very active life," Alsenius stepped in. "You may find that your king is no longer so ordinary."

Grimbolt stirred on the floor and Alsenius helped him back up on his chair. "I think I remembered something a minute ago, but it's gone now." He looked hopelessly toward Lord Farsyte.

"It's all right. You told us enough to give us a clue," the High Priest consoled him. "You will need to visit the Great Forest on your way to the North. Druid Leander probably has the key to a lot of your memories."

"We think he is the one who taught you the lore of the Goddess," said Alsenius. "We think it was your memory of him which prompted your grandfather story."

Grimbolt straightened his back. "Then we must go immediately." He turned to his mother. We shall set out early in the morning. The longer we stay here the more chance the Priestesses have of learning I am back. We aren't ready to confront them yet; we must learn more and gain more strength. Mother, you must track down the thief who stole Father's signet. I know the Priestesses cannot use it, but when I am crowned it will give me access to the magic in Father's treasury. I want that ring back when I return."

The Queen looked a little startled that her son was giving her instructions, but she took it silently. Then he went on, "Have you piled up the boxes in the store room that is used as a teleport station?"

"I gave the order."

"You might want to make sure it was carried out. It is the sort of order servants like to forget."

Lord Septimus noticed that Grimbolt remembered how easily servants forget and he reported, "As a matter of fact, I have inspected the room, and it is full of boxes," He smiled broadly at his King's attitude of command and his attention to details.

The servants arrived with a table which they quickly covered with platters of meat, fruit, breads, and pastries. As soon as they left, everyone fell to and quickly consumed the supper.

The sun had not yet risen when Grimbolt, with Alsenius, Njal, and Scrubbs mounted and quietly headed north from the palace. Nikky ranged easily ahead of them, sniffing the trail. Scrubbs held the lead reign of their pack mule while the others rode ready to grab weapons in case they were challenged.

"Nikky says my track north is too old to follow," Grimbolt warned his companions, "so we will follow the road toward Zharkovia for a couple of days and then turn off toward the Great Forest. Since we don't want to outrun Nikky, we'll take four or five days to get there."

"We won't have any roads north of the forest to the scar where the star crashed," said Alsenius. "I understand that it plowed a great furrow through the tundra before it buried itself."

Njal added, "Explorers' reports in the library talked of crushed and melted rock, volcanic glass, and a deep deposit of alien material. Hamfast Kallinar, the author of the best report, theorizes that more than half the mass of the object was ice, which vaporized violently on impact, scattering foreign material over a wide area. If he is right, we may even find alien plants from seeds which survived both the long journey and the heat of the crash. He insists on calling the object a meteor rather than a star. He says stars are all fire, but this object was solid matter which had no light of its own. He even theorizes that some of the bodies we call stars are actually huge bodies of solid matter which shine by reflecting sunlight. He insists that the moon is such an object."

"Isn't that what Eldon says he learned in the Starborn histories?" asked Alsenius.

"Yes, he says the moon is a world like ours and that the sky is full of other worlds. He even says that the Guardians and the Starborn came to our world in great flying ships which became disabled and stranded their people on our world. I have never seen any of the Starborn histories, but I more than half believe what Eldon tells about them."

Grimbolt rode silently after the dog, brooding over his elusive memories and trying to commune with the scepter, which had assumed the shape of a quarterstaff for him. It had told him the proper command words to use its powers of detection, and it had provided a few memories of his father showing him the scepter's powers. He tried to bring back other memories of his father. Did he love him? Were they close? He tried to remember how he had felt toward his mother and brother, but the blank barrier still held. "Did I ever love that imperious woman? What is she like when she takes off ger robes?" It was impossible not to like William. He struggled to remember the Druid to whom he had apparently fled after his transformation. Isolated vague flashes of his face surfaced, and of the warm presence of his voice, but nothing coherent. He felt, however that he must have loved the man.

On the other hand there was nothing wrong with his current memory. He squirmed in his saddle at the recollection of Princess Catherine gagging at the suggestion of her marriage to him, and cringed to recall his mother's distaste as she welcomed him. He looked back at Alsenius. "At least I have one friend," he thought as the black warrior grinned at him. "Apparently people who never knew me as a real human accept me." He almost smiled as he remembered how freely Clarissa had accepted him as a bed-warmer. He whistled to Nikky, who seemed almost to have forgotten he was a man as he darted from scent to scent and lifted his leg to leave his mark.

The dog piped back, "Lots of fascinating people have come this way. Last week there was even a wagon load of Priestesses."

"Any Amazons?" Grimbolt asked.

"Oh yes, about half a dozen. They rode geldings while the Priestesses went in a wagon."

"You really learn a lot by using your nose."

"It's really wonderful. The boss Amazon hates the Priestesses, and the Priestesses really resent having to travel."

"You can smell their moods?"

"Sure! How do you think a dog knows how to keep on the good side of his master? I can smell your loneliness and Njal's mischief and even Alsenius' worry. I can always tell when Njal's going to cast an illusion. He sort of giggles mentally, and I can smell it."

"Don't you miss being human?"

"It's getting hard to remember being human," Nikky answered. "When I was first transformed, I ached all the time for fingers and speech. I kept trying to read things, but my eyes won't focus that sharply. But now, I sometimes go for half a day without remembering. Njal says, if I don't find someone to break the enchantment soon, I'll begin to stop thinking like a man."

"Maybe that's a blessing," said Grimbolt. "If you can't act like a human, you might as well forget it and just be a dog."

"The trouble is, I love thinking. The only thing that keeps me going crazy is the chance to wrestle with this mystery of yours, the chance to fight the Pythoness who did this to me." He dashed off to sniff at the trail and water a bush, leaving Grimbolt to brood.

After two days the path swerved northeast, and Scrubbs signaled Nikky that it was time to leave the trail and head northwest across the open country. "You ought to pick up some tracks leading our way. Not many people visit the Druid's realm, but you ought to find some animal tracks."

The bloodhound snuffled back and forth in the new direction and soon bayed his discovery of a trail. It was little more than a deer track, but revealed signs of constant wear. As the day wore on the rolling meadow land became dotted with clumps of scrubby plant growth and even occasional groves of trees. They could see on the horizon the rising dark of the forest.

Grimbolt had no difficulty seeing the trail once it was pointed out. Presently Alsenius drew up beside him. "Any juicy news from the sniffing?" he asked.

"He says he's beginning to lose his humanity. He's afraid the transformation is becoming permanent."

"And you, my friend, are you remembering things or just wishing you could."

"Mostly wishing, I guess. I do have a few fleeting memories of the Druid teaching me, but they are too scattered to tie into a clean picture." He looked sadly at his companion. "She gagged when the Queen told her she might have to marry me. I'm so hideous she actually gagged."

Alsenius gazed back at him. "Well, you're not exactly every girl's dream," he sighed, "but Clarissa liked you well enough. Cheer up. We're making progress. The Princess didn't give me much of a look, either, and I was born this way."

"But I bet you didn't have to pay for a lay in your own country."

Alsenius couldn't help smirking. "Not even in Draecia."

They camped by the side of a brook which flowed from the forest and found the water clear, fresh, and cold.

Late in the morning of the next day they reached what was clearly the entrance of the Great Forest. The casual growth of scrub pine and juniper suddenly gave place to massive oaks, and the undergrowth yielded to reveal a broad avenue leading into the deep shadow. When Nikky frisked into the avenue, he suddenly stopped, settled on his haunches, and piped back to the others, "We must wait here. There's a powerful FORBIDDANCE."

Njal moved abreast of him. Immediately his horse shied, and he felt a sharp pain in his chest. He dismounted and took a step forward, and the pain increased. He stepped back and the pain faded. "This Druid means business," he reported. "Does it hurt you, Nikky?"

"No, it doesn't hurt, but it smells very uninviting—like jaguars and tigers."

"But we have to get in. The Druid seems to be the only one who can help us."

Scrubbs dismounted and sat down on a stone. "Don't worry, he's as curious as any man. He'll send somebody to check up on us." He waved to Alsenius. "There's no point n drawing your sword; just sit down and wait."

After about half an hour, Nikky suddenly leaped to his feet and yelped. The horses shied violently, and two massive tigers glided along the avenue. On the back of one sat a Halfling, who dismounted, gestured for the cats to pause, and approached the party. "Greetings, strangers," he said, "and I see the word fits you very well." He neighed comfortingly toward the horses and woofed at Nikky, who humbly lowered his head. "I am Handyman Greenthumb, Druid of the fifth level, henchman to he Great Druid Leander. May I ask your business in the Great Forest of the Goddess?"

Grimbolt rose to his feet and inclined his head respectfully. "My scepter tells me I am Crown Prince of Arragor, but I know myself as Grimbolt, a stranger to myself. I am told that Druid Leander befriended me in great distress, and I come begging for information and further assistance. This is Lord Nicholas of Zharkovia, who is under transformation as a bloodhound. This us Alsenius, a Fighter of Pluvia, and this is Sergeant Scrubbs, Handkrieger in the army of Arragor."

"Stranger strangers I have never greeted. May I assume your horses are not ensorceled humanoids?" The Halfling swept them a collective bow. "You are, I think, welcome to the hospitality of the Goddess and of her Druids. I ask you to keep your weapons sheathed at all times. I will not be responsible for any punishment that follows disobedience. My colleagues, Bengalus and

Bengalia, will escort your animals to appropriate resting places." he waved toward the tigers, who turned and prepared to lead the way.

Nikky piped furiously, and Grimbolt translated. "Lord Nicholas claims hospitality as a human envoy from his Majesty King Peter of Zharkovia."

"His mode of communication is most strange. Doesn't he speak *Canine?*"

"No, he is the victim of a botched spell. We are using his human voice pitch as a kind of code."

"Stranger and stranger." The Halfling shook his head. "But if he thinks of himself as human, I suppose we must humor him. Come with me, bear man, dog man, black man, and Scrubbs. It is a pleasant walk to the great tree."

The horses took to flight when the tigers approached and Handyman had to neigh and whicker vigorously at them before they would stop. He ran to them and talked soothingly in *Equine*. Hesitantly they inched back toward him, but they shied as soon as the tigers approached. Finally Handyman gestured the tigers away and sat quietly on convenient rock among the horses. Presently a chimpanzee swung into view, moving easily from tree to tree. The Halfling neighed an introduction, and the horses lined up to follow the chimp through the trees.

Handyman turned to the men and invited, "Anyone for a stroll?"

Grimbolt and Alsenius found it irksome at first to adjust their long paces to the Halfling's short stride, but Njal and Nikky enjoyed the leisure to study the forest. It was, in fact, a stroll of several miles to the huge clearing. The great Sequoia which dominated the forest towered so high that they could not, even by straining their necks, see its top. "The Goddess gave us the Sequoia when she set aside this forest for her worship several thousand years ago. The Great Druids have always made their home here." Handyman led them to a huge protruding root and tapped upon it with his staff. Immediately an opening appeared, and he led them into a comfortable dormitory room. "You may bathe in the pool and refresh yourselves until Lord Leander is ready to welcome you. I will come in an hour or so to escort you to dinner." He left them and the opening closed behind him. As was usual with Sequoia accommodations, the furniture grew out of the tree itself. There were five beds, four comfortable chairs, and a full book case. In the floor at the back of the chamber was a large depression full of surprisingly warm water, which entered in a sparkling cascade from the wall. They could not see the outlet. Without hesitation,

Nikky plunged into the pool and began swimming around. The others divested themselves of packs and clothes and quickly joined him. They found a stack of towels on a table near the pool, though Nikky preferred to shake himself dry. Soon after they had donned fresh clothes, Handyman tapped at the door, and they joined him to walk around to the other side of the great tree where they found a massive table with comfortable stools growing from an exposed root.

As they were seating themselves, two robed figures approached from a door in the trunk.

Alsenius instinctively rose and bowed as he felt their aura of authority. Scrubbs and Grimbolt quickly imitated hm, and even Njal reluctantly stood up. Handyman bowed profoundly and announced, "Leander, High Druid of the Great Forest and Miranda, High Priestess of Gaea."

The Druid and Priestess took their places on the raised stools at the head of the table. They nodded their heads to acknowledge the tribute, and everyone sat. "Welcome to the King of Arragor and to his friends." Leander's resonant bass voice effortlessly filled the area and wrapped his guests in its warmth.

"Welcome to the oppressed and to their companions—to the homeless and far from home." The Priestess' rich contralto echoed and reinforced her husband's greeting.

A troop of dryads swept around them bearing bowls of fruits and nuts. They placed a bowl on the floor beside Nukky. "We do not sacrifice beasts to our appetites," the Druid explained so the bloodhound, "What we serve you is made of nutritious grains enchanted to taste like raw meat. If it does not satisfy, we give you leave to hunt for rabbits."

Nikky piped back and Grimbolt translated, "The enchanted food is excellent; I prefer to stay and enjoy human conversation. I am, after all a man."

Miranda rose from her stool. "I would gladly restore you to your natural shape if this transformation was not of your choosing."

"Please, milady, I long to regain my humanity before I lose myself in the beast." He rose on his hind legs and struggled to bow.

"Were you respectably attired when the transformation occurred?" she asked.

"I was formally dressed for a public performance."

"Good! The counter spell will restore your body as it was clothed upon transformation."

She approached him and knelt to stare into his eyes. I see that the spell was cast ineptly or under great stress and that some protective magic further distorted its effects. It is a wonder that you retain any vestige of human thought, considering the length of time you have worn this form. You must have very great strength of purpose." She turned to the company. "If you will excuse us, we will withdraw to my rooms. This magic were best performed in private." She led Nikky to a blank wall of bark and gestured. Immediately an archway appeared which allowed them to enter before it sealed behind them. Nikky found himself in a magnificent library.

"May I read your thoughts to dispense with your rather awkward mode of speech?" she asked.

Nikky nodded and immediately felt her mind—very powerful, but gentle—present in his own. She probed delicately at his memory. "I will not intrude on your private thoughts, but I must learn what you recall of the spell's casting." After several moments of mental examination she exclaimed aloud. "Never have I observed such slapdash spell casting. The clerical protective spells preserved much of your identity from the transformation. It saved your voice—which must be very precious to you—yet it transformed your mouth and tongue so as to deprive you of articulation. Incidentally, your use of pitches as code is very ingenious."

"I sang from my infancy. Before I could master language I was singing complex tunes. When I came of age, my guardians sacrificed my manhood to preserve my voice. It has saved my sanity that I can still sing, even as a dog." He lifted his head and piped a four-octave chromatic upward scale and descended in looping arpeggios.

"Remarkable!" She paused thoughtfully. "One reason I decided to work with you privately is that my offer might embarrass you. I can, with some difficulty, untangle the magical ineptitude which has transformed you. Because you have been a dog so long, you will suffer occasional mental relapses—lifting your leg against the furniture, waking up curled on the floor, perhaps even washing your genitals in public—but those problems will fade. Lord Nicholas the canary cam be completely restored."

Nikky writhed with glee at this news.

"The Druid and I can also, at some inconvenience to ourselves, restore that part of your anatomy which your guardians removed so that you can enjoy or suffer the pangs and blisses of Aphrodite. The price, however, will be the resultant natural growth of a masculine voice box. Whether your masculine voice would be as flawless as your soprano, no one can guess, but even at best you would have to undergo the same retraining which faces any adolescent male."

"My choir master sacrificed my manhood for my voice, and you are telling me I can choose to sacrifice my voice for manhood?"

"Yes."

He thought back over the struggles and ecstasy he had observed in his friends as puberty swept over them—their agony when girls rejected them, and their swaggering glee at their successes, their inability to think of anything but their genitals. He remembered the stir in his groin when Princess Catherine met his eyes—the pounding pulse and quivering gut. He yearned for the ache of loving her and at the same time foresaw the agony of rejection that must come when her father forced her to marry Grimbolt or some other royal monstrosity. Was the possibility of unbearable pleasure, balanced with the enslavement to desire worth the loss of his voice—his livelihood, his ecstatic mastery of his world? As boys, his friends had adjusted to the inevitable change, and he to the enforced unchange. But to choose for himself?

"And if I choose to regain my manhood, no subsequent operation could never restore what I now have?"

"Once that voice box grows, there is no turning back. You would become a eunuch with a man's voice—lightened, perhaps, but the instrument would remain a man's."

"But you can restore me to what I was before the transformation?"

"Oh, yes. To neutralize the meddling of that bungling necromancer's ineptitude is the work of minutes. To regenerate your lost organs would demand time, energy, and some sacrifice on my part and on the part of the Druid. We would willingly undergo that labor if you desire, because your castration was an unnatural act which our Goddess abhors. Reproduction is the law of Gaea, yet in your unusual case, she will not compel."

"Would you be willing disenchant me now and leave me time to think about the other?"

"Yes. As I warned you, there may be mental relapses to houndhood, but I can lead you back to dine as the human Lord Nicholas, and Leander can give your dinner to the wolves. If, before you leave our forest, you decide to become a complete man, we will undertake that task also." She gestured to a lounge chair. "I suggest that you arrange yourself in that chair in as close to human pasture as you can assume. You will experience considerable discomfort as your bones and sinews rearrange themselves, but that is the price of reconstruction."

Nikky struggled to curl his tail out of the way and position his rump like a human, extending his legs toward the floor. The Priestess pressed his shoulders back against the seat, stared into his eyes and chanted a long incantation. Then she breathed heavily in his face and moved her hands firmly down his rib cage along his flanks and down to his feet. Finally she straightened: "Be as you were wont to be! I command you in the name of Gaea, Mother of earth and of all creatures of the earth."

It felt to Nikky as if every joint in his body had come unhinged; bones lengthened and shortened, sinews tensed and slacked. His gut and viscera squirmed into new relationships, and he screamed at the chaos of his face. After minutes of agony his body began to relax, and he found himself sitting comfortably in the chair with his feet planted firmly on the floor.

"As soon as your belly settles down, I would suggest that we join the company and feed you. Try to remember you are a man and don't gulp your food. Be especially careful with peaches and plums. Perhaps you would do well to start with seedless grapes and chunks of melon."

As Lord Nicholas struggled to his feet, he had to fight off vertigo before he dared move one shoe. He was grateful to discover he was clad in the finery of his recital. After a few experimental steps he staggered to a mirror he found tucked between two bookcases. It was his own face that looked timidly out at him, and he made faces at himself for a few seconds until he had covered his canine teeth and his expression of glee seemed almost natural. Then he tested his precious voice and found it sweet, flexible, and true. As he followed Miranda, he dared not swagger, but when the archway opened before them, he managed better than a totter, and his cloak swung almost gracefully about his trim ankles.

He made it to the table, schooled himself to ignore the tempting scent of raw rabbit from the bowl on the floor, and clamped his teeth on a tokay grape, feeling the seeds crunch under his grinders. The sweet-sour juice caressed his tongue, and he had to restrain himself from grabbing a whole cluster and shoving them into his mouth. He looked around the table and saw clearly the faces of his friends; at the same time he missed the heartening comfort of their scent. He flexed his fingers and carefully wrenched another grape from the stem. It was a joy to feel its cool ripeness against his finger tips as he popped the fruit into his mouth and crushed it with his tongue; then he adjusted his lips and tongue to eject the seeds into his palm. Every dextrous motion was an adventure, and the joy of humanhood swept through him. Carefully he adjusted his mouth to say, "I'm very glad to see you, though I miss your friendly smell." The words were precise and careful. "Forgive me while I learn to be a man again." He tore a sizable chunk of bread from a loaf and tried to wolf it down. Alsenius, who sat beside him, slammed his back to eject the lump, and, coughing, he sipped his water with great care to shape his lips around the rim of his tumbler. He found he had to relearn even the most familiar actions. At last, still hungry, he finished eating and they withdrew to the library.

"Lord Nicholas," asked his hostess, "you have not forgotten your gift of song?"

"No, my lady, though it has been a ling time since I twisted my mouth to sing words."

"Will you join me in a hymn to our Lady Gaea?"

"If you will set the tune, I will follow you."

By the time she finished the first stanza, he had learned the tune and his clear high counter-melody floated above her like a blessing. Leander's rich bass joined to anchor the hymn, and the listeners felt tears burning in their eyes. Njal pulled out his block-flute and romped through variations with Nicholas' voice while Alsenius finally dared to add his baritone to reinforce the melody and Scrubbs drummed his fists and fingers on the table to punctuate the rhythm. By the time the hymn ended they felt the added thrum of the ancient Sequoia that housed them.

After the silence that ended the hymn, Leander turned to Grimbolt. "You said you have memories of me?"

"I vaguely remember a grandfather—who much resembles you—teaching me the lore of the Goddess. I have tried to live by that lore."

"You remember my face?"

Grimbolt stared long at him. "No, sire. I think it is your voice that haunts me—your voice and the feel of your presence." His gaze roamed about the room. "I don't remember this library, but I remember the feeling of the place and of you."

"Very interesting. You have a wonderful sense of reality, even when you have lost all memory of material things. I suppose that is why illusions have no power over you. You have been taught by deprivation to look more deeply. Being Grimbolt has beautifully matured you."

"Then you do remember me?"

"Oh, yes. You straggled into our forest howling for help. You had been battered with cruel magic which had overwhelmed the protective magic of your signet. Apparently the evil priestess first cast a DEATH spell, which your ring partially defeated so that you were flung into a coma. Then, thinking she had killed you, she removed your ring and cast REINCARNATION, planning to imprison you in the form of a bear. Unfortunately REINCARNATION is designed to work on the newly dead; therefore its effects upon a living being are unpredictable—almost random. You were restored to consciousness and partially transformed. The resulting system shock unsettled your mind. I would guess that you surprised the Priestess by attacking her with bearlike ferocity and fleeing in panic. Again I am guessing, but I believe the animal nature of your changed form was attracted to the Forest, and you pelted over farm and wilderness in a mindless quest for relief."

Leander shrugged his shoulders. "My wife and I were powerless to unsnarl the random chaos of magic which had entangled you, and I feared that the Priestess who had wrought this insanity might pursue and further persecute you. You were pleading hysterically for release, and I gave you the only peace I could. Your consciousness was as tangled as yarn that kittens have played with; your body was half man, half bear; and the terror of your flight had practically paralyzed your reason. Right or wrong, I gave you release by blanking your memory. I then strove to teach you a way of life that would not lead you to harm. When you reached a state of mind that would pass for sanity, I carried you to a distant town, impressed a name on your consciousness, and sent you to seek employment which would comfort your spirit by exhausting your body. I then left you in the care of the Goddess and prayed that I had done more good than harm."

Grimbolt knelt at his feet. "You saved me from the Priestess who killed my father and planned to enslave my whole kingdom; you gave me peace when I was mad with fear and confusion; you placed me where I could earn a living. I can never repay you."

He and Alsenius then told of their travels with Clarissa and their subsequent return to Draecia as well as their quest in the Northwest for some clue to Grimbolt's identity.

"When King Roger sent us to Arragor to retrieve the princess, we began to find hints that Grimbolt belonged in this part of the world," Njal added. "As it turns out, our guesses were surprisingly accurate."

"The trouble is," Grimbolt added, "everybody I have talked to clucks his tongue about how interesting a problem I have, but nobody knows how to restore my identity."

"Lord Wulfstan, whom you consulted in Troxia, is reputed to be a most powerful Cleric," Miranda remarked. "We have one advantage over him, however. We know almost exactly how this magical tangle was wrought, while he confronted only symptoms."

"Since I cast the MEMORY BLANK upon you," Leander added, "I know it is not a part of the Priestess' muddle. I can, therefore, restore your memory if you can bear the agony of recalling."

"You can?"

"Yes. If you dare relive in memory of your part in your father's murder as well as your near death from the first spell, the mangling of your body by the second, and whatever other magical horrors were inflicted upon you, I can neutralize my spell. You will suffer some confusion as your old memories struggle to fit themselves into your current life, but in time, you should have a reasonably coherent recollection. The restored memories will be overwhelmingly vivid and painful when they first strike you, but if you can stay sane, they will dull with time. There will, of course be violent recurring nightmares."

"I cannot fulfill my duties as King unless I have my memory."

"One further warning." Leander laid his hand on Grimbolt's shoulder. "Your mind could never stand the strain of another MEMORY BLANK spell. Once you get your memories back, you must bear them for life. Furthermore, the REINCARNATION spell is irreversible, even miscast as it was. There is no way to restore Prince Humber's identity which was obliterated by the spell. If the priestess had succeeded in killing you, there would have been no memory at all after reincarnation. Somehow remnants of your identity and memory survived the magical mish-mash and drove you temporarily insane."

"So I can't be reincarnated again?"

"I could kill you and bring you back as a human, but that human would not be you. It would be a human without fixed identity, without memories. Prince Humber and Grimbolt would remain dead, and the body would develop its own new nature as a baby does."

"Then Lord Wulfstan was right. I cannot be restored."

"We can make cosmetic changes in your appearance," Miranda interrupted. "I could remove the hair from your forehead and between us we could reshape your face into human proportions—even move your ears back where they belong—but you will always remain part bear."

"Have you noticed a tendency near the full moon to become more intensely bearlike?" Leander asked. "There is a possibility that you are becoming a wer-bear—a creature which, at or near the full moon, changes shape from man to beast. If the balance between man and bear has been upset too far, you might occasionally have to retire from society for a few days."

"Not necessarily every month, you understand," Miranda added, "but you would have to be careful under the full moon."

"I haven't noticed any change with the moon's phases. Maybe I shall be spared that. But Princess Catherine, whom I was to marry, gagged when Mother suggested that I might be a possible husband." Grimbolt shuddered at the memory. "Is there no way I can be made presentable enough to begot children?" Suddenly a new thought struck him. "Is there an chance my children might look like me?"

"Since you are a human, and the bear traits are magically added, I would expect that you would breed true as a human," Leander answered. "I can test your seed to make sure. But I fear your wife will have to adjust to a hairy partner. If Wulfstan could not achieve full restoration, I know of no one who can." Leander shook his head sadly. "Even if the Priestess who cast the spell were willing to try to cancel it, I believe it would be impossible for her. Judging by the ineptitude of her casting, she is in no way as capable as I am. Sometimes there is no way to correct a miscast spell; the bungling introduces random factors that no human can hope to disentangle. You must decide whether what we can do is better than what you have."

Alsenius leaned forward an laid his hand on Grimbolt's arm. "Remember that you are my henchman. I will stand by you as long as you need me. I will release you if you become King, but you will always be my comrade."

Grimbolt smiled wanly. "Thank you, my friend." He looked again at Leander. "No matter what the cost, I must have my memory back before I try to decide anything else. I am grateful you saved me when I came last time, but I have grown stronger in the last two years; I must now face the memories I could not handle then."

"I shall give you a dram of something to make you sleep so that the memories will come back more gradually. You will probably first perceive them as nightmares, but those will dull the impact. It is possible that you will not recover everything at once—your mind may refuse to accept more than it can bear. It will probably be several days before your whole past fits together, so do not be dismayed if you awake in some confusion. Mental injuries like physical ones sometimes require time to heal." He went to a cupboard in the corner of the room and fetched a black ironstone bottle from which he poured a small tumbler of greenish liquid. Grimbolt tossed it off. "You should retire to your bed before this puts you to sleep. I suggest that your friends stand watch by your bedside in case you need help in the night."

"I'll curl up at the foot of your bed," Nicholas offered.

X—Mating Flight

Princess Catherine rushed down the broad corridor from Queen Elsa's office, up the grand staircase to the third floor and down the hallway to her suite. She hastily dismissed her flitterbrained maids, Tilda and Susan, and flung herself on her bed. "Are all royal males impossible? There must be somebody with royal blood who is not a freak. Why can't my father find somebody who isn't deformed, ancient, or perverted." The only man she had found even remotely interesting was that strange envoy of King Peter's, and in spite of the flutter his gaze had given her heart, she realized that he could never be her lover, even if he could be persuaded to carry her off.

"I'm just a brood mare with valuable bloodlines," she thought. "But at least they find beautiful stallions for a brood mare. Nobody really pays much attention to me. I could probably ride off for a couple of days before anybody noticed I was gone." The thought of riding off into the wilderness had a certain attraction, if only it wasn't so hopeless. "I'd need horses and food and camping equipment. I would need a man with weapons to defend me—a strong man who could use his weapons and be some use to me. I don't want to marry the first bandit who carries me off. He might be worse even than that hairy Grimbolt. Grimbolt was at least a gentleman."

She sat up and tried to imagine an escape. "Maybe I could flee to King Peter's court and put myself under his protection." For a moment she pictured Lord Nicholas riding into the night beside her. "The trouble is, King Peter would probably send me back to my father for diplomatic reasons. Damn diplomacy!"

At that moment Lady Mabel tapped on the door and came in. Seeing the princess sitting there cursing, she paused. "Oh, I was just going to suggest a walk in the gardens while it's clear. Everybody's expecting rain tomorrow. But you are out of sorts?"

"Oh, Mabel. Be glad you're not royal."

"Why what's the matter. Bad news from your father's emissaries?"

'They've brought a great hairy monster that Father wants to marry me off to. He looks like a bear."

"But surely, her Majesty isn't giving up on Prince Humber?"

"I don't know, but Father must be either suspicious or impatient—probably both. He's sent a bunch of foreigners to demand my return—there's a great black man, the hairy one, and a little Wizard of some sort with mischief in his eye. The Queen says Father wants me to marry the hairy one. I nearly puked." She flopped back on the bed. "I wonder how hard it would be to get a horse."

"Not thinking of running away?"

"I can't do it alone, and Tilda and Susan haven't got the brains of a flea between them. I'd take off in a minute if I thought I had a chance of getting away with it."

"You'd almost have to depend on a man for protection and to make arrangements." Lady Mabel amazed her by taking the idea seriously. "The only female fighters around here belong to the Pythoness, and you don't want to get mixed up with that crowd." She sat on the boudoir chair beside the bed. "My Rupert would be a wonderful protection, but he's such a stick-in-the-mud."

"You'd think of running away?"

"I've been waiting over a year for Rupert to get knighted so he can propose to me. I think her Majesty will finally approve of a wedding, but she'll make us wait through a long engagement, and probably send him off on a quest or something to prove himself. And I want him now, while he's still got his hair."

Catherine levered herself off the bed and began pacing. "Do you think there's a chance he might help me escape. I don't have much money of my own, and I don't suppose Father would reward him for protecting me—not when I'm running away."

"I've been trying to talk him into carrying me off to Zharkovia to take service with King Peter, but he still thinks he's loyal to Arragor. How much money could you raise?"

"If somebody would buy my jewelry, it's probably worth five or six hundred gold pieces. I don't have more than a hundred left from the allowance Father gave me when I came here."

"Even that would help, and I know a couple of boys in the Thieves Guild, who might be able to help fence the jewels. Let me see what you have."

The princess stooped to reach under her bed when she heard her maids twittering into the front room. She straightened up and waited for them to burst in. They were still chattering about an encounter with an impertinent footman when they entered.

Lady Mabel went to the door. "I'll consult Master Morley about possible companions at the picnic," she said. "We can talk about provisions later."

"Are we taking a picnic to the Royal Games?" Tilda demanded.

"Can we invite some of the boys to share it?" asked Susan.

"One of the guards has asked me for a favor to wear when he fights with the broadsword," Tilda added, "and I gave him that old pink glove I lost the mate to."

"Well I wouldn't want to cheapen myself, letting a man get something of mine all bloody."

"Wilbur is going to wear my glove on his helmet so it won't get soiled."

"At least there's no danger of soiling it with brains even if he gets his helmet split," Catherine snapped.

"I wonder how much we could get for the Princess' jewels," Mabel pondered as she walked away. "If they're not too distinctive, I might be able to turn a real profit." She headed to senior pages' quarters. At the reception desk she asked the duty page to tell Master Rupert Morley that Lady Mabel requested his company. In a few moments Rupert appeared and guided her to a pair of chairs in a corner of the Visitors Room. He ordered tea and scones and settled into his chair. "What brings you here at this time?' he asked.

"I'm afraid I've got myself into a mess," she confessed. Then she told him about her visit with the princess.

"You told her we would help her escape from the palace?" He looked dismayed. "You've gone mad!"

"I haven't committed us to anything, but I did offer to help her sell her jewelry to pay for the escape."

"I admit that sounds tempting," he sighed. "But she's engaged to the Prince and Queen Elsa would have a fit if anybody helped her run away. Besides, I'm scheduled to fight in the Games and win my knighthood. We can't let anything interfere with that."

"If we run away right after the games, everything will be so confused that nobody will notice we've gone. You'll be Sir Rupert, and we won't have to twiddle around for a year or two being engaged. You know how Queen Elsa is about long engagements. We can head for King Peter's court and take service with him. Then the princess won't have to marry that monster her father sent up here to fetch her.

"But once I'm knighted, there will be all sorts of chances for advancement."

"Yes, long bachelor quests where you get your head bashed in or get tangled up with some foreign princess, while I carry her Majesty's train and carve a silly grin on my face. Rupert, I want you now while I'm still pretty and you're worth being pretty for."

He stole a kiss, and she cuffed him gratefully on the ear; then suddenly she grabbed him and kissed him with her whole body. His reaction was such that she had to fight him off, but she left no doubt that she enjoyed it.

"The Princess is planning a picnic for the Games, and that means inviting boys to keep Tilda and Susan busy. You will be there as my escort. The picnic will be an excuse for having a pack mule for food, and we can have everything we need for a getaway: tents and extra clothes and all sorts of stuff. We can have our horses all saddled in case we want to picnic out in the country instead of on the crowded palace grounds. After you've been knighted, we can ride off, and nobody will notice we're gone till the next morning." She felt the resistance in his body. "You don't have to commit yourself now, but you'll at least think about it."

His grumbled, "yes," was not encouraging, but at least he had committed himself to 'think.' She rewarded him with another kiss, and darted off."

The direction of his thoughts, however, would not have pleased Lady Mabel. He had no intention of ruining his prospects at court by deserting on the day of his knighting. His family was respectable, but not noble. His father was a professional Scribe, much of whose employment was making beautiful copies of royal proclamations and important letters. Since the addition of 'Sir Rupert' to the letter head would attract upper class business, the family had sacrificed a lot to buy his appointment as a Royal Page and to support him while he progressed toward knighthood.

Master Morley had been diligent in learning court etiquette, proper speech, and protocol as well as riding, jousting, and swordplay. At sixteen, he could satisfy even his father in writing a formal document. He had an uncanny skill with seals, and could imitate individual penmanship well enough to produce undetectable forgeries. He subscribed to the knightly code of honor and often found it convenient to practice it. As a result he was never accused of improprieties as page or as scribe, nor was he suspected of deceiving Lady Mabel. He was a model of prudence and decorum.

When he promptly applied for an appointment with Lord Septimus, he had no intention of playing the informer and damaging his chances with Lady Mabel, but he rather hoped the Lord Steward would help him avoid damaging his chances at court. He had learned to trust his Lordship's skill at drawing conclusions without being told anything, and he had several times profited from his Lordship's advice in handling ethical tangles.

On the Thursday afternoon before the Saturday of the Royal Games he found himself sitting across the desk from Lord Septimus, sipping the inevitable tea and requesting counsel on the responsibilities of a knight. He began by confessing his passion for Lady Mabel and the pangs which official delays imposed. He hinted at the lady's desire to elope after his promotion to Sir Rupert.

Lord Septimus cleared his throat and suggested that newly dubbed knights usually performed services for the crown.

Master Morley wondered whether such services might include missions which might best be performed by married knights.

Lord Septimus remarked that most quests were better performed by bachelors. He trusted there were no scandalous reasons for hastening the marriage.

Master Morley reassured him, "There has been no indiscretion yet, but Milord, the lady's impatience tempts me almost beyond even a knight's honor. Furthermore some of her plans for an elopement disturb me."

"Nothing treasonous, I trust?"

"Others are involved, and my honor forbids disclosure of names, yet if your Lordship has other means of inquiry . . ."

Lord Septimus' agile mind took several intuitive leaps. "If danger threatens the royal family . . ."

"Oh, no, sir, but . . ."

"Of course if other members or guests of the court were thinking of unauthorized departures, it would be well to prevent embarrassment."

"Well, Lady Mabel was thinking—nothing actually planned, you understand—of including others in the elopement party."

"And you feared that such a departure might displease her Majesty."

"I wish to protect Lady Mabel from indiscretion, sire."

"And you also wish to possess both Lady Mabel's body and estates without unnecessary delay. You have a new knighthood and a promising career to protect, and you need to prevent your fiancee's indiscretion from compromising you."

Master Morley sighed with relief, and Lord Septimus pursued his advantage. "And you would be profoundly grateful if I should find you a quest which would honorably extricate you."

He did not need Rupert's nod and he lowered his voice conspiratorially. "It so happens that her Majesty's matrimonial plans for an absent family member have become embarrassingly entangled. Exalted guests cannot be prevented from leaving if they wish, yet a departure would threaten an important alliance. If a guest should believe she was fleeing to a foreign court and should by mistake arrive with an elopement party at the safety of the Great Druid's forest, her Majesty might be persuaded to authorize the Great Druid to solemnize the marriage of a promising young knight to an impatient maid in waiting."

"Such protective misdirection should be possible if her Majesty's approval could be guaranteed."

"And you could find cooperative male escorts for the ladies?"

"Oh, yes sire, if their absence from court were approved." Master Morley could not control a conspiratorial grin.

Lord Septimus leaned across the desk. "It would not be amiss for you to make tentative plans for an elopement after the knighting ceremonies at the Royal Games. It will be necessary for me to obtain her Majesty's approval, but I believe she will agree to a controlled escape for the princess. Come to me at the beginning of the first watch for final approval of the scheme. I believe you will not have to cancel your plans."

Master Morley, having both accomplished his desire and saved his honor, dashed smartly about the court helping Lady Mabel with her plans for the picnic. He persuaded Kit Smart and Mark Drusus, Senior Pages to her Majesty, to escort the ladies Tilda and Susan. Enlisting Ranger Eccles to guide the party due north to the Great Forest instead of northeast toward Zharkovia required not only tact, but a substantial outlay from the funds realized from Princess Catherine's jewels, which Lady Mabel had shrewdly—and profitably—fenced. He sincerely regretted the need to deceive not only the princess but also his own bride-to-be.

When he reported to Lord Septimus, he received written permission for his marriage, together with a note from her Majesty to the Great Druid requesting his hospitality for Princess Catherine until such time as she should wish to return to Arragor for her wedding.

As his Lordship watched the young knight-to-be bound out of his office, he leaned back and wondered how chance might be twisted to accomplish a meeting between the elopement party and that of Grimbolt. "Some times," he mused, "fate likes a little assistance from human ingenuity." Then he returned to the last-minute arrangements for the morrow's Games.

Nobody expected Rupert Morley to win the jousting tournament. So that his 14th place finish was regarded as respectable. Nor did anyone expect him to win the matches with long sword, broad sword, and bow, and Lady Mabel enthusiastically applauded his standings of 7th, 5th, and 12th. His performance in dressage was respectable, and his performance on the written examinations on protocol, heraldry, and honor were substantially above average. He was, therefore, sixth in the line of 36 pages dubbed knights by her Majesty late Sunday afternoon. He was delighted that she remembered him by name and congratulated him on his approaching marriage. Later, as the picnic party left the field, he was certain that he saw a pair of sentries deliberately separate in their patrol of the northward road. Lady Mabel congratulated herself on their skill in evading them. An hour later, everyone enjoyed a picnic feast which certainly did credit to her diplomatic skills with the kitchen staff. Ranger Eccles insisted on avoiding the royal road northeast to Zharkovia. Instead he led the party due north across the fields till it was fully dark, thus confusing everyone's sense of direction.

When they finally pitched camp, they found that Princess Catherine had provided two tents—one for men and the other for women. Lady Mabel and Sir Rupert, who had planned to consummate their union even before they reached the Forest, protested the arrangement, but the princess was adamant. Rupert offered to share the second watch with his intended, but Ranger Eccles agreed with the princess that the watch would be more alert if two men shared each of the first two watches while the princess and Lady Mabel shared the third. It was tacitly agreed that Tilda and Susan should sleep straight through the night, since they were unaccustomed to responsibility. Tilda wanted to share the men's watches, but Susan was content to sleep through.

During the middle watch, Rupert found time to remind the Ranger that Lord Septimus wanted the party guided to the Great Forest in spite of her Highness' intention to seek the Zharkovian court. In the process

Sir Rupert surrendered a considerable weight of coins—the rest to be delivered upon arrival in the Great Forest.

"Lord Septimus has forewarned the Great Druid that we are coming," he said. "I believe he even requested an escort of animals to make sure that we travel due north."

"We are already several miles west of the highway to Zharkovia," the Ranger assured him. "In the morning everybody will be thoroughly lost, so that I should have no trouble guiding them to the right trail." He gestured toward the tents. "I notice that you and the boys are paired off. You might have provided a woman for me."

"I'm afraid Lord Septimus intended you to guard the princess from the rest of us, but Kit and Mark aren't really paired with the fluff-heads. You're welcome to horn in on either of them. I sort of hope Lady Mabel would turn you down."

"Understood," the Ranger chuckled.

Since Tilda and Susan knew nothing of cookery, and Lady Mabel and the princess were above such drudgery, it was Eccles who prepared breakfast.

"I'm surprised that there isn't a better road between Arragor and Zharkovia," the princess remarked as he was repacking the mule.

"My instructions were to guide you safely," the Ranger answered. "If we took the main road, we would be liable to attacks by bandits and to possible interference from Queen Elsa's guards. It will be assumed that we are following either the main road to Quatch or the one to Zharkovia. By using this less traveled way through the Great Forest, we frustrate pursuit. I have covered our tracks well enough to deceive any but an experienced tracker."

"So that's why we're going due north instead of northeast. How soon do we return to the proper road?"

"The plan is to proceed to the Great Forest and travel east from there." The Ranger slapped the pack animal's rump and attached the lead line to his horse's saddle.

"And just who changed our plan? I ordered that we were to flee to Zharkovia as fast as possible."

"Sir Rupert instructed me to get you safely away from Arragor, and the only safe route lies through the Great Forest."

Princess Catherine turned on Rupert. "How dare you disobey my orders."

"Eccles and I agreed that the royal guards could overtake us if we took the direct road. The only way was for him to hide our track and seek the protection of the Great Druid."

The princess turned back to Eccles. "I demand that you turn east and take me to Zharkovia immediately."

The ranger mounted his horse and tugged on the pack mule's lead line. "The trail we are following will lead us easily to the Great Forest. We would face very difficult riding through lawless forest tangles of we try to cut east from here. I urge your Highness to mount up and continue on our way. The queen's guards will never suspect we have gone this way, and I am sure the Great Druid will help us proceed secretly eastward."

Unconvinced, but unable to compel obedience, the Princess mounted and followed the ranger. "I should have known my father's court is not the only place for double dealing." She retreated into her own thoughts, and they plodded along in silence.

"As a matter of fact," Sir Rupert confessed as he helped Mabel to her saddle, "You and I will be stopping in the Great Forest to celebrate our wedding."

Mabel darted an accusing glare at him. "You're up to something."

"I'm sorry, my darling, but I could not risk our future just to help the princess escape. Right after I talked with you, I went to Lord Septimus . . ."

"You did what?!"

I went to Lord Septimus to try . . ."

"You betrayed us to Lord Septimus?"

"Please, my dear, I didn't betray anybody. I just went to Lord Septimus to see if he could arrange a quest for me that would speed up our wedding. I didn't tell him anything about the princess."

"But you let the old demon weasel it out of you," she accused.

Sir Rupert drooped his head. "Lord Septimus is very astute, and he already knew Princess Catherine wanted to run away."

"So you blabbed the whole plan."

"No, I didn't blab anything. He just figured most of it out and offered to help us if we'd help him keep the princess from getting out of his control."

"So the he's persuaded the Great Druid to keep the princess prisoner."

"Look! Lord Septimus has arranged for Princess Catherine to go to the Great Forest instead of Zharkovia. Eccles will convince her it's just a detour to avoid pursuit. I have a letter from his Lordship asking the Druid to persuade the princess to take refuge with him. She won't really be a prisoner, but she'll have to wait around the forest for a while. Prince Humber recently came here for help, and his Lordship hopes she'll get to know the prince while they're both here."

"You slimy sneak!"

"And Lord Septimus wrote the Great Druid asking him to perform the marriage ceremony for us," Sir Rupert hastily added.

"You mean we don't have to wait till we reach Zharkovia?" Torn between anger at not being consulted and pleasure that the engagement was to be shortened, she decided that the reckoning with her fiancé should be postponed. "What about Queen Elsa? Has she approved the wedding?"

"We are performing a very special service for her Majesty, and she is allowing a wedding trip to the Great Forest as a reward." Rupert sneaked in his last argument. "This venture is to be my First Quest. Then I'm going back to Arragor and become Sir Rupert the Scribe. You will become a Matron in Waiting. So we're going to have a wonderful wedding trip in the Great Forest and start our careers as soon as we get home."

"And the princess just changes one prison for another," Mabel grumbled.

Presently the horses began to shy at the scent of a lynx following them through the bushes. Then Princess Catherine actually spotted one. "You said we'd be safer on this trail," she protested to Eccles, "but wild beasts may be a worse danger than bandits."

"He won't attack an armed party like this," he answered. "All we have to do is stay together; no straying from the trail or from camp. I wouldn't be surprised if he's one of the Druid's sentries."

"Well, he gives me the creeps, and furthermore he's scaring the horses. Can't you drive him away?"

"I can probably talk to him," said the Ranger, and he turned aside from the party and plunged into the woods. Presently he returned, looking smug. "We're perfectly safe. The lynxes belong to the Druid. I've asked them to stay downwind of the horses. They tell me if we speed up a bit, we can make the Great Forest by dark. That way we won't have to camp again."

Everybody agreed to increase speed to a ground-eating canter which the horses could maintain without undue fatigue. They noticed that the woods thickened around them and the undergrowth became sparser. The evening twilight was darkening around them when Handyman appeared in their path sitting on his tiger. "Well met," he greeted them, "The Great Druid is expecting you."

At the tiger's scent the horses panicked. Tilda and Susan were thrown and Mabel, Mark, and Kit mastered their beasts only by sticking to their backs until they tired of running. Eccles mastered his steed and the pack mule by timely use of both knees and voice. Much to his surprise, Rupert found himself still in the saddle while his horse shook with restrained terror.

Handyman obviously found the rout amusing. He laughingly rounded up the strays, speaking to them in their own language. "I suggest you dismount and proceed afoot," the Halfling urged. I have sent for Placidus, the hinny, to guide your horses to pasture. The apes will take your saddle bags to your rooms.

When the travelers had finally righted themselves, Handyman rode ahead of them to guide. It soon became apparent that Susan had twisted her ankle in falling. At first Mark and Kit supported her, but her substantial weight quickly tired them.

"You are welcome to ride behind me," Handyman offered.

"Ride that beast?"

"He's quite strong, and I weigh very little." He grinned mischievously.

"He won't eat me?"

"The Druid feeds him very well. Human flesh is all right in an emergency, but he prefers something less stringy."

"But there's no side saddle." The thought of spreading her knees horrified her.

"Actually, he's quite lean. Even I don't need a saddle." The halfling leaped to the ground and gestured for the men to hoist her aboard. After considerable screaming and protesting, Mark and Kit plopped her on the tiger's back, leaving her to arrange her voluminous skirts as modestly as she could. Handyman scrambled up in front of her, and the party proceeded again.

Thus they finally reached the great sequoia, from whose roots had grown a pair of substantial shelters in which they found beds and other furnishings. Mabel started to protest her separation from her intended, but Princess Catherine silenced her with a gesture.

"We apologize for the primitive accommodations, but we have another party in the guest chambers, and we had to grow these in haste," said

Handyman. "You will find bathing and latrine facilities in that structure closer to the trunk. The Great Druid will receive you in the morning, when you will meet our other guests."

Mabel noted that the facilities were segregated, and that Ranger Eccles obeyed the princess and kept an enforcing watch. Later in the night, the couple found that lynxes had taken over the watch. By six o'clock further sleep was rendered impossible by the trumpeting and chattering of wild life. Handyman bustled up to announce that the breakfast table was spread. He led them around the great sequoia, which had grown a huge shaded table upon which the fauns and nymphs had spread platters of fruit, piles of bread, and a cauldron of porridge. Already seated at the table were Alsenius and Nicholas, the former munching a dark roll and a dripping persimmon, the latter wolfing a mixture from a large bowl. When he saw the Princess, Nicholas leaped gracefully to his feet, upsetting the bowl as he grabbed a cloth to wipe his face. He blushed furiously as his violet eyes devoured her image. "Your Royal Highness," he murmured, and bowed at exactly the right angle for her rank.

She extended her hand for his kiss. "I am delighted to see you restored, Lord Nicholas. Rumor hinted that the Priestesses had enchanted you."

"The Great Druid restored my form two days ago, but I have not completely recovered my manners." He gestured to a seat across from him and moved a bowl of peaches in her direction. "Lord Leander has warned me that I was imprisoned in canine form for so long I forgot a lot of my humanity."

At this point Njal approached the table and shouted, "Hi Nikky!"

Without thinking Lord Nicholas barked enthusiastically and turned, wagging his rump. He stopped himself before he pounced on Njal and licked his face, but his effort at control was obvious. "I wish you wouldn't do that," he growled.

"Sorry, boy. I was never good at resisting temptation." Njal patted his head and settled down with a bowl of porridge and a fistful of raisins.

Nicholas turned back to the Princess, who stifled a giggle and started to peel a peach. Nicholas recovered his bowl and found a spoon. "Lord Leander still provides me with a gruel enchanted to taste like raw meat," he apologized. "I haven't recovered my human appetite yet."

Njal and Alsenius introduced themselves to the rest of the party, and conversation became more general. "How is Grimbolt getting on?" Alsenius asked Njal.

"Surprisingly well, considering the nature of his enchantments. He can't remember what Prince Humber looked like, so that his face is rather vague, but at least he has a forehead and a nose. I think he's going to cultivate a human beard because he definitely remembers a weak chin. He has settled down to two brown eyes this morning. His expression is still very much Grimbolt."

"Prince Humber is here?" the Princess interrupted. "I thought he was still missing."

"It turned out that Grimbolt is Prince Humber. When we were sure, we came here in hopes Leander could restore him."

Princess Catherine turned slightly green and looked pitifully at Lord Nicholas, whose violet eyes had never left her face. "And he is no longer half bear?"

"I would say his face is decidedly human now," said Njal. "The Druid couldn't restore him completely, but his new face is a distinct improvement: No hair on his forehead, a distinct upper lip and slightly aquiline human nose. The trouble is the Prince has been Grimbolt for so long that his memory has not completely come back. Since the miscast REINCARNATION spell erased his old identity completely, the Druid could only reconstruct a generalized human form. He hoped the Prince's restored memory would help give his new face character, but unfortunately Prince Humber had a low opinion of his looks and he rarely used a mirror."

"Then Queen Elsa was lying when she told me Father had sent Grimbolt to marry me?"

"I think she was trying to see how you would react to Grimbolt," Alsenius put in. "She didn't want to announce Prince Humber's return, but we already had convincing evidence that he was Grimbolt."

In a flash the princess realized her new position. "What a coincidence that I should come here just at this moment." She turned on Lady Mabel. "And you knew all along we weren't going to escape to Zharkovia," she accused. "Queen Elsa tricked me into running right into the arms of her loathsome son. You and that sneaky knight of yours duped me with all that talk about elopement. Nobody has any intention of helping me get to King Peter."

"Rupert didn't want to destroy his future by running away with me, so he went to Lord Septimus."

"And of course that serpentine bastard came up with a plan to get his own way." She drummed her fists on the table. "He twisted your puppet knight into carrying me off here. I suppose your reward was to get Sir Rupert."

Lady Mabel didn't quite manage to look her in the eye. "I didn't find out till later that the ranger was supposed to mislead us."

"But you let him get away with it. You let him trick me into coming right where that monster was hiding. You betrayed me into another prison even worse than Arragor."

Lady Mabel could muster no further defense than, "But."

"At least you're going to get what you deserve when you marry your slimy knightlet. You'll spend your marriage making fools of each other. I pray that you may grow old together." She turned back to Nicholas' admiring eyes. She felt her pulse quicken and turned sharply away as she remembered his operation. "I suppose you helped plan this trick."

"Milady, for over a month I have been a dog. Lady Miranda restored me only two days ago. How could I plot with Lord Septimus when I was nosing out plots as Prince William's pet?"

"But you were conspiring with Queen Elsa and Septimus, trying to marry me off to that monster."

"I went to Arragor as the agent of my master, King Peter. My job was to find out what happened to Prince Humber and who murdered his father. I had no concern about your marriage—that is—that is until I met your Royal Highness." He lowered his head in a sitting bow.

The arrival of her maids in waiting broke the embarrassed silence.

"My, isn't he beautiful!" Tilda giggled when they saw Nicholas.

Susan blushed lowered her eyes as she took her place beside her mistress.

The Princess haughtily made introductions. "Lord Nicholas of Zharkovia, may I present my maids in waiting, Lady Tilda and Lady Susan."

Nicholas rose slightly and bowed. "I have already had the honor of meeting your Ladyships, though we have never been formally introduced. My unfortunate transformation made that honor impossible." He deepened his voice to a warm contralto and gazed forlornly through his dark lashes. The women were suddenly confused to recognize the violet eyes of the bloodhound.

Leander and Miranda joined the company, and Alsenius asked, "Any chance our friend Grimbolt will join us today?"

"He considered coming out, but the news of our new guests frightened him," the Priestess murmured. "He is still very shy about his face."

"I thought he looked pretty good," Njal remarked, "considering he can't remember what he looks like."

"Normally this kind of reconstruction depends on the patient's memory for details, but his Grimbolt personality is much more forceful than the Prince's." the Druid explained. "Young Humber doesn't remember what he looked like, and Grimbolt remembers only his transformed body. What seems to be happening is an adjustment between selves."

"I fear that Queen Elsa so dominated the Prince that he never fully took possession of his life," Miranda added. "Even after his beard sprouted, Prince Humber remained a little boy. I doubt that the Queen will recognize her son, since Grimbolt has already impressed a rather stubborn chin and a formidable nose upon the new profile."

"You mean that the new Prince may even stand up to his mother?" Catherine interrupted.

"Her Majesty has a very harsh shock coming when she meets her new son," Njal chuckled. "Grimbolt won't fade into the background, and Humber, since he never really liked himself, is no match for him in a contest of wills."

"Ah!" Leander exclaimed, "The groom." He half rose from his seat as Sir Rupert attempted to slip unnoticed to the seat beside Mabel. The Druid smiled at the bride. "Has your Ladyship inspected the bridal finery? My dear wife and her women have been working on it ever since we learned we should host the solemnities."

Mabel avoided the Princess' gaze as she curtseyed to the Druid and Miranda. "The gown is unbelievably beautiful, and Rupert's kilt and jacket are most impressive."

"We assume that the nuptials will be celebrated promptly at noon. Miranda has chosen the peach orchard as the place. Have you chosen your companions?"

"If Princess Catherine will allow it, I should like the ladies Tilda and Susan to accompany me." Mabel responded.

"I have asked Alsenius to be my Second," said Rupert. "Since we are far from home, we must rely on new friends instead of old."

"I think my maids are the perfect companions for such a bride," Catherine acidly retorted. "Is the vanishing Prince to give away the bride?"

"In the absence of her father, I hoped that I would be an acceptable substitute," said Leander. "Priestess Miranda will preside for the Goddess."

"Prince Humber still doesn't feel up to appearing even for the wedding of a forging knight and a lady fence?" Catherine asked. "I should think he would represent his mother."

"Since he is uncrowned King, his Majesty would represent himself," Alsenius snapped, "but he is not yet disposed to appear in public. He has, however, given his consent to the marriage of the Queen Dowager's maid-in-waiting." He emphasized the Queen's title.

"Does one suspect a reshuffling of power?" Njal grinned mischievously at his companion.

"Grimbolt is beginning to think like a king," Alsenius answered. "He now has a chin to be firm with, and he's beginning to use it."

"He hasn't shaved off his beard, has he?"

"No. But he's trimmed it to emphasize the new firmness of his features. When he finishes his restoration, he's going to be a very impressive young man." Alsenius crunched a small loaf of black bread. "I don't know what Prince Humber was like, but his new face is very much like the mind of Grimbolt. My guess is that we'll be ready to take off for the fallen star within the week."

"You mean he's not going back to Arragor immediately?"

"He says, 'No!' He thinks Lord Septimus can manage the kingdom for the Queen and William. He's convinced that the star metal is important."

Njal nodded. "He's right. That star metal will take enchantment far better than iron. A few magic swords, a couple of wands, and some miscellaneous items will give Arragor enough power to stand off the Hegemony, even with their ensorceled Amazons."

After breakfast Njal went wandering in the forest to study the animals and plants. He startled a colony of monkeys with his new illusion of a tiger based on his observations of Bengalus and Bengalia. He spent almost an hour studying and imitating a patch of violets.

Nicholas stopped the Princess on her way to her room. "Your Highness." His voice trembled just slightly as he bowed, and his eyes fell an inch short of meeting hers. "May I show you the ornamental gardens in the shelter of this magnificent tree?"

She refused the support of his proffered arm, but nodded her willingness to accompany him. He hovered at her side in case she stumbled. They stood in awe of the profusion of roses, lilies, and peonies, trumpeting against a background of rhododendrons, azaleas, and wild flowers. At length he gathered his courage. "Your Highness, as you know, I am not like other men."

She smiled at him, then turned back to the flowers.

"You are aware that, when I first saw you, something happened to me which had never happened before." His eyes never left the clump of orchids which fascinated her. "You must have felt something, for magic flowed between us when your eyes met mine."

She reluctantly met his gaze, then dropped her eyes. "You are aware that I am—however reluctantly—betrothed to Prince Humber."

"But your Highness has showed no liking for his Majesty."

"Liking has very little to do with royal marriages. I am a Princess of Quatch. And my hand is not mine to bestow."

"Yet you do not deny the spell which we have shared, a spell I had thought beyond my reach."

"Were you as other men, I should possibly have made a fool of myself and a scandal to three realms. As it is, I shall always treasure that bright sprig of affection which we shared, even though it can never flower."

He dared to lay a hand upon her wrist, and his violet eyes under their black lashes sought hers. "Lady Miranda tells me she has the power to restore—at a price—that which was lost."

She allowed his fingers to capture her hand, and her voice lost its firm authority. "But the price would be unthinkable. My father would disown me; Queen Elsa would howl for revenge; and your master would cast you out of his realm. Where could even your miraculous voice find a place to provide for our needs?"

He smiled ruefully. "The regeneration of my manhood would also restore a masculine voice and appearance. I would support you by my sword and my wits, for my beard and my man's voice would conceal me. Don't you see, my masculinity would become complete." He grabbed her almost roughly and crushed her against his breast. "We could truly marry and share whatever fate decreed."

She clutch him momentarily, then drew back. "Remember that kings usually dictate to fate. Do you think my father, King Peter, and Queen Elsa would let us fade from court without revenge? How long do you think they would let you keep that masculinity if you deflowered me and upset all their plans. Is a week—perhaps only a night of passion—worth a lifetime of degradation? For they would not kill us quickly. You would see me forced into Humber's bed, and I would see you tortured for your presumption."

"I do not lack either courage or ingenuity. Surely we could flee to the east where their power does not reach. Even if we had to earn our bread as farmers or laborers, we would still have each other." He grasped her again and she melted into tears against him. "If I can feel this passion as I am, think how earth-shaking it could become if I were a man."

"And think how you would ache to see my beauty fade under the strain of hard labor. I am too accustomed to luxury—to having my own will. Even the most exquisite passion has to be fed and clothed and housed."

"Ever since I was a boy, I have ached to love as other boys loved—to wrestle in the hay; to blend two bodies into one as our blood streams beat against each other through the thinnest skin. If we can break—even for an instant—the isolation of our flesh and be at one . . ."

"We would still wake up in prison and in pain." She tore herself away from him. "I have watched my friends betrayed by romantic dreams of love, and I have held them while they wept when they awoke."

"I have ached with longing when I sang of love and read of high romance. I have even cried for envy when my friends came home and bragged of a night's pleasure."

"And I have wept at your voice. It is a wonderful gift."

"No gift. I have paid."

"But to throw it away."

"I know. I have soared to the heavens and carried many with me, but if we two . . ."

"We cannot. What we feel now is very beautiful, and I will treasure it till I die." She clasped him again and squeezed until he gasped. "I will cry over this garden and this meeting always. Now go away and let me catch my breath." She shoved him back, and when he rested his hand on her shoulder she shrugged it off.

Nicholas retreated and watched her weep for a while; then he turned and began to lope through the bushes as if he had become a dog again, feeling the whip of twigs and smelling the scent of rabbits and acacias.

*　*　*

Grimbolt stared at the stern face which looked up at him from the bowl of water. He had never really looked at himself when he was the

Crown Prince. He vaguely remembered shaving an apologetic smile, but he had never examined it. As Grimbolt the bear he had few chances for self study, and he hadn't liked what he saw in the water when the barge lay at anchor. "But this isn't really a bad face," he thought. "I'm going to have to trim back the beard. My chin has asserted itself almost too much. And that nose had better stop before it becomes a beak. Leander says I'm pretty much stuck with this face, since my memory refuses to give me back Humber's. And I suspect my face wasn't much in those days."

He had suffered through the agony of remembering his father's murder and his fears that he was guilty. He had relived the struggle in the dark against the Priestess's enchantments. He had wakened to her face and hands casting some magical horror over him and had raked ferociously with his clawed fingers. He had even thrown her down and tasted the blood from her neck before some magical force flung him away. He had fled from her bleeding body, hoping she could not follow him, and had crashed through the gardens in random flight. His face and body ached, and his mind blazed with terror. When his panic spent itself, he collapsed in sleep. It was still dark when he awoke and fled once more, putting as much distance as possible between himself and the terror of the garden. At last he had found himself in the Great Forest where the Halfling and the tigers had guided him to the great sequoia.

He remembered Leander's patient compassion, his teaching about the Goddess, and his reluctant promise to give him peace by erasing his memory.

Now he had recovered. His memories were painful, but bearable, though he knew he must face them again and again as nightmares. The first restored face Leander had showed him in the pool had looked characterless and vague, but now, after another week, this stern stranger with its assertive van Dyke beard, had clearly taken over.

"It's strange. Even though I remember all about Prince Humber, I still feel more like Grimbolt. This face is more like me than all the remembered bowing and yessing to Mother and letting the tutors and trainers push me around." He still found the borders of memory confusing, but the ache of rowing and the very different ache of Clarissa's body, the violent experience of his journeys across the continent, completely overshadowed the placid memories of court.

Later in the morning, when Alsenius and Njal joined him, he asked, "How soon do you think we can start for the fallen star?"

"As soon as you're ready to go." answered Alsenius. "We're all packed, and Leander has our horses and pack mule rested. I haven't talked with Nicholas today, but I think he plans to go with us."

"You knew Miranda offered to regenerate his balls?" Njal asked. "It will cost him his voice, but he's tempted. The restoration will be a major effort for her—even with the Druid's help—considering how long he's been a castrato. I suspect the magic will age both of them."

"I have a suspicion our bloodhound has been sniffing around your Princess," Alsenius laughed. "The way they weren't looking at each other at breakfast, I think you have serious competition."

"That's Mother's problem," Grimbolt retorted. "She nearly puked when Mother suggested she marry me. Of course I'm not so monstrous now, but she never really showed any interest in me when I was Prince Humber. A little bit like somebody offered a bowl of porridge for dinner—she'd rather have roast pork, but she'll take porridge rather than starve."

"Nikky with balls would be pretty tempting," Njal smirked. "He carries himself beautifully, that is if he doesn't stop to scratch his ear."

"My scepter keeps reminding me that I'm the King. I have a feeling it will object if Nikky runs off with Catherine."

"Well, it can't do much if you don't throw it."

"It's like Mother, it won't stop talking. I have to cover it with something to shut it up." Grimbolt grimaced toward the corner where his staff was swathed in a blanket. "It also nags me because I prefer to use it as a staff rather than a sword or mace. Mother was always throwing it around as a mace, breaking up the statuary. I think she's infected it with her temper." He stood up and unwrapped the staff. "You may take scepter form if you keep quiet." He grasped its end and it became the scepter.

"Are you finally going to do something?" it demanded.

"I'm going to talk with the Druid, and I don't want you interrupting." Grimbolt started for the doorway. "I think it's time we started searching for the star crater, and I will need your ability to detect and identify metals when we get there."

When Nicholas failed to appear for supper, Princess Catherine hesitantly turned to the Druid. "I hope Lord Nicholas has not suffered misadventure. Do you think someone should look fo him?"

Leander smiled gently. "Nicholas is suffering from a bruised heart, my dear. He won't die of it, but he needs to be alone."

"But if he's out alone in the forest . . ."

"He will finally fall asleep—uncomfortably, but safely. There is no harm for a good man in this forest, and an uncomfortable bed is sometimes helps toughen a heart."

"I'm afraid I was the cause of his pain."

"Reality often hurts. You have a remarkable sense of reality."

She looked at him accusingly. "You were listening?"

"Not eavesdropping, but I am conscious of everything that goes on in my realm."

"You know I refused to run away with him."

"I sensed a very reluctant rejection. He needs to get used to his pain. He will come back when he's ready."

After breaking his fast in his room, Grimbolt joined his companions and sought out the Druid. "I think I'm as close to cured as I'm likely to get," he said. "It's time for us to get on with our search for the star metal."

Leander looked up from a mistletoe sprig he was examining. "And you want to leave tomorrow morning? What about your fiancee?"

"I was sort of hoping you'd keep her here for Mother," Grimbolt suggested. "She wouldn't be up to going with us, and she shouldn't go back to court where her father might start a war over her."

"You don't intend to marry her?"

"I don't think she intends to marry me. I'd like to keep Nikky from running off with her because everybody will want to kill him if he does. Have you seen Lord Nicholas around?"

"His Lordship had a rather difficult interview with the Princess yesterday, and he ran off to get lost in the forest."

"She won't have him? Not even if you make a man of him?"

"Princess Catherine has a very good nose for consequences."

"What are the odds on Nikky's balls?" demanded Njal. "I'm betting that he keeps his voice."

"My wife and I offered to regenerate his manhood because his self-pity was beginning to spoil his disposition. He's a brilliant young man with a prodigious gift, but he feels cheated because his family decided that he should not father offspring. Now he must choose for himself."

"And you think he'll keep his voice." Alsenius looked pensive. "Goodness knows I have never paid any attention to my offspring. After all, a gelding can raise as long a spear as a stallion. His family left him everything but his balls. He can even have your Princess if she wants him. And it's no danger to your precious royal bloodlines if she cheats with him."

"I confess I'd rather keep my wife to myself," Grimbolt growled.

"I thought you didn't care for her," Njal objected. "So long as you put the bread in the oven, you shouldn't mind if he warms himself. That way you'd have a good excuse for finding your own lover. It sounds like an ideal arrangement. Now if I started horning in, you'd have to watch for blond children."

"You start horning in and I won't leave you as much as Nikky has." Grimbolt's jaw jutted an extra half inch.

"No fear." Njal laughed, "I don't believe that woman has a decent belly laugh in her, and I like doing it for fun." He twiddled up an illusion of a highly improbable arrangement of limbs to which he attached the caricature of the Princess' face and his own."

"Will Nicholas be all right?" Alsenius visualized his friend running thoughtlessly through the forest.

"No physical harm will come to him in my domain." Leander assured him. "The beasts won't even let him get seriously lost. He will run until exhaustion cancels pain; then he will probably fall asleep where he is. He will wake up stiff, cramped, and hungry, and his problem won't hurt so much. Then he will wear himself out again trying to find his way back here, and we'll bring him in before he starves. Of course he may even revert to bloodhound enough to catch a rabbit."

*   *   *

Leander's prediction was accurate. Nicholas indeed ran to exhaustion, forgetting that his human body, unaided by a bloodhound's nose, was incapable of running in a straight line. As a result he collapsed under a great tree less than a mile from the sequoia. Having burned off his emotional poisons, he fell almost immediately asleep. He awoke about an hour later, huddled in a chilly heap on a tangle of roots which jabbed painfully. He was hungry, cold, and still heart-bruised. His legs ached and his joints agonized as he struggled erect. He thought at first to continue his flight, but a few limping staggers dissuaded him. The he spotted a bed of moss that looked more comfortable as a bed. He found some fallen branches with enough dead leaves to provide some insulation against the breeze, and by the time he had assembled a crude nest his fatigue swept back over him and he nestled down—still chilly, but not cold, still uncomfortable, but not pained—and sleep overcame him.

When the mocking bird over his head roused him with its feisty challenge, the sun had warmed him slightly and he sat up with bearable discomfort. As he stretched his cramped body his ear unconsciously recorded the bird's song, and he found himself answering. What had been only the bird's routine warning against a casual intruder became a furious command to clear out of his territory which Nicholas heard as a brilliant challenge to his coloratura. He answered with enthusiasm and variation—his voice rising to a competitive trill. Finding himself matched in song, the mocking bird flung himself upon the intruder in a dizzying swoop which knocked Nicholas' hat askew. Then he grabbed a branch safely out of reach and berated him in still more colorful song. Not wishing to get pecked, Nicholas retreated to the next tree and matched his opponent note for note. Then he switched into a counter melody which blended with the birdsong an introduced a human music beyond the bird's experience.

Territorial challenge became vocal challenge, and the bird mimicked Nicholas' melody, introducing his own trills and flights. At this point a rival bird took station at the limit of his territory and trilled his challenge at them. Nicholas leaped from one birdsong to the other, striving to reconcile the two melodies and balance them with the counterpoint of his own. By the time a third challenge joined them, Nicholas could no longer force the pattern into the rules of human harmony, so that he gave up the struggle and abandoned imitation of birdsong. His full throated soprano asserted itself, plunging to its deepest chest tones and then soaring to the top of its register. He lost all consciousness of the world around him. He became his voice rejoicing in itself.

The birds, hearing no territorial challenge in this new song, accepted his purely musical lead and began imitating him, embracing his human warmth in the flurry of their trills. When, at last wearied, he leaned against a tree to catch his breath, Nicholas felt at peace. Somehow the pain of his love drained into the exultation of his song and he breathed deeply and freely.

He shivered as the morning breeze pierced his light blouse. He was ferociously hungry, and his body ached, but he knew how to deal with these pains. He still desired Catherine, but his pain had become part of him. He studied the ground about him until he detected his own trail. By the time ha had back-tracked a hundred yards he realized that he had run in a looping curve. Within an hour he was warming himself at a kitchen table wolfing down everything the cooks tossed to him.

"Ah, Nikky, I thought I'd find you dogging out somewhere." Njal wandered into the kitchen. "His Majesty has decided we ought to hit the road. Are you still coming with us?"

Nicholas swallowed a chunk of bread and washed it down with a gulp of milk. "I'll be ready when you are." He grinned ruefully at the mess he had made with his food. "I'm afraid I'm still a bit of a bloodhound." He got up, stretched his aching muscles into place, and accompanied Njal to where Leander was training the tendrils of a morning glory vine.

"Feeling better?" the Druid asked.

Nicholas nodded sadly. "I ran off a lot of the pain. It's funny, now that I've decided for myself, I can almost forgive my family."

"Your performance this morning was spectacular." Leander smiled encouragingly.

"You heard?"

"I was the first mocking bird. You know I can take any natural form, and I needed to keep an eye on you."

"I never really listened to bird song before—not to imitate it."

"And you cannot give up your voice?"

"I've sung for so long, I wouldn't be myself without the voice."

"You finally realize you haven't completely lost the power to love? Your operation has just dulled the appetite."

"Catherine is right. We never could escape politics. We would always be hiding." Nicholas looked down at the vine Lander was training. "But it still hurts."

"It always will," sighed Njal, "but you'll get used to it." He called up an illusion of a grey-green ocean with a ship sailing away under full sail. "Shall you be ready first thing in the morning?"

"I don't have my back pack. You remember I couldn't carry it as a dog."

Leander straightened up, "I think we can take care of that. Tell Handyman what you need."

*   *   *

Early the next morning they were all gathered at breakfast, when Princess Catherine arrived carrying a rucksack. Miranda looked up and asked, "Are you planning to explore the forest? You don't really need camping equipment for that."

"I am going north with my father's envoys," she announced casually.

"But this is not a pleasure jaunt," Alsenius protested.

"I don't expect it to be pleasant," she retorted. "My life rarely is. My betrothed and his fellow envoys are prospecting for metals which my father desperately wants for the kingdom. I believe it is my duty to accompany them and see that my father's interests are protected. You and Njal are foreign mercenaries, and Prince Humber is apparently heir to the throne of Arragor. I see no one who can be trusted to watch out for the interests of Quatch." She turned to the Druid. "Did you, sir, or did you not agree with the Queen of Arragor to allow me to be abducted to your forest where I am to be confined until I am married to the Crown Prince of Arragor?"

"Nothing was said of confinement, your Highness," Leander responded.

She faced Alsenius. "Was I or was I not abducted to this forest when I fled from Arragor to seek sanctuary with King Peter of Zharkovia?"

"Hardly abducted, your Highness. You came eagerly."

"But not here!" she stamped her foot. "You tricked me. Everybody treats me like a mindless piece of property, and I'm sick of it. The only one who recognizes me as a woman with a mind and a will of her own is that poor eunuch." Nicholas cringed as she pointed at him. "He's the only one with the manhood to offer me a choice." Once again she faced Leander. "Am I or am I not a prisoner?"

"You are not. My lady and I are your hosts, not your jailors. We promised Queen Elsa only our hospitality and protection."

"I am, therefore, free to go when and where I choose?"

"Yes."

"And you as my hosts are obligated to assist me on my journey, regardless of where I choose to go?"

"We are." Leander and Miranda spoke as one.

She spun around to face Alsenius. "Did you or did you not pledge to my father that you would protect me wherever I journey?"

"Njal and I, certainly, are bound to your father for your protection," Alsenius agreed. "Prince Humber's pledge may be invalidated by his change of identity."

Grimbolt leaped to his feet. "What I pledged as Grimbolt, I shall fulfill. Grimbolt still lives, and I shall not disgrace his word." He glared into the Princess' eyes and sat slowly down."

"Then none here dares refuse my command in my father's name that I be escorted on this exploration into the realm of the fallen star." She thumped down on a stool, broke off a man-sized chunk of bread, and bit savagely into it."

The men looked at each other in dismay as Miranda burst into peels of laughter.

Tilda gawked at Susan and sobbed, "But that means we have to go?"

"No, you silly little twit," Catherine snorted. "Nobody wants to be tied down to taking care of you two. You are no longer my hand-maids. I shall beg the Druid to provide safe escort to return you to my father's kingdom. I shall carry my own weight in this expedition. I am a capable huntress with the bow, and my daggers are quite adequate protection for my honor." She suddenly stood, and two daggers suddenly planted themselves in the table on opposite sides of Alsenius' platter. By the time they looked back at her, she flaunted another pair in her hands."

"But your Royal Highness, you must have a chaperone," Susan exclaimed.

"I have already introduced you to my chaperones." She plucked her daggers from the table. "Furthermore, my royal betrothed will be present to guard my tent against intrusion."

"But is it not required by tradition that a Princess should be chaperoned by a matron of rank?" demanded Lady Mabel.

"I fear your new husband would have the right to forbid you to sleep in my tent while he occupies a cold bed outside, your Ladyship. Remember your marriage vows." She turned back to Alsenius. "It is my will to go, and none shall prevent it."

Alsenius shrugged hopelessly. "If you insist on accompanying us, remember that the journey is long and hard. You will have no servants, and if you weary of the journey we shall not turn back to escort yo home."

"And she who accepts the king's protection must obey the king's commands." Grimbolt drew himself up to his full height. "It is our royal will that our consort-to-be shall resign herself to our authority. She shall be subject to our protection and to our governance so long as she travels in our fellowship." He extended the back of his hand to be kissed. "Have we your solemn oath of obedience?"

Catherine glared at the hairy hand.

"A just and honorable proposal." Miranda smiled sweetly.

"My lady and I resign you joyfully to the guardianship of your royal husband-to-be." Leander added. "Your acceptance of his authority is all that is needed."

"Men!" She stamped her foot again. The hand remained before her. She had won her own way, but kissing that paw accepted an implied proposal. This masterful brute was not the tame and tepid Humber she remembered, but neither was he the bearish beast she had gagged at. He lacked Nicholas' grace and charm, but he wasn't bad looking.

The hairy hand remained steady before her. The craggy face was certainly not adoring, but it was not hostile—just determined. Finally she bowed till her forehead rested on the hand. "I reserve the right to accept or reject your Majesty's offer of marriage. I accept your authority as head of the expedition and I pledge my loyalty so long as I remain in your company." As she lifted her head she saw a mischievous twinkle pass over his brooding dark eyes.

Njal suddenly pressed a ring into Grimbolt's hand. To Grimbolt it was a simple macramé circlet of golden cord, but to everyone else it was a spectacular emerald in a fantastic setting. Njal whispered in his ear, "It is a permanent illusion. I'll describe it later."

For Grimbolt, who was immune to illusions, the ring had no value, but he saw no harm in playing up to Njal's prank. Therefore, he slipped it solemnly on the Princess' finger: "While you wear this, we are affianced," he proclaimed. "Let it never leave your finger so long as the engagement is in force."

Catherine gasped at the beauty of the jewel and repeated. "While I wear this ring, we are affianced." Seeing that more was expected, she bowed her head and lightly kissed his hand.

Nicholas gasped and closed his eyes, while Mabel, Susan, and Tilda gawked enviously.

Njal pulled a scrap of papyrus frm his sleeve and scribbled a note:

Majesty:
The bearer will confirm that Grimbolt has been humanized. He and Catherine are affianced, though cool; Mabel and Morley are wed. Grimbolt, Princess Catherine, Alsenius, and I leave early for star metal. Njal

With a quick gesture he created an image of Grimbolt's new face on the back of the fragment and then folded the note, stamped it with his seal and handed it to Ranger Eccles. "Please give this to Queen Elsa. Try to report the truth of what has happened. I don't trust those courtiers to report anything accurately."

"Am I to take the butterflies home?" the Ranger asked, looking dubiously and Tilda, Susan, and their escorts.

"They are of no use to us, and I think the Druid has more important things to do than take care of them," snorted the princess.

Lord Nicholas retreated to the room and extracted from his pack a sheet of papyrus. He wrote a careful report to his master of the recent events, including the return of the Crown Prince. He concluded with, I intend to accompany the expedition to the site of the star fall. Your Majesty may well wish to send a secret force to recover some of the star metal everyone believes is superior to iron. Alsenius and Njal are formidable, and the Crown Prince is much stronger that he was before his enchantment. Even the Princess is dangerous. We also suspect that a party of the Pythoness' Amazons is active the area of the star fall I remain your Majesty's humble servant, Nicholas

He sprinkled the message with his magic powder and tossed it into the fire place. It sparkled brilliantly and disappeared without burning. Somewhat later he found the Druid at work with his mistletoe. Leander looked up and smiled.

"Sir, I am indebted to you more deeply than I can say. Your lady wife, by releasing me from the dog enchantment, saved my identity."

"We have been rewarded with the charm of your company as a human," he answered. "I think you were wise to keep your voice and travel with the explorers."

"After that wonderful morning singing with the mocking birds, I realize how fully I am identified with the voice. I was deeply grieved when Princess Catherine would not flee with me, but she is right. We cannot escape what the world demands of us, and we would torture ourselves if we succeeded in running away. Her love is not an earthshaking passion, and I must confess, neither is mine. She accepts the Crown Prince without nausea, now that he is restored, and I completely forgot her in the ecstasy of song. We are not the stuff of old romance."

"I rather thought not," the Druid agreed. "I did not think you could give up your voice for passion, but Miranda and I offered you the choice. Now you can no longer curse your family for castrating you."

"You mean because I chose to stay this way. Yes, I'm to blame now, and I have lost the excuse for bitterness. That's what I most want to thank you for. My song this morning was freer than it has ever been." He embraced Leander, turned and walked away.

In the morning Eccles set off to the south with Rupert and Lady Mabel Morley and the four courtiers. Alsenius, Njal. Lord Nicholas, and Grimbolt and Catherine headed north

XI—Skirmishes

In the morning Grimbolt's party assembled under the great sequoia. The men mounted, and Handyman gave the leading reign of the pack animal to Nicholas before he scrambled on the back of his tiger. Princess Catherine stood by her mare waiting for some man to lift her. Nicholas started to dismount, but Grimbolt stayed him with a gesture. Though she was a very accomplished horsewoman, she had always depended on servants to assist her in mounting and dismounting. She clutched her long skirt and gazed helplessly at the saddle which swayed above her. "Isn't somebody going to help me up?" she demanded.

"When you insisted upon accompanying us, you were reminded that we have no servants." Grimbolt's voice offered no compromises.

"Milady," called Njal from his mount, "Might I suggest that you ride astride for this journey? A side-saddle is elegant, but impractical."

"But . . ." She looked helplessly down at her skirts.

"The lady Clarissa wore riding breeches when she accompanied us," Alsenius suggested. "We need to depart promptly, but we will wait while you change to something more appropriate."

She started to retort, but Grimbolt overrode her voice, "We will be happy to leave you in the fostering care of Lord Leander and Lady Miranda."

She glared up at him, but saw only determination. Suppressing her rage, she stalked with Miranda back to the great tree. "This is not going to be easy," the Priestess commented as she produced a riding costume from a chest. "Men can some times be very difficult."

Catherine gritted her teeth and scrambled into the breeches and jacket which fit amazingly well.

"Your mare is going to expect you to approach from her left side. You will need to place your left foot in the stirrup—oh dear, those dainty shoes will never do. Here try these." She produced a pair of trim riding boots and let the Princess struggle into them without assistance. "Foot in the left stirrup, grasp the pommel of the saddle, and spring upward, flinging your leg high over the rump. It's a bit like a very athletic dance. You'll get quite graceful at it with practice."

Catherine stifled her tears of rage, clenched her teeth, and marched out to the party, who—still mounted—were patiently waiting. Leander held her mare while she approached warily. She got her foot into the stirrup, but found the pommel beyond her reach.

"Here, you may need a step." He led the mare to convenient stump. The Princess glared again at Grimbolt, clambered to the stump, placed her left foot and gave a mighty spring which sprawled her crosswise on the saddle. The men's faces were frozen masks of sobriety as she struggled—with unobtrusive assistance from the Druid—to arrange her limbs into a sitting position.

"If you are determined, milady, to accompany us," Grimbolt bowed from the saddle, "we are, I believe finally ready to set out."

Handyman riding Bengalus guided the party to the northern border of the Druid's domain. The forest continued for several miles after the Halfling left them, but its intense natural energy quickly faded. Grimbolt and Alsenius rode side by side in the lead and Nicholas, leading the pack pony, took the rear. Thus it was Njal who rode beside the Princess, endlessly studying the vegetation and twiddling his fingers to produce illusions with more accurate details. Catherine found riding astride both awkward and uncomfortable, but she gritted her teeth in silence. At their first stop, she looked down in horror at the distant ground.

The little illusionist swung himself effortlessly to earth. "There isn't enough of me to lift you down." he apologized, "but I'll try to ease your fall."

She steered her mare beside a small rock, loosed her right foot from the stirrup, and strove mightily to fling her leg over the rump. Her weight overbalanced Njal, and they tangled awkwardly on the ground. Alsenius and Grimbolt moved into a clump of bushes to relieve themselves, but Nicholas rushed to her side, offering brief assistance before he had to run back to make the pack pony fast to a scrubby tree.

When it came time to remount, Nicholas sneaked a boost toward the saddle which sprawled her facing forwards. As they proceeded, Alsenius and Grimbolt discussed their route, while the Princess rode in silent rage by Njal. "They do have logic on their side," the Illusionist reminded her. "This is going to be a rough trip, and nobody will have the energy to wait on your Highness."

"Arrogant brutes. I know they're sniggering."

"Alsenius is a soldier. He has little experience with high-born ladies."

"But Prince Humber knows better."

"For over two years as Grimbolt he has known nothing but hardship. The only woman he knew was that wild Priestess Clarissa who crossed the continent with him and Alsenius. He may even have loved her."

"But his mother brought him up better."

"From what I have seen of her, she is more a force to be reckoned with than a mother. I'm afraid she will have a hard time when he takes the throne." He paused and listened to Nicholas beguiling the pack pony with birdsong. "Now there's a real oddment."

"I'm beginning to realize how wonderful he is," she sighed. "He's just a big boy, but . . ."

"He's a remarkable man. You realize he was given to King Peter as a slave toy, and he's fought his way to a top position in a wolf-pack court. He may have the voice of a canary, but he has the balls of a bull."

She tittered in spite of herself. Then she glared ahead at Grimbolt's back. My husband-to-be is a bully." She tried to pull off her ring, but had to grab her reins again.

"He's stuck with a wife he has no interest in, and you forced him to take you along. He's going to let this journey toughen you or kill you, and he doesn't much care which. If you're as stubborn as I think, you'll concentrate on toughening. Nikky and I will help you when we can, but you'll have to work your delicious butt down to pure muscle."

She grimaced. "Right now it is pure ache. I never realized riding could be so painful."

By noon the canopy of tall trees thinned, and heavy undergrowth narrowed the path. By evening the brook they followed had become a substantial stream and began to veer eastward toward the northern lakes. To the west they could see the mountains that marked the border of the Hegemony of the Pythoness. They camped on the west bank in a grove of birch and pine. The men silently divided up the chores: Nicholas unpacked the ass, then went off to gather firewood, while Alsenius dug the fire pit and latrine, Njal laid out the food and utensils, and Grimbolt tethered and fed the horses and arranged the sleeping bags. Then he and Njal put lines into the stream in hopes of fish.

When Grimbolt took the reins from her hands, Catherine realized that she had to dismount for herself. Desperately she loosed her right foot and flung herself off. She ended up on her back with her left foot still caught in the stirrup. With frozen face, Grimbolt skillfully released her. "You are undamaged?"

She struggled to her feet. "I'm fine." She turned her back as he led the mare away. She watched as the camp shaped into order and Njal wrapped the fish in clay to cook in the hot coals. Then she realized that her tent still lay outside the circle of light. Nobody was going to set it up for her. She forced her aching joints to approach the package and timidly unfold it. There was a lot of canvas to open and a great number of carefully coiled lines which spread in all directions. She looked desperately for Nicholas and spotted him staking out the animals to leeward of the camp, trying to find adequate browse for them. Njal looked up from his cooking.

"I can't figure this thing out." she was close to tears.

"Might I suggest that you spread a sleeping bag near the fire and forget the tent. Everybody's too tired to molest you, and nobody wants to wrestle with that thing. I'll help you wrap it up again later." He turned his attention back to his kettle of tea, which threatened to boil and spoil the flavor.

Alsenius and Grimbolt returned to the fire and flung themselves down. Shortly after, Nicholas came back from the mounts and bowed as he settled wearily beside her. "The riding has wearied you?" he asked.

"Yes. I have always thought of myself as an excellent horsewoman, but riding all day astride has left me aching."

"Njal is right about the side saddle," he assured her. "It was designed to keep a lady dependent on men. Riding like a man means you can mount and dismount by yourself. I can give you a boost until you get used to it, but Grimbolt means to make you independent."

"I suppose that means no tent."

"I can put it up for you, but your fiancé won't approve."

She glared down at her ring. "Damn my fiancé!"

He placed his arm gently around her waist. "I would agree, but you wear his ring."

She moved reluctantly away. "I know I have to go through with it. Father *will* have me married to somebody profitable to his realm, and Prince Humber is the least revolting of my choices. That's why I insisted on coming along. If I have to marry him, I have to make him like me. Maybe when I get him away form his mother, I can civilize him."

"I think he's a very good man, but he doesn't really know himself yet. TRANSFORMATION is hell. I know. And he had a lot worse time and for a lot longer than I did." He gently squeezed her hand. "I hope I can be a friend to both of you."

"And you're right about the tent. I'll use a sleeping bag."

Alsenius yawned and stood up. "I suppose I have first watch again. Njal, have you cast our defensive spells?"

"You have an invisible magical beast marching around the camp to attack any intruder, and a magical voice that will scream if anything comes within a hundred yards. Your eyes and ears ought to be enough for the human watch." He wrapped himself in a blanket and curled up near the fire. Grimbolt, who had already stripped to his breech clout, strode to patch of dry leaves, flung himself down, and was asleep almost before he landed. Nicholas arranged Catherine's sleeping bag on top of the packaged tent to cushion the lumpy ground and then spread his own at a respectful distance. Alsenius paced among them, humming an old folk tune of his native Pluvia.

Catherine gazed at Grimbolt's hairy body and wondered whether it would be possible to snuggle against such a pelt. "He really isn't bad looking, now he has a forehead and a proper nose and chin—a much more stubborn chin than he had before his transformation. There are a lot more muscles under that hair. I never saw him naked before, but after all that rowing he has a beautiful build now." She giggled to herself. "Alsenius says he's great as a wrestler." The thought of wrestling with that hairy body sent fearful tingles along her spine. Then she looked at Nicholas sprawled out under his blanket like a hound. She marveled at his grace, even in such an awkward pose. "I know I can't have him," she sighed, "but I'll always want him. It's easy for him. He has his voice, and his springs aren't wound up so tight as the others. Even Njal looks at me sometimes like a plate of beef, but Nicholas appreciates me like a beautiful statue." She indulged the fantasy of crushing Nicholas against her body and felt very warm in spite of the growing chill of the evening. It was in that warm glow that she drifted into sleep.

After about three hours, Alsenius spoke softly to rouse Grimbolt; then he sheathed his sword, wrapped two blankets around him and curled as close to the banked fire as he dared. Even after years away from his tropical home, he still shivered when other men enjoyed brisk weather. Grimbolt stood and shook himself awake. As he needed no blankets for sleep, so he needed no clothes to stand watch. He grabbed his staff and stumped resolutely around the camp. He paused for a few moments standing over Catherine. He felt his body respond to her. It would be no sacrifice to bed her for the good of the realm, but he wasn't at all sure he could live with her temper. His mother was bossy, but at least she loved him. Even with his new body, she looked proud of him. When she hugged him, he knew she meant it.

He strode once more on his rounds. "I shouldn't blame her for gagging. After all I was pretty gruesome before Leander fixed me up. The way she looks at him, Nicholas must have made quite an impression on her, but she must know he's useless that way. She looks at me like a dose of medicine. She knows she can't escape, so she puts up with me."

He laughed ruefully as he remembered his mother's cliché: "Throw any healthy young pair into bed together, and nature will do the rest." His own body told him she was right, but unfortunately marriage was more than bed. Even if she stopped gagging, she was still a spoiled, calculating cat, and he didn't like the role of mouse. Of course she couldn't bully him the way his mother did. He could always pick her up and shake her. Furthermore, now he was King, his mother would have to curtsey. Now that he was Grimbolt, nobody pushed him around. He picked up a substantial fallen limb, snapped it over his thigh, and tossed the pieces into the dying fire.

At the first crack, Njal was suddenly standing with his fingers already atwiddle. "Grimbolt?"

"Sorry! I was just thinking."

"You have the noisiest mind I know."

"Go back to sleep."

"I'm awake now. Can I help pick up the pieces of your brain?"

"No. I've just made a decision. I'm not going to become King Humber VIII"

"Abdicate rather than marry the woman you can't love?"

"No. I'm not going to abdicate. Everybody thinks King Humber will be easy to manipulate, but I'm going to fool them all. I'm going to be crowned King Grimbolt I."

"Mother won't approve."

"I know. It's my challenge to her and Septimus, and to all the royal neighbors. It's my challenge to the Pythoness who caused all this mess."

Njal looked up at his massive body. "The name still suits you. I suppose it was Leander who gave it to you."

"Yes. He gave me a new name when he gave the chance to find myself without the old memories. The Pythoness gave me a new body that I can't get rid of. Leander gave me chance to make up my mind."

Njal performed a careful court bow. "Hail King Grimbolt! I believe the Northwest Kingdoms have just suffered a revolution." He twiddled his fingers and produced the illusion of Grimbolt clad only in his own fur and a golden kilt, bearing the royal scepter and crowned with Arragor's diadem.

"What are you up to?" Grimbolt demanded as Njal bowed ceremoniously to the image.

"Oh, I forgot you can't see illusions. I was just looking at what you will become."

The sound of their conversation penetrated Catherine's slumber, and she looked up to see Grimbolt's crowned image staring imperiously down at her. She yelped nervously and checked frantically to make sure she was covered. Her cry roused Alsenius and Nicholas, who were on their feet with drawn weapons before they were fully awake.

"What tomfoolery are you up to now?" Alsenius demanded.

"Just idle speculation," Njal laughed. "His Majesty just announced that he is to be crowned King Grimbolt, and I was trying to imagine him at his coronation.

"He needs a gold chain and medallion of office," Nicholas protested. "Anybody else would have to wear an ermine robe, but at least give him a chain and some rings."

Njal obliged with a great chain and a massive signet ring.

"The guild of tailors is gong to assassinate him," Alsenius remarked. "He'll put them out of business if he sets the fashion."

"Damned Illusionist!" Grimbolt growled, looking every inch the disapproving king.

Njal gestured and the illusion vanished. "Sorry, your Majesty," he smiled. "I'm so used to visualizing my thoughts, I forgot you don't see illusions."

"Well, now everybody's awake, we might as well have breakfast and go on," said Alsenius.

As a result, Nicholas was soon leading them along the trail through the long northern morning twilight. As the days passed, the trees became fewer and scrubbier. Since the mountains to the west cut off the rain clouds from the ocean, all the vegetation was stunted and grey, and the rolling hills monotonously defined the horizon in all directions. The sun swung lower across the southern sky, rising late and setting early. Alsenius and Catherine wore fur cloaks all day, and even Njal felt the need of a jacket.

"Nobody has bothered to define borders out in this stretch of tundra," Nicholas remarked. "My master claims the whole territory up to the Brieland border, but so do the Pythoness and Arragor. As a result the Barbarians roam the whole countryside without much interference except for occasional armed parties from the civilized claimants. Anybody we meet is likely to be hostile."

"Can you tell how far we are from the star fall?" asked Alsenius.

"I'd say Markov—our capital—lies almost due east. The Hegemony of the Pythoness is west on the other side of the mountains. We ought to see some signs of the star fall about fifty miles north of here. The maps don't agree up here, but everybody places the crater northwest of Markov and south of Brieland."

"Except the Brie, who claim Brieland includes it," Njal added. "I saw a Brie map in your library," he remarked to Grimbolt, "and it puts the southern border of Brieland at the edge of Leander's forest."

"For that matter, the maps in King Peter's library include all of this territory north of the Great Forest in Zharkovia," said Nicholas.

"Well, Mother always talks about our border with Brieland being in the frozen north," Grimbolt laughed.

"I think somebody's fighting over it right now," Nicholas interrupted. "I can hear a lot of yelling and screaming off to the northeast."

"You still have bloodhound ears." Njal remarked. "Can you guide us?"

"Are you sure we want to be guided into a battle?" Grimbolt protested.

"I'd like to see what's going on. We don't have to fight, just look. I still have my Invisibility ring." Njal put it on and disappeared. Presently he appeared again, ringless.

"We'd face less danger watching a battle than running into either side unexpectedly," Alsenius added. "If they're fighting each other, they won't be watching for strangers."

Nicholas started off at an easy canter and within half an hour they could all hear the clash of arms and the screams of combatants. Princess Catherine observed, "They sound like a lot of women. I'll bet its some Amazons."

"I'd think I hear some Barbarian war whoops," Nicholas answered. "Let's go up that hill over there and see what we can see." He dismounted almost before his horse stopped. Njal stopped, disappeared, and followed. From the top of the hill they could clearly discern a disciplined band of about thirty armored sword wielders in a square, fighting off a mounted whirl of horsemen armed with short bows and spears.

"It looks as if a Barbarian hunting party ran into a platoon of Amazons."

"They'll get badly mauled if the Amazons have cavalry in reserve. I think we should help them." Nicholas ran back to report while Njal began gesturing.

"We can assume the Amazons are bad news," Alsenius observed. "They'll have a priestess or two casting spells, and Nikky's right—they'll have cavalry backup and more foot soldiers coming up. This must a have been a foraging party that ran into some hunters. What's Njal up to?"

"I think he's chanting a spell," Nicholas answered. "I couldn't see him."

"Catherine, you get up on the hill and stay with Njal," Grimbolt ordered. "Nikky, you'd better go with her as guard. I think Alsenius and I should charge in and disrupt things."

"I'd feel better if I had a warhorse," Alsenius grumbled. "Charging on a palfrey against a shield wall . . ."

"If we can get the Barbarians to follow us instead of just milling around, we can break the square."

"Njal must have the same idea," shouted Nicholas. "There goes a magic cavalry charge."

"Where?" Grimbolt demanded. "It must be one of his damned illusions."

"Well, it's a good one," Alsenius answered. "They're charging down the hill with lances set and banners streaming, yelling fit to rout the enemy by the noise. I'm gong to join the charge and give it some added substance." He kicked his horse and dashed around the hill brandishing his sword. Grimbolt and Nicholas dashed after him.

As the charging illusion approached, the Barbarians on that side of the square scattered to join their comrades on the other sides. The Amazons facing the charge planted spears in the ground confronting the charge while a robed figure in the center of the square began gesticulating toward them. Njal cast a Dispel Magic over the Priestess, hoping to neutralize her spell before it took effect. Alsenius and Grimbolt focused their charge on the corner of the square, hoping to flank the Amazons facing the Barbarians while the illusory charge preoccupied those facing Njal's hill.

Njal's **DISPEL** was too late to neutralize the **FLAME STRIKE** which crashed down in the center of his cavalry charge, but it neutralized most of the defensive spells which protected the Amazons. As a result, Barbarian arrows began to strike down warriors on the square.

Alsenius, meanwhile, struck the Amazon at the end of the south face of the square just as the remnant of the illusory charge hit the east face. As a result, Grimbolt, brandishing the magical Scepter of Arragor, was able to burst through the shield wall at the corner and slam the Priestess, disrupting her second spell. Nicholas followed and addressed his rapier to the backs of the Amazons. Njal's third spell was a **HOLD PERSONS** on the north face of the square, which put three of the Amazons out of action and left a gap through which the Barbarians could penetrate. Thus, by the time the supporting Amazon cavalry arrived on the scene, the square had dissolved into individual struggles between Amazon foot soldiers and Barbarian horsemen with Grimbolt and the Priestess battling in the center.

At the approach of the Amazon cavalry, the Barbarians scattered out of the path of their charge. Alsenius swept in behind the Priestess, grabbed her off her horse and whirled after the Barbarians with Grimbolt in close pursuit. While the Barbarians regrouped on both sides, Njal created the illusion of an additional dozen struggling to organize a frontal charge. The Amazon Cavalry focused their charge upon the illusion, thus giving the Barbarians a chance to pepper their flanks with arrows and close in behind for a counter charge.

Grimbolt turned and hurled his Scepter at the Amazon Lieutenant in charge of the cavalry. The blow stunned her and knocked her from her horse, so that the Amazons were suddenly without leadership. As a result, when the Barbarians swarmed against them, the surviving Amazon cavalry carried as many infantry women as they could out of danger. The rest of the Amazons fled in total disorder, pursued briefly by the Barbarians, who quickly returned to loot the bodies of the fallen. Alsenius slashed the Priestess' throat with his sword and returned to what remained of the melee. Grimbolt's Scepter returned to him, and he waded into the fight.

When Njal's illusory Barbarians faded quietly in to the atmosphere, he took off his **INVISIBILITY** ring and rode with Catherine toward the leader of the Barbarians. "Hail, mighty Chieftain! May we join you as friends?"

"Who in blazes are you?" The Chieftain dropped a gory Amazon head to raise his right hand in salute.

"I am Njal, a humble merchant-explorer, and this is my cousin, Princess Catherine of Quatch. We and our body guards have taken the liberty of joining your attack upon the hated Amazons."

Catherine decided to go along with Njal's fiction and swept a sitting curtsy from her horse. "Your Lordship will excuse my cousin's impetuosity, but we cannot abide the arrogance of the servants of the Pythoness."

The Chieftain felt somewhat awkward at the approach of royalty, especially with bloody hands and a horse adorned with Amazon heads. Still he managed a courteous nod. "Where did all those horsemen come from . . ." He looked vaguely around for them. "And go?"

"I dabble in illusions," Njal confessed. "It isn't really magic, but it fools some people who are not prepared for it." He waved toward Nicholas, who rode up looking only slightly less gory than the Chieftain. "My friend, Lord Nicholas of Zharkovia."

Nicholas saluted with his rapier. "Congratulations on your glorious victory. I hope you don't mind our stepping in."

Since the Chief knew he had been getting nowhere until the strangers intervened, he thought it worth while to be gracious. "Oh, there is plenty of glory to go around. We welcome the enemy of our enemies."

When Alsenius and Grimbolt rode up, Njal carefully introduced them as his and his cousin's body guards. Grimbolt snorted irritably but commanded his scepter to appear less royal. Alsenius, who was used to Njal's humor played his part with good grace.

At this point a young man strode up leading a horse on which were draped two captive Amazons. "Father, most of the enemy have been slain either in battle or during the raping afterwards, but these two aren't much damaged. Do you want me to cure them?"

The Chieftain appraised the bodies. "They don't look good enough to be worth a fight with your mother," he grumbled. "Do you want them?"

"No, I'm sure Flora would make a fuss. Maybe you should give them to the strangers. After all we'd never have captured them without help." The Chieftain nodded, and the young man flung them to the ground and arranged their limbs in the semblance of order. "Any of you want a woman to keep off the cold?" He gestured toward them.

"Oh, the poor dears, you've beaten them unconscious, and now you want our men to rape them?" Princess Catherine became a royal ice block.

"They're not likely to make good serving wenches," remarked the young man. "I'd give one to my betrothed, but all they're trained for is fighting."

At this point the dark haired Amazon opened her eyes and sprang to her feet in defiance. Her armor had been stripped off, and she looked like a kitten defying a large dog. When Alsenius knelt to look in her face, and she raked at him with her nails, but he brushed her hand aside. The second Amazon—a tall blond—struggled to sit up and glared ferociously.

"I would guess that these women have been ensorceled to make them good fighters," Njal observed. "Notice the fixed expression." He closed his eyes and gestured toward the sitting girl, muttering under his breath. Suddenly she relaxed and gazed up at him.

"There, that takes care of that one." He turned toward the other, who was still trying to claw Alsenius.

"What did you do to her?" demanded the Chieftain.

"Just a simple incantation I learned from my old mother," said Njal. "It's an old formula for breaking spells." He repeated his performance on the second Amazon, who lowered her hand to a defensive posture and dropped her eyes.

"That's quite a wonder," exclaimed the young man. "I am Shaman as well as Sub-Chief of our tribe now that old Brancour, my master, has died, but he never taught me anything like that. Could you show me how to do it?"

"I don't know. How were you trained, as a Mage-Shaman or a Cleric?"

"I think both. I can CURE, and I can cast MAGIC MISSILE."

By this time, the blond Amazon had crawled forward to clasp Njal's knees in supplication. "My lord, my deliverer, save me from these Barbarians," she sobbed.

"There, there!" Njal struggled to retain his balance as he detached her. "The Lord Chieftain has not yet decided what he wants to do with you. You'd best not call him a Barbarian."

She clutched his legs again and began weeping over his feet.

"I suppose I'd better give the slaves to you, since you seem to have tamed them," the Chieftain responded. He looked appraisingly at Catherine. "Perhaps we might persuade your cousin to join our tribe and accept my brother as her husband."

Catherine bristled. "I've had enough of this."

Njal hastily tossed off another fiction. "Oh dear, I'm afraid she doesn't understand about the fate of women in battle. We are traveling on a peaceful mission."

"I don't see any problem," returned the Chieftain. "Both slaves are yours. Since you have befriended us in battle, I'll present the princess to my wife, who is Senior Judge of Southmark—our tribe. She will decide whether to invite you all to join Southmark. In that case—if my brother finds favor in the princess' eyes, Our mothrt will probably approve my brother's marriage to her. If the Senior Judge accepts you only as allies . . ."

Catherine's reaction to this talk of marriage was to brandish her daggers; at the same time Grimbolt hitched his scepter to his saddle and swung off his horse. He shrugged off his breast plate and shirt, and advanced in hairy menace. "If you want my betrothed, you'll have to fight me for her," he challenged, flexing his rowing muscles. "Get down off that nag and face me chest to chest."

At the same moment, Nicholas kicked his horse forward and swished his rapier under the Chieftain's nose.

The young Shaman turned and commanded, "Here! Stop this nonsense." He cast a clerical **HOLD PERSON** on the trio. Grimbolt, since he was not holding his scepter, immediately froze on the spot as did the Chieftain. Nicholas was unaffected by the spell, but when he saw his opponent suddenly immobile, he stopped in mid flourish and subsided.

The Shaman advanced to face them. "Father, you're behaving like a boy. These people have just helped us win a nasty battle, and you treat their Princess is if she was a common foreigner. Now just sit there till the spell wears off and think what a fool you've made of yourself." He turned to Grimbolt. "Sir Grimbolt, I apologize for casting a spell on you, but I cannot allow you to attack my father. You'll have to stand there for half an hour, because I don't know how to cancel the spell. Prince Njal, I apologize for my father. I'm sure he will see reason by the time he is free." He bowed deeply to Catherine. "On my honor as Sub-Chief and Shaman I pledge that no harm nor insult shall affront you. Please accept the hospitality and gratitude of our tribe."

Nicholas leaped from his horse and swept him a graceful bow. "Most nobly done and spoken, sir. I am Lord Nicholas of Zharkovia, and I gladly accept the hospitality of so decisive a prince." He turned and bowed to the immobile Chieftain. "I bear milord no malice and crave pardon for drawing my rapier." He sheathed his weapon with a snap.

Catherine extended her hand and the Shaman bowed over it. "I am sure I speak for all our company in accepting your apology and your hospitality. "I am Princess Catherine of Quatch, and this is my bastard cousin Njal—who is not a prince."

Njal winced at her revenge for his mischief.

"This," she continued. "is Sir Alsenius, who is our comrade, not a mere guard, and that—she waved toward Grimbolt—is Grimbolt, my betrothed."

Though marveling at the princess' taste, the young Shaman managed a respectful bow. "I am Aethelstan Moonflower's son, Sub-chief and Shaman of Southmark, and this is my father, Sven Mist's Son, Chieftain of Southmark.

"Then you must be men of Brie," Nicholas observed.

"We pay tribute to the Overlord of Brie," Aethelstan answered, "but otherwise the people of Southmark are independent. We acknowledge no king—only the Lady Judge and the Chieftain whom she has chosen. We range freely over our Mark, having no need of city or farm."

"You are aware that other powers have laid claim to this same territory?" asked Nicholas. "My master King Peter of Zharkovia holds clear title to this expanse of wasteland."

"He's welcome to claim it," laughed Aethelstan, "but we occupy it, and it is not such a waste as you think. We harvest meat from the tundra, fish from the lakes, and fruits and grains from the water holes. Your King Peter and the Pythoness may march troops over it once in a while, but we remain."

"Are you acquainted with the scar of the fallen star?" Njal asked.

"Oh yes, that's where we get the star metal. We find lumps of the metal and trade them with the Rockborn of the mountains for finished daggers which neither break nor rust." He drew from his belt sheath a long dagger—almost a short sword—of dull grey metal with a beautiful scrimshaw bone handle. "I broke the iron sword of one of the Amazons with this blade today. It is my most valued possession." He sheathed it lovingly. "If you will accompany us to our camp, I will introduce you to my mother, Moonflower, who sits in judgment on the tribe."

"What about . . . ?"

"The men will lead my father's horse and carry your comrade respectfully."

"What do I do with this?" demanded Njal, whose ankles were still imprisoned in the Amazon's grasp.

"Whatever you wish. Father gave her to you."

Njal pulled the woman to her feet. "I suppose you might as well come along," he said. "Just don't keep grabbing me." He started to remount, and she immediately gave him a boost which nearly tossed him over the horse. "Hey, stop that. Here climb up behind me and don't choke me."

She leaped up on his horse's rump and clung to the saddle as he followed Aethelstan.

Alsenius stared at the Amazon who now crouched confused in front of him. "Now that Njal has canceled the spells on you, who are you?"

"I am Reina. My father is a smith in Tainville, a village of Arragor near the border of the Hegemony. The servants of the Pythoness enchanted me and carried me off to serve as an Amazon."

"I am Alsenius, Fighter 13th level. Perhaps you'd better mount behind me till we find out what these Brielanders have decided to do with you."

She looked appraisingly at his dark physique and formidable armor. "I think they have given me to you."

"I don't keep slaves, but I suppose you might as well ride behind me. We can't just leave you on the battle field to starve." He swung himself easily into his saddle and leaned down to assist her. A moment's hesitation convinced her that she was better off with this powerful stranger, and she swung up behind him.

They had reached the fourth rolling hill when Grimbolt became mobile and demanded to mount his own horse. They waited while he donned his shirt and armor and, ignoring the revived Chieftain Sven, swung into his saddle. Sven grumbled as he recovered motion, but made no attempt to interfere with his son's plans. From the flat top of the next hill they saw the encampment a few miles away. Along the shore of a small lake were four wooden structures grouped in the center with tents of skins scattered around them.

"The big one is our Council Hall." Aethelstan said. "The one to the right is my mother's lodge. My Grandmother, Mist, has the one behind the Hall, and the mother of my betrothed has the one to the left. When we are married, I will move to the house of my mother-in-law until I have slain enough beasts to make a tent for Flora."

"You speak of your mother's lodge," Njal observed. "Doesn't it belong to your father?"

"Oh no, Mother sits in judgment in the lodge my father built for her. All property belongs to the wife, except what her husband can carry on his horse. A man builds the home for his wife, and she lets him live there so long as he pleases her. Now Mother is Senior Judge, and she has appointed Father Chieftain. She and your cousin will decide how you will relate to our tribe."

"I thought your father already decided that when he invited us as guests."

"As Moonflower's husband, he has the right to extend hospitality, but the council of judges will determine your permanent relation to our tribe. When he became incapable of command, I as Sub-Chief acted for him. I am sure the Council will allow my decision to stand."

"And your mother is in charge of this council."

"Yes. When Grandfather was killed, Sven, his eldest daughter's husband, became Chieftain and leads the men to hunt and to war. My grandmother yielded the senior judgeship to her daughter when Sven became Chieftain."

"But you will become Chief when your father dies?"

"Oh, no. Unless he is disgraced, my eldest sister's husband will be elected Chieftain. Since all pass through the womb, all must be traced through the womb. My father may give his horse and saddlebags to whatever man earns his respect, but position and property pass through the womb."

"But your father gave me this prisoner." Njal jerked his head at the Amazon behind him."

"He determines who gets the fruits of battle. All the swords and armor will be distributed among the men. Of course, if you have a wife, you will give the slave-girl to her. Otherwise you may use her as you will."

"Is that why your father didn't take this woman for himself?"

"Mother does not like slaves—especially women slaves. If Sven brought her home, Mother might kill her or turn her loose in the wilderness, but she wouldn't keep her around the lodge to tempt the men."

"So she has other men living in her lodge?"

"Of course. All my brothers live there until they marry and build tents for their wives. Then there's Uncle Sigurt. His wife put his bag out on the common, and Grandmother wouldn't take him back."

"I don't understand?"

"When a woman puts her husband's sleeping bag and saddle out in the common, she has divorced him. Unless one of his relatives takes him in, he has to sleep outside."

"That seems pretty rough."

"It's her tent. If she doesn't want him, out he goes."

"But he built it for her."

"It was his bride gift to her."

Njal shook his head in bewilderment. "What if I decide to sleep with this slave girl?"

"So you sleep."

"That doesn't make her my wife?"

"No, silly, she isn't your wife unless she takes you in marriage."

"How would that happen?"

"Why her mother would have to invite you into her tent to share her daughter's bed. You would give her mother gifts to prove that you were worthy, and she would ask the woman whether she wants you. If you please both women, the mother would give a bridal feast and announce she was accepting you as her son-in-law. Then the woman would give you night shirt she would make for you. The men would take you out in the common to strip you and dress you in the shirt. You would leave your horse and bedroll with your Best Friend and walk barefoot to your mother-in-law's tent. That way, the daughter would recognize you by your shirt and would and take you to her bed. If you pleased her on the wedding night, she would let you bring your bedroll and saddle bags to her space and your horse into her paddock, and you would be her husband. Within a year you would be expected to provide her a home, and she would set herself up as a judge."

"But as things stand, she can't marry me?"

"Of course not. She has no mother in the tribe. She doesn't really exist in law; that's why she's a slave. Everything passes through the womb, but her womb is not of the tribe."

Njal felt her hands cautiously clasp his waist; her voice murmured in his ear: "I lost my family when the Amazons raided our village and they pressed me into their service. You have rescued me from their spells. Please let me be your slave."

Wondering whether he would regret the action, but always ready for new amusement, he asked his host, "Will she be included in your hospitality, since she is Sven's treasure gift to me?"

"If you wish to share your bedroll with her, she is part of your equipment."

As they approached the camp, Sven took the lead and greeted the home guard with news of the victory. The men dispersed to their quarters and Sven led his guests to Moonflower's lodge. It was a substantial wooden structure, ingeniously constructed so that it could be dismantled and carried on a large wagon designed for the purpose. At the door, his wife greeted him with a quick embrace; then he introduced his guests. Aethelstan knelt briefly before his mother and she clasped him to her breast. She gestured her welcome to the guests with both arms. "My husband's guests are my guests, and we welcome you to the sanctuary of our home."

Grimbolt spoke for the party: "We gratefully accept your hospitality and pledge our obedience to your laws while we remain. Your enemies re our enemies and your friends are our friends."

Each of the party clearly spoke the response, "So be it." Then they were free to enter the lodge, and were shown to the guest area, where they could spread their sleeping rolls. Young men of the family took their steeds and led them to the enclosure behind the lodge, where they unloaded them, brushed them down, and turned them loose to graze. The two Amazon prisoners quickly spread Alsenius' and Njal's possessions and retired to a corner while the party joined the family in the central area. "I am Emma Thorwaldsdatter," the blond girl muttered as Njal passed her. "I shall wait here with your gear?"

"I will see that you get fed," he answered. "Have you any clothing?"

"I have nothing but what I wear."

He nodded and followed the others into the hall, where a long trestle table was set up, bearing a substantial meal. Njal found Aethelstan and asked, "Does my woman eat here or in the sleeping room?"

"Everybody eats here. We don't want bugs in the dormitory."

"Can I purchase clothing and equipment for her?"

"We'll talk later. Fetch her now, and she can sit behind you at table."

"She looks pretty scruffy after the battle and the long ride."

"So do we all. Don't fret."

The meal was extremely informal: the hunting party and guests were still soiled with battle and the women had come directly from daily chores. Moonflower presided with gusto, hacking strips of roast meat with her dagger and slurping her ale from a horn mounted in a scrimshawed frame designed to hold it level. Everyone speared chunks of meat from platters placed conveniently on the table and laid them on slabs of bread to soak up the juices. Njal watched Alsenius hack off chunks for his Amazon and followed his example in providing for Emma.

After the meal everyone dashed across the compound to the Community Lodge where they stripped and gathered in a large sealed room in the center of which blazed a huge bed of hot coals. They distributed themselves on tiered benches to absorb the oppressive heat. Princess Catherine crouched in a corner where terror at the close confinement battled with heat exhaustion. Finally she struggled to her feet and staggered for the door, fumbling dizzily with the fasteners. It was Nicholas, to whom the experience of a sauna was familiar, who leaped to her aid and steadied her while he refastened the door. "Run to the pool," he commanded, grasping her arm and half dragging her to a large bathing pool which was fenced off from the lower end of the lake. He unceremoniously shoved her into the glacial water and leaped in after her. She screamed as the cold water struck her overheated skin and struggled to keep from drowning until she felt his steadying arm under her back.

"It's a bit chilly at first," he encouraged, "but if you keep swimming you'll warm up." When he let go of her, she sank, then struggled to the surface and began to swim. Nicholas was already standing at the shallow end of the pool rubbing himself with yellow soap. As she struggled to his side, he tossed her the lump and plunged into the deep to rinse himself. He had emerged and was rubbing himself with a coarse towel from the pile on the bank as a group from the sauna raced across the compound and plunged with gleeful howls into the water.

Catherine rinsed herself and grabbed a towel. The chill breeze seemed almost warm as she dried her hair and watched the natives frolicking in the icy pool.

"You'd better head back to the lodge and put some clothes on," he urged. "You're not used to this." He guided her back, then turned at the door and headed for the sauna for another bout with the heat. She gratefully pulled on some warm clothes, wrapped herself in her blanket and burrowed into her sleeping bag. For more than an hour she listened to the others yelling with delight as they pelted back and forth from sauna to pool. At last naked bodies began pelting into the lodge. Most of them paired off into sleeping rolls. She saw Nicholas shrug off his towel and plunge into his bag. Alsenius and Reina, his Amazon, carefully dried each other off before they shared his roll. Grimbolt shook himself vigorously and stretched out on his blanket looking more like a bear than ever. For the first time his shaggy pelt looked inviting as he sprawled at ease and snored.

Everybody was up at first light, and Aethelstan guided the travelers to the hall where several men were setting up the boards on the trestles. After a breakfast, which was a repetition of supper, the men cleared the benches and table and placed a substantial chair at the upper end of the room. Moonflower took the chair and waved her guests to stools scattered nearby. For Catherine she provided a chair placed close to her own.

"My husband tells me that you fought valiantly and well, despite the suspicion that you used magic in the battle." She addressed herself exclusively to the Princess, tolerating the men as spectators to the negotiations.

Catherine looked helplessly toward her companions. "I was at some distance from the battle," she apologized. "I couldn't really see what was going on. I think Njal used some illusions to confuse the enemy."

"I am informed that your Highness is a princess of Quatch. Are you at war with the servants of the Pythoness?"

"I don't think there's ever been a declaration of war, but Father suspects them of trying to undermine the kingdoms. His policy is to make defensive alliances against them."

"Does your mother permit such an aggressive policy?"

"Oh, Mother has nothing to do with policy. She's too busy keeping th palace in order."

"Do you mean that you are not the daughter of the Queen? Surely her Majesty would not permit the child of a servant to succeed her."

"Of course Mother's the Queen, but Father runs the country."

"Oh." Moonflower looked as if she has tasted an overripe fish. "Another of those male monarchies, like our neighbor Zharkovia. And you are betrothed to this male?" She gestured rather dismissively toward Grimbolt.

"Father wants me to marry him to cement an alliance. At least, that was the original plan. Alsenius and Njal came with instructions to take me home for a different marriage, but that was just because Prince Humber of Arragor was still missing. Now that he's come back, I suppose I have to marry him."

"You suppose!?" Moonflower stood up and paced around her chair, then slammed herself down again. "You suppose you have to marry him? Have you invited him to share your tent or not?"

"You don't understand Kingdom politics," Grimbolt interrupted.

"And you think that you, a mere man, can explain?"

"I at least have the facts," he snapped back.

"And you may keep them. When I desire your facts I will demand them." She turned back to Catherine. "Can you explain your remarkable statement that you suppose you are betrothed to this impertinent male."

"When we were babies, King Humber, his father, and my father agreed on an alliance between the kingdoms. As a pledge of their faith, they betrothed Prince Humber to me. When I became a woman, Father sent me to Arragor to fulfill his pledge. Of course, if the Prince or I found the match intolerable, either of us could have refused, but we didn't object, so the marriage was planned. Then a Priestess of the Pythoness murdered King Humber and kidnapped the Prince, so I stayed in Arragor waiting for them to recover him."

"What did your mother the Queen say about all this nonsense?"

"I don't think anybody ever asked her."

"This is blasphemous!"

"Oh no, Ma'am. That's the way things work."

"Your mother never examined this man to see whether he is suitable?" She glared at Grimbolt. "From what I saw of him in the sauna, I would never have approved him for a daughter of mine, even if she chose him."

"But he wasn't that way till after the Pythoness carried him off. Prince Humber was a very ordinary young man. He wasn't much of a man, but nobody could really object to him."

"And your mother allowed you to be betrothed to a nonentity."

"He was only a baby when we were betrothed, and Mother had nothing to do with it."

Grimbolt stood up and glared down at Moonflower. "You are ignorant of the ways of the kingdoms. Furthermore you have no business meddling in the private affairs of your guests." She tried to interrupt, but he roared through her protests. "Princess Catherine is an ignorant, silly woman who happens to be Princess of Quatch. I am a battered and deformed victim of Pythoness tyranny. We don't particularly like each other, but for the good of our kingdoms we are willing to marry. Since my hairiness was magically induced, there is no danger I will pass it on to my children. It's a damned poor way to run a courtship, but we're stuck with it, and we thank you to mind your own business." He sat down.

Moonflower was speechless with fury. Grimbolt had pointedly reminded her that he was her guest, and she felt a twinge of guilt as hostess. Alsenius cleared his throat and stood, remaining respectfully silent until she nodded to him.

"I apologize for the brutality of my friend's analysis of his affairs. Your honor could justifiably resent his mode of speech, but I beg you to remember that we are strangers, ignorant of your customs. Grimbolt suffers the agony of incurable transformation; he has very recently recovered the agonizing memory of humiliation and deformity. May I crave your indulgence toward our bungling." He bowed and sat.

She almost smiled. "You are all my husband's guests and mine. I may deplore the barbarity of your customs, but the laws of hospitality forbid that I should resent what was not intended as an affront." She turned her gaze toward Grimbolt. "I compassionate your sufferings and wonder at what passes in your country for devotion to duty." She then addressed Catherine. "I assign my son Aethelstan to see to your needs and those of your companions. If you will excuse me, I would hear the story of your travels and the nature of your needs from your servant Alsenius, who seems more conversant with the courtesies of discourse." She stood and watched as everyone except Alsenius retired. Then she gestured him to the vacant chair and sat to listen to his story.

He told of his meeting with Grimbolt when they rowed together on a river barge, of their travels with Clarissa to Augustia, of the failure of Eastern clerics to break the spell which made Grimbolt bear-like and deprived him of his memory. He told of their clash with the priestesses of the Pythoness in Draecia and of their subsequent journey northward from Megalopolis and of the discovery that Grimbolt was Prince Humber. "He has courageously suffered much. He is a noble, and loyal friend. I am sorry he has ignorantly offended your customs."

"You are an amazingly eloquent friend," she smiled. "If your skin were not so conspicuously dark, I would urge one of my daughters to claim you. As a matter of fact I might put Sven out and take you as my own husband, but I'm afraid you haven't been properly trained. At any rate, I am disposed to help you in spite of your alien ways. Go and let my men folk teach you something of our civilization. I shall welcome you all at our noon meal." She gestured dismissal and signaled to her guard that she was ready to judge the next case."

Alsenius found his friends with Aethelstan at the swimming pier. He noticed that Reina, his captured Amazon, was with the group, as was Njal's Emma, clinging possessively to the Illusionist's arm.

Njal was just asking, "Do your people often wander north to the country of the fallen star?"

"Never as a tribe, for the region is most inhospitable, but hunting parties sometimes go that far north to look for star metal. Our smiths cannot work the stuff. It requires more heat than we can get from charcoal, but the Rockborn weapon master who lives on the side of the smoking mountain will fashion weapons from half the metal we bring. He keeps the other half as his fee. My grandfather had a beautiful short sword fashioned of the grey metal, and I have my dagger."

"Do you find it in large chunks?"

"Not usually. I gathered most of mine from sifting dirt at the entrance to a deep cave. Father dared to explore deep into a cavern dug out by a piece of the star, and he found a fragment so heavy he could not lift it. He had to use the dogs to drag the metal on a sledge. The metal is very dense. Feel how heavy my dagger is." He drew his weapon and laid it across Njal's hands. "It's heavier than gold."

Alsenius drew his long sword. "That is why not many men can wield my weapon," he said. "It was fashioned from a star fall off the coast of my homeland. My prince gave it to me in gratitude for my saving his life."

Aethelstan hefted the sword with difficulty and then stared in wonder as Alsenius swept the blade through the motions of a complicated royal salute.

"I don't know whether I marvel more at the blade or at the arm which masters it."

Alsenius sheathed the blade, and they sauntered to the end of the pier. "Did your father get a star metal weapon?"

"Not yet. He suffered a strange illness after he came out with the metal. We had to camp for several weeks while I fought his fever and bloody flux. All his hair fell out, and it seemed almost as if her had suffered burns under the skin. All the dogs who were used to pull the fragment out died of the same disease, and it took all of my Shaman's art to save Father. I ordered the men to bury the metal fragment and Father concealed it as well as he could. We couldn't drag the chunk with us since we needed all the surviving dogs to get Father home. I think the fallen star must have left some poison in the cavern with the metal.

"Njal and Aethelstan stood silently thinking for a long time. Finally Njal asked, "Has your mother had any children since your father's illness?"

"Come to think of it, no. Do you think his illness has affected his powers?"

"I heard about an expedition which fell ill with a similar plague, and none of them had children after that, even though several had been frequent fathers on different women. I would suggest that Sven be persuaded to visit one of the major temples and seek healing from a high level Cleric. I'm sure it was only your prompt labor as a Shaman which kept him alive."

"You don't think the curse comes from the metal, do you?" Aethelstan paled as he looked down at his dagger."

"I doubt it," Alsenius volunteered. "I've carried this blade for years and left a trail of dark bastards all across the continent. It's probably something else that came down with this star."

"And the closed atmosphere of the cavern concentrates the effect of the curse," Njal added. "As I remember it, the people I heard of had been exploring a deep cave just before they became ill." He twiddled his fingers briefly. "Somehow I think I shall stay out of caverns made by fallen stars. I don't think the metal is worth the risk."

"Does your father plan to try to recover the fragment you buried?" Alsenius asked. "If he does, he might be willing to let us help him."

"I'm not sure Mother will let him. She believes the metal is connected with his disease, and she fears a relapse. She has even raised the question with Flora's mother in connection with my dagger. That's the last thing that stands between me and my betrothed. Her mother wants me to give up my weapon, and I won't. She wants to make Flora demand surrender of my dagger as a condition to the marriage."

"And if she does?"

"I'm probably a bachelor for life. If Flora rejects me for disobedience, no other woman will even look at me, except maybe as a temporary mate."

"What's that?"

"Some widow might get horny enough to take me in to keep her bed warm." Aethelstan shuddered. "What I'll do if Flora refuses me will be to get Mother's permission to take off as a mercenary. That way I might find a woman in another tribe who will marry me for my strength as a hunter and fighter."

"Why not come to the kingdoms and win a woman who won't be so bossy?" Alsenius suggested. "Join with us and seek your own fortune. After all men hold the property in most of the world."

"I still hope Flora wants me enough to put up with the dagger. Maybe you could talk to her about your sword and convince her the metal isn't dangerous."

"Is that banging sound by any chance a call to food?" Njal asked as from every lodge came the sound of massive gongs.

"Yes, and we should make haste. Mother doesn't like to be kept waiting." Aethelstan led the way back to the lodge.

Njal offered Emma his arm. "Would you be willing to serve as my body guard if I bought your armor back from the tribe?" he asked. "I've been thinking that we would make a formidable pair. You could keep people from hitting me, and I could cast spells to protect you."

"I would become your henchman? I would be a free woman?"

"You'll be a free woman as soon as we get away from here anyhow. I don't like slavery, and I won't keep a slave," Njal answered. "I'm not sure I want to be tied down to a marriage, but we did manage to warm up the bed last night, and I thought we might make a long-term partnership. You protect me from fighters; I cast spells behind your shield; and we share body heat at night? Does that sound reasonable?"

"And you always make the decisions?"

"We could work that out. I couldn't make you do anything you didn't want to—you're too strong. And you can't boss me around because I'm too smart."

"You think I'm stupid?"

"I couldn't put up with you if I did, but you're not as bright as I am. What I'm hoping is that you're smart enough to listen to reason and I'm bright enough to recognize a good idea if you have one."

She smiled down at him. "I'm glad you saved me from the Pythoness' spells. Her priestesses made me a slave right after they raided my village and carried me off. They decided I was big enough to be a soldier, and an OBEDIENCE spell was one of the things you."

"I promise you that I'll never cast a serious spell on you unless you consent, though I won't guarantee not to make an occasional illusion for fun."

She squeezed his arm as they entered the lodge.

Grimbolt had laid aside all clothing except his kilt. Early in the meal, he brushed aside the his hostess' reluctance to mix business with the important activity of feeding. "If your Excellence is willing to assists us, we should like to be on our way tomorrow morning," he said.

Moonflower looked up from the bone she was gnawing. "I will discuss the matter with Princess Catherine at the appropriate time," she answered and returned to her bone.

"Our mission is of some urgency," Grimbolt persisted, "and we should be grateful if you would permit one of your men to guide us."

She stiffened and pointedly addressed Princess Catherine. "It is appropriate to discuss women's business in private—certainly not to raise such matters at meals. If you will instruct your betrothed in patience and decorum, I shall be happy to talk with you alone this afternoon."

Grimbolt refrained from hurling a slab of bread at her and savagely attacked his meal. Njal and Alsenius maintained a decorous silence. Catherine looked helplessly at Nicholas, who picked up the conversation as if nothing had been dropped. "Yours is the first comfortable sauna I have enjoyed since I left my homeland."

"We have always enjoyed the fellowship of the sauna," Dewblossom, the eldest daughter, responded. "We noticed that Princess Catherine and you departed our company in some haste."

"The Princess is from the South and her constitution is not adjusted to the sauna's heat. I feared she might lose consciousness."

"Your delicacy for another's betrothed is most sensitive."

"I am a Zharkovian diplomat. I am trained in sensitivity."

Moonflower looked up from her bone and snapped, "One wonders whether this diplomatic sensitivity is not the flower of your deficiencies."

"At least Lord Nicholas' deficiencies did not disable him in battle." Sven braved his wife's withering glare.

"Yes," Alsenius added, "his rapier is as ready as any man's."

"Does Arragor enjoy the pleasures of the sauna," Aethelstan asked Grimbolt.

"No, but I am seriously tempted to install one in my palace. The problem for us is a reluctance to discard clothing in mixed company. My mother would be horrified to bathe in my company."

"Yet you flaunt your naked chest at mealtime." Moonflower reposted.

"Among us, only women's breasts are concealed. We men have nothing there to hide."

"We in the Northeast have bathing customs very like yours." Njal jumped into the conversation before it became more dangerous. "We heat rocks in a great enclosed fire, but we then douse them with water, so that out sauna becomes a steam bath. Then when the pores of the skin are opened by the steam we dash across the snow to plunge through the ice into the ocean. Yet, like you, we swath ourselves in clothing on all other occasions."

"Perhaps," Princess Catherine interrupted, "if the rest of us were so warmly clothed in fur, we would share King Grimbolt's freedom from artificial cover." She rose from the table and stalked out, turning in the doorway to add,. "I shall be happy to confer with the Lady Moonflower at her convenience."

The meal had by this time obviously ended.

Alsenius and Grimbolt spent the afternoon with Sven, Aethelstan, and several other fighting men practicing their craft. Grimbolt surprised the Brielanders by fending off their sword attacks and punishing their heads and bodies with his staff, while Alsenius dazzled them with his brilliant swordplay. On the other hand Sven and his comrades demonstrated their skill in attacking with bows from cover and from horseback. "We can stall a conventional military formation and throw them on the defensive. If the force is not too large and well trained, we can even break a defensive square. The key is mobility and using the terrain."

"Not much use in an attack," Grimbolt grunted.

"But we don't attack," Sven answered. "We only fight to defend our wilderness against those who would fence it in. Once in a great while we march on a border town and sack it just to discourage invaders. But mostly we fight to be left alone."

"I suppose that's the advantage of letting the women run things," Alsenius laughed. "Women are natural conservatives. They need to protect their young and preserve their homes. It's the men who get big ideas about glory and power." He turned to Grimbolt. "You notice that Arragor has been peaceful and anxious for defensive treaties since your mother took over."

"Oh, I don't know. Dad wasn't much of a fighter either."

"And he let his wife run things most of the time, I'll wager."

"True," Grimbolt laughed. "Mother must be a Brielander at heart. I suppose that's why we've been at odds ever since we learned I was king. She really likes to run things."

"And it takes a wily old fox like Septimus to keep her in line," Njal remarked. "He always suggests and reminds. He'd make a great Brieland husband."

"He makes a great Lord Steward," Grimbolt returned. "I know I'm going to keep him when I take over."

"You are going to take over?" Alsenius queried.

"Oh yes! Mother won't like it, but I'm going to be King Grimbolt, not King Humber. She's not going to smother me in court costumes or in court ritual. If my courtiers want to wrap themselves against the cold, that's their business, but this kilt is as far as I'm going. Furthermore they're going to learn to hear 'Yes' and 'No,' not 'I'm not sure.' That's one thing I learned from my old Boatswain. You always knew what he wanted and what it would cost if you didn't give it to him."

Alsenius grinned at the memory of their life as oarsmen. "With him you knew where the line was and what would happen if you crossed it."

"Yes, and that's the kind of King I'm going to be."

"In some ways your mother has a bit of that," said Njal.

"I don't agree. Oh you knew if she got mad she'd throw the scepter, but you never knew when she was going to blow up. I want my people to know when they're sailing near a rock. I don't intend to have to throw my scepter."

Meanwhile Princess Catherine joined Moonflower in the Hall. She managed a court curtsey and waited for the matriarch to start.

"Your man Grimbolt seems impatient to quest for metal. I am not sure I would recommend such a quest. Nor is such impatience seemly."

"King Grimbolt chafes under the restraints of a culture unlike his own."

"As a guest of that culture he runs dangerously close to impropriety. We have given him appropriate clothing. He might at least wear it."

"As your Ladyship has observed, his body is ill suited for clothing. He wears the kilt as a concession to modesty."

"He encourages improper thoughts in our males."

"That is why he wishes to leave immediately. He realizes that a clash of cultures threatens our friendship."

"Why do you permit him to flaunt himself?"

"By the customs of the kingdoms, he is his own authority."

"But you have claimed him as your betrothed."

"Madame, my father, who by our laws has authority over me, has commanded that I marry him. The match will cement a peaceful relationship between our kingdoms. My father will be Grandfather to the next king of Arragor."

"What does Grimbolt's mother say? What is your will in this matter?'"

"We were betrothed by law in our infancy. This man is the least objectionable candidate for my hand. We of royal blood are not free to please our fancy in marriage. After I have borne proper heirs to the throne, we shall be free to entertain ourselves discretely."

"Yet you encourage that abomination who helped you out of the sauna."

"Nicholas cannot endanger the succession. Even if I slept with him, there could be no issue."

"Your so-called culture is insane. The mother is the natural protector of the family. Even your kings cannot be certain of paternity: a man must accept his wife's word that he is the father. The need to establish paternity places intolerable limits on a woman. Sven teaches Aethelstan to be a man because I assure him that they are kin. I teach my daughters because I know I am their mother. All passes through the womb, and the only true line of descent is through the womb."

"And if I try to compel that great brute of a man, he will pick me up and toss me aside. I can govern him only by his desire for me and his early training to protect women."

"But you haven't even leashed him in your way."

"We are trying to work out an arrangement. It's not easy for either of us. Look, your way may make more sense, but it can only work if you have the males trained from infancy. Our males are trained for dominance. I would suggest that you give Grimbolt what he wants before he teaches your strongest men to use their strength. The only hold you have over Sven is your authority to throw him out of the house. But if you throw him out, you've lost him and he's free to go anywhere else in the world and capture a submissive woman. Look at the way that Amazon crawls over Njal? What kind of example is she. If you don't give Grimbolt what he wants, he'll destroy your little paradise without even intending to."

"But what do you want?"

"I am not a very bright woman, and I have been trained for only one thing—to entice and keep a man. I can't out-fight him; I can't out-think him. What I want is to capture the loyalty of the strongest, smartest man I can catch. Then I want him to protect me and my children for the rest of his life. If that means guaranteeing that the children are his, that's a price I'll have to pay. Grimbolt is a very good man. He's honorable; he's intelligent; he's strong and skillful; and he's surprisingly gentle. He does not make my body tremble with desire for his, but now I know him, I can imagine even the ultimate intimacy without revulsion. What I'd really like would be Nicholas with a mustache in a world that would let us live together. I know I can't have that, so I'm willing to settle for being

Grimbolt's queen. He'll never give me ecstasy, but he'll keep me and our children safe and perhaps sometimes happy."

"I never before realized how fragile our way of life is." Moonflower shuddered as she visualized the influence Grimbolt and Alsenius might have on the men of Southmark. "You have convinced me that we must get rid of Grimbolt and his companions immediately. Go and tell your betrothed that I will provide supplies for his journey north. As to his request for a guide, I must think about that. One question I must ask. This star metal—is Alsenius honest when he tells me that wielding his weapon has not diminished his manhood?"

"Court gossip says that he's very virile. His companions indicate that he has left a trail of bastards behind him. Furthermore, my father has worn a star metal dagger all his life, and I have a horde of half brothers and sisters."

"Thank you, my dear. I wish you faced a brighter future, but I fear you are too much the slave of your court. Believe me, I wish you happiness with your compromise betrothed."

Within an hour of this interview, while Aethelstan was at swordplay with Alsenius, a boy interrupted with an urgent summons from Flora. Excusing himself, he hastened to bathe in the pool and return to Moonflower's lodge to don his best leggings and blouse.

"I see Flora has finally made up her mind," his mother remarked.

"What made you give up your objections?"

"My objections?"

"Mother dear, you know very well Flora made up her mind months ago. You've kept her mother from approving our marriage because of your silly fears about my dagger." He adjusted his sheath on his belt and straightened up for final inspection.

"I wonder whether that hairy brute is right about blouses. I admit that naked chest of his is very impressive." She nodded her approval of her son. "Still, you have to save some surprises for the wedding night. "I assume Violet has inspected you on her daughter's behalf."

Aethelstan shuddered. "She even had the gall to squeeze my balls to make sure they were sound. I hope you don't do that to my sister's men when their time comes.

"Lady Violet is a lecherous old vixen," snapped Moonflower, "but a mother has to inspect her perspective sons-in-law to make sure there are no hidden flaws."

"She'd a lot better let Flora look for herself."

"Don't argue with custom, my dear. A mother can't trust a young couple's self control that far. I'm sure Judge Violet did you no harm."

"But it was damned embarrassing." Aethelstan kissed his mother and strode from the lodge to Violet's tent and Flora's enthusiastic welcome.

Shortly afterwards Sven responded to his wife's summons. She seated him next to her and placed a hand on his bare knee. "Husband, I have decided that you should go with the strangers tomorrow and guide them to the star metal they want."

He stared at her blankly.

"They want Aethelstan to go with them, but he needs to settle down with Flora. Those foreign ideas of Catherine's are much too dangerous for a boy to handle."

"They're letting him keep his dagger?"

"Catherine says her father has carried one for years and still remakes the court in his own image. If by any chance I'm wrong and he fails Flora, she'll just have to send him off in disgrace."

"I confess I enjoy the company of the alien warriors, but why are you sending me?"

"My dear, you have been a very satisfactory husband and I do not wish to spoil your reputation, but you must realize that I have had no children since your illness, and my rhythms have suffered no change. The family needs more children, and I shall soon be compelled to take a new husband. This is an opportunity for me to yield reluctantly to your wanderlust and let you take a spotless reputation on this quest."

"But I don't like the idea of sharing you with another husband when I come back. I know the law allows it, but . . ."

"Unless you find yourself miraculously cured, you should not return. I will send a young man as your aide, and he can bring back all the treasure you amass. I do not wish to condemn you to spend the rest of your life in the old men's tents, and that's where you'll end up if you cannot give me children. We must sacrifice our marriage to the welfare of the tribe. You will send back treasure to enhance your reputation and your new friends should be able to find you satisfying work as a mercenary."

He looked longingly at her. "I have loved you, my wife, and enjoyed every night of our marriage. I must bow to your will about the children, and I thank you for saving me from disgrace." His hand covered hers on his knee and slid gently up her arm. "Could we at least have one more night warming the same bedroll?"

She looked carefully to make sure no one was spying on them. Then she took him in her arms. "After the sauna we shall share our flesh once more. I shall miss you very much, my husband."

Aethelstan was absent from his mother's table at supper. In the evening, when the clans gathered in the sauna, Flora announced that she had taken Aethelstan as her husband, and Violet announced her acceptance of her new son-in-law and father of her grandchildren. When the couple fled the sauna for the pool, no one followed them, so that they had the pool to themselves. Poor Catherine nearly fainted in the sauna heat, but Nicholas found a way to jam the door slightly open, and she crouched in the cool draft that sneaked in. When they were sure that the newly-weds were safely in their bedroll, she and Nicholas were able to slip away while the tribe celebrated long and late.

It was an hour before the morning twilight when half a dozen horsemen pounded down the hill and ignored the sentries' challenges. They dismounted at the Community Lodge and beat upon the gong at its door. They were quickly surrounded by armed men and led to Moonflower's lodge. She threw on a robe and took her place in her judgement chair to receive the strangers. The men were from a neighboring clan whose camp lay about fifty miles to the west. They reported that a large army of Amazons was marching east from the Hegemony of the Pythoness. Several tribes had been overrun before they had time to flee. Warned by fugitives from the western tribes, their own people had succeeded in loading their tents and moving camp northward out of the Amazons' line of march. Their Senior Judge had assigned such men as she could spare to join the informal band of fugitives who were harrying the flanks of the enemy. She had also assigned a few men to warn the rest of the clans and to raise a resistance force.

Moonflower immediately chose three men to mount and ride one north, one south, and one east to spread the warning and to summon the militia. "You will remain with us to rest yourselves and your horses while we break camp. Did your judge give you orders about what to do after you warned us?"

"Only to see that all the tribes are warned and beg for reinforcements."

"Good. My men will carry the word to the next tribes, and those tribes will send fresh messengers to carry the word from there. I shall beg them to send as many fighting men as they can spare to reinforce us here. Unless your orders forbid it, I urge you to join the resistance force we shall dispatch westward to begin harrying the enemy." She turned to Alsenius, who stood near her. "Mercenary! Do your commitments make it impossible to help us?"

"Unless King Grimbolt objects to the delay, I believe we are as committed to the defeat of the Pythoness as you are."

"The Pythoness is as much of a threat to the kingdoms as she is to the Brie," Grimbolt answered. "We are ready to ally ourselves with you."

"Good! Although my husband Sven will remain in charge of our men, I hereby appoint Alsenius as general of the united defense forces. He is far more experienced in warfare than any of our men, and we need someone outside tribal rivalries to coordinate our defense." Her look to Alsenius dared him to refuse command.

"Will the men of other tribes accept your general?" Alsenius demanded.

"We accept the ruling of the Senior Judge," the spokesman for the visiting men declared. "And I am certain that all of our men will agree. Our own judge was too busy evacuating the camp to worry about military affairs."

Alsenius turned to Grimbolt.

"Don't look at me. I'm an oarsman, not a general. You're the only one around who knows about tactics."

"Please take over," Sven urged. "You gave us our success in the last battle."

"Very well." Alsenius looked back at Moonflower. "My first order as General is that you get this settlement on wheels ready to take off. We can't beat a large trained army in a set battle. We need to make the countryside fight for us, and that means no fixed settlements they can loot. The farther they march without winning anything, the harder they'll find it to supply their army."

He questioned the messengers. "How big a force have they?"

"I'd estimate about a thousand Amazon infantry and two or three hundred horsewomen. The horses don't stay still to be counted. The cavalry almost caught us in camp, but our wagons went north and left a sacrifice force to keep them busy."

"Horse or foot?"

"Our defenders were on fast horses. The idea was to hit and run south in hopes they'd chase the horsemen who attacked them and not bother with the main body of the camp."

"Did it work?"

"We think so. The Amazon cavalry was still chasing our horsemen when we separated and came west."

"Moonflower," Njal challenged, "all the Pythoness' soldiers are women. Why do you send men against them?"

"I should think that was obvious. Men are expendable; women are not. If we lost ninety percent of our men, we could recover our population in one generation by sharing the surviving males. Seed is cheap, wombs are not. Furthermore, preparing to fight keeps the men out of mischief. We women have more important things to do."

Orders were promptly given to break camp while Alsenius gathered the men assigned to him. "Njal, how big an illusion can you create?"

"That depends on how complex you want it and how long I have."

"Could you create the illusion of a camp here surrounded by pike men?"

"It wouldn't be as big as this one, but I could make a very convincing tribe of a dozen tents surrounded by 100 pike men. Of course if you could give me fifty real pike men to build on, I could double the size of the camp and make the defenders look like 300."

"Done! Sven find me fifty men who won't run away from a cavalry charge and furnish them with spears about eight feet long. Teach them to station themselves like this." He knelt to support a pike at the right angle to impale an oncoming horseman. "Make sure they know how to brace the butt of the pike so it will hold firm even against a charging horse."

"Teach them to take station about ten feet apart." Njal added "That way I can fit my illusory warriors between and behind them. The enemy horses will probably believe the illusion and become difficult to control. Once blood is shed, we should fool the whole charge. The horsemen who run on the illusion will think they're injured and fall down just as fast as the ones who take real damage."

"Excellent," Alsenius continued. "I want to spread the rumor that a camp is standing fast here. If I can lure the cavalry into racing ahead of their foot soldiers to loot the camp, we can harry the infantry with horse bowmen. Even more important, we can attack their supply wagons." Alsenius turned back to the messengers. "When you get back to your own horsemen, try to impress upon them that hitting the supplies is more important than breaking their squares. If their cavalry runs out of browse, they'll have to quit, and even Amazons won't fight very well on empty bellies. This countryside will be deadly to a big army, while our men can draw supplies from the roving camps."

He turned to Moonflower. "Can you find a dozen boys too young to fight but capable of riding fast as messengers?"

"Finding boys to get into mischief? I'll have to fight off volunteers."

"I'd like half a dozen within call, but out of the way. You had better have a batch on hand near you. Communications are going to be very important."

Njal volunteered, "I can enchant animals and birds to carry notes. They won't be as good as the boys, but the enemy won't notice them."

Grimbolt approached Alsenius. "If you can persuade Sven to turn his pike men over to me, I can probably train them and serve as their officer in battle."

"Sven needs no persuading," Sven interrupted, "I'll send the men to you right away."

Within minutes Njal and Grimbolt were training pike men and getting them accustomed to the apparent presence of imaginary comrades. Some of the men saw through the illusions almost immediately and had to be reminded not to tramp through them. Others actually convinced themselves that their brother pike men were real.

"What I'm hoping," Alsenius explained, "is that the Pythoness' general is as rigidly disciplined as most of the servants of the Priestesses. They like obedience and dependability, and I'm going to depend on imagination. If she is thoroughly trained in traditional battle technique, she will be very uncomfortable with an army that rides away from battle and sneaks up on the supply train. The last thing we want is a classic pitched battle where discipline wins every time."

"Shall we leave the piers and bathing pools for you to anchor your illusions?" asked Moonflower.

"Oh, yes! Anything you leave, I don't have to dream up. I can always use real things to hang my illusions on."

As they were planning, Nicholas retired behind a wagon and wrote a swift note to King Peter:

> We are at a water hole almost due west of Markov at a distance of about a hundred miles. A large army of Amazons—about a thousand foot and several hundred horse—is headed east across the tundra. Alsenius is

organizing the Brieland tribes into a resistance force of a few hundred. They plan to harass the flanks and supply lines of the enemy. We cannot hope to defeat the Amazons in a pitch battle, but should weaken them as they march eastward. If your Majesty should dispatch a substantial force westward, it would have an excellent chance of defeating the Amazon army and winning the good will of the nomads who wander and camp over the wilderness. I am negotiating for military cooperation from the Brielanders in exchange for our assurance that we do not plan to colonize.

He approached the fire and casually tossed the note into the embers. It vanished in a flash and almost immediately floated from the fireplace to the floor of King Peter's study in his palace. Two days later, a Zharkovian army of fifteen hundred foot soldiers and five hundred cavalry marched westward from Markov to meet the invading Amazons.

Nicholas caught the attention of Moonflower just before the wagon train of her people left the pond. "Lady Moonflower!" He bowed from his horse and gestured a desire to talk. She turned her steed to approach him. "Milady, I have notified King Peter of the advancing Amazon army. I expect that his Majesty will dispatch a sizable force to assist your people in their defense of this territory. You realize that, while King Peter claims all this tundra as part of his Kingdom, he has no intention of occupying it permanently. If your people would assist, or at least avoid, the Zharkovian army marching from the east, they would be able to defeat the Amazons and leave the country to you."

"And what does King Peter propose to gain by this invasion?"

"Primarily it would weaken the Hegemony of the Pythoness. Her Priestesses are plotting against the kingdoms, and any opportunity to weaken them will strengthen him and his allies. A second benefit would be to strengthen his claim to this area, which he desires, not to occupy—for it is too inhospitable for his subjects—but to deny it to any hostile power."

"And you offer us, on his behalf, a passive master in place of an enslaving mistress?"

"His Majesty has empowered me to negotiate on his behalf."

"Then you may tell his Majesty, by whatever means of communication you possess, that the free tribes of Brielanders will not oppose the advance of his army into our territory, but will not encourage fraternization nor welcome permanent settlers."

"On behalf of his Majesty, I think your Ladyship." His bow was conspicuously profound.

As the exodus of the camp began, Alsenius gathered his officers. "I want to leave the pike men and the illusory camp in charge of Njal and Grimbolt. They should put up as convincing a defense as possible. I will gather as many horse bowmen from the tribes as I can. We will divide into two main forces. Sven will command the force who harry the flanks of the Amazon infantry and their supply line. And remember that you are not to play heroes and sacrifice yourself trying to break their defensive squares. Pepper them with arrows, kill off any scouts or stragglers, and lead their cavalry a merry chase, but don't get yourselves killed. There's a Zharkovian army coming westward, and they will probably fight a formal battle. Your job is to be the mosquitoes—bite and fly, but don't get swatted.

The force with me will try to surprise the cavalry who attack Njal's illusion and Grimbolt's pike men. I hope that a flank attack just as they're making their initial charge on the illusion will break up their formation and perhaps rout them.

By the time the horse bowmen had started westward, the watchword was "Make like mosquitoes!" Many of the men were even heard practicing a loud buzzing battle cry."

Moonflower was sure that someone among her companions was a spy for the Pythoness. Since she didn't know who, she called a meeting and told them all that she had some treasure which was too heavy to conveniently load on the wagons. Therefore she had decided to leave it concealed at the camp site and to use the men under Grimbolt's command to defend it. She expected that the men would be able to protect the site against a troop of cavalry. When the main Amazon army arrived, they could flee to the north. She trusted the treasure was well enough hidden to escape notice if the campsite was finally overrun. She did not know who reported the information to the enemy or how it was done, but she trusted the priestesses to have an efficient spy system.

Within an hour, the Amazon general received a report that there was a considerable treasure—possibly a cache of star metal, since it was very heavy—hidden in the deserted camp and defended by only fifty men. The general promptly dispatched a hundred cavalry under a junior captain of horse to precede the army and capture and loot the camp. The rest of the cavalry was deployed to protect the infantry and the supply train as it swept irresistibly over the rolling hills. They had already sacked two small settlements and routed with small casualties several disorganized forays of horse bowmen. Using a gifted psionic novice, she reported to the High Priestess that, since resistence was disorganized and scattered, she planned to march swiftly to the camp where the treasure was reported.

The psionic reply came quickly. "Remember that the horse bowmen actually broke the defensive square of our recent attack. Be sure you keep sufficient cavalry in support of your infantry. Do not allow your cavalry to be lured away from the main body in pursuit of fleeing Barbarians. Do not detach cavalry units."

The general congratulated herself that she could not recall the cavalry unit already dispatched and obediently drew the rest of her mounted troops into closer formation around her foot soldiers. Thus, when Alsenius had organized his horse bowmen, he found the main army virtually impregnable, but the baggage train very lightly defended. He assigned a small group of swift-riding bowmen to pepper the main force and keep them busy while he led the main body of his bowmen to sweep down on the lightly protected supply train which stretched for several miles behind the main force. As a result, by the time the Amazon cavalry had rushed to defend the supplies, the bowmen had totally disorganized the train—destroying wagon loads of food—and had vanished unscathed among the hills.

While Njal was preparing his illusion of a defensive force, Grimbolt managed to buy the armor and weapons of Emma and Reina, the captured Amazons, from the tribe. As he paid for the equipment, he asked, "Where is Aethelstan serving.? Did he ride with Alsenius?"

"Oh no, sir," the bursar answered. "He is Lady Flora's new husband. No woman is separated from her husband during the first year. Her right to her first child takes precedence over any other duty. Of course, if we were digging in to protect the settlement, everybody—men and women—would serve in the battle, but since we are escaping the enemy, his duty is with his bride."

Grimbolt watched the last of the wagons trundle over the northern hills and then returned to the lake.

One of his pike men asked him, "How are we supposed to escape when the Amazons ride us down?"

"We're expected to hold the line until our mounted bowmen sweep down and drive off the cavalry. That's what Njal's illusion is going to do"

"Where shall we fight?" Emma demanded of Grimbolt.

"I'm going to stand with the pike men and give substance to the illusion," He answered. "I suggest that you and Reina stand behind us and shoot arrows."

"Good," said Njal. "Take your places on the western side, and I'll reinforce you with a dozen or so illusory duplicates. I'd be grateful if you would place your people now so that I can begin to weave the whole illusion around them. It's going to take all my concentration to keep all the appearances working smoothly."

"What if they hit you with an arrow or break through and charge you?"

"I'll wear my Invisibility ring and be standing well away from anything they're likely to attack. If I have to start casting defensive spells, we're all in deep trouble." He moved out into the pond until the water rose to his waist. "This will be a bit uncomfortable, but I don't think anybody's going to attack the water."

"Why not use a boat?"

"Too suspicious. Somebody might suspect an empty boat rocking as I gesticulate."

Grimbolt strode to his position and braced his scepter as a pike. He placed the two Amazons behind him, so that they had human brawn rather than illusion standing between them and the attack. When he saw the enemy cavalry topping the hill to the west, he asked," Has Njal got his damned illusion working yet?"

"Oh yes," answered Emma. "We are surrounded by bowmen, and you are part of a solid line of pike men. When they get too close for arrows, we'll be swinging our swords over your head, so don't straighten up without warning us."

"After they charge us, I'll use my scepter as a staff. We may have to swing through illusions."

They watched the hundred Amazon cavalry form up at the top of the hill for its charge. The horsemen formed into a line, their lances erect and steady; then on command they couched their weapons and started down the hill like a living avalanche. They held their formation with amazing discipline, and the defenders felt the thunder of their hooves as they neared. Three of the pike men dropped their pikes and fled, but the rest, encouraged by the steadiness of Njal's illusion, stood their ground so that a hedge of bristling points confronted the charge. The Amazons—supported by the enchantments of their Priestesses—faced the barrier and the cloud of arrows from the illusory archers behind it with determination. A number of the horses, however, shied at the last moment. They were borne forward by the pressure of those behind, but they caused the line to falter. Several attempted to leap over the pike men and received both arrows in the face and pikes in the belly. The charge broke through the line at several points, but no formation remained. The pike men were able to turn to face the disorganized horsemen, in several cases pulling the riders off their steeds. In the center a pile of fallen horses and riders rose in front of Grimbolt and the women, who formed a small square with neighboring Southmarkers to fend off the attack.

It was at this point that the reserved horse bowmen swept down from the northen hill, showering the Amazons not actually in melee with arrows. Those Southmark horsemen wielding swords and maces pounded against the Amazon cavalry surrounding the square and forming again after the charge.

Njal's pike men began to waver and lose coordination as the Illusionist turned his attention to casting a new spell. Many of the Amazons still attacked the illusions, but the Brielanders, who had been warned, were able to ride and shoot straight through them.

When Njal's second illusion of a horde of horse bowmen charged over the hill from the south, the Amazon attack fell apart. The commander managed to rally about half of her unit into ragged formation so that they could beat a fairly organized retreat, but they left behind many bodies. Some of these were killed or wounded by real weapons, but about thirty were unconscious from imaginary damage. Grimbolt's pike men dashed among the fallen in order to tie up and loot the victims. The horse bowmen rounded up the enemy horses, treating the real injuries and calming the terror of the deluded.

Njal cast **DISPEL MAGIC** on all of the Amazon prisoners; then Sven and his horse bowmen marched them north to Moonflower's temporary camp. There were enough captured horses to mount Grimbolt's pike men, and he set off with them immediately to join Alsenius. Having done all he could at the settlement Njal, with Reina and Emma, mounted and traveled with Grimbolt.

When Sven triumphantly marched his weary prisoners into the temporary Southmark camp, his wife welcomed him as conquering general and promptly sat in judgment on the prisoners. Eleven of the Amazons had found themselves released from Pythoness' magic sufficiently to plead for refugee status rather than to continue in the Amazon service. These, Moonflower provided with tents and supplies, instructing them to camp apart from her people under guard. The rest she stripped of arms and armor and placed under their Amazon officers. "You may camp on the side of the hill to the south of our camp; there you will be fed and allowed to rest for the night. In the morning you will be provided with enough short bows to enable you to hunt for food. Your officers will then march you eastward until you either unite with the Amazon invasion force or reach the borders of the Pythoness' Hegemony. We have neither personnel to guard prisoners nor the resources to feed you. Since we are too civilized to slay you, we must send you home to your mistress. You will swear an oath never to enter the territory of the Southmark again, and if you are ever again found within our territory, you will be executed.

"For the night you will confine yourselves strictly to your designated camp ground and strays will be executed by the guards. You will inform your mistresses that the Southmark of the Brie are not barbarians to be brushed aside for Amazon convenience. We are an independent people who will defend our homeland against all comers. You may go."

She stalked from the tent, and Sven's men escorted the prisoners courteously, but firmly, to the designated campground.

After supper, Moonflower summoned the eleven and Aethelstan. "If Njal were with us, I would punish him for meddling in our affairs by giving all of you to him as slaves. Your presence as refugees is an embarrassment to us and a threat to our way of life. We have no time to teach you our ways, even if you were capable of following them. You are innocent victims of the Pythoness' policy of raiding the kingdoms for magically enslaved servants. Your education in a male-dominated society renders you socially incompatible, as does your Amazon training as seducers and soldiers. Therefore, we cannot offer you a home among us. In the midst of a war, we cannot undertake to restore you to your homes in the kingdoms, and in our society dedicated to the freedom of the individual is unthinkable to keep you as slaves.

The solution I have to offer may not please you, but it is better than death or enslavement. You will be provided with a tent and supples adequate for your needs. You will elect a leader from your number who will keep me informed of your decisions and needs. You will then decide whether you shall form yourselves into an independent military unit to join Alsenius and united army or into a work unit to earn your keep by laboring for the good of our camp, or into an independent colony to wander and support yourselves as you can. If you choose the first, we shall provide you with captured horses and military equipment; then you will depart immediately to serve under Alsenius. After the war you may go where you will outside our territory. If you choose to serve us here, you will be absolutely segregated to your own tent and field of labor. If you become independent, you will remain at all times no less than ten miles from any Southmark settlement. Under no circumstances are you to mingle with our people. If any of our young men become sexually involved with any of you, they will become exiles from our community—disowned by their mothers' houses—and will share your isolation. Please inform me as to your choice in the morning. You will be escorted to your tent."

The interview was over.

In the morning Mahla, the elected chief of the eleven appeared before Moonflower. Reina and Emma were standing to the Judge's side. "Your honor, the eleven prisoners elected me to speak for them. We choose to be provided with horses and equipment to serve as an independent force under your general Alsenius."

"Good. I thought you would. Alsenius is both considerate and intelligent. He will figure out what to do with you after the Amazons are driven off." Moonflower turned to the other two. "Reina, it is my understanding that you are willing to travel with this independent unit to join Alsenius, who is your master. We shall equip you like the others. You will inform Alsenius that we forbid you to come again into the camps of the Southmark. He indicated that he intended to free you, but that is not our affair. I will send with you a letter instructing him, when the victory is won, to surrender command of our men to the officer Sven designates as his successor. You will be escorted by a man of Southmark who will carry Sven's sleeping bedroll along with a letter divorcing him as our husband and exiling him to the outside world. Your escort will also bestow on Sven my gift of five horses with their tackle, a complete set of armor, and a purse of gold coins as a gift of gratitude for his service as a satisfactory husband. You will convey to him my blessing and my hope for his success." She turned her attention back to Mahla. "If any of you renegade Amazons wish to marry or otherwise comfort my divorced husband, you are welcome to him. I fear he cannot give you children, but he can provide great pleasure, and I wish him well."

She turned to Emma. "You have indicated a desire to continue as Njal's companion. Except for his burdening Southmark with unwanted prisoners, he has done us great service. I shall place in your care an appropriate expression of our gratitude together with a letter ending our grant of hospitality. We suggest that he, along with Grimbolt and the Princess Catherine rejoin Alsenius. The Princess and Grimbolt have received their gifts and are awaiting you to the west of our camp. We are grateful for the help you have given us, but we cannot risk further contamination of our way of life. If you can find means to transport the star metal which Sven discovered, you are welcome to remove it. My son Aethelstan says that he has taught Njal a **FLOATING PLATFORM** spell, which should solve the problem of transporting the metal. You may travel over our territories wherever you will, providing you all avoid our settlements. Are there questions?"

"On behalf of Njal, I wish you and your people well." Emma responded. "I understand that he was turned away when he came to your camp and that he is waiting with Grimbolt and the Princess. May I ask where Lord Nicholas is?"

"He was escorting the Princess when last I saw him. By your insane customs he is a man of consequence in his kingdom. He has been rewarded for his service."

Within an hour the liberated Amazons and Grimbolt's party were riding westward to join Alsenius' army.

XII—The Ambassador

A year after the Royal Games, a platoon of brilliantly caparisoned Amazons marched into the Arragor City flaunting the banners of the Ambassador from her Supreme Sanctity the Avatar of the Pythoness to her Majesty Queen Dowager and Regent Elsa of Arragor. Enthroned in the Great Hall with most of her nobility standing in attendance, her Royal Highness received the ambassador's herald.

A gold-clad acolyte knelt at the foot of the throne and presented the formidable credentials of Her Sanctity High Priestess Bodvarka, Ambassador Plenipotentiary. Queen Elsa accepted the documents and passed them to Lord Septimus, who stood behind her to the right. He perused them and muttered that they seemed in order. Her Royal Highness announced, "Arragor grants an audience to her Sanctity the Ambassador."

Six golden trumpets played a fanfare and her Sanctity entered like a parade, clad in a massive golden cloak which required twelve pages to carry. She progressed to the foot of the throne staircase and bowed just enough to condescend without offending. For a long silence the two women measured each other; then Bodvarka spoke: "On behalf of her Supreme Sanctity we greet your Majesty." He voice, like the whisper of scales over a path of dry leaves, carried effortlessly through the hall.

"We greet her Supreme Sanctity though your ears," the Queen answered.

The Ambassador clapped once, and the gold-clad acolyte slid up the aisle to present, on bended knee, a large silken pillow upon which rested a massive necklace: two golden serpents whose tails were designed to circle the neck of the wearer. Their two heads grasped between them a huge blazing fire agate surrounded by six two-carat stones, two diamonds, two rubies, and two emeralds.

"In token of the cordial relations between the Kingdom of Arragor and the Hegemony of the Pythoness, her Supreme Sanctity sends this NECKLACE OF PROTECTION. No missile—not even a great rock

thrown by a giant—can harm your Majesty while she wears this jewel."
She clapped her hands again, and the acolyte rose to her feet, started up
the steps to the throne, and extended the pillow.

Instantly, Lord Septimus stepped before his queen. "Have care!" he
muttered, "The . . ." He froze in place at a gesture from Bodvarka.

"Your servant presumes," the High Priestess rustled. "Shall I remove
him for you?" Her eye captured the queen's, and Elsa unthinkingly nodded.
The acolyte laid the pillow at her feet, picked up Lord Septimus, and
carried him down the stairs, depositing him at the feet of a guardsman.
"You may find some place to store him," Bodvarka murmured, fixing her
gaze upon the soldier. He carried his Lordship into an anteroom.

The queen stared fixedly at the necklace as the acolyte glided up the
remaining steps and lifted the pillow within her reach. Without looking
away from Bodvarka, she reached for the jewel. Slowly she raised it to her
throat where it parted automatically and settled itself, adjusting itself to fit
exactly the contours of her neck. "I thank you for this priceless gift." She
inclined her head and extended her hands, palm up.

"If your Majesty would grant an audience for tomorrow afternoon, I
should be grateful to rest after the rigors of my journey." Bodvarka repeated
the condescending bow, and with cloak and pages progressed toward the
door. There a servant met her and conducted the procession toward the
State Guest Suite.

The queen beckoned dreamily to Lord Crabhook. "Take Lord
Septimus to his quarters and join me in my office," she commanded. She
raised her hands to caress the necklace. "If there is no further business, this
audience is ended." She descended the steps and marched regally to her
chambers, where her maids began divesting her of her court finery.

Therese started to unclasp the necklace, but could find no fastener.
Madame, how does this new jewel unfasten? I have never seen it before."

"Oh, it's a gift from the new Ambassador from the Hegemony." She
reached back to feel for a clasp, but found none. "That's strange."

"It is too small to slide over your Majesty's head. Perhaps we should
send for one of the Ambassador's train to assist us." She stepped to he
door and sent a messenger scurrying down the hallway. The boy returned
shortly with the message, "Your Majesty has no need to remove the circ. It
will adjust itself to your comfort even while you sleep."

Queen Elsa tugged at it sharply and exclaimed, "But I don't want to
sleep in the damned thing."

"Perhaps the Ambassador can give you a magic word of unclasping in the morning."

Elsa drew blood from her neck with a vicious yank. "Ouch!" It's a hell of a gift—a magic slave collar."

At this point the guard announced Lord Crabhook. "Lord Septimus appears to be suffering from total paralysis. We have placed him on his bed and summoned Sir Grendal."

"The Ambassador cast a spell on him. Sir Grendal won't be needed." She stared at the dour lord for a moment. Finally she said, "I need your absolute discretion and loyalty, Lord Crabhook. Do I have it?"

"I know you do not enjoy my company, your Royal Highness, but I have always been a loyal subject and I can keep silence."

"I believe the new ambassador from the Hegemony has worked magic against me. She paralyzed Lord Septimus to keep him from warning me against accepting this necklace, and I now believe it is enchanted. Therese and I have been trying to remove it from my neck, and it won't come off."

"May I try, your Royal Highness?"

She nodded, and he examined the circlet closely, trying to unhitch the chain which joined the serpents' tails. He even tried to break it with his fingers. "It has no clasp. It must be magic."

"Exactly. Now, I believe it may have enchantments on it which will enable Ambassador Bodvarka to influence my decisions. I want you to get Lord Septimus out of the city as soon as he recovers from the HOLD spell. He will need transport to the Great Forest, where Prince Humber went for help."

"Lord Septimus has no love for me, nor I for him," Crabhook observed.

"You have been a pain in the arse for years, milord, but I believe you are loyal and less of a fool than you seem. Will you bury your resentment and help me save the kingdom?"

"I love the old law and customs, and I will do anything I can to preserve them. I believe Lord Septimus is a schemer, a twister of the law. He's forever changing things that are better left alone, but I will help him if you command it. Shall I go with him?"

"No. I need you here. The Priestesses must know we are not on easy terms, and I need somebody she won't bother to enchant. If Bodvarka enslaves my mind, I need you to act intelligently to save the realm. Protect Prince William and send Septimus to warn Prince Humber. If I lose control, you must do whatever seems best to protect Arragor. I fear Ambassador Bodvarka is more dangerous than an army."

Lord Crabhook knelt and kissed her hand. "I may not be overly bright, and I'm no soldier, but I'll do what I can."

"No sovereign can ask more." She raised him to his feet and turned to Therese. "If this collar is what I fear it is, you must work with Lord Crabhook to keep me from harming the realm. Whatever happens, protect Prince William."

Lord Crabhook set about his business; the Queen finished her desk work and retired to her bed. As she lay down, the circlet faded flexibly into the skin of her neck so that it seemed not to be there. Yet all night she felt its pressure on her mind.

When Crabhook returned to Septimus' quarters, he found the High Steward conscious and furious. "What do you want, Crabhook?" he demanded. "I don't have time for trivia right now."

"The Queen's commands are not trivia, Lord Steward," Crabhook snapped back.

"Forgive me, I am vexed and frightened beyond bearing. You were there in the Throne Room when that unspeakable Ambassador cast a spell to keep me from acting. The Queen was going to make a fool of herself over that bauble. Did she put it on?"

"Unfortunately yes. I have just came from her study where we both tried to remove that cursed neck piece. The Queen is fearful that is will put her mind under the Ambassador's will."

"That confirms my worst fears. And that demonic Priestess knows I'm suspicious."

"Her Royal Highness commanded me to get you on your way to the Druid's forest. You must warn the king. I have horses saddled and two guards ready to escort you. I beg you trust me to watch over the Queen while you ride out before the Ambassador stops you."

Septimus stared at Crabhook. "You actually understand the danger?"

"We have very little time. You must escape before the Ambassador gains control."

Septimus gazed intently into his eyes, then shook his head. "Somehow I must have misjudged you. You are truly loyal to the realm?"

"I am loyal o the old order. The King must be crowned and warned, and we must forget our enmity in the face of this crisis."

Septimus grasped his hand momentarily, then turned to stuff clothes and documents indiscriminately into a leather bag. "I will apologize when I return. Take care of Prince William. Where is my horse?"

They swept out of the room, and Crabhook led the way to the postern door where the guardsmen and Septimus' horse waited. "Try to talk with young Harper. He's taken over most of the Seneschal's duties since old Harper retired. Tell him to try to keep control over the Palace Guards."

"I planned to get young Harper as soon as I sent you off. I also need to catch Prince William's Tutor before the palace awakes. I'm afraid this attack has been well planned."

Septimus mounted and reached down to grasp Lord Crabhook's hand. "Take care of Elsa and be careful for yourself."

"I'm too old and unpopular for the Ambassador to bother about. Have a safe journey."

Sparks flew from the horses' shoes as Lord Septimus and his guards lunged across the plaza and off to the north. Crabhook hurried back into the palace and sought out Prince William's quarters. He found the Prince struggling with a manual of protocol while Dothokles, Royal Tutor and Governor, puttered at a work table with an experiment on motion. "Your Royal Highness did not attend the audience at which the new Ambassador from the Hegemony of the Pytheness presented herself?"

"I am excused from most of that stuff," the Prince replied. Dothokles rolled a red ball across the floor of a large flat box and carefully measured the angles at which it bounced from the sides before it collided with a blue ball. He then noted the deflection of the red ball and the track of the blue one until they came to rest.

"Nobody from the Ambassador's train has come to you?"

"Nobody usually comes to me except the guard to escort me to military lessons. They call me 'heir presumptive,' but they still treat me like a child. I might get to be king if my brother gets himself killed before he has a son, but nobody pays much attention to the understudy."

"Well, things have changed." Lord Crabhook banged on the back of the Prince's chair. "The new Ambassador gave your mother a necklace which she can't take off. Lord Septimus has fled to warn the king, and you will probably be a target for more alien magic."

William dropped his book and jumped up. "Mother's in danger?"

"We're all in danger. Nothing has happened to your mother yet, but that necklace undoubtedly gives the Ambassador magical power over her."

"Some kind of control device," the tutor interrupted. "That means the Queen's decisions may be influenced by the Ambassador."

"Exactly. I sent Septimus off because he is certainly a target for villainy. The question is whether we should get the Prince out of the palace."

"Can't I stay and help?" demanded the Prince. "I'm almost a man now, and I proved I could be helpful with Nikky."

"You have no experience against magic. Having the Queen enchanted is bad enough. If the Ambassador gets control of the heir presumptive, she might succeed in killing the Crown Prince. Then she would be completely in charge."

"You're thinking about the King's Magic." William sat down again. "If Brother died, I would be King, and the door of the Secret Treasure Room would open if I wore the King's Signet."

"Exactly. The Priestesses have the King's Signet as well as the Crown Prince's ring. The only reason nobody can get into the King's secret treasury is that your brother lacks the ring and the Priestesses don't have the King."

Dothocles rolled his ball vigorously across its box. "You said Septimus has ridden north to warn the King. I think it would be best if Prince William and I ride with his personal guards in the opposite direction. If we take refuge in the court of King Roger, we might be able to raise some support against this aggression. At least the heir presumptive would be safe."

"I'm sick of being safe. I want to get into the fight."

"And become the Ambassador's pawn." snapped Crabhook. "Remember she has magic."

Dothokles dragged the guard in from the doorway. "I relieve you of guard duty. Report to the guard captain that the Prince and I are to ride south within the hour with all of the Prince's retinue. The mission is absolutely secret. No one must know except the men actually riding with us."

The guard repeated his instructions, saluted, and trotted off. "Prince William, you will consult with Lord Crabhook while I pack your things for the journey. Make sure you have some official message from the Queen to King Roger."

"I'll go get the Queen to write something immediately." Crabhook headed for the door. "My Lord Prince, I know your courage revolts at this flight, but the brave fool often dies."

"I know. I'm sill a minor and I'm no match for magic. I'll do the best I can as an ambassador to Quatch."

"Thank you my Prince. You have made the truly brave choice." Crabhook bustled out and Prince William joined his tutor in packing.

Lord Crabhook hurried through the castle until he reached the quarters reserved for the lesser nobility. He found young Sir Archibald Harper, Master of the Palace Guards, playing chess with his Senior Captain. "You are the Seneschal's son?"

"Yes, Milord."

"And you have taken over all of his duties since he retired to the country?"

"Her Majesty has never appointed a successor to my father. In fact she has never accepted his resignation as Seneschal."

"And you have taken charge of palace security in the absence of the Seneschal?"

"Yes. Milord."

"Very well. May we speak privately?"

"Captain Manly, Senior Captain of the Guards, is my right hand. If you wish to speak concerning the security of the palace, he needs to hear."

Lord Crabhook sat. "You are aware that a new Ambassador from the Hegemony of the Pythoness arrived late this afternoon."

"We were both present at her presentation."

"Did you observe the necklace which Bodvarka gave to the Queen."

"Yes, Milord."

"And the spell which she cast on Lord Septimus to keep him from interfering?"

"I was not aware of a spell, but the Lord Steward's behavior was very strange."

"Lord Septimus tried to prevent her Majesty from accepting the necklace, and Ambassador Bodvarka cast a spell on him to keep him from warning the Queen. Unfortunately the Lord Steward was right. The necklace is enchanted so that her Royal Highness cannot remove it. We suspect it will give Bodvarka power over the Queen."

The two men stared at each other. "If that is so, it creates a unique security problem," Sir Archibald observed.

"Lord Septimus has fled northward to warn the King, and I have sent Prince William and his Tutor to take sanctuary with King Roger of Quatch."

"Very prudent." Sir Archibald studied the older man for a full minute. "Pardon my question, Milord, but what do you expect of me?"

"I can expect nothing from you, young man, but I assume you are old lord Harper's son."

"So I am, but my father has never found you particularly interested in the security of the realm."

"Your father was, in my opinion, a fumbling incompetent as Seneschal, and he's worse than useless now he occupies his office *in absentia*. The fact remains that you are *de facto* Seneschal. And the kingdom needs somebody to take responsibility for its safety. I know I am an unpopular relic of ancient grandeur. I have never been at home at court since Humber VII started changing everything, and therefore nobody likes me. But that's not the point. At this moment I'm preparing to face a foreign menace alone, and I need you and anybody else who will stand for the kingdom against the Pythoness. Will you swallow your dislike and help?" His lordship wanted to stamp his foot and bellow, but he kept his voice steady and quiet.

"What do you want us to do? Try to arrest the Ambassador?"

"Kill her, if you think you can beat her magic. You control the guards. Do whatever you can do to keep your men and the army loyal. I'm trying to figure out ways to keep Bodvarka away from the Royal Magic. The queen may be ensorceled into working for the enemy. I'm going to try to gather a core of loyal courtiers. I need you to do the same for the military. Ordinarily I wouldn't trust Septimus with a used bum wipe, but I'm sure he's on our side in this. He'll get to the King if anybody can. Prince William is a spoiled child, but I am trusting him to appeal for help to the south. At least I've got him out of danger. What can you do?"

"I can talk to the High Priest. He can probably strengthen the men against magic. Manly, go rout the old man out of bed and beg him to join us."

The Senior Captain dashed out. "I assume the Ambassador is going to start trouble in the morning. We need to do everything we can tonight."

"That was my guess, too."

"Let's persuade the High Priest to visit the Queen tonight and strengthen her against the magic as far as he can. Then I'll muster the guards and have him bless them. I'd better send a messenger to General Bludger. He's never fought a battle, but he looks very impressive in his uniform and he can really bellow at the men. I thought old Plotz was a fool, but at least he was courageous. Still, maybe we can get Bludger to muster the army for a blessing. We'd better call him." He opened the door and sent the sentry to fetch the general.

"I would guess that assassination won't work," Crabhook went on. "Those Priestesses are magically armored, and they always PURIFY what they eat and drink. If we had an Assassins Guild in Arragor, I would try to hire one, though using evil, even to cure evil, corrupts the psyche. If we hadn't gone soft on fornication, impiety, and embezzlement, we wouldn't be vulnerable to the Pythoness now."

"You really are a relic, aren't you? I haven't heard that word *fornication* since I was a kid. Everybody likes a nimble tumble once in a while, but you don't want to get stuck for life just because you plug a leak."

"And a bit of your soul dribbles away with every tumble. My wife is a very difficult woman to live with, but we made a contract for life and we both trust each other because we know that oath is still intact. Our estate prospers because we are both honest in all things. We don't cheat over money; we don't cheat over confidences, and we don't cheat in our marriage. A man who will cheat on the most intimate of contracts will cheat in all things."

"But I have made no contracts with the girls I've plugged."

"The very act is a contract between you and the woman and her children."

Young Harper smiled tolerantly at the older man and changed the subject. "Do you think we can trust old Farsyte?"

"He has the mind of a child, but I trust his heart. He'll be little help in plotting, but he's loyal to his Guardian and his kingdom."

"It's the same with the General. I'd trust him to die for his Queen, but unfortunately we need someone to stay alive and beat the enemy."

At this point Captain Manly returned with Lord Farsyte. The High Priest had thrown on a loose robe over his night shirt and he seemed still half asleep. "Perhaps," Manly suggested, "I should brew up a pot of tea."

"Good idea," Harper responded, "and you might find some tea cakes in the cupboard."

"Oh dear, I do believe a cup of tea would help focus my wits." The High Priest sank into a chair near the fire. "The nights are getting brisk." He arranged his robe over his knees and stretched his hands to the heat. "Manly tells me that you think the Ambassador is up to no good."

"You saw what she did to Septimus."

"I presume it was a **HOLD** spell. I trust the Lord Steward has recovered."

"We have got him out of the country to protect him," answered Lord Crabhook.

"Probably a good idea. These Priestesses are a very nasty bunch, and Septimus has interfered with some very disagreeable plots. You know they turned that Zharkovian eunuch into a hound. Septimus was very angry with them about that."

"You do realize that they were using that concert to cast a mass spell over our people."

"Oh, yes. Lord Nicholas really queered that spell for them. He changed the music and made the spell turn back on the casters. A very clever bit of musicianship." He extended his hand for a cup, and almost drained it at one slurp. "Oh, that was just what I needed." He held his cup for a refill. "I suppose you realize that necklace Septimus was trying to make the Queen refuse is enchanted."

"I know. She can't take it off." Lord Crabhook sipped. "That's what this meeting is about."

A knock at the door announced the arrival of General Bludger. As soon as he was seated and provided with a cup, Lord Crabhook summarized what they knew of the problem. The General cleared his throat several times. "You have notified the King; you have sent Prince William out of the country; you are planning to protect the Queen's guards magically as far as you can. Ahem! You plan to bless the army in hopes that will neutralize any generalized spells. But the army should not be used as a police force because thieves and murderers won't stand up and fight. Therefore, it seems to me the best thing for the army to do is get out of town and deploy on the border of the Hegemony. Ahem! The trouble is, the priestesses use women as soldiers—call them Amazons. It's damned unfair to expect my soldiers to fight women; their training has always been either to rape them or take care of them—sometimes both. Ahem! Bad show, really ramming a sword into a perfectly good lay. Well, can't be helped. We have to fight the army that's sent against us." He drained his cup and stood up. "I can't do anything about the menace inside the city; that's your problem. I will have the whole army drawn up in formation at 0800, and you and your priests can go through the motions of blessing them. After that I'll march them westward to the border and try to get them ready to face a damned batch of fighting women." He pushed back his chair and headed for the door muttering under his breath about the difference between stabbing a woman with a spear and raping her. "They mustn't take time for the wrong kind of stabbing."

"I thought an army was supposed to have an information gathering division," Crabhook grumbled. "How do they find out what to attack?"

"Theirs not to reason who: Just march out and do and do." Young Harper made an obscene gesture on 'do.'

"I'm afraid the army is worse off than we are," said Lord Farsyte. "At least we can pray." He yawned and adjusted his robe again. "Now, if there's no more urgent business, I should like to return to my bed. I don't want to fall asleep in the middle of blessing the army." He drained his cup and dragged himself from his chair. "Just as a precaution, let me cast a protection spell which should keep Bodvarka out of your minds for the rest of the night." He steadied himself and pronounced a blessing, then followed the guardsman who carried a light to guide him to his chambers.

"An impossible bore," sighed Crabhook, "but at least he's on our side."

"I think his advice is sound. We all need to rest if we're to have our wits about us in the morning. Do you need Manly to guide you back to your rooms."

"No, I can find my way around the palace blindfolded." Lord Crabhook let himself out.

Harper leaned back in his chair. "How that old hedgehog survived into old age, I'll never know."

"He's as charming as a patch of poison oak," Manly replied, "but he's stubborn. Since he's on the right side, at least we can count on him." He yawned again. "It's time we turned in. I'll call you early in the morning."

"I suppose I really am acting Seneschal," sighed Archibald. "It seems strange the Queen has never appointed anyone to take Father's place." He doused all the lamps but the little one he carried to his bedchamber.

Early in the morning, before the court was awake, General Bludger mustered his army on the Parade Ground a mile from the palace. Lord Farsyte, the High Priest, solemnly blessed the assembly, including in his blessing a mass resistence to magic. Sir Archibald Harper strode through a superficial inspection and dismissed the men. The general gave the order to march, and the entire force was on its way yo the western border before the Queen yawned her way to breakfast.

Lord Crabhook joined her and reported that the Lord Steward had departed on a mission to seek His Majesty at the Great Forest. "Does your Royal Highness intend to appoint an interim Lord Steward to keep the palace in order during Lord Septimus' absence?"

"Would you be so kind as to serve for the present?"

"I should be honored." The new Lord Steward bowed ceremoniously. They were, at this point, joined by Sir Archibald and Captain Manly, who reported that the Palace Guard had been blessed by the High Priest. Sir Archibald asked. "Has your Royal Highness seen Prince William this morning? The Senior Guard Captain reports that he, his guards, and his tutor are all absent from the royal quarters."

Queen Elsa stared at her Steward for a moment. "I assigned the Prince to your care, Lord Crabhook."

"He is, to the best of my knowledge traveling with his most trusted servants to a place of safety in accordance with your Royal Highness' instructions." Lord Crabhook answered. "Under the present circumstances it was deemed inexpedient for him to remain idle in the palace, where he seemed in danger of encountering immoral influences."

"His Tutor is in charge of the traveling arrangements?"

"Yes, your Royal Highness."

"Then I can rest easy on his account. Have provisions been made for entertaining the Ambassador?"

"She expressed no displeasure at her accommodations. She will, no doubt, speak more in detail at the royal audience this morning."

"I see your Majesty is still wearing the Ambassador's necklace," Harper observed.

"We have not succeeded in removing it. The attempt was rather painful." She moved her fingers cautiously over the scabs on her neck.

Manly asked, "May I examine it, your Majesty? I'll make no attempt to remove it."

The Queen nodded, and he studied it for several minutes. "There is no doubt that the clasp is magically hidden. Unless Lord Farsyte can create a NULL MAGIC ZONE to work in, I believe it would be unwise to meddle."

It was almost noon when word came from the Throne Room that the Ambassador was approaching. "I shall wait until I until a messenger officially informs me that the ambassador desires an audience. I mustn't seem to be worried or eager. You gentlemen shall accompany me. I wish I had Septimus."

The messenger was not long in coming, and the Queen delayed to arrange her attire for about half an hour before she sent Therese to announce her royal approach. Bodvarka stood easily near the foot of the throne and bowed her minimum obeisance as Elsa ascended the steps and sat. "We trust you rested well."

"The accommodations are adequate." Bodvarka responded.

"We appreciate the beauty of the necklace which you brought us," said Queen Elsa but we were distressed to discover that we could not remove it."

"The necklace is not designed to be removed," Bodvarka smiled. "It is designed for comfort, as my messenger informed you, even at night. You suffered no discomfort while you slept."

"It scratched my neck when I tried to take it off."

"It will do that." Bodvarka smiled more broadly. "It is designed to be worn at all times, and it will resist any attempt to remove it. There are blades magically embedded in the gems. They extend upon command or upon any attempt to remove the necklace. In fact, if someone tried to break it open, the blades could even pierce deeply enough to remove the head." She muttered a syllable, and Elsa felt pinpricks from the necklace. This necklace is called THE CIRC OF OBEDIENCE. The prototype was first used in training animals, but Her Sublime Holiness, the Avatar, designed this one especially for the training of humans. Let me demonstrate."

She pointed a finger at Queen Elsa and commanded, "You will immediately order the execution of your presumptuous High Steward, Lord Septimus." There was a dramatic pause; then the Ambassador spoke a syllable, and the necklace drew blood from the Queen's neck and throat. "You will give the command for the execution within two minutes." Bodvarka turned away and sat down on a convenient chair and watched the blood trickle over the Queen's dress. When Elsa grabbed the necklace to ease the pain, the blades sank in slightly further.

"So long as you remain disobedient, the pain will continue. To try to remove the Circ will increase it. As soon as I hold Lord Septimus' head in my hands, the pain will cease, and it will be possible to cure you." Bodvarka tapped her foot gently.

Lord Crabhook stepped forward and knelt before the Ambassador. "Please, your Grace, the command cannot be carried out. We discovered this morning that Lord Septimus has fled the court."

"Where has the scoundrel gone?" Bodvarka stood so suddenly that Lord Crabhook ended up on the floor.

"I don't know," Queen Elsa gasped. "My messenger found his chambers empty when they summoned him to council."

"The Lord Steward was ever mindful of his own safety." Crabhook scrambled to his feet and retreated. "I have often advised her Majesty to remove him from office."

"You were always jealous of his abilities," Elsa snapped back.

"He was ever greedy for power. He prevented me from being promoted to Lord Seneschal when Lord Harper retired."

Bodvarka observed the tension between Lord Crabhook and his sovereign. "Lord Septimus and you were not on the best of terms?"

"Lord Crabhook resented my husband's respect for Lord Septimus' judgment." The Queen fluttered her hands helplessly around her throat.

Bodvarka gestured toward the Queen and muttered. The blades of the circ retracted and the gashes in her neck closed. She muttered a CLEAN cantrip, and the bloodstains vanished from the royal dress. "I will not punish you for this disobedience, but this demonstration of my power should suffice. I command you to appoint this faithful servant to the post of Lord Steward." She paused. "Did Lord Septimus abscond with the chain of office?"

"No, your Grace," Crabhook answered. "I found it on his desk when I went to his chambers." He pulled the massive gold chain from his pouch and displayed it."

Bodvarka pointed her finger again at the Queen. "You will take the chain of office and appoint Lord Crabhook as Lord Steward."

Crabhook knelt before his sovereign and extended the chain. She took it and glared down at him. "We designate you, Lord Crabhook, as our High Steward. In token of your rank, I bestow upon you the chain of office." She dropped the chain over his bowed head and sat down again. Lord Crabhook stood, bowed deeply, and retreated to his position a step below the throne on the right side.

"Now," said Bodvarka, "We can get on with the important business of the realm. Lord Steward, your first assignment is to remove all the boxes of stores from the basement store room designated on this map of the palace. Our Priestesses have memorized that room as a place to which they can **TELEPORT**. Your predecessor filled the room in hope of destroying anyone who **TELEPORTED** in."

"Yes, your Sanctity." The new High Steward scuttled out of the throne room.

"And now, your Majesty, we come to the important business. We understand that you have not been able to access the Royal Magic of the realm because you have lost the King's signet."

"The king's signet was stolen from our study and has not been recovered."

"Further evidence of the incompetence of the late High Steward." Bodvarka allowed herself a small gloat. "Before I came to your court, I was able to apprehend the thief, and obtain the signet ring from her. You will, therefore, now be able to access the King's Treasury and to use the magic. Our intelligence officers have failed to learn the exact nature of the Royal Magic, but we understand it is of considerable potence."

"The Kings of Arragor never divulge the nature of the Royal Magic," Elsa confessed. "The information, along with access to the King's Treasury, is magically imparted to the rightful King at his coronation. He can, then, use his signet to enter the chamber and use the magic."

"Your husband, King Humber VII is dead, and his eldest son, Prince Humber, has, I believe, disappeared."

"Yes."

"Then why has not your younger son been crowned?"

"Because the Royal Signet and scepter refuse to recognize him."

Bodvarka betrayed impatience at such nonsense. All you have to do is crown him; then they will recognize him. I should think your fool of a High Priest would realize that."

"Lord Farsyte says he cannot crown anybody whom the scepter rejects."

"But you have been throwing the Scepter around for years. You're notorious for breaking up the furniture with it."

"It will function as a weapon for anybody—at least anybody of royal blood—but it will do no other magic except for the lawful sovereign." Queen Elsa felt the first glimmer of hope, since the Ambassador seemed to know very little about the Royal Magic. Furthermore she had said nothing of Grimbolt's return. "I can get no satisfaction from Lord Farsyte. All he tells me is that my son still lives, and no one else can be crowned."

"It seems that your High Priest is nearly as stupid as the Arch Priestess of the Hegemony. She has botched the operation so badly that her Sublime Holiness, the Pythoness Incarnate, sent me to straighten things out."

"You don't come from the Hegemony?"

"No. The Arch Priestess bungled the enchantment of your son, magically aged herself into senility, and came dangerously close to TELEPORTING herself into that room your High Steward filed with boxes. Once I have settled this mess in your kingdom, I am certain I shall be appointed Arch Priestess in her place."

"Then it really was the Arch Priestess of the Hegemony who murdered my husband and carried off my son?"

"Now that you are wearing the Circ, I suppose there's no danger in telling you. Apparently your husband was a stubborn fool. He defied the Arch Priestess when she offered him an alliance. When she approached your son, he refused to replace the King. Her plan was to kill King Humber and so enchant the prince that he would do her bidding. Apparently the Prince had some form of magical resistance which caused her spell to mal-function. She thought he was dead, and, since she intended to subdue his will and put him on the throne, she needed him alive. So she cast a REINCARNATE spell to bring him back as a bear. Because he wasn't actually dead and his magical protection was still imperfectly functioning, she suffered extreme aging and fell unconscious. He became a half-human monster and fled beyond her power to trace him."

"And that's why Lord Farsyte can't crown young William. All the coronation magic still recognizes Prince Humber as the rightful heir."

"I shall probably have to replace Lord Farsyte as High Priest of Arragor. In fact, that's is my next command. Summon him now and demote him."

"I don't think I have the power to replace the High Priest," Elsa protested. "I'm only Queen-Regent."

Bodvarka stood in preparation for another point. The Queen clutched her throat and cried, "I'll try! I'll try! Don't jab me with that necklace again. I'll do my best, but don't blame me if I fail."

"Very well, summon him immediately. If I have to I can kill the old goat."

Queen Elsa called a messenger and sent him to fetch the High Priest. Then they settled back to await his arrival. Shortly afterward Lord Crabhook bustled in.

"Your Grace, all the boxes are being moved out, and the room is being prepared as an indoor drying room when it rains on laundry day. That way nobody will put anything in there except on a rainy Monday."

"Why not just keep it empty?"

"Because an empty room is always a temptation to young people. Since there's always danger of somebody coming in with laundry and surprising them, they'll find some place else to couple."

"I suppose we can teach the priestesses not to TELEPORT on Mondays," Bodvarka grumbled.

"They could learn to scry before they came," Elsa remarked.

"Not all of my colleagues are foresighted or careful. If they were, I would not have been sent to subdue your realm. This part of the continent was supposed to have been brought to heel two years ago; instead, the Hegemony is still bickering with four independent kingdoms while half the area is given over to chaos. We are behind schedule in practically all areas. Her Sublime Holiness is highly displeased."

"Why not just leave us alone?" asked the Queen.

"The Pythoness cannot become the supreme Guardian unless she subdues the earthbound kingdoms. The Guardians draw much of their strength from the humanoid races."

"But the other Guardians leave us pretty much alone."

"That's why we shall overcome them. My Lady Pythoness will absorb all the life energy of the world and become supreme."

The queen felt nervously at her throat and gave up the argument.

"What becomes of the rest of us when the Pythoness absorbs all the energy?" Lord Crabhook asked.

"Oh, I'm sure she'll find something to do with you. After all, you do produce psychic energy whenever you experience extreme pain or pleasure, and she will always need plenty of that. Extreme pain produces more energy, but tends to destroy the source. We also have techniques for stimulating extreme sexual pleasure, which is very productive of energy. You will all be assigned whatever tasks produce the most useful energy, and we holy Servants will always need servants."

"So we are to become slaves."

"Oh no! Slaves are compelled to serve against their will, but our servants will have no desire except to serve. You will rejoice to do what we decide you want to do." She turned scornfully back to the Queen. "Your majesty, for instance, will learn from the collar to perceive what I desire before I command it. Thus what I will becomes your most intense desire."

Elsa shuddered.

Bodvarka smiled. "Since Crown Prince Humber is either dead or incapable of ascending the throne, and the Queen-Regent is unable to use the Royal Magic, it is time to crown a monarch who can. You will now summon Prince William. It is our intention to have him crowned immediately."

"But the Prince is not yet of age," Queen Elsa objected. "I would still be Queen-Regent, and he would not be able to use the magic until he comes of age."

"I'm sure we can change any laws which stand in the way. If nothing else works, you will appoint me regent, and I will bend the magic of this kingdom to my will. You will send for the prince now." She glared at Elsa and pursed her mouth to utter her magic syllables.

Lord Crabhook quickly interrupted. "I will go to the Prince at once, your Excellency. It may take some time to get him dressed for a court appearance."

"I have no interest in his attire. I want his body here. **NOW!**"

Lord Crabhook scuttled out.

Bodvarka's face relaxed again into a smile as she turned back to the Queen. "It happens that the king's signet ring has come into my hands. Therefore it will be a simple matter to crown your son and place the signet upon his finger. You do recognize the ring." She drew the Royal Signet from her belt pouch and held it before Elsa's face."

"I recognize the ring, but I assure you that the ring will not recognize Prince William. Like the royal scepter, it is attuned to my husband and to his eldest son. Those royal artifacts will serve no one but the rightful king."

"And when we crown him Prince William will be the rightful king."

"I have tried to explain to you that coronation is only possible if the scepter accepts the candidate. At Prince Humber's birth, the King forcibly took him away from me and presented him to the people and to the scepter, the crown, and the ring. If we try to crown Prince William, the ceremony will fail because Prince Humber is still alive."

"Balderdash! I can overrule such local magic. As soon as I have the Prince and the High Priest here, we can proceed with the coronation. You!" She pointed imperiously at Captain Manly. "Have the court assembled in the Throne Room within the hour. We shall have the coronation ceremony this afternoon, and I will have control of the Royal Magic by supper time."

"Yes, your Excellence." Manly bowed to the Ambassador and sent several messengers about the palace.

"You, as Queen-Regent, will issue such commands as are necessary to the accomplishment of our will. You will also make the young king understand that our will is his command unless he wants me as his Regent. As soon as the coronation is accomplished, you will guide us to the King's Treasury where King William will use the Royal Signet to open the door for me. You understand?"

"I understand and will have to obey as far as I am able, but it won't work." Elsa volunteered no information about the Crown Prince's whereabouts. Nor did she confide that the scepter she held in her hand was a carefully crafted fake. She saw no way to defeat Bodvarka, but at least she could play for time in case fate had something unexpected up her sleeve.

The guard tapped on the door and admitted Lord Crabhook, who was wearing his most imbecilic and confused expression. "You Royal Highness," he ignored Bodvarka, "I went to Prince William's suite to summon him, but he isn't there."

"Well, find him and fetch him," demanded Bodvarka.

"Where is he?" His Lordship looked blankly at the Queen.

"Didn't you ask his tutor or his guards?" Queen Elsa asked.

"I couldn't ask them. They're not there either."

Bodvarka's voice dropped dangerously. "The prince is not there? His tutor and guards are all gone? Find them!"

"How? The Lord Steward has fled. The Lord Seneschal has retired to his southern estates. There's nobody in the Prince's suite." Lord Crabhook wrung his hands helplessly."

"I instructed you to provide for Prince William's safety," Queen Elsa rebuked him.

"I was very careful to instruct his Tutor to double the guard and take special care of the Prince because your Royal Highness was afraid the Ambassador might harm him. I was very careful to make sure his Tutor knew the Prince was in danger."

"You cretin!" Bodvarka howled. "You frightened his Tutor so badly he must have run off with the boy and his guards. Who commands the guards? You?" She pointed at Captain Manly.

"I am the palace Guard Captain, but the Prince's private guards have their own commander who reports directly to Sir Archibald Harper."

"Then summon him. I want to know where Prince William has gone."

"Yes, your Sublime Excellence." Lord Crabhook dithered out.

The ambassador glowered at the queen for a full minute, then demanded, "Hand me that scepter."

"The scepter will respond only to a member of the royal family."

Bodvarka advanced threateningly. "I ordered you to hand me the scepter. I can master any protective magic." She raised her finger and started to mumble orders. Queen Elsa obediently crept down the stairs, extending the scepter toward her enemy. Bodvarka gestured impatiently and the royal mace flew obediently to a point inches form her hand and hung motionless while she examined it. The queen quickly retreated to her throne.

The ambassador gestured at the scepter, and her expression changed from haughty irritation to wrath. She pointed and spoke unintelligible syllables. Queen Elsa felt the blades of her collar jabbing again at her throat. "Where is the scepter?"

Elsa grabbed her throat and pointed.

"Don't quibble with me." Bodvarka increased the pressure of the circ. "This is a very well crafted fake. It has no magical properties. Where is the true scepter."

Bleeding, Elsa sank back on the throne and choked out, "Humber."

Bodvarka eased the blades of the circ and bored in verbally. "You mean the Crown Prince has the scepter? He has come back?"

Elsa curled up in the throne and whimpered. "Stop it!"

The ambassador pointed again, and the blades retracted. "You will tell me everything you know or I'll keep you on the brink of death for a week. Where is the scepter? Where is the Crown Prince? Where is Prince William? Where is that worm of a steward? You say that the Crown Prince has the Scepter? How did he get it?"

"I threw it at him, thinking he was a monster attacking Prince William. He put out his arm to protect his head, and the Scepter forced itself into his hand."

"And you assumed it had accepted him."

"It conferred protection against spells, which it never did for me. It converted itself into whatever weapon Prince Humber wanted to use. My husband always used it as a sword; the Crown Prince prefers a staff. For the rightful king, the Scepter becomes his weapon."

"If Crown Prince Humber is here, why are you still Regent?"

"He isn't here. He went north to the Great Forest. He thinks the Druid can help him."

"Help him?"

"He's lost his memory and he's been horribly transformed. You ought to know. It was your priestess that did it."

"That monstrous senility! The Pythoness will take care of her." Bodvarka glared murderously at Queen Elsa. "The Crown Prince is away in the north with the scepter; Prince William has run away with his guards and his tutor; Lord Septimus has run away to warn the Crown Prince. Where is the Princess of Quatch?"

"She fled the court. Lord Septimus tricked her into fleeing north to the Great Forest. I think she is with my son."

"Married?"

"I don't know. They were not married when they left. They don't like each other."

"They ran off together because of their dislike? Is this whole nation insane?"

"I know I'm on the edge," Elsa sobbed. "Life at court used to ne so comfortable."

Bodvarka abruptly changed course. "You have tried to use the king's signet to enter the King's Treasury?"

"Both Prince William and I tried before the ring was stolen. The royal signet will only work for the true King." Elsa nervously fingered the Circ and felt a sharp pain jab her finger.

"Do not try to loosen he Circ." Bodvarka cautioned, "It is ever alert."

Lord Crabhook blundered in leading Sir Archibald. The Ambassador immediately demanded, "Are you responsible for Prince William's guards?"

"Their captain reports to me, but only as a matter of courtesy. In the absence of the Lord Seneschal, the captain is sole commander of Prince William's guards. Of course, the Queen Regent has overriding authority over the whole kingdom, but she normally leaves the prince's safety to the professionals."

"Where is the prince?"

"His guard captain reported to me last evening that he believed the prince was in danger. I believe the Tutor and the Guard Captain planned to take refuge in Quatch. The captain said he was instructed to invoke our alliance with King Roger against an expected attack by the Hegemony."

"How dare he accuse the Hegemony? I am here as a friendly Ambassador."

"I suppose he acted on instructions from Lord Septimus. I am told his Lordship has fled to the north. The Army has marched to protect the western border. If your Excellence is not at war with us, somebody had better make a peace proclamation."

Bodvarka turned furiously toward the Queen. "You will proclaim a firm alliance with the Hegemony of the Pythoness immediately," she commanded. "You will recall the army and Prince William's guard." She pointed directly at Queen Elsa. "I command your immediate compliance."

At this point the guard knocked and showed in a messenger.

"Where is the High Priest?" demanded Bodvarka.

"His Grace says he won't come. He says he has wrapped the Temple in a protective spell which he will not leave." He turned away from the Ambassador to the Queen. "He says your Majesty may visit him in the protection of the temple."

Bodvarka leaped to her feet and gestured at the messenger, who screamed and dropped to the floor in pain.

"You can't do that!" yelled Queen Elsa. "You can't punish him for just telling you what the High Priest says. Stop it!" She bolted down the steps of the throne and grabbed the Ambassador by the shoulder. Bodvarka knocked her hand away and bellowed a command at the Circ, which jabbed Elsa cruelly.

Lord Crabhook pulled a dagger from a sheath in his boot and flung it with deadly accuracy at Bodvarka' breast. The missile stopped a hair's breadth from her gown and quivered, embedded in her invisible armor. She gestured at him and spoke a few words of command, and he froze in his place. "I can do what I will." She glared down at the screaming boy and Queen. Presently they dropped into unconsciousness, and she realized she was no closer to killing the High Priest.

The guard opened the door and rushed to his mistress' side. "Your Majesty!" He stared at her bloody throat and dashed for the door. "I'll fetch Sir Grendal." He raced down the corridor shouting "Help her Majesty! Sir Grendal help! Captain!"

"Within moments Therese and Captain Manly with drawn sword dashed through the door followed by reserve guards. Therese rushed to her mistress and frantically attempted to staunch the flow of blood from the Circ. Manly thrust his sword into Bodvarka's side, piercing even her magical armor with his attack. Without thinking Bodvarka evoked a **FLAME STRIKE** from her wand which seriously burned Captain Manly and in the process set fire to the carpet and the furniture near him. Heedless of his own anguish, the Captain thrust again, drawing blood from Bodvarka's breast.

By this time the guards had surrounded her. Most of their swords were stopped by her armor, but a deflected blow to her head so jolted her in spite of her invisible helm that she staggered and fell to the floor. Immediately the rest of the guards fell upon her in a bruising pile. From this position she was unable to cast spells, so that she was quickly subdued.

Into this confusion strode Sir Grendal, the Court Physician. He hastened to the fallen Queen. "Who in blazes put this thing on her? Go get a blacksmith."

"It's magical," Therese objected. "You can't get it off without killing her."

"Well if you don't get it off it certainly will kill her. These blades are deadly."

"Release me at once," Bodvarka demanded, "or I'll cut her head off."

"Turn that damned thing off, or I'll cut your throat." Captain Manly slid his blade into an opening at the gorget of her armor and started to thrust."

Fearing for her life, Bodvarka gave the command to retract the blades of the Circ. Sir Grendal began to bathe and bandage the gashes in Elsa's neck. The guards started to unpile themselves from the Ambassador, but Manly stayed them. "Cancel the rest of your magic." he gestured toward the fallen messenger and the immobile Crabhook. "And I think I'll take charge of this." he picked up her wand frm the floor. Even through the metal and leather of his gauntlet gloves, he felt a wave of anguish. He managed to endure the pain long to enough carry the wand to the queen's desk, where he dropped it.

"Your stupid messenger will be all right when he wakes up. My **ANGUISH** spell has run out. I'll release the idiot Crabhook. You'll have to put out the fires yourselves."

"I demand that you cure her Majesty." interrupted Sir Grendal. "Those gashes are dangerous, and they will take a long time to heal naturally."

"And you'd better do something about my burns," added Manly, busily smothering the burning floor with the carpet." Then he turned back to the guards who were rising from Bodvarka. "Tie that vixen up before you do anything else," he directed, "and if she starts to cast spells, gag her." He smothered a burning chair with the woolen table cover.

"You will release me," Bodvarka demanded. "I can speak the word that kills her before you can gag me."

"And they'll kill you before you can do any more harm," the Queen retorted. "It might be worth getting killed if it put an end to you."

"My mistress would rescue my body from your grasp and bring me back, so it will hardly be an end of me." She looked uncomfortably at the drawn swords surrounding her. "Though I confess, dying is not a pleasant experience. Perhaps we can come to some agreement." She spoke a word to release Lord Crabhook.

"The trouble is, your word isn't worth the air it costs to speak it," Queen Elsa observed. "As soon as we let you go, you can control me with this Circ. I tell you what I'll do. I will promise to release you and to treat you with the respect due to a genuine Ambassador if you remove this Circ from my neck and promise to behave like an Ambassador instead of a conqueror."

Bodvarka squirmed under the weight of two remaining guardsmen. "Unfortunately the Circ is much easier to put on than to put off. My mistress did not teach me the spell which opens the Circ. Your release did not enter into her plans for Arragor." She smiled patronizingly. "Your term of servitude to the Pythoness has no end. Even if I am dead, you cannot remove the Circ without decapitation, and even if you succeeded in killing me before I could speak, my mistress, when she rescues my body, will speak the words which control the Circ. Your only hope is to trust my mercy. Release me and we will negotiate the surrender of your kingdom to the Pythoness without rancor and pain."

Manly had been frantically fumbling Bodvarka's invisible armor in search of a release catch. At last his fingers found the catch and he quickly stripped off her armor, leaving her vulnerable to the cross bows which the guards now aimed at her. Lord Crabhook moved to murmur in the

Queen's ear, "I believe we can kill her before she can speak the magic words. With her out of the way, we at least have time to act before any rescue force can come."

"Wait," she whispered.

"Do I have your word that you will not allow me to be attacked while we negotiate?" Bodvarka demanded.

"You will cure my wounds and clean my clothes." answered the Queen. "If you speak a hostile word or activate any magical item, my soldiers will make you into a porcupine. If you make no attempt to harm anyone, we will discuss the stand-off."

The Ambassador quickly cured the gashes on Elsa's neck and removed all traces of blood from her clothes. She even cured Captain Manly's burns and gashes. "You are surprisingly courageous and resourceful for a man," she remarked. "I don't suppose you could be persuaded to change mistresses? A High Priestess of the Pythoness can fulfill your every desire."

The Captain turned his back to avoid her gaze.

The guard at the study door knocked and then showed in a young temple acolyte. "Brother Tam comes from his Grace," the guard announced.

The acolyte slipped hastily into the room and pinned a small golden button to the Ambassador's gown. He stepped quickly away from her and knelt before the Queen. "Your Majesty, Lord Farsyte urges you to take immediate refuge in the Temple. He told me to pin that button on the Ambassador. He cast a **SILENCE** spell on it so that she won't be able to cast any spells or even make any noise for half an hour. You can leave the room without her hurting you with magic."

"You have done nobly, Sir Tam. I will heed the counsel of the High Priest. Lord Crabhook, you are empowered to negotiate for me. I am trusting you with the fate of the realm." She picked up her crown from the desk and set it carefully on her head. She nodded politely to Bodvarka, whose mouth uttered silent maledictions, and strode past her into the hallway. Brother Tam—still wondering whether she had really knighted him—followed her, and the guard firmly closed the door.

Bodvarka tried frantically to get her bound hands on the button and continued her silent cursing. Manly placed an upholstered stool behind her and gestured an invitation to sit. Lord Crabhook approached, unpinned the button, and silently carried it to the far corner of the room. Bodvarka's fulminations burst on their ears. When he had moved back out of the range of the Silence spell, he interrupted. "Your Grace, we are now free to discuss any business which The Hegemony wishes to transact with the Kingdom of Arragor."

While she continued to scream, he instructed one of the soldiers, "Go pick up that button and stay in the corner. If you see any sign that the Ambassador is casting a spell, you are to fling yourself upon her, so as to stop the spell. Do you understand? You won't be able to hear or speak while you hold the button."

The soldier saluted. "I understand." Then he marched to the corner and picked up the button.

When Bodvarka finally paused for breath, his Lordship quietly suggested, "I am instructed to negotiate. Her Royal Highness is safe in the Temple, even though she still wears your slave collar. I believe the temple is adequately protected from your magic. Have you any proposals to present?"

"Come! Immediately!" Bodvarka shouted before the soldier with the button could act.

"I gather that you are wearing a device to summon aid," Lord Crabhook said. "Is someone **TELEPORTING** into the laundry drying room?"

"You will regret this defiance," she roared. "Even if you silence me, my sister Priestesses will find me."

"Oh, dear!" His Lordship clasped his hands anxiously. "I suppose the reinforcements are **TELEPORTING**."

"They will be in that room you cleared before you can do anything about it."

"More than one? Oh, that is very bad—**very bad**." He turned to Manly. "Captain, will you send some men to the **TELEPORT** Room to take care of the problem?" He signaled the soldier with the button to approach."

"Swordsmen or bowmen, sir?"

Bodvarka began another incantation, and the soldier with the button jumped in. As the silence spell reached them, Crabhook pulled Manly to the back of the room. "Not soldiers, my boy, footmen with mops and pails. When I had the boxes taken out of the room, I had them string wires throughout the space. A quick scrying of the room will reveal that the boxes are gone, but only a minute inspection will discover the wires. When the Priestesses **TELEPORT** in, the wires will occupy the same space that parts of their bodies occupy, and the tiny explosions will slice them

up. With the SILENCE spell covering Bodvarka, she can't call off the
TELEPORT."

The Captain left the room and hurried to the servants' wing to gather
recruits. By the time they reached the TELEPORT room, the wires had
explosively blended with the flesh of the Priestesses, spattering ecclesiastical
fragments from floor to ceiling. Manly instructed his gagging crew to
replace the wires before they attempted their grisly cleanup.

"Can you tell how many bodies there are?" Manly asked the lead
footman.

"We've found five hands, sir. That ought to mean three bodies, but
there's enough blood for a platoon. It looks like they was all women. Seems
like an awful waste, sir."

"Find a Priest when you have them all cleaned up. We ought to
provide a civilized cremation. I'll ask the Ambassador if she can give me
their names. It's hard to send them off properly without knowing who
they were." Manly left the footmen to their work and headed back to the
Queen's study. When he arrived, he found Lord Crabhook still weathering
Bodvarka's storm of curses and threats.

"The cleaning crew say they have five hands," he said casually. "That
probably means three Priestesses Teleported in."

Bodvarka stopped on mid-obscenity.

"Do you happen to know their names, ma'am? I hate to cremate them
without knowing who they are."

"Three?" The Ambassador seemed on the brink of explosion. "Dead?
I checked that room myself, and all the boxes were gone."

"Perhaps they didn't make allowance for air pressure," suggested Lord
Crabhook.

"The footmen are making the room exactly as it was before the
accident," Manly reported. "They found no wreckage of boxes in there."

"You incompetent imbecile," she screamed at Lord Crabhook. "You
must have left something in there." Then she glared more closely at the
bland innocense of his face. "You cringing, fox-hearted mammal. What
did you put in there?"

"There wasn't any laundry in there," he protested. "The weather has
been beautifully clear all day."

Bodvarka's voice dropped an octave. "What, you unmitigated idiot,
was in that room."

"Nothing."

"There had to be something in there." She mastered her rage with super-human effort. "Three of my sister Priestesses were dismembered because they Teleported into a room where something else occupied the space their bodies tried to occupy. What was in the room?"

Lord Crabhook looked as stupid as possible. Captain Manly intervened, "Perhaps she means the wire strung up to hang clothes on when it rains."

"You strung wires in there?"

"Of course. You can't hang clothes without wires or lines. We prefer wires because line always stretches when it gets wet and then the clothes drag on the floor."

"I don't care a fart about your laundering habits, I told you to have that room empty."

"But we didn't hang any . . ."

Bodvarka began mumbling under her breath, but the soldier with the button was alert and flung himself upon her, upsetting the stool and tumbling himself and the Priestess into a bruising tangle. Because of the **SILENCE** spell, Crabhook's and Manly's laughter went unheard.

The guards carefully disentangled Bodvarka and the soldier. Suddenly the **SILENCE** spell wore off and Bodvarka's curses rang clear.

"I think," suggested Crabhook, "that your men should remove the Ambassador's jewelry. It is obvious that some of it is magical."

Since her hands were restrained, the men had little difficulty removing necklaces, brooches, and bracelets. Rings, however, were extremely difficult. When Bodvarka finally sat unadorned upon her stool, she and the guards were close to exhaustion. "Thief!" she hissed.

"Not at all, your Excellence." his Lordship replied. "Your valuables are all in this padded box, which I shall deposit in her Royal Highness' desk for safe keeping. Everything will be restored when you return to the Hegemony." He leaned wearily on the desk as he placed her jewels in a drawer. "Perhaps your Excellence would prefer to rest for the night. We can resume negotiations in the morning."

Bodvarka shrugged as she gazed at her bound wrists. "You dare to imprison the Ambassador of the Pythoness?"

"You will be escorted to your chambers, where the guards will be instructed to loose your bonds as soon as magical restrictions are in place. We regret the necessity for your restraint, but you must admit our caution to have been prudent. Tomorrow you have but to send one of your guards, and I will attend you to discuss harmonious relations between our two nations."

As soon as the guards had led Bodvarka away, Lord Crabhook sent for Wizard Quackenthorp. It took less than half an hour for the two men to agree on a price for the Wizard's services. He was to set up and maintain a non-magic zone in the ambassador's quarters through the night. He would also inspect the magical jewelry taken from her and detect its powers.

"Perhaps you might see something which would compensate you for your trouble and save the royal treasury the expense of your fee. Everything is in this box except the wand, which nobody wants to touch."

Quackenthorp was trembling with greed as his hand quivered over the wand, but before he touched it he jerked back in dismay. "This is a very powerful **WAND OF SPELL STORING** which I lust to possess, but, alas, it is magically tied to the Priestess with a bond I cannot break. I suspect it would kill anyone except its mistress who touched it. As soon as she steps out of my **NULL MAGIC ZONE**, she will be able to summon this wand wherever it is hidden and cast whatever spells she has stored in it."

"The we had better destroy it," Lord Crabhook urged.

"Unfortunately I do not have the skill to disenchant so powerful a wand, and if you should protect your hands with enchanted gloves to pick it up and break it, the wand would release all its magical energy in a blast which would gut the palace."

"You mean that thing would have killed Manly if he hadn't been wearing gauntlets?" asked Sir Archibald.

"Yes, his gauntlets saved his life."

"Then how do we keep her from summoning it as soon as she leaves the Null Magic Zone?"

"You can't." Quackenthorp quivered with greed as he cast the identifying magic on the jewelry.

"But . . ."

"Face it, young man. The ambassador is going to get her wand back no matter what you do, so you might just as well stop dithering and take care of problems you can solve." He plucked a massive golden ring setting a very large star ruby surrounded with diamonds. "Now this is a very powerful protective ring. Anyone can wear it, and it will guard against both spells and blows."

"Why didn't it protect her from my dagger?" demanded Manly.

"You were very skillful and very lucky. The ring's protection is not absolute, but it makes the wearer very difficult to injure either with magic or weapons."

"Perhaps we should send this to Queen Elsa," Lord Crabhook suggested, "unless this is what you choose for your fee."

"No, What I want is this brooch and this plain platinum ring. The brooch will make me immune to the life draining power of the undead, and the ring will enable me to Teleport safely and unerringly even to places I imperfectly remember. Had one of the priestesses whom your wire clothes line destroyed been wearing this ring, it would have steered her into unoccupied space. It would even have found a safe target space when you had the room filled with boxes."

"I had thought you would be content with one magic item," Lord Crabhook objected.

"I am performing two services for you: IDENTIFICATION and NULL MAGIC. I believe my price is not excessive in view of your helplessness without me."

"He has us by the balls," Captain Manly put in. "Without him we'll lose the queen and perhaps the kingdom."

"Exactly." Quackenthorp pinned the brooch to his blouse and slipped the ring on his finger. The ring immediately adjusted itself to a perfect fit. "Now to the rest of the jewelry. This necklace of yellow gems produces energy missiles. When you detach one of the beads and throw it, the bead becomes a ball of energy which will wreak a ten-foot radius sphere of destruction. Incidentally you must throw the bead promptly or it will center the destruction on you. This pink tourmaline necklace will protect you from magical missiles. This amethyst brooch increases your attraction to the opposite sex." He grimaced as he set it down on the desk. "I would use this brooch with extreme caution. A swarm of admirers is not always a blessing." He signaled to Captain Manly. "If you will show me the way to the ambassador's quarters, I will cast my NULL MAGIC field so that you can safely untie and ungag her. I believe I have been assigned a room across the corridor so that I can renew the spell in the early morning."

Manly led him out. Lord Crabhook gathered the remaining magical jewelry into the box. "I shall deliver this to her Majesty and then retire for the night. It will be a busy day tomorrow."

The others withdrew, and lord Crabhook locked the door of the study.

Early next morning Queen Elsa received Lord Crabhook and Sir Archibald Harper in her quarters at the Temple. "You say the Ambassador from the Pythoness has **TELEPORTED** home? In spite of the **NULL MAGIC** zone?

"I fear she picked the lock of her suite. Then all she had to so was walk a few yards down the corridor to escape the zone," Sir Archibald explained. "As soon as she could use magic, she mst have summoned her wand and **TELEPORTED** home."

"Even with her escape," Lord Farsyte consoled the queen, "She has suffered a major defeat."

"Let me get this straight. When you took the boxes out of the **TELEPORT** room, you stung wire instead. As a result, when Bodvarka summoned three Priestesses to help her, they were sliced up by the wire? Then you silenced her, took away her magic jewelry, and then offered to negotiate in the morning?"

"It seemed the only way to negotiate on equal terms," Lord Crabhook apologized. "I thought we would have to give back her jewelry in exchange for removing the circ from your Highness' neck."

The Queen sadly stroked the circ. "I think you did remarkably well. I fear I'll have to live here in the safety of the Temple as long as there's any danger of a Priestess appearing and making the thing cut off my head, but you two can take care of court business. I suppose I had better appoint you to your father's position as Lord Seneschal, Sir Archibald, and I think Captain Manly has earned a promotion to Major. Lord Crabhook, You had better put the military on a wartime footing and declare a state of siege in the capital. I should feel a lot better if Lord Septimus came back with Prince Humber, but we have done all we can to repel invasion."

"Your Majesty can take comfort in the fact the we killed three Priestesses during the attack," Sir Archibald pointed out. "They will have trouble bringing them back from the dead, since the bodies were shredded by the wires and then cremated. It is to be hoped that it will take some time to replace them."

"True, we can hope for breathing space."

XIII—Explorations

As the Amazon cavalry attack unit fled to rejoin their main force, Njal and the small group of pike men, along with Grimbolt's horse archers and the converted Amazons, gathered to the west of the Brie camp and rode rapidly to join Alsenius' army.

About a hundred miles to the east of Moonflower's evacuated camp an impressive army of Zharkovians began their westward march. Their orders were to defeat the Amazon army, but to leave the nomadic tribes undisturbed.

If they succeeded in routing the Amazons, they were to detach a platoon to head north and scour the star fall for deposits of the grey metal. They were warned to avoid caves dug by the impacting star, as there were rumors of poisonous materials underground. The platoon commander had secret instructions to watch for a party of explorers including Lord Nicholas. If he encountered Lord Nicholas, he was to deliver a message from his Majesty, King Peter. Assuming victory over the Amazons, the remainder of the Zharkovian army was ordered to return home without disturbing the natives.

The Amazon army regrouped to the west and pressed eastward again in defiance of Alsenius' horse archers. Alsenius kept his liberated Amazons and nomad footmen together as an infantry force marching to shadow the Amazon advance. Alsenius hoped to be able to liberate more Amazons in the lightning raids of his horse archers.

Alsenius soon found that Sven and about fifty nomad bachelors and rejects regarded themselves as exiles from the disrupted tribes. These men absorbed the reformed Amazons into a loose independent force and separated themselves from the horse archers still dedicated to Southmark. Mahla and Sven approached Alsenius after a skirmish on the fourth day of the Amazons' eastward march.

"Do you realize that your army is dividing into two parts?" Sven asked.

"I know that a lot of the bachelors are sticking pretty close to you and the rest of the horse archers prefer to work with your brother Lars, who is still respectably married."

"It's more important than that. Lars' men are going back to the tribe as soon as the fight is over. My bachelors and the Amazons don't have any place to go back to."

"What he means," Mahla interrupted, "is that you have an unattached army of well over sixty who have begun to look to you as their leader. Sven is a good man, but he doesn't know about running an army. I'm Amazon trained, but I've never been a officer."

Sven grabbed the conversation again. "What we're trying to say is that we've become a substantial group of exiles, and we need a leader. Will you take us on as a mercenary force after we beat the Amazons?"

"Njal will disenchant more of the Amazons before we finish," Mahla added, "and some of the bachelors from the tribes are going to think twice about going back to mama after they've tasted independence. There's going to be more of us before we finish."

Sven suddenly laid his sword at Alsenius' feet. "I've always obeyed my mother and my wife. I'm no leader, but I'd make a very good second in command. I'll pledge you my sword as a henchman if you'll take the exiles and me."

Mahla presented her sword and knelt beside him. "We Amazons are in the same pickle. We need a leader, and my women agree that you're the one."

Alsenius stepped back a pace and wiped his forehead on his sleeve. "I've been a loner ever since my Prince left me a slave in Troxia. I've never been a chieftain."

Njal wandered up and laughed, "I'd assume a proposal if it was just Mahla, but what's all this kneeling about?"

"We want Alsenius to be Chief," Sven answered.

"Well, so he is," said Njal, "your ex-wife made him General of the Brie army."

"Not general for that woman—Chief in his own right, elected Chief of the exiles," Mahla interrupted.

"Good idea. He's a great swordsman, and he has a good head. Let me get out of the way and you go on with the ceremony."

"But . . ." Alsenius stared down, bewildered.

Reina gently tapped him on the shoulder. "If you're worried about how to feed us, remember you can always set us to hunting and fishing."

"A lot of the men can even farm if you settle us down in one place." Mahla reminded him. "Most of us women had peaceful skills before the Pythoness enslaved us. We don't have to fight all the time. All we want is somebody to tell us what to do and keep us from fighting among ourselves."

Sven reminded him, "None of us of Southmark are full-time fighters. We can live off the land and support ourselves, but if we don't have a judge to run things, we want a man who can figure out what we all want to do and then tell us."

Njal broke into a spasm of chuckles. "Nobody wants to think. All these people want is somebody to make them do what the know they ought to so they can gripe while they're doing it. You don't see Lord Paramour or Ambloq slaving over chores, because they know how to get somebody else to do them better. Nobody expects Ambloq to hunt or dig a latrine. He plans how to get the work done and asks the people who are good at it to scurry around while he does the thinking for them. If we think he's messing it up, we tell him, and he usually can give a good reason for what he asks. So long as we all think he knows what he's doing and that he'll listen and try to be fair, we'd rather obey than think."

"Well, if you still want me after this war is over, I'll give it a try." Alsenius still looked worried. "One thing we'll have to face is hunting a place for headquarters. We certainly can't stay around here in competition with the Southmark. Moonflower and the other judges won't put up with a tribe where men share the authority. For the present Sven will continue in charge of the men and Mahla has been elected by the women, but in the long run we're going to be one band."

"That's why we need you," said Sven. "Somebody has to bring us together without a fight."

"We all hate the way the Priestesses run things," Mahla put in, "and you're the only man with any experience. As for getting together, most of us are already planning to marry, so somebody's got to decide whether we name the kids after the mother or the father."

"But not in the middle of a war," Alsenius exploded. "Right now we need to keep ourselves in training and alert so that we can keep the Amazons off balance."

"Fine, but what about prisoners?" Mahla demanded. "Moonflower sent all the prisoners back to the enemy except the few Njal had a chance to liberate from the Pythoness' magic. It's not fair. She should have given them a choice to join us."

"Are you suggesting that we recapture the women marching east from Moonflower's camp" Alsenius asked.

"Yes!" Mahla and Reina spoke as one, then Reina continued the argument. "Your Illusionist, Njal, cast a general **DISPEL** on all the prisoners and then paid attention only to those who appealed for refugee status. I know enough about the Pythoness' spells to understand that a **DISPEL** would have to cancel three enchantments at once before a woman might appeal for release. Only eleven of us were completely freed and dared to risk slavery from new masters rather than continue serving the Pythoness. There must have been some more women who were freed, but feared their conquerors more than they hated the Pythoness. I think we ought to meet those Amazons before they reach the enemy army and offer them the deal we have."

"Furthermore," Mahla interrupted, "If you cast **DISPEL** on a smaller group. You'll rescue more of them."

Alsenius turned to Sven. "Do you think the men would agree?"

"Anything that will get us more women," Sven answered. "Our main trouble under the old system was that we couldn't remarry if our wives threw us out. We left the tribe in hopes of finding women."

"Can you find a way to intercept the released prisoners?" he asked Sven.

"Simple. We know where they started and which way they were going. We can guess pretty well how fast they can march." He paused for a moment, then pointed roughly west-southwest. "Go that way, and we should meet them by noon tomorrow."

"Good. Make it so." Alsenius stooped to pick up Sven's sword at his feet. "Sven, I accept you as my Henchman and return your sword. Use it in obedience for the good of the tribe." He picked up Mahla's sword and returned it with the same words. "You are now my sub-chiefs. Use your authority justly and wisely. Make sure everybody knows what we're doing and why. If there's a serious protest against any decision, we'll have a meeting to find out what everybody wants."

"There won't be any protests." Mahla bowed slightly and Sven saluted. "If you always command us to do what we want to do anyway, you'll have no trouble being obeyed."

Suddenly Njal interrupted. "Alsenius, I think your mew tribe needs a name. Why don't you call yourselves *The Liberated*?"

"I like it," Mahla exclaimed.

"I like it, too. I'll ask the men," said Sven.

As they headed back to their followers, Njal remarked, "I think you've started a major force to support Ambloq at the final battle with the Pythoness. You'll need to recruit a cleric or two and a mage to support your army, but these people know the enemy, and I think they'll stay with you."

Leaving the foot soldiers and most of the mounted bowmen to continue harassing the Amazon supply lines, Alsenius found horses for Mahla and twenty of her liberated women and took them with thirty of his mounted men and sped past the slowly slogging Amazon army in search of the captives Moonflower had sent away.

It was late in the afternoon of the next day when they met the released captives straggling, hungry and exhausted, across the rolling wilderness in search of their army. When they spotted Alsenius' band, they formed their defensive square with the six short bows in the center prepared to sell their lives as dearly as they could. Alsenius sent Njal—with Emma to protect him—to cast spells and Mahla to speak for his tribe. Njal promptly cast **DISPEL MAGIC** on the square while Mahla tested her skill as an orator.

"Fellow Amazons, we come to you in peace," she shouted. "Will you choose someone to speak for you and discuss the possible terms of honorable surrender?"

The horse bowmen conspicuously maneuvered their steeds in combat formation, and the women formed up behind Mahla and Njal. Presently an Amazon in clerical robes strode outside the square, bearing a pennant of truce. As she approached, Njal targeted her specifically with another **DISPEL**.

"I am Sister Aspasia, Priestess of the second level, in command of this unit," she announced. "I recognize you as one of those who deserted to the enemy."

"I am Mahla, sub-chief of the Liberated. Our Chieftain, Alsenius, has authorized me to offer peace, liberation, and the opportunity to join our band to any woman who renounces her enslavement to the Pythoness." This offer was shouted loud enough to be heard by all the women in the square. Mahla noted the restlessness that passed through the square as Aspasia strode to meet her.

"Those of us who surrendered have been liberated and have joined a free band under General Alsenius. We come to offer you the chance to join us, unless you are determined to rejoin the Amazon army."

Aspasia sadly shook her head. "The general will be furious at our defeat. She'll probably have us executed, or at best be reduced to slaves. I suspect that you have a spell caster who has negated most of the spells which bound us to obedience. As a result there is no discipline among us. We are all hungry and exhausted, but we have agreed to fight as well as we can to keep from being enslaved."

"But we don't want slaves. We want you to join us. We have agreed to help the native barbarians to fight off the Amazons. Then we're going to join with the exiled barbarian men as a free mercenary tribe under Alsenius."

"You are offering us freedom?"

"What's more we're offering you food," Njal broke in. "Food, warm sleeping equipment, and men. There are about fifty more bachelors than women."

"So we'll surrender and get raped." Aspasia drew herself up, prepared for battle."

"Nobody has been raped," Mahla assured her. "I'm sleeping with a very civilized barbarian because I like him and he asked me to share his bedroll, but nobody has been forced."

"I've been accepted as Njal's free henchman in spite of the fact that the barbarians gave me to him as a slave. This is a genuine offer of freedom."

"If any of your women want to go on wandering by themselves, they'll be free to leave us," Njal added. "But we hope you'll join the tribe and add to its strength."

Mahla took Aspasia aside and added, "I don't now how far Njal's magic has released you from enslavement by the Pythoness, but we are offering you freedom to choose and the chance to build a life with our tribe."

"I realize that I have just been freed from a magical compulsion to obey and serve the Pythoness, but I have been enchanted so long that I don't really know what I want for myself. I freely confess that we are completely at your mercy. The Barbarians left us no armor and only six short bows for hunting. The Amazon general will have no use for us, and we have no more heart to fight. I believe that most of the spells that bound us to the Amazons have been broken, so that we have no desire to return to our mistresses. We would be grateful to surrender if the terms are bearable."

"Freedom, full partnership, men if you want them." Mahla answered. "Njal will remove all the enslaving spells he can, and he is a powerful

Illusionist. Alsenius, our chief, has authorized me to offer you full membership in The Tribe of the Liberated. There are a lot of bachelors who have either left or been exiled from a tribe of mother-dominated Barbarians. They are used to being bossed by women and will probably make biddable husbands. There are only a dozen of us, so the tribe needs women. Any of you who do not choose to join us may go wherever you wish, so long as you swear not to fight for the Hegemony."

"I suppose we'll have to fight if we join you," sighed Aspasia.

"We're pretty well committed to fighting until the Amazons are driven out. Alsenius has committed us to help the Barbarians in exchange for help in picking up some star metal, but he comes from a tribe where the men normally do the fighting. I would guess that most of us will give up battle and take to raising children when the war ends."

Aspasia quickly walked back to her band. Immediately the formation shattered as all thirty-eight Amazons broke ranks and crowded around her. When the Amazons learned the terms offered, the vote to surrender was unanimous. None of the women wanted to go back to the Pythoness and they all preferred the safety of an established tribe to the dangers of wandering alone. For most, the idea of finding a husband added to the appeal. Aspasia and Phyllis, an acolyte who served as her second in command, led them toward the horse bowmen. The women from the Liberated moved quickly to intercept them and guide them first to Njal for another **DISPEL MAGIC** and then to Alsenius.

Njal's magic was strong enough to neutralize most of the Pythoness' spells. He warned Aspasia and Phyllis that there were probably hidden Clerical webs of obedience which he could not guarantee to remove. "I would suggest that you let Grimbolt introduce you into the service of Gaea. As soon as we are free to travel freely, we can take you to the Great Forest where you can train with Leander the Druid and Miranda, the High Priestess of Gaea.

Alsenius was delighted to find two Clerically trained women. "You can do important healing work for us, and you can train others to bind and clean wounds. "You are immediately appointed Shamans of the Liberated. As soon as you are comfortable with the service of Gaea, you will be able to bless the army, cast occasional auguries, and even perform marriages. Though many of the couples will want to be married by the chief, there will be some who would prefer a Cleric. You have been taught by the Pythoness to **CURE**?"

They assured him that they understood both curing and binding. When Grimbolt told what he understood of the service of Gaea, they both easily accepted her demands for life in tune with nature. That evening the Liberated celebrated with a feast which convinced the newcomers of the hunting prowess of their new tribe. The next day Alsenius distributed the tribe's stock of horses, armor, and weapons as far as it would stretch. Most of the new recruits had to join the pike men, but everyone had at least some equipment, and Alsenius' strategy of raiding the enemy's supply train would provide more. They established their base camp at a water hole to the north of the Amazons' advance so that hunting and fishing parties could provide food and the horse bowmen could strike at their own speed, leaving the pike men to guard the camp.

Alsenius made no attempt to slow the Amazon advance, since his plan depended upon a confrontation between the Amazons and King Peter's army. Sometimes a raid provided a few extra horses. Occasionally they captured a wagon load of food. Once they captured a small wagon on which a number of Amazons had deposited their armor, bows, and swords. Alsenius promptly turned this load of booty over to Mahla and Aspasia. "I am making you responsible for distributing this equipment where it will do the most good. You know the individual strengths of your women, so I trust you to make the best use of it."

Grimbolt grinned at his comrade. "You're beginning to behave like a king," he laughed. "Old Septimus always used to tell me, 'Delegate, delegate. Especially delegate what somebody's likely to resent.'"

Njal chuckled as he added, "A good Captain always wears a worried look on his Executive Officer's face."

"That's what Mother never really learned," Grimbolt mused. "She was always trying to tell Septimus how to do what he did much better.

The Amazon force plodded inexorably eastward. Their reduced cavalry was forced to hover along the flanks of the supply train—no more raids against the Southmark camps they passed en route—but the infantry slogged forward always seeking a decisive battle. Alsenius' army shadowed them to protect local camps, always prepared to join a ring of pike men around a settlement. As a result the Pythoness' forces occupied a moving patch of the wilderness without changing anything, while they constantly drained supplies from the Hegemony's economy. For them to occupy was not to control.

Alsenius' tribe could trade their booty with the locals while they shielded the settlements. Their freedom of movement allowed them to hunt and fish while they harassed and raided. They cleared forage out of the path of the invaders, so that the Amazons grew more and more dependent on an ever lengthening supply line. They picked up a few stragglers, whom they could liberate and often recruit, yet they never committed themselves to a full-scale battle where the Amazons' armored infantry, powerful Priestesses, and lumbering catapults would have been decisive.

Several times the Amazons tried to detach a small force to the north where they hoped to discover deposits of star metal, but the horse bowmen forced these detachments to retreat.

"Are you certain that King Peter has sent an army to attack these Amazons?" Alsenius demanded as the Amazon army approached the neighborhood of Mistflower's tribe.

"If I know King Peter, he couldn't resist a chance like this to surprise the Hegemony's army. He can't send me any messages till I have a permanent fire to receive them, but unless I've lost my skill as an advisor, he sent an army as soon as he got my last note."

Alsenius nodded. "I'll still bet on your skill," he laughed, "though I don't know how we can deal with this Amazon army unless King Peter comes through."

As the armies advanced, so did the season, and the Southmarkers harvested their modest crops before the frost could nip or the soldiers destroy. Ice glazed the water holes at night. Then one day a band of Sven's horse bowmen sighted the advanced guard of the Zharkovian army. After half an our of challenges and counter challenges the bowmen finally convinced the Zharkovians that they were not hostile. When the Liberated leader finally gained General Gorchov's presence, he promptly named Lord Nicholas.

"Describe him," the general demanded.

Reference to his voice and his dark violet eyes convinced the general that the bowman knew Lord Nicholas. General Gorchov quickly scribbled a brief note on a scrap of papyrus, folded and sealed it. "Give this to Lord Nicholas. As soon as I have talked with him, I will be able to trust you."

As soon as he learned that a Zharkovian army was in the immediate neighborhood, Lord Nicholas wrote a detailed report of everything he knew about the composition, location, and condition of the Amazon force. He also briefed General Gorchov on the activities of the Southmark harriers.

As the armies drew even closer, the Liberated pulled out of the potential battlefield and concentrated their entire attention on the western end of the Amazon supply train. Their scouts were, however, still able to feed up-to-date information about Amazon movements.

Amazon scouts met and clashed with Zharkovian patrols, and both armies began the laborious reforming into battle array. Indecisive cavalry clashes enabled both generals to estimate the power of the opposing forces, and the Amazon High Priestess began to fear a major battle against a superior force. She communicated by spell with her superiors at home and was told that reinforcements were not available. The situation in Arragor was approaching crisis, and Queen Elsa's army had been deployed along the border.

As a result of this news, the Amazon force pulled back into a pattern of defensive squares. In the center were the catapults and the spell casters. The archers stood behind the long swords. And the cavalry ranged along the flanks. The larger Zharkovian force seized the hills in front of the Amazons and also those on the left and right flanks. Their cavalry patrolled the area between the armies, seeking to entice the Amazon cavalry into a melee. Alsenius withdrew to the north, watching and waiting. The horse bowmen from Southmark continued to harry the Amazon supply line, while their foot soldiers occupied the highest hill in the area and began to fortify it.

For two days the armies probed each other's perimeters; the third night, the Amazons withdrew about five miles to occupy a group of hills through which a small river wound. When the Zharkovian cavalry pounded in to test the new line of defense, the Amazon catapults lobbed rocks into their charge. As they regrouped to attack again, a Priestess summoned a succession of Griffins which soared over the field causing panic among the horses. Since the Zharkovians had neither catapults nor offensive magic, they continued their 'block and surround' approach—gradually advancing their infantry to occupy high ground on the flanks and blocking the center with massed troops. They found a grove of trees and set about constructing catapults, while their cavalry tried to maneuver around the Griffins.

In the Liberated camp Nicholas sought out Njal. "Our general doesn't dare commit his army in an all-out battle against Amazon magic. Do you think you could neutralize the High Priestess? We believe there's only one high level spell caster, but she has already summoned five Griffins which are terrorizing the cavalry."

"There's a storm brewing in the west," Njal noted. "My guess is that she will station herself on the highest hill and try to CALL LIGHTNING. Then she'll summon either more Griffins or other monsters. That way she might throw the center of the army into enough confusion to allow a combined cavalry charge and infantry rush. If she can break the center she might put the larger Zharkovian force to flight."

"With lighting bolts on our headquarters and monsters disrupting the cavalry, they might just succeed." Nicholas agreed. "Can you help?"

"Ride down with me to introduce me to your general. If we can persuade him to vacate the headquarters, I can create the illusion of a large flock of crows to attack the Griffins, and . . ."

"Come on, let's ride." Nicholas mounted, and Njal and Emma quickly followed. By the time they reached the Zharkovian lines, the storm had darkened the western sky. Nicholas' signet ring provided instant identification when presented to the Guard Captain at the northern camp, and they received an escort to the headquarters of the central camp. General Gorchov recognized the Royal Bloodhound and embraced him immediately.

"Njal is convinced that the Amazon Priestess is going to attack your headquarters with a barrage of lightning bolts. You have barely time to evacuate before this storm provides her with the power. We think she's going to support an attack on the center with griffins and other monsters. She'll have her catapults aimed at our center as well."

"It wouldn't take many more griffins to demoralize our cavalry, and destroying headquarters might weaken our defensive line. I'll move everybody out of this part of the camp and place our most experienced commanders at the front. Can you do anything about the magical attacks?"

"Griffins are pretty vulnerable to large numbers of crows," said Njal. "I can create the illusion of a big flock that will concentrate on pecking the eyes of the griffins. The other thing I can do is distort their perception of the terrain. If they think they are passing through a tangle of briars, that will break up their formation. If your cavalry can function without fear of monsters, and without believing the illusions, you ought to be able to rout an attack."

The griffins summoned by the Priestess were real and very angry at having been summoned. Since they were not very bright, they believed that the illusory crows were real. As a result, their fear of the crows and their resentment over the summoning overcame their fear of the Priestess. They turned away from the battle and concentrated their rage on her. This attack compelled her to abort her lengthy CALL LIGHTNING spell and expend time and spell energy in banishing the griffins. The crows remained a nuisance until she realized they were an illusion; then she had to dispel them. Meanwhile Njal's ILLUSORY TERRAIN—a bramble and insect infested swamp—disorganized enough of the Amazon attackers to enable the Zharkovians to capture one of their central hills—catapults and all. As a result the Amazon army had to retreat and reform defensively on a new group of hills.

By the time the Priestess had competed her new CALL LIGHTNING, Njal had masked the Zharkovian headquarters from her sight and produced an illusion of tents a few hundred yards below it. As a result most of the lightning bolts crashed into the illusory headquarters and buried themselves in the swamp. Njal tried the illusion of a gold dragon, which scattered the priestess' guards but had no effect of the priestess. She answered with a series of FLAME STRIKES, which caused limited damage, but were able to stop the Zharkovian advance.

Njal flung a genuine FIREBALL at the hilltop where he perceived the Priestess, intending to follow it with a barrage of illusions, but her defensive magic neutralized the spell. Although nothing Njal did seemed able to harm the priestess, his presence forced her into a magical duel with the Illusionist. Thus she was a little use to the army she was supposed to aid.

"The Amazons don't dare attack without magical support," the General noted. "If you can continue to keep their spell caster busy, our superior forces should drive them back to the Hegemony."

"You don't intend to attack their homeland?" Nicholas sounded worried.

"King Peter has more sense than that," chuckled General Gorchov. "The fact is, he ordered us to return home as soon as the men we sent north come back with the star metal. The main reason for this force is to keep the Priestesses from turning north. All we need to do is keep pushing them toward home and wait for our expedition."

"Good," said Nicholas. "My mission to Arragor has accomplished its purpose. I shall return with you and report to his Majesty in person."

"I will inquire of his Majesty," answered the General. "He gave no orders for escorting diplomats."

"But surely . . ."

"His Majesty was very explicit about what we were to do and how we were to do it. Terminating your Excellence's mission to Arragor was not in his instructions. Unless you can provide specific orders for your return, it would be imprudent for me to act upon your authority. I think it would be extremely unwise for you to leave Arragor without direct orders."

"But I have already left Arragor."

"Whether you had authority to do so, only you and his Majesty know, but I will not assist your possible disobedience. I have a letter for you from his Majesty, and I will write request new instructions. If you have in some way embarrassed yourself with the Barbarians, you may remain with us until I receive an answer. I will instruct my men to erect a tent for you." The General turned aside, indicating that the interview was ended.

Nicholas knew he had always been given a longer leash than most courtiers. Only once had he been checked, and he remembered King Peter's sharp jerk when he strayed. His orders on this mission had been explicit: "Find the young king and see that he is properly crowned. Keep an eye on the Queen Dowager."

His new letter from King Peter contained no change in his instructions. Surely Grimbolt's coronation was assured. Alsenius' new tribe was certainly adequate protection while he traveled. Nicholas still ached over Princess Catherine, and a free trip home with the army seemed to offer a relief from the pain of watching her.

"Grimbolt certainly doesn't act like a lover. He never visits the women's section of the camp. He greets her with casual courtesy when they met. On the other hand he has refrained from taking an Amazon to his bed." Nicholas knew that the royal engagement was no love match, but still he was sure Catherine regarded herself as betrothed, and he longed to escape from the futility of his love. He followed the soldier who came to show him to his tent, and flung himself heedlessly upon his pile of straw.

An hour or so later, Njal stopped in to discuss the sort of illusion which would be most likely to distress the Amazons. "I have decided on mosquitos for tonight." the Illusionist grinned. "I'll start by summoning a real swarm; then they'll be sure to believe the illusions. I think about midnight, I'll switch to field mice. Even disciplined Amazons won't enjoy sharing their blankets with mice." He sat cross-legged beside his friend. "I thought about scorpions in their boots when they get up, but I'm afraid that might be suspicious. I think I'll settle for mildew." He waited for an appreciative chuckle. Then he looked sharply across the tent. "You all right?" he demanded.

"I want to go home," Nicholas sighed.

"Still mooning over the Princess? I thought your operation saved you from that kind of heart-ache."

"I thought so too. But it still hurts. She's determined to marry Grimbolt, and I don't blame her. I don't have much to offer her."

"She loves you, but doesn't dare run away with you."

"She's right," Nicholas sighed, "but that doesn't make it feel any better. I want to go home with the army, but General Gorchov says 'No!'"

"Well I'm glad. I'm sorry you're unhappy, but we need you to keep the Princess from coming apart. She's not up to camp life, and nobody but you has time to keep rescuing her. Of course what she needs is a good roll in the blanket, but I don't suppose you can do anything about that."

"As a matter of fact, I probably could. They took only my testicles; I can still get rigid. That's why I wanted to run away with her. We could never have children, but . . ."

"But that's ideal," Njal crowed. "You can give her romance and Grimbolt can take care of begetting the children in his spare time."

"Don't be silly."

"I see what you mean. The court would never put up with it, and you'd lose your job with King Peter. Life's a vixen."

A soldier appeared at the opening of the tent. "Sir, a message from the General." He thrust a packet into Nicholas' hands.

"He doesn't want me?"

"No sir." The soldier thumped his breast in salute, turned about sharply, and marched off.

Nicholas fumbled with the seal, got it open and found a scrawled note and a smaller sealed packet. He read the note: "Enclosed are your orders from his Majesty. You will return to the Barbarian force in the morning."

"Bad news?" asked Njal.

"Orders from King Peter."

"You have a very efficient way of communicating."

"Oh, yes. I can report to his Majesty whenever I need to. He can't send me messages because I'm moving around, but he knows exactly where to find the General." He broke the seal on the smaller packet and read: "We forgive your failure to watch the Queen-Dowager while you guard the king. Continue with the king until he is properly crowned; when possible watch Queen Elsa. Instructions will follow. Do not desert your post." He sighed and smiled wanly at Njal.

"No getaway?"

"I go back to the Liberated tomorrow morning. King Peter has jerked my leash."

"I wonder whether I could make a believable illusion of leeches in their stream," Njal returned to his planned mischief. "It ought to upset them when they bathe." He looked sympathetically at Nicholas' drooping face. "At least you can enjoy her company for a while longer." He patted Nicholas' knee and stood up. "Now I have to think up some new way to convince the Amazons they ought to go home." He stepped out, leaving Nicholas to his brooding.

Nicholas and Njal returned to the Liberated in time for the singer to serenade the enemy with a chorus of wolf howls which started the local wolves into competition, so that the night was eerie with song. Njal provided a menacing dance of hostile shadows which tempted the Amazon sentries with hysteria and kept the officers awake with repeated reports of hostile raiders.

In the morning the Amazons found leeches in their bathing pool, mildew on their boots, and a large a large flock of geese who flew over them at morning inspection. Even the officers had to change their uniforms after the flight. Later in the day, when another flight passed over, those in danger broke ranks to avoid contamination

By the time General Gorchov was ready to advance, the Amazons were almost eager to retreat.

At this point, Alsenius detached the Southmark men under Lars to carry their share of the Amazon booty back to Moonflower. With his band of the Liberated—Southmark exiles and freed Amazons—he turned north toward the impact site of the fallen star. The Zharkovian cavalry took over the job of harrying the Amazon supply line. Njal provided a parting illusion of the horse bowmen charging the northern flank of the Amazons to hasten their retreat and to weaken their rear guard against the Zharkovians. There was, by this time, no question that the Amazon invasion had become a retreat.

For the first time since the invasion, Grimbolt was able to lay aside his armor and rejoin his friends at headquarters. Alsenius had commandeered several impressive tents from the booty, so that his command center looked surprisingly formidable with its silken sleeping tents surrounding a central tabernacle where the new tribe could dine and plan in style. He found the appointments of his personal royal tent—though too feminine for his austere taste—very luxurious. As a bachelor king affianced to the Princess, Grimbolt had to sleep alone. Alsenius shared his substantial headquarters tent with Reina; Princess Catherine had an elaborate tent complex to herself; Njal and Emma had a smaller tent on the outskirts of the compound; and Nicholas' Spartan shelter was pitched near the main tabernacle.

They traveled at a leisurely pace so that the hunters could keep the tribe provided with meat. They had regular reports on the activities of the Zharkovian star metal expedition, and Sven was relieved to find that they had not approached his cache. He was beginning to adjust to bachelorhood, and had even persuaded Mahla to visit his tent.

Soon after they started north, Princess Catherine pulled Grimbolt aside after supper. "We should talk about our arrangements," she said. "Our parents have officially engaged us, but we've never really been consulted. Will you come to my tent and discuss it?"

"I thought you had some kind of understanding with Lord Nicholas." He lowered his eyes. "You showed everybody what you thought of me when we were introduced."

She blushed slightly at the memory. "They caught me by surprise. Your mother . . ."

"Mother likes her own way, and she's not always tactful," he conceded. "I must have looked pretty dreadful. As a matter of fact, I guess I still do."

"No, you look quite human now, but not at all the way you did when I first came north to meet Prince Humber." She examined his face in the lamp light. "Your face is much stronger than it used to be."

"I'm a lot stronger in every way," he asserted. "Being an oarsman and an adventurer has changed me. I don't blame you for being put off."

She lifted the tent flap and invited him inside. They sat on cushions near the fire that flickered under the smoke hole. A freed Amazon brought them steaming cups of kvatch and discreetly withdrew. "I was resigned to marrying you when I first came to Arragor because there wasn't any graceful way out, and there was nothing especially disagreeable about you. I'd always known I would be given to whoever would do Daddy the most political good, and I thought I could put up with you."

"You were very beautiful, and Mother always told me that if you toss any presentable young couple into bed together, they would manage to get on. We weren't much interested in each other, but I figured we wouldn't have to spend a lot of time together. Then the Priestess enchanted me, Leander freed me from my memory, and I became Grimbolt." He looked down at he Draecian carpet. "And then you saw me and gagged."

"You're much changed since Druid Leander restored you to human form."

"But I'm still not Prince Humber. Nobody recognizes me. I'm still hairy, and my face has changed. I'm not really the same man. That's why I'm going to reign as King Grimbolt. I'm not Humber any more, even though Leander has given me back Humber's memories."

She gazed at him steadily. "You're right about being a stranger, but at least you're a lot more interesting than Humber was. You do things. You make up your mind, and your mother can't change it."

"And you gagged at the thought of taking my hairy body to bed with you." Grimbolt straightened and inflated his great furry chest.

"I'm not gagging now."

"You are well trained."

"No, you've become human again. I can't say I find all that fur beautiful—and you make sure nobody overlooks it—but it doesn't turn my stomach." She leaned toward him and placed her hand on his furry knee. "I've seen a lot of more handsome men, but most of them are pretty boring."

"What about Nicholas?"

Tears gleamed in her eyes as she looked away from him. "I can't have Nicholas. I'll probably always carry that ache in my heart, but we can't escape the world we were born into. I'm a Princess, and Nicholas is no prince—he's not even a complete man—and if the Druid restored his manhood, he'd lose his voice and we'd have no money. We've faced that, and he understands."

"Poor Nikky," Grimbolt sighed. "He's lost even more than I have."

Her tears escaped, and she dabbed them impatiently away. "Are you still pining for that girl you kept warm while you were traveling?"

"Clarissa? Heavens no! She was closer to Alsenius than she was to me." He almost laughed. "She was a wonderful companion and a very experienced woman, but there was no romance."

"What about all these liberated Amazons. Have you found a wife among them?"

He shook his head. "They're well trained like Clarissa, but you don't lose your heart over a good lay. They find my body exciting because they've never had such a mattress before, but my wife has to have a mind—she's going to have to be Queen."

"Ah-ha! You're up against the same wall." She fixed her eyes on his. "You have a job to do and you need a partner."

"You mean, 'Daddy knows best?'"

"Daddy is a fool. He'll marry me off to any oaf who can deliver an alliance." She glared at him. "Damn it, I'm not supposed to have to do this. Now that you've recovered human shape, you are the only royal male I can marry without disgust. I don't burn for your body, and I sometimes wonder whether you've developed much of a soul even now, but you're the least impossible choice. The question is, 'Can we manage a decent life between us if we marry. You're mother is right about throwing young bodies into bed. I'm sure I can bear you the heirs you need for the succession, but can you and I be good enough friends to put up with each other for the rest of our lives?"

"You're right. I'm the one who should have raised the question." He scrambled to his knees, adjusting the pillow to cushion against the rough canvas floor of the tent. "You are a very lovely woman, and I should enjoy begetting heirs with you. You have spirit and you're even beginning to show some sense. You have better control over your temper than my mother. The thing is, we're supposed to cement an alliance with our bodies. If you can you put up with my appearance, I beg you to regard that illusion-soaked ring as a true pledge of our betrothal. If we find that we like each other well enough to risk a permanent friendship, I'll ask you to marry me as soon as we can get our lives unsnarled."

"Thank you for taking the responsibility of proposing, even of it was a back-handed sort of proposal." She took his hand and smoothed its hairy back. "I accept you as my betrothed and, if we do not hate each other as we get acquainted, I will wed you as soon as your mother can arrange the ceremony. I suppose we must wait till we are married before we snare a tent."

"That may get to be a problem. Chastity doesn't agree with this new body." There was lechery in his glance. "Unfortunately it is politic to wait. Incidentally, I can't see what sort of illusion Njal cast on that ring. What does it look like to you?"

"It's a very large emerald surrounded with six large diamonds; it's very beautiful."

Grimbolt shook his head, "Illusions!" he snorted. "It's actually nothing but fancy tied-up string, but I'm sure Mother can find something decent we can use when we get back home."

"Njal said the illusion is permanent. I like it."

"A good thing, since it's all we have for now."

They sealed the agreement with a kiss which was becoming almost enthusiastic when they heard Alsenius cough outside. They sprang apart, and the princess demurely opened the tent flap.

"If this is a bad time . . ." Alsenius looked appraisingly at them.

"Not at all," Grimbolt grinned in reply. "We were just settling some affairs of state. We have decided to announce our betrothal in obedience to the treaty agreement between our parents. The princess finds my new body acceptable."

"The princess is sick of being shoved around the game board," Catherine added.

"I'm sure you could both do lot worse," Alsenius laughed. "I'm sorry for Nikky."

"Lord Nicholas understands." Catherine's eyes misted, but Alsenius saw no sign of hesitation.

"What I came for was to ask your royal Highness if you would award the crown of victory to the winners of the horse bowmen's competition. The Amazons have woven a beautiful chaplet and they want to present it with a royal flourish. We planned on presenting it at supper, when all the tribe is together."

"I am honored," said Catherine. "I will even permit the winner to kiss my hand."

"I shall announce our betrothal tonight," said Grimbolt.

That evening Sven and Mahla visited Alsenius in his tent. Mahla accepted a cup of tea and immediately raised the problem. "This organization of the army isn't working."

"I thought we did pretty well in the battle with the Amazons. Nobody expected us to beat them all by ourselves."

"I'm not talking about fighting order, though we are going to have to talk about that too. It's the sleeping arrangements."

"That's the trouble with female soldiers," Alsenius grumped. "If you take a batch of men out on campaign, each one figures out what to do with his prick and does it. Everybody minds his own business; everybody has something to gripe about, and we get on with the war. Then when it's over everybody goes crazy and we spend the next week getting over it. But women! How did the Priestesses handle it?"

"Magic. They just cast spells on everybody."

"Well, that's no help to us, is it?"

"The trouble is, there's no privacy," Sven put in. "If a man sneaks into the women's tent, everybody knows who's getting laid, and the rest get jealous. And it's the same way if the women sneak into the men's tent, only worse because the lonely men try to horn into the action, and we get all sorts of fights."

"Well, we don't have enough small tents to pair everybody off," said Alsenius.

"What's worse, we don't have enough women." Sven reminded him.

"A lot of the women don't mind that. They were trained to live generously, but sex isn't supposed to be a spectator sport." Mahla corrected him. "A woman needs her own space. She wants to make it look like her personality. She want's her own nest, even when there's no babies. If she wants to entertain a man, she wants to be able to invite him in, and if she wants to be alone, she wants to be able to shut him out."

"Furthermore," Sven added, "she doesn't want a lot of other women crowding her. A man doesn't mind having another man beside him pissing into a bush, but crowded women get quarrelsome."

Mahla nodded.

"I suppose we can solve that problem when our tribe settles down," Alsenius said, "but on campaign . . ." He visualized the chaos when they moved camp. "What about partitions? Would it help if we let the women hang something around each bed area? It would be a nuisance for the packers, but everybody could decorate her own partitions."

"Not exactly sound proof," Mahla mused, "but it might help. We could issue orders making every woman responsible for stowing her hangings in her pack. We'd have to set up aisles so people could get around without intruding on anybody's space. Let me see, Divide the dormitory tent into thirty-five spaces. I'll have to sit down and draw a plan. It just might work."

"We still have a couple of spare tents on the pack mules," Sven added. "I suppose we could set them up to provide a little more space."

Mahla headed for her own tent busily counting on her fingers. Sven watched the swing of her hips as she left, then turned back to Alsenius. "We do have some problems with the division of the army between my cavalry and her infantry," he said. "A few of the women are complaining that they're not allowed to join the horse bowmen. We don't yet have mounts for all the men who are trained for that duty, and no matter what we do it's going to be bad for morale. The men will say untrained women slow our maneuvering, and the qualified men without horses will complain if we mount women before them."

"We can't do anything about that until we get more horses. For the present any new mounts have to go to those trained to shoot bows from horseback. That gang is remarkably sharp, and we can't weaken our best corps. Later, I'd like to train some regular cavalry, and we could use mounted women for that."

"What about the men who don't like serving as pike men? Mahla says they are bad for morale."

"We need to train all the foot soldiers to use javelins and short swords. With just pikes they're no good on the offensive. All they can do is break up a cavalry charge. They're no good against enemy swordsmen. Maybe we should start that training right away. Soldiers are always better if they're learning something new.

Two days later they came upon a sudden lake carved into the tundra. Around it the grass was still green, and substantial trees had sprung up in clumps along its edges and on its substantial island. Njal was fascinated with the variety of vegetation. "Friend Sven, could this be a scar from a fallen star?" he asked. "I see no stream that could have carved this lake, but if a missile from the sky had struck here, it might have made this shaped mark."

Sven answered, "There are several lakes like this in the area. They are all isolated as if something from the sky hacked them out, and they are the only open water in a huge dry stretch."

"It's almost as if a great chunk of ice smashed into the ground here and melted. It must have hit an underground stream to replenish the lake. See, off to the east there seems to be an overflow stream. I wonder if pieces of the fallen star broke off while it hurtled down. Then these lakes would be impact craters from the fragments."

"If that's the case, there might be a core of star metal imbedded in the bottom of the lake," said Sven. "I wonder if it would be worth stopping to dive."

"The water is warm." Emma had dismounted and knelt on the shore. "Feel it."

Njal joined her and thrust his hands into the water. "Amazing! There must be hot springs at the bottom." He gazed across the lake, searching for signs of inhabitants. "I can't understand why nobody has claimed this place for a settlement."

Sven dismounted in time to overhear. "It's because most tribes don't settle. Southmark is unusual in always coming back to the same water hole and building a permanent bathing area and lodge sites. Most of the Brie are completely nomadic." He swept his gaze around the lake. "This would be a perfect place for us to settle. We could build a permanent camp out there on that wooded island and make enough boats to keep raiders from landing. Then we could cultivate the shores and have plenty of space to grow." He turned to Alsenius, who had joined them. "Why don't we pitch a permanent camp here. We could search for the star metal from a permanent home and use it to trade for what we need to get started."

"And I suppose you'll have to find a new wife to run things for you," Alsenius laughed.

Sven watched as Mahla directed her women in setting up their camp near a pebble beach a hundred yards to the west of them. "No, I don't want to serve another Moonflower. I want to have my own stake in the settlement. After all, our men are all exiles from a tribe where the women own everything. None of us will ever put up with being chased off again." He straightened up and gathered his men to set up camp not too far from the women's

"Are you tempted?" Njal asked Alsenius.

"Tempted? Yes, but not sold. They'll want to make me chief, so I'll have to solve everybody's problems. I've been a wanderer too long, to take up farming."

"But Sven is right about a settlement," Njal urged.

"Oh yes. Sven's right. The idea of a nomadic army of exiles never looked very good as a permanent arrangement. Those women were abducted from towns and farms. Now you've broken the Pythoness' spells, almost all of them want to settle down to a fixed home with a husband to do the heavy work and children all over the place. Look at those partitions in their tent. They want their own possessions—their own place."

Camp was already settled, and everybody was rushing to plunge into the lake. Emma tugged at Njal's arm. "Don't you think we should set up our tent and go for a swim?" He laughed and joined her in domestic labors.

Alsenius found his own tent already set up beside the big tabernacle. Reina had already established order and was on her way to fetch him. "Are we going to settle here permanently?" she asked as they eased into the water.

"I think it's what the tribe wants," he answered.

"Sven says we could build a permanent camp on that big island and be safe from raiders."

"I think he's right. There's plenty of wood for lodges, and the tribe could build war canoes that could fend off even a full army. The warm water would take the curse off the northern winters, so that you could raise abundant crops. I don't understand why nobody has claimed this site already."

"Are you going to order the building of a permanent camp?" Her voice vibrated with an almost wheedling longing.

Alsenius shook his head. "I'm not going to order anything. Tomorrow I shall call a meeting of the tribe and let them decide what they want. If they decide to settle here, I shall resign as General and let them choose how they want to be governed.

She looked up at him sadly. "You aren't going to settle down with us?"

"I'm not a settler. I am a traveling mercenary. I've committed myself to helping Grimbolt until he's established on his throne. Then I shall return to Ambloq's service. I dreamed of leading a small independent army, but your people aren't really suited to the life of mercenaries. I hope, when the final battle comes against the Pythoness, you'll be at our side, but I can feel that everybody has fallen in love with this place."

"And what happens to me?"

"You are free. I accepted you as a slave only to keep you from worse slavery. You are free to stay and work out your future among the Liberated. If you want to wander with me, you are welcome—no promises and no conditions. You are welcome to share my tent for the present and to leave it when either one of us wants a new bed mate."

"I am not your slave?"

"You know you have never been my slave I will publicly renounce any claim to ownership at tomorrow's meeting."

"But you will not accept me as either a wife or a henchman."

He looked at her sadly. "You are a pleasant companion, but my heart is not enslaved. I cannot pledge you my life's love, and for me a henchman of less than tenth level would be a liability rather than a help."

"You have a cold heart."

"At least it is honest. Shall you share warmth another night?"

She gazed longingly at his sleeping bag, but walked slowly to the tent opening. "I thank you for my freedom. If I have not won your heart, I must find one who can love me." She opened the flap. "I part from you in your debt."

Alsenius watched the flap drop, sighed gently, and settled into his sleeping bag. In the morning, true to his word, he called a meeting of the leaders. Sven, Aspasia, Mahla, Reina, Njal and Emma, Nicholas, and Catherine gathered in the tabernacle.

It was Sven who opened the meeting. "I think I know the reason you've brought us together," he said. "Everybody I have talked to has fallen in love with this place. Are you going to order us to build a permanent camp?"

"No." Alsenius grinned at him. "I'm through giving orders. The first order of business is for you to accept my resignation as General. Our part in the war with the Amazons is over. Lars and the men of Southmark have returned to their tribe. General Gorchov's army is driving the Amazons back, and we have turned north to seek our own futures. My job as General is ended, and it is time for the Liberated to decide what they want to do. If you decide to continue as a wandering mercenary army, I am willing to continue as your Chief and lead you from contract to contract, earning such profit as our military prowess deserves. Last night I became convinced that the people want to settle peaceably here by this lake. I urge you to call a meeting of the whole tribe and learn whether they do, in fact, want to settle here. If they do, they must elect new leaders, for I am committed to assist King Grimbolt until he is crowned. I believe that Njal, Princess Catherine, and Lord Nicholas are similarly committed to searching for the Star Metal and escorting his Majesty back to Arragor."

Njal stood to speak. "I am indeed committed to King Grimbolt until his coronation and after that to Lord Ambloq, whose henchman I am. To dispel any question about Emma's status. I proclaim that she has been my slave only in word. I now declare her to be free and unfettered by any commitment to me."

Emma leaped to her feet. "Njal declared me free at the time I was awarded to him by Judge Moonflower. I have already pledged my sword as Njal's henchman and he has accepted me. I claim my rights and acknowledge my responsibilities as a henchman."

Njal took her hand. "I acknowledge your rights as my henchman and accept your service to guard my body with your sword as I will guard you with my spells. Your duty is to me, and I accept responsibility for you." They moved to Alsenius' right and sat.

Alsenius then rose and proclaimed Reina's freedom. Then he said, "As my final command, I instruct Sven to summon a meeting of the tribe that they may determine whether they choose to wander with me as a mercenary army of to settle here to claim this gracious homeland under their own leaders."

Sven, Aspasia, Mahla, and Reina withdrew frm the tabernacle and left Grimbolt and his companions to make their own plans.

XIV—Experiments

No one was surprised when the Tribe of the Liberated voted almost unanimously to settle on the wooded island and to claim the entire shore of the newly named "Lake Harmony" as their dominion. Because the men were the majority, they elected Sven as Lord Chieftain and Aspasia as Lady Shaman. Sven immediately proposed marriage to Mahla and she accepted him on the spot. Aspasia promptly solemnized the union, and Sven appointed his new wife Lady Judge. It was clear that the scope of this office would have to be defined by later action, but the women accepted the appointment as a recognition of their equality

Inside their tent, the companions discussed their own plans. Grimbolt insisted on the importance of his quest for star metal.

"The trouble is that Sven has first claim to the cache he left to the east of here, and my countrymen are actively searching for deposits," Nicholas pointed out." This lake seems to be about the westernmost strike of the star fragments."

Njal mused on what they had so far observed and heard. "My best guess, from what I've seen of the pattern of scars, is that a large chunk of matter plunged toward earth and broke up during its fall. This lake and probably several others in the area were struck by fragments composed of lighter materials—mostly ice. The heavier core landed east of here and plowed a deepening furrow through he earth until it embedded itself in the deep hole where Sven contracted his disease. That probably marks the easternmost deposit of metal, although some ice fragments may have struck farther on."

"I've noticed that you study the way things are built and the way things move pretty closely," Alsenius said.

"I have to study the way things are and how they behave so that I can create believable illusions. As a result I've learned a lot about making buildings, roads, and bridges just because I know how things work."

"And you have some theory stewing in the back of your mind," Grimbolt observed.

"We know the air is thicker in the valleys than it is on the tops of mountains where it's a lot harder to breathe." Njal was obviously enjoying the chance to explain. "When I was younger, I tried to see how high I could go with a Fly spell, and I finally got so high there wasn't enough air to keep me alive, so I figured that there isn't any air a few miles up where the stars are. We live at the bottom of an air sea, and if we go too high we run out of air just as a fish would run out of water if he swam too high.

"Now we know there are two kinds of stars. Most of them are some kind of fire, and the disturbance of the air makes them seem to twinkle. These stars stay fixed in their constellations. There are some, however—philosophers call them planets because they wander around among the stars—that don't twinkle. I think that's because they are rock, and they only shine because they reflect the sun. In all probability the planets are much closer and smaller than the stars. I believe the moon is the closest of these planets. I've done a lot of arithmetic about the way the moon changes shape, and I think the explanation is that part of the moon's face is in shadow when it goes around the sky."

"So you don't think these fallen stars are stars at all. You think they're little planets that get too close to us and fall down," Princess Catherine crowed. "I had a tutor who thought the same way."

"Exactly. As a result, these tiny planets may contain metals not found on earth. They may also contain seeds of life unknown to earth"

"Well, I wish I could hold my breath for half an hour at a time," Grimbolt grumbled, "so I could explore the bottom of this lake. The fallen star that gouged the lake might have had left a lot of stuff on the bottom."

Njal suddenly lapsed into silence.

"You have an idea?" Alsenius asked.

"There are potions of Water Breathing which would enable us to explore the bottom of the lake, but unfortunately I have only one, which I'm saving for study and analysis. Furthermore those potions allow only a very limited time under water. There is also a spell of WATER BREATHING, but I do not have it in my spell book. I may have it in my collection of scrolls, but I haven't had time to hunt for it."

"I don't how that takes us any closer to a solution," snapped Grimbolt.

"I'm trying to explore possibilities. Be patient." There was a long pause while the Illusionist scowled at the ground. "I remember Glitchby sometimes cast **METAMORPH** spells, which changed him into other creatures temporarily. He even had a spell which could change another person's form permanently, though it only works if the victim consents or the spell caster is able to overcome the victim's will. Ambloq often tells about being changed into a dolphin once, and it was probably a **METAMORPH** spell that the priestess used on Nikky."

"But Glitchby isn't here and I'll bet anything that you don't have the spells in your book." Princess Catherine sneered.

"True." Njal ignored the jab and rambled on. "So I ask myself, 'What do I have that might work?'"

"And does yourself come up with an answer?"

"I wonder whether an illusion might work."

"Now why am I not surprised that your answer to any problem is an illusion?" Grimbolt laughed. "I'm sure that answer leaves me out."

"You think somebody might be able to breathe water if you cast an illusion that he has gills?" asked Alsenius.

"Exactly. I can use **SHADOW MAGIC** which actually gives an illusion a kind of shadow substance, and I can prolong the life of the illusion by using Extension spells. Suppose I found some people who are very susceptible to illusions and convinced them that I was going to do a transformation."

"It might be worth a try. We could send a couple of strong swimmers along to pull them out if the illusion doesn't work." Alsenius got up and began to pace. "We could ask Sven to call for volunteers."

"I can prepare myself overnight to cast the spells." Njal headed out toward his own tent. "You and Grimbolt can work on Sven."

The next day it was announced that Njal was going to enchant volunteers so that they could explore the lake bottom by breathing water. On each of the six volunteers Njal cast an advanced illusion of gills, webbed fingers, and a dolphin's tail. Four of them floundered in the shallow water and laboriously adjusted to the use of hands and tail until they managed to swim very well on the surface, still breathing air. But two of them choked and gasped until they immersed themselves in the water and breathed with the gills. These two dived quickly toward the bottom and commenced exploration.

"What happened?" Grimbolt demanded.

"The illusion deceived all six of them, but only two believed so completely that they are able to breathe water with their gills. These two have, in belief, so thoroughly become mer-humans that my illusion has the effect of a METAMORPH spell. The other four have simply become very good human swimmers." Njal grinned with satisfaction. "I suggest that you have your best swimmers shadow those two and be ready to pull them out if the illusion wears off before they surface."

"How long should the illusion last?" Sven demanded.

"I cast the spells with a spell extender attached, so that they should be good for at least a couple of hours. I warned all of them to be back in shallow water after an hour just to be on the safe side. We'll experiment carefully with those two who completely believe and find out how long they dare explore, and we'll have swimmers with a boat at the ready whenever we're actually searching. That way the boats can carry out anything the divers find, and the divers can stay down."

"But you've found only one couple who believe the illusions so completely that they can actually breathe under water?" said Sven.

"So far." Njal nodded. "And be sure you never mention *illusion* when you talk about this project. The moment those people realize it's all an illusion, they will lose belief. From now on, make sure you refer to them as METAMORPH spells. That will make people more ready to believe them. I'll try the spells on some more people tomorrow, and I'll keep studying and experimenting. Somewhere in my scrolls I have a true METAMORPH spell, but I haven't studied it recently enough to dare try to cast it."

The deluded 'Mermen' reported that the lake bottom deepened gradually for about half a mile; then it plunged precipitously below the depth to which they dared dive. When they explored to the east, they found that the water became uncomfortably hot when they went deeper. They also noted that the fish population diminished sharply as they approached the eastern end of the lake. Jon Chowter, the more observant of the two, reported that the few fish they saw were "queer-looking."

When Njal demanded more precise information, Jon answered. "I didn't pay too much attention, but they were a kind of sickly purple color and their skin looked queer."

"I think it would be a good idea not to swim too far east until we've had a chance to study the lake more carefully," Njal said. "I would like to have you examine the bottom for any little solid lumps. Next time see whether the channel shallows as you explore toward the west. We think this lake was gouged out by a piece of fallen star that was mostly ice, and it might have left some chunks of rock when it melted."

While the swimmers continued the exploration of the bottom, Njal began a detailed study of fish gills in order to make his illusions more accurate. About a week later Grimbolt brought back an amphibious lizard from his explorations of the northern lake shore, and the little Illusionist plunged into the investigation of its complex breathing apparatus. Working from the other end of the problem, he analyzed his potion of WATER BREATHING until he could duplicate it. The ingredients were difficult to find, and he had only a limited supply of the magical gem dust which gave the potion its power. Nevertheless he repeatedly tested the potion on himself, studying the way it changed his lungs to permit them to breathe the small quantities of air dissolved in water.

During the months he labored at his experiments, his illusions improved, and he found six volunteers especially susceptible to illusions who were able to explore the bottom of the lake without using the expensive potions.

Meanwhile the Tribe of the Liberated commenced construction of their settlement on Liber Isle, while a group of volunteers under Alsenius explored the shoreline. Sven decided that any star metal deposited in the lake was probably concentrated in the dangerous eastern deeps where searchers would face the unacceptable peril of the mysterious disease which afflicted the fish observed there. He approached Alsenius and Grimbolt one evening in the sauna. "How important do you think the star metal is?"

"Do you mean, 'Is it important enough to risk exploring the eastern depths?' I should say 'No.'" Grimbolt frowned. "I desperately want to have the superior weapons, but your experience with the star disease indicates the price is too high. You nearly died and you ended up as sterile as Nikky. Maybe some time the Priests will figure out a way to cure or avoid the disease, but nobody wants to look like those fish we caught near the hot spot."

"Didn't you say you left a cache of the stuff near the cave where you caught the disease?" Alsenius asked. "Was it far enough away from the cave for you to pick it up safely?"

"I think so. I got sick and a couple of my men died because we went deep into the cave to bring it out. Nobody else had any trouble. I've been wondering if the metal is worth my marching back with a working party to fetch it."

"I'll guarantee to find 10,000 gold pieces in the my treasury if you can find enough of the metal for five long sword blades," Grimbolt volunteered. "I'd offer to buy more if I knew for sure I wouldn't bankrupt the country."

"Before you become known as a source of star metal, you will need alliances with the three kingdoms to protect you from the Hegemony," Alsenius warned.

"King Peter's army sent a platoon north to look at the big cave where you found the core deposit," Grimbolt added. "How well is your cache hidden?"

"Soldiers don't know anything about hiding and finding," Sven laughed. "I may have been sick, but not sick enough to let anybody find my cache. If I could find out how to work the metal for myself instead of having to pay a Rockborn Weapons Master, I could make at least a dozen long swords out of what I buried."

"I think you'd better fetch the metal before the landscape changes so much that you can't find it," said Grimbolt. "The only trouble is that you're needed here to direct the building operation. Can you make a map so that somebody else can find the stuff?"

"Bengt, Son of Evenstar, was with me on that trip. I probably owe him my life for the way he took care of me during my sickness. He can probably remember the area where we camped until it was safe to move me. I'll go ask him." Sven moved through the sauna fog among the sweating bodies.

Soon afterwards Grimbolt noticed that Catherine and Nicholas were preparing to leave the sauna, and he decided to join them in the lake. Hoping to reduce the friction Alsenius signaled Njal and Emma and grabbed Reina. "The princess and Nikky are heading out of the heat, and Grimbolt is going to follow them. I suggest that we go splash in the bathing cove with them.

The next morning Sven and Bengt caught up with Alsenius and Njal on the way to breakfast. "Bengt says he can find our old camp with no trouble. He even guessed the place where I buried the metal."

"Old Sven thought he was being very secret," laughed Bengt, "but he was too feverish to be sly. Actually I thought I was going to have to finish filling up the hole under the hackmatack bush, but he stuck it out and even did a pretty good job of covering his tracks. I went out later and planted a few sprigs to hide the bare spot. I didn't see what he hid, but I guessed it must be star metal."

"I'm afraid he's going to have to take a couple of strong men to help him carry the load," said Sven.

"Not if he takes one of the women who can cast spells," Njal put in. "I can teach her to cast a simple **TRAVOIS** spell that can handle up to four hundred pounds easily. I would suggest Carla. She's a second level mage and not bad looking in case things get lonely on the journey."

By the next morning Bengt and Carla slipped quietly from the camp heading east.

That evening in the sauna Njal noticed that several of the women were complaining that Sven had taken two people out of the labor pool to risk the dangers of a long trek just to fetch his personal cache of treasure. "So much for the privileges of being chief," he quipped to Emma.

"Oh, he's popular enough to get away with it," she laughed.

By the end of the month Alsenius' crew had produced a rough map of the coast of Lake Harmony. A fragment of fallen star had apparently gouged a trench about twenty miles long from west to east, shallow at the western end and deep under ground at the eastern. Most of the fragment's mass must have been ice, which had melted to form the lake. The gash must have opened innumerable thermal springs, for the lake spread to a width of five miles at the astern end before it overflowed and poured a sizable stream eastward across the tundra. Most of the deep cavern at the eastern end of the lake, where the core of the fallen fragment buried itself, had caved in. About two miles west of the outflow a solid granite outcropping resisted erosion to form Liber Isle, where the settlers were building their permanent headquarters. Over several centuries flood, bird droppings, and erosion had formed a deep enough covering of soil on the island to support not only a dense ground cover but also clumps of larch, birch, and aspen.

The underwater explorers along the southern shore of the lake found that the bottom sloped gradually for several hundred yards and then dropped off in precipitously. They dared not plumb the eastern depths, but they surmised that the core of the fallen fragment lay buried under the substantial mound north of the exit stream. When they had gained sufficient skill and confidence to explore the western end of the channel, they found that it deepened sharply to the east. They discovered occasional chunks of rock, which Njal appropriated as 'star stones.'

"No sign of star metal?" demanded Grimbolt.

"These rocks may be ore, but we've found no nuggets of pure metal," Njal answered. "I'm afraid the metal is connected with the unnatural heat and diseased life that we've observed at the eastern end of the channel. I've told the divers to stay away from there."

As Njal focused more and more on his underwater experiments, he had little need of Emma's assistance. She found herself relegated to building and exploring missions with the other ex-Amazons, while Njal puttered over his papers or plunged into the deeper water. One day she silently followed him as he headed for the water with a couple of potions. He stripped and laid one potion beside his clothes, then waded out to the drop-off, drank his potion, and surface dived into the deep. Emma grabbed the spare potion of Water Breathing, peeled off her armor and clothing, and splashed to the place where he had disappeared. Quickly quaffing her potion, she plunged into the deep and felt her lungs accepting the water. She soon found him following a sizable bream. At first he imitated its undulations; then as she watched he shifted to a dolphin's up-and-down leg stroke. The bream objected to Njal's attempted scrutiny of its gill structure and with a flick of its tail evaded him.

Emma swam swiftly under him and rubbed her body against him. He goggled at her and lurched upward. Since his vocal apparatus was unchanged by the potion, speech was both slow and difficult. "What you do?"

Her reply was to twine her body around his and run her hands suggestively along his sides and loins. His body reacted swiftly, though he protested, "Wasting potion."

Her body indicated that she had no intention of wasting anything, while her hands spoke her intentions. His intellect raged at the distraction, but he could neither voice his protest nor control his body. He reached out to fend her off and found his hands full of the pleasure of her body. Still grumbling over the waste of a precious potion his intellect soon surrendered to the fascination of weightless gymnastics. They writhed harmoniously for over an hour before the potions wore off and they suddenly found themselves having to streak for the surface to breathe.

As they waded back toward their clothes, Njal started to berate her for interrupting his studies, but a well-placed caress silenced him.

"A henchman is supposed to help her help her boss," she interrupted him as her hands reminded him that he had cooperated. "You'll think a lot clearer now."

"But . . ."

"Just think how much you learned about the anatomy of swimming."

Meanwhile Grimbolt found that the concentration required for exploration and the hard labor of helping to construct the settlement distracted him from his own problems and allowed him to bring his Grimbolt and Prince Humber identities closer together. Daily he dragged his weary body back to camp and collapsed while waiting for those on cooking detail to prepare supper. He watched his promised bride as she struggled between the boredom of lounging in her tent while everybody else worked and the frustration of trying to help with the camp chores.

At night he watched more as more of the workers paired up. Several ex-Amazons eyed his body appraisingly, but none of them signaled a hunger for his pelt and he dreaded the possibility of rejection. Yet his body told him it was time he took care of its needs. His education as Prince Humber demanded that he honor his betrothal to Princess Catherine, while his bearish instincts snarled at frustration. When he hinted to Catherine that they need not wait for the wedding, she looked shocked and bustled off about her attempts at cooking. After that she watched him jealously.

"The Princess," he mused is pretty enough, but she is certainly not my heart's ideal. She is silly, self-centered, and uninformed. She has little to talk about except gossip, and she seldom listens. Yet she has showed a level-headed skepticism about court life, and she is trying to adapt to camp life. Perhaps she is capable of growth."

Grimbolt wistfully remembered Clarissa, who had shared the journey across the continent with Alsenius and him. Not that he had fallen passionately for her, but she was an interesting companion as well as a very skillful bed-mate. His body reminded him how skillful she was.

He visualized dreary years with Catherine as his queen—days without wisdom to help him rule; evenings of banal conversation; nights of dutiful pleasure. What if her children took after her?

Then he thought of the political consequences of refusing her, and knew he had no right to deprive his country of the favorable alliance she represented. She had half-heartedly agreed to the match, even though she obviously still ached for that singing eunuch.

"Can a husband be cuckolded by a man with no balls?" He almost laughed. "Nicholas can be no danger to the succession—almost a perfect lover for a royal wife. Furthermore neither of them has the courage to run off." The thought that his betrothed lacked courage was not encouraging. Then he paused. "Give the wench her due," he corrected himself. "She understands politics. It's not cowardice but good sense that keeps her from running off. Maybe she's not as stupid as she seems. She refused to flee with Nicholas because she's not a sentimental butterfly. She has a mind after all. Still, the temptation of passion is always there. If I push for the marriage now, she'll be committed to the alliance. Nikky is too sound a politician to elope with the queen. His master would throw him out and ruin his chances for life. If I'm going to sell myself for the alliance, I might as well do it when I need a woman. We'll have a chance to get used to each other without family interference and political pressure. Sort of a working honey-moon." He rubbed his forehead and stared as Catherine stumbled around the fire trying to transfer the chunks of venison from roasting sticks to slabs of bread. "I can get Sven to perform the ceremony right away; and if Mother wants to go through it all again when we get to court, we can put up with that nuisance. At least we'd get things settled. Her father won't be able to back off and peddle her to somebody else, and Mother will have to move out of the king's quarters into the Dowager's suite."

He accepted a slab of bread with its dripping chunk of hot venison. "Thank you, my dear. How would you feel about getting married tomorrow?"

It was fortunate she had nothing to drop. She stepped back and stared at him. He bit into the meat, burning his tongue in the process. He spit it back on the bread and sucked cool air into his mouth, wiped the juice from his chin and cleared his throat. "I'm sorry to shock you, but I need a woman, and I feel guilty about taking one of the Amazons. If we're going to marry because of the treaty, we might as well get started while it might be fun."

She dropped to her knees and stared him in the face. "You're serious!"

"I'm always serious about sex." He smiled sadly at her. "When we get home to Arragor, we'll both be so tangled up in politics at court that we won't have a chance to get adjusted to each other. You're in love with Nikky now, and I can't blame you. I like and respect him, but he's not exactly the ideal lover. Furthermore, if you were going to run away with him, you'd have done it before this."

"My father and King Peter would never let us. We talked it over, and we couldn't have a life." She kept her eyes dry. "You're right about politics."

"Then let's make the best bargain we can. I'm still struggling to find out who I am, and being starved for a woman doesn't help. I can't stand the loneliness of playing in an empty bed, so either I take one of the

Amazons or we consummate the marriage we can't avoid. We're already engaged to marry, so it would dishonor you for me to take a mistress. You don't find me attractive, and I don't blame you. I'm not much of a beauty and I'm hairy as a bear, but you're going to have to give me an couple of heirs before you can safely look for a lover. Some time you're going to have to trust me to be gentle and to make things as pleasurable as possible. I'm asking you to do it now when I'm suffering."

"You suggested once before that I become your mistress before the marriage?"

"But now I'm suggesting that we get Sven to perform the ceremony. That way you save your reputation, and if we have a baby it will be legitimate."

"You know I don't love you."

"At least you don't gag any more."

She flushed and shook her head. "You're so damned reasonable about it."

His eyes bored into hers. "I'm trying to be honest with you. Women who have shared my bed tell me I am a satisfactory stud. I'm not in love with you, but I can offer you gentleness and consideration. I am sure I can make the experience physically pleasurable. That's the best I can offer. When marriage is inevitable, take pity on your husband and make the best of it."

Tears clouded her eyes as she gazed at his burly pelt and bulging breech clout. "There really isn't any way out of it."

"Your father will find you another husband if you reject me."

Catherine remembered the catalog of candidates Queen Elsa had enumerated, and shuddered. At least this man was honest. She reached out and touched his chest with her fingers. The pelt was soft, and she felt the warmth of his body beneath it.

"It's my fur," he said sadly. "You can't stand to think of lying next to all that hair."

She opened her hand and stroked him with her palm. He held himself still, and lightly leaned his chest toward her as her hand moved slowly to his shoulder and upper arm.

"Come to my bed tonight and feel the warmth of my body against yours. I promise to do nothing unless you are willing. Find out whether my body really revolts you. He took her hands and pressed them on his pectorals, then slid them gently down his flanks. "You might find you enjoy a warm body on a cool night. We'll wash in the lake and dry off in the sauna; then take a quick run through the chill night to my cabin. I promise absolute obedience for the night."

Her hands strayed across his muscular belly and withdrew almost reluctantly. "You promise not to force me?"

"You shall wear your daggers at your side. If I offend, you may plunge them where you will."

"No, I know you. I can trust your word." She straight-ened up and backed away. "If I find your body acceptable, you may talk to Sven in the morning."

He devoured his bread and meat, washing it down with strong tea. He watched her striving to be useful around the fire. "At least she has a good body," he murmured to himself.

That night when they joined the throng in the sauna cabin, Sven pulled Grimbolt aside. "I want you to come up with me to the north side of the island. We found a hot spring bubbling into a deep pool. The water is almost too hot for my hand, and it smells sulphurous. I want you and Alsenius to see if you think it might be safe to bathe in. I know he's convinced the hot water at the east end of the lake comes from a submerged cave and might make us sick the way the star cave poisoned me, but this seems different."

"He's probably right about the eastern water. There's very little life around there. Njal is convinced that something in the fallen star is poisonous."

"But there's no sulphur smell around the east cave. Nikky says the hot springs in Zharkovia smell like sulphur and sick people bathe in them to get well. Besides, there's a thick grove of trees around the pool we found today."

"I know what Njal will say," Grimbolt laughed. "He'll tell us to see whether the animals use the pool. If it doesn't harm them, it's probably safe for men. I'm not going near it because I've got to provide Arragor with an heir or two. Let Nikky check it out."

Sven laughed ruefully. "I suppose it can't do me any harm." He nudged Grimbolt with his elbow. "I notice your betrothed took a long time to give you your supper. Is she warming up?"

"I think she's almost resigned to the marriage. As a matter of fact, I was going to ask you tomorrow if you would perform the ceremony. I'm horny as a devil, and I might as well do it with my own wife as try to tame one of the Amazons."

"You think she'll finally take you?"

"Keep everybody away form my cabin tonight. We're going to see whether she can put up with my pelt."

"What will your mother think if you come home married.?"

"She may make us go through the ceremony all over again at court, but she'll be so glad about the alliance with Quatch that she won't complain about a little haste."

"I'll get Aspasia to help me with the ceremony. It's always good to use a Cleric even with a civil wedding."

Later in the evening Grimbolt and Catherine slipped down to the bathing pool and washed. Back in the sauna they dried off, and Grimbolt applied a stiff brush to his pelt. To his surprise, Catherine volunteered to brush his back. As the crowd began to thin, Sven and Alsenius slipped out and took station to follow Grimbolt and Catherine when they left. The princess retired with several of the other women to their quarters, and Grimbolt hurried to his cabin. He did not light the fire in his fireplace, but stripped off his breech clout and kept himself warm by brushing himself vigorously. Then by the light of s single small lamp he curled up on the blanket which covered his bed of fragrant balsam fir boughs.

A few minutes later Princess Catherine tapped at the door, lifted the latch, and slipped in. As soon as she had entered, Sven and Alsenius returned to Sven's quarters to arrange that no one disturb Grimbolt's cabin. Sven also sent for Aspasia to make arrangements for a possible wedding.

Catherine had a cloak wrapped tightly around her as she sat on a stool to remove her boots. When she rose to her feet, she looked hungrily at the cold hearth and shivered.

"We sha'n't need a fire," he rumbled. "Do you want to put the lamp out?"

She hesitated for a second, then answered, "No. I think I want to see."

"Take off your cloak and let me warm you. You can throw it over us if you like."

As she approached the bed, he uncurled himself and lay back to reveal his urgency. She stared at him and felt a panicked urge to run away.

"You'll get used to it." His voice was very soft and dark. He lifted his arms toward her. "Come, take off that cloak and let me warm you properly."

She turned her back to him as she slipped out of the cloak. She turned shyly toward him, dropped the cloak over his feet, then straightened to show her body. His hungry grin pleased her, and she came to the side of the bed. The chill of the room began to raise goose flesh on her arms, and she shivered.

"Come," he murmured. "It's all right."

She sat tentatively on the edge of the blanket and let his arms pull her against him. His body hair felt almost silky, not harsh as she expected. She let him draw her down against his flank and pull the cloak over their shoulders. The heat of his body soothed her as his arms drew her against him. Instinctively she nestled closer to his comforting warmth; then he turned toward her and clasped her protectively against him.

"It's all right," he said. "Just let me drive the chill away."

She felt his entire body envelope her, yet she felt no fear, only warmth and safety. Gradually her body relaxed against him as his hairy chest slowly expanded against her with his deep slow breath. Her own shallow gasps slowed to match his rhythm: her hands unclenched, and her head relaxed in the hollow of his shoulder.

Grimbolt felt her drop off to sleep and lay very still to cradle her. He curbed his own urgency and kept his breathing deep. She was accepting him, trusting him. He must be patient as a fisherman enticing a trout. He must wait till she wanted to come to him. He forced the tenseness from his shoulders and strove to quiet the churning of his belly.

Nearly an hour passed before she stirred. Gradually she became conscious that her pillow was very warm and fuzzy and that it rose and fell rhythmically. After a moment of panic, she remembered where she was. Yet she felt somehow safe and comfortable. She nestled closer to his warmth. Even when she felt his hairy arms feathering down her back and along her flanks, she accepted them as part of her vague sense of well-being. When the stroking strayed to her buttocks, a twinge of alarm made her lift her head and stare up into his bearded face. He moved against her and brought his lips down to brush hers while his palms moved to cup her breasts. Even this intimacy seemed comfortable and protecting.

He shifted his weight to ease his cramped muscles without losing his contact with her body. It was over a half hour before she realized how intimate the presence of his body, his arms, his mouth had become; yet somehow she felt no jab of fear, only an increasing unease as she felt her body responding to his. The trout drifted closer to the lure, but he was using no hook—only the deft caressing of his hands as his body moved cautiously to enfold her. Even when the sharp pain of his first entrance pierced her, she was so far under his spell that she clutched him tighter as she drove her nails into his hide and they blended into nature's timeless dance.

The autumn night was long, and the harmony of their blending repeated more than once the change from *largo pianissimo* to *presto furioso*. They warmed each other's dreams late into the morning, and Sven made sure no one disturbed them.

When they joined the company for the noon meal, Sven signaled Grimbolt to approach. He noted that the princess followed him closely, even touching him as he leaned to talk.

"Is there to be a wedding?" he asked.

Grimbolt turned toward Catherine, and she nodded shyly. They took seats at the table, and Sven rose in his place to announce, "Today we are going to have a half holiday. Aspasia and I are going to perform a royal marriage ceremony joining Crown Prince Grimbolt of Arragor and Princess Catherine of Quatch. You are all invited to the wedding, and we shall have a special feast and sauna gathering before we carry the bride and groom to the bridal bed."

"Something tells me," Njal muttered to Emma, "They've already shared the bridal bed."

"They do seem better acquainted," she smirked. "She can't keep her hands off him."

"And he looks pretty smug," he added.

Lord Nicholas applauded with the rest, but huddled within himself as he watched the royal pair. He had known the wedding would come, but being warned 'This is going to hurt,' doesn't lessen the pain when it comes. Nevertheless, when Sven asked him to sing at the wedding, he consented gladly, though his heart still sang a small threnody of its own.

Sven's ceremony was simple adaptation of his mother's. He charged both partners to be faithful, to share all property, and to defend each other from danger. Knowing Grimbolt's devotion to the Goddess, he blessed them in her name. The couple pledged monogamy and faithful care for all offspring. They promised physical, emotional and financial sharing and support. Aspasia invoked the favor of the Guardians. Nicholas sang a hymn to Alfather at the beginning and one to the Mother Goddess at the end. During the climactic kiss, everybody noticed that the bride pressed close against her husband's furry chest.

At the festival supper congratulations blended with bawdy cliches which became increasingly anatomical as repeated toasts relaxed the crowd.

Everybody slapped Grimbolt on the shoulder and hugged Catherine, so that by the time they adjourned to the sauna, both were sore and weary. The boisterous bedding of the bride would be anticlimactic, but they both knew how to disguise their feelings, even in the hurly-burly of public celebration.

The couple sipped sparingly, as did Alsenius, the Chief Groomsman, and Mahla, the Matron of Honor. When the party adjourned to the Sauna, Nicholas led the songs of fertility and pleasure. Njal's illusions inspired imaginative horseplay among the men, while the women disapprovingly egged them on.

"You can join our exploration team tomorrow," Sven consoled her, "and we can get away for a few days with a small band of friends. I want you, Njal, and Alsenius to look at the hot spring we found yesterday. I think Emma and Njal are in pretty much the same boat with you two. A couple of Njal's amphibians saw them doing some athletic swimming off the south beach."

As early as they dared, Mahla and the bride's attendants vanished from the sauna and took over Grimbolt's cabin, which they decked with greenery and supplied with baskets of eggs, wild asparagus, and other aphrodisiac dainties. They built a roaring fire in the fireplace and wove fresh balsam for the bed. When Catherine arrived, they carefully folded her bridal garments and washed and perfumed the bride before placing her in the bed, covered with a blanket.

When the signal from the women reached the sauna, Alsenius and Sven stripped the bridegroom and carried him off to the lake, where they scrubbed him and dried him off with rough towels. As they curry-combed his pelt, the spectators commented. At last he donned the ceremonial white robe, and they carried him to the door of the cabin. Alsenius knocked three times and Aspasia demanded, "Who comes?"

"The king is come to claim his own." Alsenius roared, and thundered on the door.

"Let him stand and be recognized." She opened the door. They stood Grimbolt on the threshold and stripped off his robe at the same time Mahla flung back the blanket from the bride.

"This is indeed my husband," Catherine affirmed.

"This is indeed my bride." Grimbolt replied.

The women withdrew, and Sven and Alsenius escorted Grimbolt to the bed and placed him beside the bride.

"We witness that this is the true bride," the groomsmen testified. "We witness that the true bridegroom has joined the bride," the women answered, and they pulled the blanket over the couple and filed out. Grimbolt embraced Catherine, and spectators from the doorway and the windows testified, "We have seen the true bridegroom embrace the true bride. Let none disturb the secret of their joining." Alsenius closed the door and the women hung reed mats over the windows, Most of the party paired off and wandered into the woods to celebrate. A few confirmed bachelors stayed by the cabin and chanted bawdy songs, but soon even those departed and left the couple in peace.

A few days before the wedding, Njal was poking through his null-space box searching for a the scroll of a **METAMORPH** spell which he vaguely remembered tucking away several years before. The box took up only the space of a normal scroll tube in his rucksack, but the pocket dimension to which it opened would hold hundreds of scrolls. Since he was a child of imagination and impulse rather than of order, he had never bothered to develop an indexing spell. As a result the floor around him was strewn with dozens of scroll tubes which he had pulled out and cast aside.

Emma was trying vainly to bring some order to pile. "Why don't you make bundles of the same kind of scroll so you won't have to waste so much time rooting around in there?" she demanded.

"Too busy." he muttered as he deciphered the label on another tube.

"But think of the time you'd save in the long run." She grabbed a tube at random and tried to decipher the label.

"Here, leave that alone. You can't read it. It's written in *Magic*." He turned again to his scrutiny of the scroll in his hand.

"If you'd label them in Common, I could catalog them for you. As it is, it takes you an age to decipher the labels."

"I can't always remember which dialect of *Magic* I used for a particular label. For instance, this one is labeled in Norse runes because I happened to get it from a Norse wizard. But those," he gestured toward a small pile, "are scrolls I got from my mentor Siegmacht the Bull, so they're labeled in Acadian Norse."

"Well, at least let me sort out the ones from Siegmacht." She studied the labels on the Siegmacht scrolls, hoping to be able to recognize the script.

"What kind of scroll is that?" She grabbed it before it got lost in the pile.

"It's a spell for summoning bees."

"Are there any other SUMMONING spells around here?"

"Oh yes, lots. I got a whole batch of them from Germond the Bald."

"And how were those labeled?"

"He used a local dialect of Common."

She studied the label and then set about collecting others in the same script. Njal pulled another scroll from his box and tapped it thoughtfully. "This is a spell for turning people into frogs. I'd better examine this one." He stuffed it into his blouse with four other tubes.

"Here! Let me take those before you rip your blouse." She pulled the tubes from his bosom and stuffed them into a sack, which she promptly labeled. "Who are you going to turn into frogs?" she demanded.

"Nobody. I'm trying to adapt my mer-folk illusions into spells which will actually change physical structure. I have half a dozen people who want me to make them permanently into amphibians. They want to found a new race who can live as comfortably in the lake as they can on the island. I have studied amphibian anatomy so that I can adjust the lungs to breathe either air or water and I have built retractable webs for their hands and feet. I have even developed erectile tissue on their feet so that they can enlarge to swimming flippers in water and shrink to normal feet for walking. I haven't worked out an underwater adjustment for the vocal mechanism yet, but that will come. What I want now is a way to combine the METAMORPH magic with Illusion and SHADOW magic so that I can achieve the accuracy of my SHADOW-ILLUSION spells with the permanence of METAMORPH."

"And those six want to become permanent amphibians?"

"Yes. They are three couples who don't get on very well with the rest of the Liberated. Jon Chowter and his wife found four others who want to separate without having to move away from the protection of the rest of the tribe."

"Will their children be amphibians?"

"I don't know whether magically acquired characteristics will breed true or not. I shall have to write out a scroll of the spell when I perfect it; then they will have to train one of their number as a Mage. If the children are born normal, the Mage can cast the spell on each as it comes along."

"I suppose he could delay the spell and see whether the child chooses to be normal or amphibean."

"Having the scroll would also allow for conversion of any other adults whom they want to adopt." He dropped the scroll he was scanning and pulled out another. "Another summoning spell—this time tigers."

She grabbed it, and stuffed it into the bag with the other summoning scrolls. By noon Emma was bored beyond enduring. She snatched his box away from him and placed it on a shelf beyond his reach. "Time for a swim and lunch and a nap" she announced.

Njal protested, but she was both stronger and more stubborn. "I'll race you down to the lake," she challenged, "or do I have to carry you?" She started to strip off her clothes.

While she was pulling her blouse over her head, Njal slipped on his **RING OF INVISIBILITY** and created an illusion of his naked body running toward the lake. The illusion won the race and swam swiftly beyond her reach. Meanwhile Njal had leisure to strip and stroll. Presently he waded out and directed his illusion to join him.

"You cheated," she grumbled as she splashed out to him. "You used magic." She grabbed him in both arms and plunged under the water.

After their nap. They returned to the null-space box of scrolls. Njal took time to announce the kind of scroll he had before he tossed it aside, and Emma tried to find others of the same sort. By the time he had emptied his magical box. Njal had found seven scrolls of interest, including one labeled **METAMORPH**. This scroll he studied for the rest of the day and all the next day, taking notes and even drawing diagrams of patterns of magical force. After this—using a special pen and magical ink—he laboriously copied parts of three scrolls; then he added sections of his mer-folk illusion.

"Can't I help you with all that copying?" Emma demanded. "I write a much more elegant hand than you do."

"But you don't understand magic," he reminded her. "One wrong word or gesture—one false inflection of the voice, any error, however minor—will cause a spell to fail or even to misfire."

"I suppose that's why you take so long about copying."

"This writing material costs five gold pieces a sheet, and the magical ink contains frightfully expensive ingredients, and one can't correct a mistake. One error wastes the whole sheet."

"I'm glad I'm a warrior maiden."

"A warrior what? After what you've been doing to me, you're no maid." He leaned toward her to pinch her buttocks, and she answered by kissing him firmly.

Three weeks after the royal wedding Njal finally announced that he was ready to try the new spell. He took his first volunteers—Jon and Helmwege—to a deserted beach. "This is an extremely complex and difficult spell." Njal warned them. "Are you certain that you want permanently to change into Mer-Folk? The changes in your bodies will be complicated and profound. Even I cannot reverse them if you should change your minds, so you must be certain that you wish to remain in your new form for life. After I have gone, no ordinary Priest or Mage can safely attempt reversal."

"We are certain."

"I do not know whether this transformation will pass through you to your children. Magically acquired character-istics sometimes become part of the essential chemistry of the body and therefore breed true, but often they act like surgical changes, which cannot be inherited. I rather suspect than your children will be Mer-Folk, but I will leave you a copy of the spell, so that you can change your children if they are born human."

"Does that mean we can change other adults if they want to join us?" Helmwege asked.

"Yes, but make sure the spell is cast by a Mage or Illusionist of at least seventh level, preferably higher. This is a difficult spell which blends different types of magic. It is not a spell for dabblers."

"You promised you would transform the other four who have been helping us with the underwater exploration," said Jon.

Njal nodded.

"Miriamne is studying to be a Mage. We'll make sure she gets trained to a high enough level."

"If you are sure you desire this permanent change, you should strip and wade out till the water reaches your waists." Njal waited until they were in place; then he commenced the long, complicated incantation. After several minutes a blue-green globe of light formed in his hands. Still chanting he carried the globe carefully out to the couple and placed it so that it engulfed Jon's head. The globe expanded downward until it covered his entire body—pushing aside the water and even the sand on which he stood. His features blurred for the count of a hundred and seven; then the his body seemed to suck in the light. He cried out—not in pain, but feeling a convulsive churning throughout his body. Finally he re-appeared with a massively enlarged chest and webbing between his fingers and toes.

"Try swimming," Njal commanded.

As Jon plunged his head into the water and inhaled, he felt the water filling his lungs as his feet expanded. With a dolphin flip of his legs he surged forward into the deep water and arrowed easily toward the island. They could hear him howl from the depths to prove that he had underwater speech. He turned sharply and sped back toward them, lowered his feet and stood. Water poured effortlessly from his mouth. "It's perfect," he exclaimed. "Do it to Helmwege."

Njal repeated the ritual, and he and Emma watched as the couple streaked to deep water, cavorting and shouting to demonstrate their power. Shortly they waved to the couple on the shore and disappeared in the depths.

That evening, Njal reported his success to the assembly and congratulated Sven on becoming leader of the bi-racial Tribe of the Liberated. The next day he performed the transformation on the remaining four volunteers. After a few days of observation, he reported to Sven that his work was done.

XV—Homewards

A week after Njal's triumph, Bengt and Carla returned to camp trailing a large canvas package on a magical travois. A ripple of excitement ran through the tribe, and Sven decided to hold an open meeting to make sure everyone understood why he had sent two of their number to retrieve his private hoard of treasure.

Those who questioned Bengt and Carla about their journey found the pair unenthusiastic about their burden.

"The whole trip was a waste of time," Carla said to the women who crowded around her. "It was a long hard ride, and we had to go out of our way to get around all the soldiers. Bengt says they came from the Zharkovian army that fought the Amazons. He said they were looking for star metal and they'd make prisoners of us. That meant we had to sneak in to get Sven's junk and sneak it out again before they caught us."

Bengt, meanwhile, told the men that the so-called star metal was practically useless. "Heat doesn't soften it up, so you can't make anything out of it, and it's so hard you can't even make coins out of it. It's just a lot of hard, heavy, ugly lumps."

"What about the Zharkovian soldiers?"

"They found a deep chasm where the fallen star crashed. I sneaked into their camp and talked with some of them, and they said the men who got sent in to dig out the metal all got sick. And most of them died. They said they got some heavy nuggets of the stuff, but it was so hard it broke their hammers when they tried to break the lumps down so that they could carry it. Then when they tried to melt the nuggets down to purify the metal, they couldn't even soften them."

"How did you get away?"

"They were so busy taking care of the sick and dying they weren't paying any attention to discipline. The soldiers were camped miles from the place where Sven hid his stuff. We managed to dig it up and load it on the magic travois without being bothered, and we skirted around the

Zharkovians without any trouble. The mission wasn't really dangerous, it was just a waste of time."

When Sven had the twenty-three greyish lumps spread out for inspection on a large table in front of the central cabin, the rest of the tribe were unimpressed. Strong men commented on their weight and hardness, but everybody agreed that sending the couple on a two-month's mission to fetch his private bag of 'stuff' was an abuse of Sven's authority.

In the privacy of their cabin Mahla grumbled, "Why did you bother with that junk in the first place? We can't make anything out of it."

Sven explained again that the metal was rare and valuable. "Grimbolt is willing to give me more than their weight in gold for five of those chunks. A Weapons-Master can fashion mighty swords out of this metal."

"Then you should have kept the stuff hidden and paid Bengt and Carla out of your own pouch. Everybody's mad at you now. I'll bet there's a motion at tonight's meeting to vote you out and elect somebody else chief. You don't have the sense of a new-born."

"Trust me, my love, I'm not as innocent as I look." Sven went out and stood on the box which had been set out for him. The rumbling tribe crowded around, and Chief Sven smiled benignly down at them. "Doesn't look like much. Does it?"

"I'm sorry, friend Sven, but it looks like a long hard journey for nothing." Bengt gestured scornfully at the table.

"You know I sent you because the tribe needed me here whole we were building. Would you have been able to organize the work while I went off to fetch my treasure?"

Bengt looked at the neatly arranged cabins and public buildings and shrugged. "You always had a gift for organization, Sven. That's why Moonflower let you get away with so mich back at Southmark."

"If you'd brought back a sack of gold and jewels, you wouldn't have minded going, would you?"

"Real treasure is one thing," one of the Amazons interrupted, "but these lumps aren't good for anything."

"Do you still have your iron sword?" Sven asked.

"Sure." She pulled a massive bastard sword from its scabbard.

"Will you try to break one of those nuggets with your sword?"

She suspected a trick and approached the table warily. "You think those lumps of metal with nick my blade."

"I know they will. Here, Alsenius, will you bring your sword here?"

Alsenius pressed to the center and drew his long sword. "This blade is made from star metal like those lumps. The star metal is so hard that only the heat of volcanic fire can make it workable. It I struck your sword with mine, the iron sword would break like a clay pot. Do you want me to prove it?" Alsenius raised his weapon."

The Amazon promptly sheathed her sword. "Your sword is magic, and your arm is mighty. I've seen you in battle."

"My sword is magical because the star metal is tough enough to stand the strain of enchantment. No wizard would charm that iron stick of yours. How often do you have to sharpen it?"

"It gets pretty dull every time I hit something with it," she confessed.

"When I have fought all day, smiting metal armor, swords, and maces, all I need to do is wipe off the blood. This star metal cannot ne blunted. I have not sharpened it in the ten years I have wielded it, and behold!" He flung a scarf into the air and held his sword out to intercept its fall. The scarf landed on the sharp edge and fell in two pieces to the ground. "So much for my mighty arm!"

"Here let me show you a real weapon." Grimbolt waded through the crowd and flourished his scepter. "The royal Scepter of Arragor is a simple club made of star metal. It has been fancied up to look royal, but underneath all the glitter you can see the substance." He spoke the command and revealed the dull grey metal in which the gems were embedded. "The star metal has stood up to all the rigors of enchantment so that it not only strikes with irresistible force, but also takes any weapon form the wielded wishes. At his command it became a flaming sword, a menacing mace, a massive pole-arm, and a formidable lance. "No other metal can take such massive enchantment. I have offered Sven 10,000 gold pieces for enough of his metal to make five sword blades."

The crowd backed away in awe of the two weapons. Sven drew his dagger and held it aloft. "I wield a simple weapon made of star metal. My dagger is not enchanted, yet this little blade has broken iron Amazon swords in battle."

Reina cried out from the crowd. "I saw it happen in the attack on Southmark. One of my war-sisters swung an iron sword down at his head, and his dagger snapped her blade when it blocked the stroke."

Sven quickly capitalized on this advantage. "You see what a valuable treasure Bengt and Carla have brought home for us. Think what a prize it will be if we can entice a Weapons-Master to come and live with us and work our metal." He waited for the weight of his words to impress them. Then when the hubbub died down, he struck his final blow. "Dear friends, this is too valuable a treasure for one man. I sent Bengt and Carla openly to fetch my treasure because I wanted you to know that it is no longer my private hoard. This treasure of star metal belongs to all of you. This treasure which cost me my power to beget sons and daughters I freely give to The Tribe of the Liberated who become the sons and daughters I can never have."

If he at that moment had demanded kingship, they would have crowned him gleefully. They chaired him around the camp followed by the table with its precious load. They screamed and shouted until their voices failed. Finally they put him down beside his wife and dashed off to collect supplies for a celebration.

It was during the party the Grimbolt announced his departure. "Princess Catherine and I thank you for your hospitality. We have had time after the wedding to get accustomed to marriage, and we must now return to Arragor. We must be crowned and prepare our kingdom for renewed hostilities from the Hegemony." He placed his arm around Sven's shoulders and added, "We pronounce our royal will that my kingdom of Arragor and the Tribe of the Liberated are henceforth both friends and allies. We shall indeed purchase a share in your star metal treasure, and we shall strive to defend you from the aggressions of the Hegemony. If we are successful in liberating more of the Amazons, we will offer them freedom to join your ranks."

After the cheering had died down, Alsenius, Njal, and Emma announced their intention to accompany the royal couple. Nicholas then rose to announce that he still had official business with Queen Elsa of Arragor and that he too would be leaving.

"What business do you have with my mother now that I am King?" Grimbolt demanded as they sweated in the sauna.

"I am sure that your Majesty will need to approve the matter, but . . ."

"Nikky, I shall be crowned as soon as I reach home." Grimbolt's stern voice distanced him from his friend. "I shall deal with all business myself. The regency is at an end."

"I don't question your authority. It's just that my business with the Queen Dowager is of a rather personal nature."

"You're not having an affair with her? I regard you as a friend, even though my wife still hankers for you, but I don't want you hanging around the court as my father-in-law."

"Great Guardians no!" Nicholas exclaimed. "She's old enough to be my mother. It's just that King Peter's instructions are that I should talk with her first."

Grimbolt's tone deepened. "About what?"

Lord Nicholas hesitated. "You place me in an awkward position. Protocol requires that I address you in the presence of your council."

"Council be damned! I plan to send them all packing except for old Septimus. What are you and your tricksy master plotting?"

"Very well." Nicholas surrendered. "Arragor has become allied with Quatch by virtue of your marriage to Queen-designate Catherine. King Peter is apprehensive. He does not wish to confront the Hegemony of the Pythoness without allies, nor does he wish to play odd-man-out to your alliance. He is proposing an alliance with Arragor cemented by a marriage between himself and the Queen-Dowager of Arragor. The Queen of Zharkovia has been long dead, and King Peter has instructed me to assure her Majesty that he will dismiss his concubines if she accepts his offer. He is a few years older than her Majesty, but he directs me to assure her he can perform the office of a husband with vigor and enthusiasm." Nicholas smirked self-consciously. "I know several of his mistresses very well, and their only objection to his attentions seems to be the frequency of their pregnancies. He instructs me to promise the royal succession to his legitimate offspring out of her Majesty. There has long been bitter speculation about which of King Peter's bastards will be the designated heir. Young Peter, Justin, and Igor hold the rank of Prince, but he refuses to elevate anyone to Crown Prince. If his Majesty were to die suddenly Prince Igor is the oldest, but Peter has his father's name and Justin has the strongest following in the army. Everyone at court wants the King to marry again while he is still able to beget a true heir."

"And you have instructions to offer my mother the throne of Zharkovia?"

"Yes, your Majesty."

Grimbolt flung his arms around Lord Nicholas, almost smothering him. "Nikky, Nikky, I can't think of a better arrangement. If she can be persuaded to accept, we establish a blood alliance among the three great kingdoms; furthermore you get Mother out of my hair while I'm learning to govern. I pray that you are as skillful a diplomat as you are blood hound and canary. You have just given me another reason for leaving immediately."

The Liberated used the departure as another excuse for a party, and the sauna rang with toasts to the travelers on the night before the departure.

"I assume you'll be stopping at the Great Forest on your way home," Sven said.

"Oh yes, I want Leander's blessing on the marriage. Can I take any message?"

Please ask him if he could send us a junior Druid to help us with hunting and fishing procedures as well as with the farming. We plan to follow the way of the Goddess toward nature, and a Druid's guidance would be very helpful."

"He should be able to tell you definitely about the hot springs," Alsenius put in. "I think those on the north shore are safe, and I suspect the hot cave at the eastern end of the lake is deadly, but a Druid should be able to tell you at a glance."

"I'll keep you informed if we learn any more about the star metal." Sven added. "You're right about other things being more important, but it would be helpful to have a few superior weapons in case we're attacked."

"The metal will also be valuable for trade." Alsenius turned aside to take his leave of Reina.

"Unfortunately if rumor gets around that we have the metal, it will tempt our neighbors to try to conquer us instead of trade for it." Sven worried.

"I meant what I said in the sauna about an alliance." Grimbolt rode back to Sven and grasped his hand. "I don't think King Peter is interested in conquest. He must really want peace if he's willing to marry my mother on Nicholas' recommendation. If you have trouble with the Pythoness, send immediately to me. Arragor will not stand by and watch those witches expand their dominions."

Nikky leaned gracefully down from his horse and offered Sven a sheet of papyrus. "In an emergency, write a message on this and throw it into a fire with the command 'Zharkovia!' It will appear in King Peter's study immediately, and he can forward it to Grimbolt. King Peter is also determined that the Hegemony of the Pythoness shall not expand."

Alsenius hugged Reina closely. "I wish you were going with us, but you are right. I would be away too much for a husband, and there is too much difference in our levels as Fighters for you to adventure with me. You are only a second level Fighter and I am now 14th. You could not protect yourself against my enemies, and I would be too busy fighting to defend you. As a result, you would be left alone when I went out on a quest, and my absences might ne very long."

"And there would be children to take care of, so that I could never catch up with you." Reina looked up at him sadly. "It has been wonderful, and I will never forget you. Here I can progress at my own speed, and The Liberated can use my abilities."

"We've been good comrades together. You'll find a proper mate in the tribe."

She looked dubious.

"Yes you will, just as I will find new companions wherever Lord Ambloq leads me. Now that you're free of the Pythoness, you need to settle down to a normal life. You were a farmer lass before the Priestesses kidnaped you. You've enjoyed the chance to go adventuring, but that's no life for a sensible woman like you."

She nodded sadly, kissed him again, and held his stirrup as he mounted his palfrey.

"Is she pregnant?" Njal asked as they rode off.

"Great Guardians! I never thought to ask." Alsenius looked back, but Reina had already blended in with the crowd returning to the encampment. "If she's stuck with a child, I hope it's not too dark."

"Cheer up, it can always volunteer for Amphibian service," Njal laughed. "Nobody will notice skin color under water."

To make sure the party got stared in the right direction, Sven accompanied them until they stopped for the noon break. After the meal he repeated his travel advice. "Remember that traveling in a straight line is very difficult when there are no trails. You need to keep an eye on the sun, or you'll find yourselves going in a circle. Keep the afternoon sun ahead of you and to the right. In a couple of days these rolling steppes will level out into the coastal plain; then you'll find trails you can follow. Keep going south, and you'll find more trees."

"I know," laughed Grimbolt, "keep going south till the woodland grows into the Great Forest. And I know all about the Druid's guards."

With a last arm clasp, Sven turned his horse north-ward and the royal party continued on its way. The next morning, Catherine struggled from the sleeping bag and confessed that she dreaded the thought of breakfast and mounting her horse. "I hardly slept at all last night. The ground hurts my back, and all that roasted meat disagreed with me."

"You'll get back into the swing of traveling," her husband reassured her. "Maybe I can find a second sleeping bag to pad your saddle. There was nothing wrong with dinner. We all ate it, and nobody's sick. I'll get you a plate of the bacon Njal is cooking. That will settle your stomach and build you up for another day's riding."

She gagged at the thought of bacon, but finally Grimbolt persuaded her at least to nibble on a crust of bread. By noon she was able to wolf down some jerky before she collapsed into sleep. It was with great reluctance that she mounted her horse for the afternoon's ride. Alsenius had to dash forward and catch her when she fell asleep in the saddle; after that Grimbolt had to ride close to her side so that she could doze as she rode.

"There is no fever," Emma reported when they stopped for the night and Catherine dropped into a limp heap. "She doesn't have any difficulty breathing, and her pulse is strong." She glared accusingly at Grimbolt. "Don't tell me you've got her pregnant already?"

"I suppose it's possible. We've been pretty busy since the wedding. After all I hadn't had a woman for a couple of months. That's why we decided to get married."

"Well it was stupid to make her pregnant just before a long ride."

"Now look, it takes two to make a baby. I didn't rape her, you know."

"Well, you're supposed to take care of your wife."

"Oh, stop fussing," Catherine wailed. "Can't you do something to make me feel better?"

"Perhaps," Njal suggested, "a cup of tea and a few cushions to sit on." He grabbed some dry wood and started a fire while Grimbolt dumped everything out of the saddle bags looking for something soft. Within half an hour, she was propped up against a small tree padded with blankets. The tea had settled her stomach and she was nibbling with ravenous caution at a carefully roasted leg of a chicken.

Suddenly she had become the focus of the entire party, and she reveled in the attention. Her slightest qualm sent tremors through the whole expedition, and her whim became law. She was pregnant, and the world was hers.

When Grimbolt crawled into the sleeping bag with her, he was diligently subservient. In the morning the whole party cosseted her nausea, and her husband found himself riding with her cushioned on his lap. The journey to the Great Forest took nine days instead of the expected six, as the expedition adjusted itself to her metabolism. When they arrived at the Druid's massive Sequoia, they were amazed to see Lord Septimus of Arragor.

"What brings you here?" Grimbolt demanded. "I thought you were protecting the kingdom from my mother."

"Unfortunately the kingdom needs more protection than I could provide," the Lord Steward confessed. He briefly told of Bodvarka's arrival as the Pythoness' Ambassador, of the gift of the magical circ, and of his failure to keep the Queen from putting the jewel around her neck. "The ambassador stopped me with a **HOLD** spell before I could prevent her Majesty. Lord Crabhook was convinced that the Ambassador intended to kill me, and he insisted on getting me out of the country immediately both to save my life and to find and warn your majesty. The Druid assured me that you would stop here on your way home and persuaded me to wait for you."

"Probably the best thing you could do. You would have found me difficult to overtake with all the armies tramping through the northern steppes. Have you got any later news from Arragor?"

"Leander has used animal spies to keep check on the kingdom, and your mother and Lord Crabhook have been amazingly successful. They've stationed the army on the border of the Hegemony but the priestesses have not sent any Amazons against them. Apparently your mother has succeeded in driving the Ambassador out. She is still in grave danger from the circ, but Lord Farsyte has her sequestered in the temple under protection of a **NULL MAGIC ZONE**. The result seems to be a stand-off between Arragor and the Hegemony. We must get you home as quickly as possible. If ever a country needed her king, it's Arragor."

While Lord Septimus and Grimbolt were conferring, Miranda, the Priestess of Gaea, carried Catherine to her quarters and quickly confirmed that her malady was indeed pregnancy.

"You're as healthy as an elephant," she reassured the Princess, "though you'll soon feel like one. Just make sure you don't sit around feeling sorry for yourself. As soon as the morning sickness passes, you'll want to eat like a cougar. That's fine, but don't fatten yourself up with sweets and dainties. Eat plenty of plain nourishing food and keep busy. You want to feed the baby well, but you don't want to lay on a lot of lard. Birthing is no picnic, but it will be a lot easier if you keep your muscles supple and your figure as trim as the baby permits. If you want to stay here till the lying in, I'll find plenty of useful work for you around the Forest and get you fit for the battle."

Grimbolt had his mouth open to accept the invitation, but Catherine overbore him vigorously, "I'm afraid I have obligations at court. My mother-in-law will want a formal wedding, even though we're already married, and my new duties as Queen will demand all of my attention."

"I'm sure . . ." Grimbolt tried again.

"My dear, you know you have to get back to Arragor and take up your kingly duties. You've been fretting all along the journey about the reforms you need to make and the magic you need to learn. Our kingdom needs us, and I am not going to let anything keep us from our duties."

"But your first duty is to give us an heir." Grimbolt finally got a word in, "and Arragor is in crisis."

"Nevertheless the heir should be born in Arragor so that everybody will know he's really ours," the Princess insisted. "What would the court think if I marched in about a year from now and presented them with a strange child. It's bad enough that he was conceived abroad."

"But the ride to Arragor!"

"I'm sure Lord Leander can provide me with safe transport." She looked pleadingly at the Druid. "Surely you can spare a couple of apes to carry a sedan chair. I'm sure I can trust your ingenuity to get me home safely." She turned back to Grimbolt. "Think what my father would say if you told him you had left me to give birth in a forest."

Miranda smiled wisely. "I am sure your Majesty will manage everything for your own ease, but remember the birth channel is a narrow passage into life, and a fat baby won't shrink to get through."

The Princess swayed uncertainly as a sudden wave of nausea swept her, and the men quickly carried her off to a comfortable guest chamber.

Leander took Grimbolt aside into a nearby glade. "Young man, you have a very determined bride. Pregnancy is a very difficult time, and she is going to need a tremendous amount of support as well as a firm guiding hand."

"I'm going to be very busy taking over my kingdom," Grimbolt protested. "My mother is used to running things, and she's not going to like yielding power."

"And yours is not a love match?"

Grimbolt shrugged. "She's still in love with the canary. I've given her some genuine pleasure in bed, but she doesn't particularly like me."

"And you?"

"She's not a bad bedfellow now she's learned the ropes, but she's a spoiled brat. Furthermore she's ignorant. She has a fixed opinion on everything and information about nothing. I'd like nothing better than to leave her here with your wife to take care of her."

"Maybe it's just as well you don't dote on her. She's going to need a lot of intelligent support. She's very fearful and very good at getting her own way. Can you keep your temper?"

"I think so."

"She's going to be completely unpredictable. One minute she will cling to you and need intense affection; the next moment, nothing you do will be right. She will go from brainless joy to suicidal gloom. She will hate you and then drag you to bed in the middle of an important meeting. She will scream, weep buckets, and giggle uncontrollably. She will demand the impossible and then not want it when you provide it. But remember she is sharing her body with a creature that has no mercy—no consideration—no consciousness beyond its own needs. The baby will take over her body, ruin its shape, its coordination, and its predictable rhythms. If you provide her with steadfast consideration and stability during this time, you may well win her devotion for life."

"That's asking a lot."

"She's giving a lot. If you were in love, it would be easier for her, because she desperately needs love."

"So do I." Grimbolt turned aside to regain control.

"If you are a faithful partner in this struggle, comrade-ship will grow. You will discover her strengths and appreciate them. You will discover her weaknesses and learn to compensate. If you become a fellowship, love of a kind will grow."

"Well, at least she plays the game in the sleeping bag." Grimbolt laughed ruefully.

"And that's important." Leander squeezed his shoulder. "If you give her a good time there, she'll put up with a lot elsewhere."

"Ah, Grimbolt, I'm glad I found you." Miranda strode up. "Your wife is settled in bed, and she wants you."

He shrugged out of Leander's grip. "I'll try," he murmured. He bowed slightly to the Priestess. "Thank you, milady. I'll see what she wants."

What Catherine wanted was her own way, but unfortunately she hadn't yet figured out what that way was. She was uncomfortable and afraid, and the hairy oaf who had talked her into marriage was responsible. When he strolled into her room, obviously not suffering from either discomfort or fear, she lashed out at him. "How dare you talk about leaving me behind while you go back to Arragor and king it?"

Grimbolt started a logical explanation that she could get better care here and she wouldn't have to suffer the discomfort of the journey to Arragor.

"Better care? Bullied by that Priestess-Harpy? You just want to get rid of me so you can go back to your mistresses."

"But . . ." He wanted to remind her that he was too homely and hairy to attract mistresses, but she gave him no time.

"You got me into this mess and now you're going to desert me. You don't love me, and now I'm too sick to satisfy that raging appetite of yours."

"Now wait a minute . . ."

"All I'm good for is to give you that damned heir your mother wants, and you can wallow with a harem of whores."

"But . . ."

"I'm going to get fat and ugly and maybe die while your precious mother gloats over her Crown Prince. And you don't even care if I die."

Grimbolt could feel his control weakening. He could not imagine where she dreamed up the "harem of whores." He had been a diligent husband and hadn't even had a chance to look at another woman. Her semi-hysterical plaints beat upon his ears and allowed no answer. Suddenly he understood. He remembered his own moments of terror when he stood on the barge's gangway with no memory and no guidance—no mother to hug him and tell him it was all right. Without thinking—ignoring her fists beating on his shoulders—he grabbed her out of the bed and clutched her to his hairy chest. He squeezed as gently as he could, but he squeezed.

Her fury quickly spent itself in pounding his back, and he sank to the bed and adjusted their position till her face neared his. Then he stopped her protests with his mouth.

She collapsed against him, pouring her frustration and panic out first in curses, then in tears. Suddenly she felt his embrace as protection, and she clutched him as defense against the world. His grasp eased into a stroking clasp which reminded her of his patient exploration of her body on their first night together, and she began fumbling with the ties on his kilt.

That evening Njal had a long conversation with Leander about his AMPHIBIAN spell.

"I marvel that you were able to accomplish anything building from an illusion," the Druid rumbled. "I should certainly have started from the biology of breathing. You have created a very complex spell with a lot of variables which could go wrong. See how much simpler it would be to start here." He grabbed a large sheet of papyrus and began scrawling upon it.

"But you're losing sight of the original vision. You want to let nature take its course, and we need it to take ours. After all I did study the anatomy very carefully." Njal protested, and he drew a careful sketch of the foot.

"That's the difference between a Mage and a Cleric, I suppose," Leander conceded. "You always work from human will and we trust nature or the Guardians. Even the Guardians interfere too much in most magic. You're much better to let the goddess decide."

"But nature is so often crude. Creation is littered with failed experiments."

"And she doesn't try to cover them up." Leander drew a number of quick sketches.

"True. But I was dealing with humans who trusted me with their lives. I couldn't leave them with a mismatched bodies."

"You concern yourself too much with individuals. You may be upsetting the balance of nature with those creations of yours."

"But you do admit my spell is sound."

"Oh, it's unbelievably ingenious. But I should certainly strengthen it here." He pointed to Njal's formula. "If you bolstered this incantation with a graft from a naturally webbed foot—say of a frog—you would make a more natural joining."

Njal nodded, and they continued to argue well into the night. By morning Njal had simplified and strengthened his formula and had persuaded the Druid to teach the revised version to the Acolyte he was sending to Sven's kingdom to teach the lore of the Goddess. "This spell is not really something a Druid ought to mess with, but I confess the creation of a new race of amphibian humans is fascinating. I shall watch their offspring with eager interest. I can't believe that a spell like this, based on illusion, can possibly breed true, but Gaea is capricious, and I shall add my prayers to your incantations."

Grimbolt closeted himself for hours with Lord Septimus, meticulously going over every grain of news which his Lordship had gleaned during his exile. "I'm amazed at how intelligent Crabhook can be when he's pushed," the old man confessed. "There's no question he saved my life by chasing me out of the country, and he was absolutely right in sending young William to Quatch."

"Farsyte certainly saved my mother with that NULL MAGIC ZONE of his," Grimbolt added, "and Manly deserves to be ennobled for stringing laundry wires in the teleport room. The defeat of the Amazons in the north and the loss of three priestesses in the laundry room must certainly have slowed the Hegemony down a bit. But I swear there's going to be a shake-up in my High Council."

"Your mother will take it hard if you make too many revolutionary changes."

"Not if Nikky has his way with her. King Peter proposes to make her Queen of Zharkovia, and I think our canary is just the man to sell her the arrangement."

"I think she would hardly look with favor on marriage to so profligate a man as King Peter. Her views on chastity are very strict. After all she remained faithful to your father even after his hunting injury."

"Nikky says King Peter promises to give up his mistresses. If she gives him a son, he'll even make him Crown Prince over his bastards."

Lord Septimus sighed. "Too much 'if and when' for my taste."

"Well the fact remains: I shall be my own king, and Mother will have to make the best of it. Did your last messenger say something about William coming home?"

"Lord Crabhook's last messenger said Prince William came home with the new Ambassador from Quatch. It seems that King Roger is still hesitating about the alliance."

"I'll have to trust Catherine to hold her father to his word," Grimbolt mused. "She took me as the least disgusting of her father's candidates for her hand, and she's determined to get value for her bargain."

"His Majesty is only slightly less stubborn than his daughter, but I think she will probably have her will there."

"Well one thing is certain, we must get home as quickly as we can. The interim government has done amazingly well, but I don't want them tying me to the wrong policies."

When he located the Druid, Grimbolt found him giving final instructions to Morgan app Gwydd a fifth level Druid whom he was sending north to assist Sven with his farming and forestry.

"I understand the new tribe has settled into virgin land," Morgan said to Grimbolt. "Is it true that these people truly desire to live in harmony with nature?"

"They may not be as enthusiastic as you Druids are, but Sven wants someone trained in the ways of Nature to teach them the best way to preserve their woods and to cultivate their farms."

"I am taking with me a collection of choice seeds, several pairs of fish in tanks, and a pair of brown bears who will carry me on my way and then set up their home in the wild. I will try to teach Sven and his people the way of the goddess."

Leander blessed both the bears and Morgan and sent them on their way.

Grimbolt begged the Druid to hasten their departure, and Leander swiftly arranged the details. When Grimbolt's party was ready to depart for Arragor, they included a sedan chair for Princess Catherine supported by two long poles resting on the shoulders of a team of oxen. It was Handyman Greenthumb himself who went along to govern the beasts, so that the Queen-elect and the heir *in utero* could enter the capital in style.

XVI—Coronation

The journey with the ox team would take at least a week; therefore Grimbolt sent Lord Septimus ahead to give Queen Elsa time to prepare a public welcome for his Majesty King Grimbolt and her Majesty Queen Catherine.

His Lordship arrived on the second day and was immediately escorted to Lord Crabhook in the Royal Study. "You finally dared to come back?" Lord Crabhook sneered. "Just remember, I wear the Lord Steward's chain now.

"You have worn it with great credit. Arragor should salute you as savior of the realm." Septimus turned Lord Crabhook's challenge aside with his praise. "I have warned his Majesty of the danger from the Pythoness and come as his harbinger. You may announce to her Royal Highness that King Grimbolt approaches Arragor with his bride, Queen Catherine, and should arrive on the fifth day from today.

"His bride? The Crown Prince has married in the wilderness without even telling the Queen?"

"There is much news. I should be grateful if you could arrange an appointment for me to tell her Royal Highness his Majesty's instructions for the coronation."

"Because of certain magical perils, the Queen has taken up residence in the temple. I will inform her of your desire for an audience."

"Don't you think it's about time someone removed that necklace?"

"Lord Farsyte has been studying the circ to make sure in is not physically trapped t kill her Majesty if it is removed—even in a **Null Magic Zone**."

"Surely the Queen-Regent does not wish to remain imprisoned in the temple."

"Her Majesty has yielded to the judgment of her counselors."

"That doesn't sound like Elsa."

"Her Majesty has been rather impatient, but no one is willing to risk . . ."

Lord Septimus restrained himself from tapping his foot. "Will you please arrange for an audience at her Royal Highness' earliest convenience. I have vital news to impart."

"Her Majesty's High Council and he Queen will welcome you in the Royal Chapel tomorrow at the fourth hour." Lord Crabhook tapped a small gong on his desk to summon a messenger. "Escort Lord Septimus to the Garden Suite and make sure all of his needs are attended to."

"You need not trouble about a suite in the palace," Lord Septimus answered. "I have no official position in her Majesty's court, and I am anxious to return to my wife."

As an afterthought Lord Crabhook added. "Ambassador Feltran of Quatch is staying in the Purple Suite. Lord Feltran escorted Prince William back home only three days ago. He reports that King Roger is mightily irritated at the absence of his daughter and demands her immediate return so that he may dispose of her hand in more profitable fashion."

Lord Septimus paused in the doorway. "Please tell my dear friend Queen Elsa that her daughter-in-law is not only married, but pregnant. King Grimbolt has been diligent in his duty to provide the realm with an heir. Queen Elsa will, of course, choose her own time to inform Lord Feltran, but Queen Catherine's apartments must be suitable to her condition."

Lord Crabhook's jaw slackened as he watched Lord Septimus' back retreat into the corridor. As soon as Septimus had gone, Crabhook grabbed his cloak and set out for the temple. He found Queen Elsa still up and fuming about her necklace. There was evidence that she could throw her scepter with deadly accuracy even though it had no magic.

"Your Majesty, Lord Septimus has returned. I have scheduled an appointment for tomorrow morning, but there is news which you mast have immediately. Crown Prince Humber has married Princess Catherine in the wilderness and she is already pregnant. His Royal Highness intends to be crowned with the princess immediately—Lord Septimus carries detailed instructions from Prince Humber about the coronation."

Elsa dropped back into her chair. "Lord Feltran will have a fit," she exclaimed. "King Roger has already promised the Princess to Prince Schlarr of Grand Island, and this wild gesture of Humber's is going to throw negotiations into chaos. How dare he take such a step without consulting me?"

"Lord Septimus speaks of him as King Grimbolt already, your Majesty. I fear that he has dared a number of steps."

"And Septimus?"

"Seems very confident that Prince Humber is in charge."

"Did he ask you to return the Lord Steward's chain?"

"No, your Majesty, he showed no interest in claiming office, but he was much put out that I refused to scheduled his appointment before tomorrow. He seemed to think you should see him immediately."

"I'm sorry you delayed things. His news won't wait." She banged her scepter on the on the table beside her. "I have to face Lord Feltran again tomorrow, and I don't know what I'm going to tell him. Did Septimus seem to be in health?"

"Well rested and very confident, your Majesty. His visit with the Druid has been good for him." He flinched at the joyful smile that flashed across Elsa's face. "I fear, however, that Lord Septimus is plotting something. He seemed very smug."

"Lord Septimu usually has plans." She mused happily over her old friend's practical confidence in the face of problems. "I shall be happy to see him."

"Pardon, your Majesty, but I thought I had been a satisfactory Lord Steward."

She suddenly wished she could like this man who had served her so faithfully in crisis. She tried to smile affectionately at him. "You have saved both my life and my realm, and we all owe you a deep debt of gratitude, Lord Steward. Nothing can take that from you. My joy to see my old friend takes nothing from your glory."

Lord Crabhook brightened at her words, but he still envied the warm affection the thought of Septimus brought to her face.

"Can you stall Lord Feltran until after my meeting with Septimus. Perhaps you could hint at the importance of the news from the north."

"Perhaps I should hint that the news is of the Crown Prince's marriage. That would force him to seek new instructions from Quatch. Your Majesty ought to have several days of peace while King Roger is making up his mind how to deal with the fact of the marriage."

"Thank you, Milord, I should be very grateful for any breathing time you can win me." Her smile showed such genuine appreciation that his Lordship straightened up with his accustomed self-importance as he bustled out of the room on his errand.

Before he retired for the evening, Lord Septimus sought out Archibald Harper, who greeted the old statesman enthusiastically. "You have been sore missed, Milord," said the young Seneschal. "Bodvarka nearly took the kingdom away from us."

"You, Manly, and Lord Crabhook managed things very well."

"And Lord Farsyte with his **Null Magic Zone**," Archibald added. "Frankly I was amazed at Lord Crabhook. Most of us thought he was a useless old busybody, but he really came through in the crisis. He had the ambassador completely fooled with that pompous idiot act of his."

"He has proved himself a stalwart prop to the throne." Septimus agreed. "It's a shame he is so difficult to like."

Young Harper poured a cup of tea for his senior and they settled into comfortable chairs. "What can I do for you? You look like a man with something on his mind,"

"I need a tool for quickly cutting through a thin piece of metal in a crowded space."

"Her Majesty's necklace?" Archibald's quick insight amused Septimus.

"Exactly. She cannot function—she probably can't even think straight—with that death-dealing circ around her throat. Everybody's so scared of the thing they don't dare cut it off even in the **Null Magic Zone.**"

"We're all afraid it has a mechanical spring which will jab those knives out even without magic."

"Queen Elsa doesn't agree with you, does she?"

"No, but she can't do anything at the back of her own neck."

Septimus drained his cup and held it out for a refill. Can you find me a tool? If I cut the circ and you pull it off very quickly, no spring can act fast enough to do harm. Frankly I don't believe there are any springs. I think you've let that priestess make fools of you, but we must get that thing off before the Queen goes mad with frustration."

Young Harper chuckled. You have described a tool which I use for cutting strands of the wire fences we sometimes use to keep a bull fenced in. We've learned that a bull can break a wall just by running his bone head into it often enough, so someone came up with the idea of a wire fence which will flex and hold when he hits it and at the same time give him a painful cut when it stops him. Even a bull learns after a while." He went into his workroom and came out with a long handled cutter. "This thing ought to snip through whatever the circ is made of."

"Have you anything I can practice on?"

"I have some pretty strong pieces of wire in my workroom."

"Good. Make about a dozen loops about the same size as the circ, and twist one around your neck."

Even the first time, Septimus cut through the wire at one snip. After six tries he could do it very quickly without damaging the back of Archibald's neck. Before he started on the last six loops, he directed Archibald to yank the loop downward on command. By the time they got to the last three loops, they had the timing worked out exactly for a safe removal.

"Good," said Septimus. "Tomorrow you will accompany me when I visit the Queen Elsa. I will explain and get her permission to cut the circ while you pull down from the front. If I know my queen, she will be eager for us to do it. You had better carry the cutter, since the guards might argue with me about taking anything so lethal looking into an audience. They'll never question you because you're always running around the palace with odd equipment."

The next morning at the fourth hour Lord Septimus and Archibald Harper presented themselves at the door of the Queen's retreat in the temple. Elsa flung herself across the room to embrace her old friend. "Oh Septimus, it's so good to see you again." She backed off an gazed at him. "Crabhook was right, you do look rested, you lazy slacker. Here we are sweating blood trying to keep the realm from falling apart, and you waltz up without a care in the world."

"Well we're going to remove one care right now. Archibald and I have been practicing, and we're going to snip off that bauble you insisted on taking from Bodvarka."

She grabbed the circ defensively. "Everybody says it's trapped."

"You are surrounded by a bunch of timid ninnies. In the first place that thing is too small for an efficient mechanical trap. In the second place Archie and I have practiced till we can whip it off before anything non-magical has time to go off. Now are you going to sit there and let us work or are you going to be scared of that thing for the rest of your life?"

"Now that sounds like my Lord Septimus." She grinned at him nervously and sat down in the straight chair he had indicated. Young Harper knelt before her and grasped the circ firmly in both hands.

"Now I am going to snip and yell. When I yell, Archie is going to pull down on the circ. You aren't going to feel a thing."

She set her mouth and stiffened her back bone. "Do it."

It took but a second for Septimus to sever the circ, yelling to Archibald as he cut. The young Seneschal whipped the circ clear of her neck, and Queen Elsa burst into tears of relief. Septimus immediately turned, grabbed the circ from Harper, and raced to the window which opened above the temple moat. He thrust his arm outside, and dropped the severed circ.

"Hey! Stop!" shouted the queen, jumping up to stop him. "The gems in that . . ."

Her protest was cut off by a massive explosion which shook the temple to its foundations, shattering the glass in those windows which were glazed and upsetting pleasure boats in the moat below.

His Lordship turned back from the window and explained, "Many powerful magical devices have a protection built into them which causes all their magical energy to release at once when the device is broken. I feared that as soon as anyone carried the broken circ out of the NULL MAGIC ZONE, it would produce a devastating explosion of magical energy. I thought it prudent to release the energy outside the temple."

"You might have warned me," the young Seneschal growled. "After all I am charged with protecting the city's buildings from damage or destruction."

"I'm sorry, but I wanted to get rid of that thing before it exploded. Somebody might have been tempted to try to save the gems." He looked meaningfully at Elsa, who said nothing. He turned to Harper. "While you're inspecting for damage, you might look around to see if anything valuable survived the blast."

"You're right. I need to inspect. I hope nobody was killed."

"I hope somebody is fishing those people from the boats out of the moat. I didn't really look too carefully when I threw the circ away." Septimus turned his attention to the queen as Harper marched out of the room. "Are you going to see Ambassador Feltran here, or shall we adjourn to the palace?"

"It had better be here. That's where I scheduled the audience. I would feel more comfortable in my own study, but any change would ruffle Lord Feltran even more." She looked carefully in the great pier glass on the wall and adjusted her neckline, examining her throat for possible scars. "Did the blades snap out when you cut the circ?" she asked.

"No, the only trapping was magical, and as soon as the circ dropped out of the NULL MAGIC ZONE all the magical traps took effect at he same time."

At this point the High Priest flustered in. "Is everyone all right? There was a horrible noise outside. Did you see what happened?"

"I'm afraid I caused what happened," Lord septimus confessed. "Young Harper and I removed the circ from the queen, and it blew up when I tossed it out the window. Harper is out inspecting the grounds now."

Lord Forsyte looked at Queen Elsa and sighed with relief. "At last you are free. I suppose we can let the NULL MAGIC ZONE lapse, now that the circ is gone." He dithered about the table, tut-tutting about the scepter scars and adjusting the cloth to cover the worst of them.

"You will stay, I trust, to support me when Lord Feltran comes," her Majesty settled back onto her chair. "I feel totally unprepared for his appointment."

"I shall be happy to support your Majesty. Has anyone arranged for refreshments?"

"Great Guardians no, and I feel desperately in need of tea." She whacked a gong that hung at the head of the table.

When the messenger appeared, the High Priest dispatched a him for tea, turned from the door, and rearranged the chairs around the table. Septimus sank into one of them "Let me summarize the news for your Royal Highness. I believe you have not been told that the Great Druid has restored King Grimbolt's memory and has done what can be done to civilize his appearance. His Majesty will never resemble Prince Humber, but his features are less ursine and quite regal. He will always retain the heavy fur which the priestess put upon him, and his attire is, therefore, unconventional."

"You mean he still won't wear a blouse?"

"I fear so."

Queen Elsa sighed. "But Lord Crabhook said he has married Princess Catherine."

"He and the Queen apparently came to some sort of agreement in the northern wilderness, and they were married by a local chieftain. Furthermore, by the time they reached the Great Forest, Lady Miranda declared that her Majesty is with child."

"Lord Feltran will have kittens all over the room."

"I fear that Lord Feltran will have to send to Quatch for new instructions. King Roger will not be amused."

"Well, that is something of a relief. I suppose I shall have to send a personal representative to pacify him."

"I think, your Royal Highness, that his Majesty has already made plans for that contingency."

"His Majesty?"

"I know this comes as something of a surprise, but King Grimbolt has already assumed authority. He has provided me with detailed instructions for his and Queen Catherine's coronation; he has indicated major changes in the High Council; and he has forwarded orders that the Royal Apartments are to be made ready for himself and the queen. I fear that he will designate his own personal representative to King Roger and that his message to his father-in-law will be peremptory. I am afraid I must inform your Royal Highness that the Regency is at an end."

Queen Elsa was so taken aback that she did not even reach for her scepter.

"Dear Elsa." Septimus spoke with the gentle intimacy of long friendship. "We have labored for this moment ever since his Majesty was murdered. The rightful heir has returned stronger than you can imagine. Our struggle has succeeded beyond our most optimistic dreams. Your son has survived a maturing struggle that would have destroyed most men. He will be a magnificent king, and we must get out of his way."

She dissolved into tears, and Septimus struggled from his chair to place his arms around her. "I know it's hard to give up authority. I confess that I ache to see Crabhook wearing my chain of office, but this is your dear son who is going to be a great king. What more can you ask."

"But it's so lonely. I've been alone so long, and now my son is going to take everything and leave me alone in the Dower House. Ever since King Humber's injury, I've had nobody except the children. I didn't mind too much when he moved me out of the royal apartments, because I found I had to take charge of the kingdom as soon as I recovered from William's birth. Humber never picked up the reins of government after the boar slashed him. I had to move out of the royal quarters while he was bed-ridden, and I've lived alone since. At the same time I've got into the habit of signing documents and chairing meetings whole the king remained in his quarters or rode out hunting or wandered in the orchards."

"You could have married after the murder."

"You were the only man I could have loved," she confessed, "and you have Lady Constance."

Septimus backed away, startled. "I have always loved you, Elsa, but I've never thought of you in that way."

"I know. Even that loyal devotion has been a prop—not only a political support, but personal."

"But perhaps you might make another royal marriage?"

"Don't be silly. What young prince is going to marry a thirty-two-year-old queen-dowager?"

A tap at the door sent Septimus back to his chair, and Lord Crabhook escorted the ambassador from Quatch into the room. As he bowed to the queen and took his seat at the table, three acolytes came in with tea and cakes. When they were settled, Queen Elsa introduced Lord Septimus.

"Oh, we have met back in the days when you were Lord Steward." Lord Feltran seemed prepared to dismiss the former Lord Steward from the conversation.

"Lord Septimus has just come from the north with important news from our son—" She hesitated before she finally forced herself to acknowledge the truth—"from our son King Grimbolt, who will be returning in a few days for his coronation."

"I beg your pardon, Majesty, what has become of Crown Prince Humber."

"Lord Septimus, since you are bearer of the news, will you explain to his Lordship?"

Lord Septimus sipped his tea, giving the ambassador time to adjust. "When I left his Majesty two days ago he was already on the road home with her Majesty Queen Catherine." He paused to allow Lord Feltran time to choke over that news.

Finally the ambassador managed to ask. "What majesty? Did you say Queen Catherine?"

"When the Crown Prince returned from his travels and recovered his memory and identity, he proclaimed that he would reign under the name of King Grimbolt I, because his adventures had so transformed him that the name Humber no longer suited his new identity."

"But he has not yet been crowned."

"His Majesty declared that upon his coming of age, he automatically became king. He permitted the Regency to continue during his absence in the north, but has empowered me to declare that the regency is now at an end. His coronation is to be celebrated next week." Seeing that Lord Feltran had been reduced to speechlessness, Septimus continued throwing lightning bolts of information. "When King Grimbolt talked with King Roger several months ago, neither was aware that they were brother monarchs and that King Roger's instructions were not, in fact, valid. His Majesty intends, therefore, to send his personal representatives to the Court of Quatch as soon as his coronation ceremony is accomplished. He has, however, instructed me to inform King Roger through you that he recognized his obligation under the treaty of alliance between his father and King Roger to marry Princess Catherine of Quatch as his Queen. Therefore he empowered Chief Sven of the Tribe of the Liberated to perform the ceremony which united him and Princess Catherine as man and wife."

"You tell me that Princess Catherine has already married the Crown Prince?" Lord Feltran jumped to his feet. "How dare he without King Roger's permission."

"King Roger's permission at the time of the initial betrothal of the children was the foundation upon which we have built the treaty of alliance," Lord Septimus reminded him "If, in his haste to fulfill the conditions of the treaty, King Grimbolt has surprised all of us, your master should be gratified at his prompt fulfillment of an agreement which cost King Roger and me many hours of negotiation."

"I shall present King Grimbolt with a copy of the treaty as soon as he reaches the palace." Lord Crabhook interrupted. "I am sure he will sign the document immediately."

"And you are authorized to sign for King Roger," Queen Elsa added. "It will then be binding on both parties even before it reaches Quatch for his Majesty's confirming signature."

"But the treaty hasn't been finalized. There has been no formal signing. His Majesty is still weighing other options. This is most irregular." The ambassador collapsed in a paroxysm of bleats and throat clearings.

"I regret that Prince Humber has changed much from the accommodating young man who visited Quatch with his family before his ensorcelment," The queen tried once more to sound conciliating.

"But that is no justification for . . ."

"My dear Ambassador," Queen Elsa interrupted, "King Roger and my husband, King Humber VII agreed upon a Treaty of Amity and Alliance while the prince and princess were children. The Crown Prince assumed that King Roger is a man of his word."

"But King Roger abrogated that treaty after Prince Humber's disappearance and ordered his personal representatives to bring Princess

Catherine back to Quatch." Lord Feltran sprang to his feet, upsetting his tea over the table. "This whole proceeding is illegal."

"I am not empowered to negotiate for his Majesty, nor is the Queen-Dowager. I am authorized to inform King Roger through the person of his ambassador of the existing conditions." Lord Septimus smiled blandly. "His majesty's arrival has been unavoidably delayed by the travel arrangements dictated by her Majesty's pregnancy."

"Pregnant?!" Lord Feltran collapsed back into his chair. "The situation is impossible."

"Reality is never impossible. The facts are clear. The marriage of Princess Catherine to King Grimbolt fulfilled the conditions of the treaty of alliance between Quatch and Arragor. Therefore the treaty is still in force. Furthermore the marriage is being fulfilled in the expectation of an heir who—if male—is by treaty Crown Prince of both nations. I suggest that you inform his majesty of these facts."

Lord Feltran still sat stupefied when Queen Elsa rang for a messenger and instructed him to escort the ambassador to his quarters. She spent the rest of the day transferring her residence from the temple to a comfortable suite in the palace.

When, four days later, King Grimbolt's entourage approached the city of Arragor, they were met by a guard of honor headed by the Lord Seneschal Archibald Harper and escorted to the palace. A huge crowd of cheering citizens lined the streets, and Queen Elsa with the High Council welcomed the royal pair at the steps of the palace. The royal suite was spotless—radiant with flowers—and the guest suites for Alsenius and Njal were luxurious.

When he had seen the Queen Catherine comfortably settled in the royal suite, King Grimbolt dressed himself in his crown, his most massive gold chain, his gold-embroidered scarlet kilt, and his most ornate, but comfortable, shoes. He then indicated his intention to hold an audience in the Throne Room.

A step below the king's broad throne seat and to its right sat Queen-Dowager Elsa. On the same level to the left was Prince William's seat. Two steps lower were empty chairs for the High Council. As soon as King Grimbolt mounted to his throne, his mother and brother faced him and knelt. He embraced and kissed each of them, and they returned to their places.

At the foot of the throne steps the Herald announced, "The king summons his High Council. First Minister of State—Duke Septimus."

Septimus, clad in new ducal finery, climbed to kneel at Grimbolt's feet.

"In gratitude for long and faithful service to the crown, we hereby elevate you to the exalted rank of Duke of the Realm and First Minister of the High Council." He raised the new duke to his feet and embraced him. "Dear Septimus your wisdom has preserved the kingdom through its long night. May it continue to grace us in this dawn of a new reign."

Duke Septimus carefully descended and took the center chair of the High Council.

"The king summons Lord Crabhook—Lord Steward of the Realm."

"We confirm the Queen-Dowager's appointment of the Lord Steward to the High Council." Grimbolt raised Lord Crabhook and embraced him. His Lordship stifled the sneeze which afflicted him as his nose encountered the royal pelt, and he took his place at Duke Septimus' right.

Next came Archibald Harper's elevation to Lord Archibald—Lord Seneschal of the Realm. He took his seat at Duke Septimus' left. Here the king once more confirmed his mother's appointment.

The next two appointments augmented the Council to five members. Lord Farsyte was confirmed as Lord High Priest of the Realm and took his seat at Lord Crabhook's right. The elevation of Manly to Lord Manly—Lord Marshall of the Realm—surprised everyone.

The Herald now stamped three times with his staff. "The assembled liegemen and women of the realm will now kneel in homage to our rightful lord—King Grimbolt, son of King Humber VII." The Herald turned and joined the assembly in kneeling.

King Grimbolt stood and extended his arms over the crowd. We, Grimbolt I, accept your homage and confirm your rights as citizens of Arragor. We rejoice in your loyalty and we pledge ourselves to rule with equity, humanity, and love. Your safety and welfare is our charge We shall to the best of our ability judge with justice, legislate with wisdom, and listen with humility. The Guardians bless and keep my people of Arragor."

The assembly arose and responded, "The Guardians bless and keep the king and people of Arragor."

It was at this point Grimbolt intended a brief address and the introduction of the ambassadors from Quatch and Zharkovia, but as he stood waiting for silence, a messenger dashed through the crowd and up the throne step to present him with a note. A frown of annoyance crossed his face—well hidden by his beard. He hesitated for a few moments to calculate; then he smiled broadly and extended his arms to the people. "My friends, we had thought to postpone this news until you had time to become accustomed to a new king and a new High Council, but good news perhaps should not wait. Our journey from the Great Forest has been long and arduous, and we judged that our dear wife—your new queen—should not bear the added fatigue of this meeting. We are now informed that her Majesty has mustered her energies and is at the doorway waiting to meet her new subjects. You have, we are sure, noticed that our throne is unusually broad. We now have the pleasure of introducing you to her who shall share this throne during our reign. We order the Lord Herald to summon to her place on the throne Her Royal Majesty Queen Catherine of Arragor—born Princess Catherine of Quatch.

"The king summons Queen Catherine to approach the throne." the Herald intoned, and through the double doors of the throne room four footmen carried an open sedan chair in which her Majesty rode in a magnificent gown of scarlet embroidered with gold which perfectly matched and far outshone her husband's kilt. The bearers ascended the throne stairs; then the queen gracefully stepped out and knelt before her husband to pledge her fealty. He raised her to her feet, embraced her, and gestured her to the left side of the great throne chair.

"We give you Queen Catherine of Arragor!"

The crowd burst into applause, at which Catherine stood gracefully and curtsied. From his seat on the main aisle Lord Feltran rose in fury and stormed down the aisle. Elsa stood and warned Grimbolt, "It's King Roger's ambassador."

His majesty grinned with mischief as he stepped forward on the throne platform and extended both arms to the approaching rage. "We see the Ambassador of Quatch approaching. Even without summons, come up and let us embrace our royal father-in-law's representative. Bring him to my arms that I may salute our noble ally."

Lord Feltran found himself borne up the steps in the Herald's grip and practically flung upon the hairy bosom of the king, whose bear hug deprived him of breath; then the king passed him to Queen Catherine, who promptly stopped his protests with a resounding kiss.

"We welcome the blessing of our dear father and long for the time when we can embrace him in person." Grimbolt took the ambassador back from Catherine, hugged him very thoroughly, and passed him to the Herald who practically carried him down the steps and out of the hall.

Since the audience was still enthusiastic, Grimbolt continued in an informal vein. "Having welcomed the ambassador of our father-in-law and brother monarch King Roger of Quatch, let us summon the Personal Representative of our mighty ally King Peter of Zharkovia. Herald summon our dear friend and trusted companion Lord Nicholas of Zharkovia.

King Grimbolt's embrace was gentler and Queen Catherine's kiss was far tenderer as Nicholas greeted his old friends.

After a few moments Grimbolt gestured with his right hand, and the scepter produced the overwhelming tone of a great gong. "My ministers inform me that I am to be crowned Grimbolt five days hence, and my dear wife—Queen Catherine—will be crowned immediately afterward." The company roared approval.

The scepter gonged for silence again as Grimbolt returned to his chair. "I proclaim my gratitude to my courageous mother who has heroically held the kingdom together since my dear father's murder by the Priestesses of the Pythoness. I give you Queen Elsa the Magnificent." He gestured toward her and seated himself, leaving the floor to the Dowager Queen Regent.

Even though Queen Elsa scrupulously referred to her son as The Crown Prince and to herself as 'we,' she graciously acquiesced in the inevitable. At last she dismissed the assembly and led the royal procession around the city. She and Grimbolt mounted palfreys and Princess Catherine took her place in her gorgeous sedan chair. The court transformed itself into a magnificent parade through the city which finally returned, exhausted, to the palace.

During the banquet which followed, they could at least sit down and allow the musicians to entertain. Lord Septimus and other dignitaries rose periodically to propose the toasts. Grimbolt and Catherine were expected to lead the first dance, giving the Crown Princess a chance to display her gorgeous court gown and her graceful footwork. Grimbolt provided a formidable anchor for her performance.

Immediately after the assembly in the Throne Room, Lord Feltran sought out Wizard Quackenthorp to establish a magical conference with King Roger.

"You say that hairy brute I sent as an emissary with the black man is now king of Arragor?" His Majesty looked unsettled.

"And what's more, your daughter appeared publicly with him and affirmed that she is his wife."

The king's profanity was eloquent and imaginative.

"King Grimbolt insists that I must ratify the treaty of alliance in your name tomorrow morning. He has scheduled his coronation along with Princess Catherine's for the end of the week. What must I do?"

The extreme expense of the magical meeting forced King Roger to rapid decision. He was not unhappy that the alliance was at last to be ratified, though he regretted the lost opportunity to be obstructive and then reluctantly magnanimous. He had been maneuvering for protracted negotiations, but they were suddenly ended. His mouthing of expletives required no thought and provided the delay he needed for decision. "You say Princess Catherine has publicly confessed to the marriage?"

"There is no doubt about the marriage. There is not even a possibility of annulment. The brute has publicly announced that his queen is with child."

"So short of going to war and leaving ourselves open to the Hegemony, we have no choice but to implement the alliance."

"No, sire."

"Then sign the damned treaty and stop wasting my money on magic." His Majesty gestured imperiously to the image of Quackenthorp that the magic was to stop."

The next morning King Grimbolt summoned Lord Feltran to meet with the High Council to ratify the treaty. While they waited for the Quatch ambassador Grimbolt heard reports.

"The coronations are scheduled four days hence," Duke Septimus said. "I assume there will be no need for a second marriage ceremony."

"For the queen to carry her child to the wedding would be an invitation to scandal," said Grimbolt. "We have the testimony of Chief Sven and the entire Tribe of the Liberated as well as Njal and Alsenius that the wedding took place before the consummation. It is important to establish that the child was conceived in wedlock."

Lord Feltran was introduced and the treaty document appeared upon the table. When he attempted a last protest, Queen Elsa silenced him: "King Roger's demand for the princess' release was based on the false assumption that Crown Prince Humber was no longer available. We wrote his majesty of the Prince's restoration and of our plans for a prompt fulfillment of the conditions of the alliance. You must have departed

Quatch before our letter arrived. We assume that you have by now received new instructions. Since it is desirable that Queen Catherine's coronation should immediately follow her husband's, it is proper that the Treaty of Amity and Alliance should be in effect before the coronation. You of all people should be aware of the breach of protocol which could result if King Roger were not at peace with his daughter."

As the summoned witnesses took their places by the desk, young Harper remarked to Lord Bascom, the senior attache to Lord Feltran, "I admire Lord Feltran's shrewdness in persuading our Queen to sign the treaty. She has questioned both to the treaty and to the marriage. I wonder that she could be brought to sign so quickly."

As was intended, Lord Feltran overheard the remark and noted his colleague's sage nod. Such praise from a foreign dignitary reassured him of his own importance, and he plastered a conspiratorial smirk over his face as he confronted the treaty.

King Grimbolt signed with a flourish, and the witnesses confirmed that he had signed. Lord Feltran's smirk broadened as he spread his bold, clear signature over twice the area of parchment devoted to the king. As a result, his witnesses had to squeeze their confirmations into a very small space at the bottom of the page.

As soon as the document was signed and the seals affixed, Lord Harper grabbed a bottle of wine and poured tumblers for the signers while Lord Crabhook signaled from the window that drums should sound and fireworks should proclaim to the countryside that the treaty of amity was signed.

The next day Lord Nicholas presented a formal document offering a treaty of Amity and Alliance between Zharkovia and Arragor to be cemented by the royal marriage of King Peter and Queen-Dowager Elsa. The king enclosed a portrait of himself and a solemn commitment to abstain from concubinage for the first five years of the marriage. King Peter also promised that the first son of the marriage should be Crown Prince of Zharkovia and that all children of the marriage should take precedence over King Peter's princes out of concubines.

"I notice he doesn't promise to declare them illegitimate," Elsa objected, as she studied the portrait. "How recent is this picture?"

"It is a very recent portrait," said Lord Nicholas. "He was sitting for it when I left on my current mission. Part of my assignment was to observe your Majesty to determine whether you would indeed be a fitting consort for my master. When I reported that your Majesty is both beautiful and intelligent, King Peter instructed me to study you as a serious candidate."

"Humph! You've been taking my measurements ever since you came here."

"And you found my mother a suitable consort for his Majesty?" asked Grimbolt.

"I assumed that her Majesty was about 14 when she married King Humber, that you were born within the first year of that marriage. That would place her age at about thirty to thirty-two, giving her another seven or eight years of child-bearing potential."

"Actually, I am only seventeen, and my mother was thirteen when I was born," Grimbolt volunteered. "My brother arrived two years later, and it is believed that an injury to my father's stones explains why I have only one brother."

"Now wait a minute!" Elsa interrupted. "I will not have my son hawking his mother on the marriage market. Why should I leave my home and family to go off to Zharkovia and start having babies again."

"Because your Majesty is still a young woman," snapped Lord Crabhook, "and Lord Septimus—the only man around court for whom you have any real affection—is happily married."

Septimus glared at his Lordship.

Grimbolt picked up the argument. "Most of the time since Father's death you have been Queen-Regent. Now that I am King, you are going to be colossally bored. I have no intention of letting you run the kingdom while I strut in my uniforms and butcher venison. I shall both reign and rule, and my wife will be the partner of my reign. You will fret in the dower castle and resent me because I won't let you run things. You'll either make a fool of yourself with a young lover or drive me to distraction with your meddling—probably both."

"That's a terrible thing to say to your mother!"

"But it's true. Remember I have become a different person from the boy you knew. My change of name is no mere caprice, it is a recognition that the biddable boy, Prince Humber, is as dead as Father. I have rowed a barge, wrestled with brutes, traveled the world, bedded powerful women, and borne the agony of a blanked memory in a transformed body. I do not need and will not tolerate a regent. You are my mother and I honor you, but from now on I shape my life, rule my kingdom, and make my own mistakes. You are a stubborn, domineering woman with a short temper, and you won't enjoy watching me run things. Here you are offered your own husband to fight with, new children to rear, and a new court to take over."

"But I still have young William to bring up."

"My brother has proved that he is ready for a man's education. I don't know whether he wants to train for the army or the priesthood, but he must be trained as my right hand until he goes forth and conquers or marries a kingdom of his own. He'll break your heart if you try to clutch him to your bosom and smother him."

Elsa grabbed a heavy bronze vase and flung it very accurately at Grimbolt's head. He fended it off with the scepter, and it clattered across the room.

Duke Septimus rose from his chair and crossed the room to her side. "Dear Majesty, he has told you brutally, but he has told you the truth." He sat beside her and placed his arm around her shoulders. "The world is cruel to a capable woman. Everything—even the magic of the kingdom which only works for the king—conspires to take power out of your hands. Think of the possible advantages of this marriage. King Peter is a man of proven virility, and he promises to devote that strength to your service. You will be Queen. Your husband will reign, but you can influence."

"I suppose I must give the offer careful consideration," she conceded. "I'm sorry I threw the vase at you," she faced Grimbolt and added, "but you are a terrible disappointment to me. You were such a gentle, polite little boy—always anxious to please." She gave a little sniffle, but refused to let it take control. "I think I should withdraw to my chambers." She stood up, patted Duke Septimus on the head, and started for the door. Nicholas intercepted her and handed her a packet wrapped in tissue of gold.

"King Peter entrusted this to me when I first set out from Zharkovia. He instructed me to give it to you if his proposal was delivered at court." He gazed searchingly at her, and then continued. "This whole business is pretty messy—proposal by proxy and having the proposal tied to an alliance. But I can tell you King Peter is really a very great man, and a very sensitive one. He understands music and loves it even as I do. He's not just a soldier and a politician. He is courteous and considerate, a man you can love."

"Thank you, Nicholas. He must have some good qualities if you can love him." She accepted the package and made a stately exit. She waited to open her packet until Therese had helped her undress, stowed her clothes, and tucked her into her great canopied bed. She opened it carefully so as not to tear the gorgeous wrapper. Inside was a magnificent cochineal-dyed silk shawl with a carved amber fastener and a substantial epistle. She adjusted the candle stand at her bedside and opened the letter.

Dear Queen Elsa:

Your reading of this proves that you are considering my proposal of marriage. You have seen my portrait; Nicholas has testified to my character; and you have not rejected me. There is no question that a marriage between us is sound diplomacy. It remains only to persuade you that my person and my nature are such that you may hope for a happy union.

I am a king and soldier; I am also a musician and a lover of beauty. My reputation as a womanizer can argue both for and against me, for it testifies to my capability as a lover and against my constancy. For this reason I have pledged myself for a five-year period to eschew concubinage. Of course if our marriage is congenial my pledge becomes permanent. Nicholas will testify that I am a man of my word.

May I offer a word of explanation for my record. For my twelfth birthday my father presented me with an experienced female slave named Athalie who instructed me very thoroughly in the physical arts of love. I now suspect that he took the trouble to train her himself—such is a father's love for his son. As a result I approached my marriage with considerable optimism.

My queen was delicately reared and came to me knowing nothing of organs of generation except that they were used for purging of wastes and were, therefore, nasty. When on our wedding night I presented mine in a rampant state, she was horrified and offended. She fled. The next day our High Priest explained the reproductive function of our organs and convinced her that children could be engendered by no other process than the merging of these organs. Unfortunately he said nothing of affection or pleasure, so that while she tolerated my intrusion, she permitted neither anticipatory caress nor amatory maneuvering. It is not surprising that our coupling produced neither pleasure nor off-spring. I confess my marital intrusions were few.

Elsa caught herself grinning at King Peter's plight. The man himself reached out from the formal rhetoric, and she began to understand his inconstancy. His 'rampant state' contrasted with her memory of her husband's rather proper approach. She even wondered whether her own dutiful responses might have contributed to King Humber's lack of fire. Suddenly a monstrous thought hissed at her. Had Humber perhaps become 'rampant' for some more responsive woman?

"Good heavens," she exclaimed to herself, "those night meetings of the Royal Council? His 'injury' while I was pregnant with Prince William? Could that luke-warm, proper politician have combined the hot blood and cool cunning to be 'rampant' on the sly?" She looked for something to throw. "Did that insignificant dunce fool me and the whole court?" Then a worse fear attacked her. "Could the whole court have known about it while I . . . ?" She blushed with scarlet fury. "He couldn't have made a fool of me. He hadn't the brains." She squirmed into several uncomfortable postures before she succeeded in turning her attention back to the letter.

Athalie's children were no problem. When they came of age I freed them and arranged for appropriate apprenticeships or marriages. On the other hand my affair with Countess Veronica caused a scandal. Her first three children passed for the Count's. He mounted her occasionally and asked no questions, but he took seven months to recover from a battle injury, and we could not explain young Igor, who arrived three months after the count's recovery. I suppose I should have had him executed, but I am not without conscience. He denounced the Countess and proclaimed me a lecherous tyrant. I gave him a province in the far northeast and acknowledged Prince Igor as my bastard. He took Veronica, who had begun to bore me, with him.

When my queen first learned about reproduction, she demanded that I abandon Athalie. I yielded to the extent of exiling my teacher to a comfortable tower on the far side of the capital where she could rear the children and entertain me more or less in secret. While I was distracted by the scandal over Igor, my wife succeeded in poisoning Athalie. I was grieved to distraction.

Scandal mongers spread the tale that I had the Queen killed, but the truth is that she died in childbirth. I was so furious at Athalie's death that I compelled the queen to submit to a proper mating before I exiled her to a tower. I suppose one could say that our coupling caused her death, but that was not my intent.

For several years after Athalie's death I despaired of happiness and opened my bed chamber to any woman of the court who wanted solace. The result was complete loss of reputation and serious neglect of my duties as king. I became enslaved to a skillful priestess of the Pythoness and alienated even my loyal subjects. What roused me was plot to overthrow my government. Two of my generals proclaimed Prince Igor as king, seized the palace and invaded my bed chamber during the night.

By a strange fluke of luck, I had quarreled that day with my priestess and was nested in Athalie's Tower with Adriana, the wife of one of the rebelling generals. As a result the priestess killed both of the generals with a spell. Fortunately she was so busy with them that some common soldiers who were sacking the palace overcame and slew her. Even her insatiability was not sufficient to satisfy the regiment's lust.

When the rebellion collapsed, I confined Prince Igor to the dungeons for a few months to teach him humility; then I married him to a whore and gave them a suite in the palace where I could keep an eye on him—a very entertaining eye, I might add.

Out of gratitude for my deliverance, I appointed Adriana as Royal Concubine and acknowledged Peter, who arrived a few months later, as my second bastard Prince.

Elsa shook her head in dismay as she pondered the man who used confession for seduction. "Well, at least he isn't sneaky." She thought again of King Humber's tepid love making and wondered what it would be like to mate with a confessed scoundrel. "At least he's 'rampant,'" she mused.

She closed her eyes and shuddered as she tried to visualize the rampant king. As she pondered, her thoughts drifted into dreams, and the letter dropped from her fingers.

It was late in the morning when Therese brought her morning tea and pulled aside the drapes and bed curtains.

"Important documents, your Majesty?" She gathered the scattered sheets and stacked them on the side table.

"How would you like to move to Zharkovia?"

"Zharkovia?" Therese slopped tea in the saucer and had to tidy up before she could present the cup. "Surely Prince Humber didn't take that vase so seriously."

"Oh, you've already heard about that." Elsa sipped and warmed her hands around the cup.

"Oh yes, Ma'am, everybody's heard about the meeting last night."

"I suppose the servants hear about everything."

"Pretty much, ma'am. Nobody pays much attention to us if we does our jobs right."

"And they know I throw things, so they stay on their toes around me."

"It ain't so bad now that Prince Humber has the scepter. We used to be scared to death when you was smashing statues."

"I suppose you heard all about King Humber's injury."

"Well of course, him being laid up all them months, poor man."

"But everybody knew just how far up his leg the boar's tusk gouged."

"Oh yes, Dr. Grendal was that worried."

"So you all knew that he wasn't crippled?"

"Dr. Grendal said he might have a little limp, but the tusk never got all the way."

Elsa felt her temper rising and carefully softened her voice. "So the wound wouldn't keep him from giving William a little sister."

"Oh no, ma'am, the tusk didn't get up to his . . ." Therese froze. "That is, ma'am, nobody thought . . ."

Queen Elsa sat up and planted her feet on the floor. "Everybody except me knew that the king escaped with his balls intact?"

"Oh, your majesty!" Therese fell on her knees and clasped the queen's legs.

Queen Elsa glared into the maid's eyes. "And those late night Council meetings?"

The eyes dropped as Therese whimpered, "He was always so hard working. Morning and night, day after day."

"Everybody but me knew he had a mistress even before Prince William was born. That mealy-mouthed bastard fooled me for years." She grabbed Therese by the shoulders and shook her ferociously. "You let him make a fool of me."

"We never saw nothing for sure," she protested.

"Oh, I'm glad you didn't stand by and hold his night shirt. Who was she? Was it one of my ladies in waiting?"

"Oh your Majesty, we never knew anything for certain. It's just that this priestess came and took a little cottage on the edge of the orchard and some of the men used to see his Majesty out walking that way of a night. We never knew anything."

The Queen shoved Therese to the floor and stamped past her to began flinging on her clothes. The maid crawled toward her. "Oh, your Majesty!" Queen Elsa aimed a kick at her and struck her toe on the brooch that held her gown. She grabbed her toe and hopped around the room cursing imaginatively. "Get out!" she screamed, looking frantically for something to throw.

Therese scrambled out, not even pausing to close the door. Elsa sank into a chair and glared miserably at the tangle of her clothes. Suddenly she realized that she was going to have to call Therese back if she was to make herself presentable, and she shredded her dressing gown with her fingernails and smashed the chair against the bedstead. Then she flung herself back on the bed and howled.

Half and hour later Lady Mabel entered the room to find out why the Queen had missed dinner. When she approached the bed the Queen awoke and glared. "Well, are you going to help me dress or not?" she demanded.

Lady Mabel disentangled the Queen's garments from the shreds of her dressing gown and began presenting them to her in order. "Your Majesty slept badly?" She deposited the tatters in the corner.

"I made some very disquieting discoveries." Elsa gathered the scattered sheets of papyrus from the bed and the floor, looked under the bed to make sure none were missing, and covered her nakedness. "You have no doubt heard of my son's plans to get rid of me."

"You mean King Peter's proposal? The servants all think it's wonderful. You'll be Queen in your own right."

"And subject to another damned man." She lifted her arms to allow a silken shift to rustle over her head.

"But what a man!" Lady Mabel arranged the under skirts in order and held the first for the queen to step into.

"A lecherous old fart with a wandering prick."

"Well, if gossip it true, there's enough of it." Lady Mabel looked furtively at the papyrus sheets. "Did he propose in writing?"

"Yes, and I'll see to it the servants don't get a look at it." The Queen grabbed the letter, wound a piece of ribbon around it, and shoved it into the hidden pocket in the bosom of her under-gown. "I've had enough of court gossip to last me a lifetime." She thought about King Humber's deception and blushed with renewed rage. She wanted to throw something, but found nothing heavy enough. Suddenly she stared at Lady Mabel. She crossed the room and grabbed her face, glaring at it. "How old ore you?"

"Almost fifteen, your Majesty."

"Just a little younger than my William. You look a little like him, but then again you're unusually dark. Who were your parents?"

"My mother was a widow who lived in a cottage near the orchard. Her name was Thespia. My father was killed in a duel before I was born, and Lord Harper arranged for Mother to have the cottage free of rent. It was Lady Harper who introduced me into court."

"You must know young Archibald rather well."

"He's been like a brother to me. Because of the Harpers, everybody always treated me like a princess."

"You may go." Queen Elsa restrained herself from pulling out Lady Mabel's hair, but the dismissal was not friendly. The thought that the widow Thespia in the cottage was probably Humber's priestess infuriated her. "No wonder you're so useful for trickery," she snarled.

"But . . ."

"Get out of my sight. I shall come when I please. If anyone is waiting for me, let him wait." she turned her back and stood motionless until she heard the door close. Then she exercised vocabulary which neither Duke Septimus nor her sons had ever heard from her. Presently she pulled Lord Peter's confession from her bosom and read his account of a servant girl for whom he apparently entertained real affection. When she became pregnant, he sent her to the country to give birth. Then he found her a prosperous husband and acknowledged the boy as Prince Justin in spite of his low birth.

"He's a damned scoundrel," she muttered, "but it's an honest letter. I swear he's a better man than that self-righteous prig, Humber. You know, I'm glad the boy isn't going to take his father's name. Serves the old hypocrite right. King Grimbolt I. It sounds like a lot to live up to. I suppose the Druid gave him the name." She stuffed the letter back into her hidden pocket and stared out the window. At last she stiffened her back, carefully drew on King Peter's cochineal shawl, strode to the door, and commanded the two sentries, "Escort me to the Royal Study and announce me."

In the study Grimbolt and Septimus were startled when a sentry opened the door with a formal announcement, "Queen-Regent Elsa." The Queen marched in and curtsied, just barely deep enough, to her son, nodded to the new Duke, and swept into the formal chair Grimbolt had vacated to pace the floor, leaving the Crown Prince to find another.

"Summon Lord Nicholas of Zharkovia." Her command would have felt more imperious if she could have slammed her scepter on the desk, but the scepter had deserted her.

"Have you come to a decision, Mother?" Grimbolt tried to be patient, but her hostile formality irritated him.

"We have."

"Might we hear some inkling of what you have decided?"

"You may not. We will permit you and the First Minister to hear what I have to communicate to Lord Nicholas."

"Mother, this decision involves the welfare of the realm. I insist . . ."

"When you are King, we shall obey you in all matters concerning the realm even as we obeyed your infamous father. While we are Queen-Regent we shall manage our own affairs."

"Infamous?!" Duke Septimus and Grimbolt exclaimed.

"Infamous, treacherous, deceitful, lecherous, venomous, and detestable!"

Both men shrank back from the vehemence of her denunciation. Duke Septimus suddenly realized that she must have discovered the 'Court Secret,' and he squirmed in his chair.

"That's what I thought. You were all in on it." She stood up and advanced on Septimus.

At this point the sentry announced, "Lord Nicholas of Zharkovia." Nicholas the impeccable glided into the room, swept his graceful bow to the Queen-Dowager and bowed more profoundly before the King-Elect.

"Your business is with *us*." The queen gestured imperiously to the floor at her feet, and Lord Nicholas—unruffled—transferred his obeisance. "Your master, King Peter, did us the honor of offering us his hand in matrimony—promising equal partnership in his throne and absolute fidelity of his person in exchange for our own obedience, loyalty, and devotion. The words which you spoke in his name, he has confirmed in this epistle." She drew King Peter's letter from her pocket and extended it to Lord Nicholas. He noticed that she was wearing King Peter's gift. "You acknowledge this as his Majesty's seal and signature."

"I so acknowledge."

"From this letter I conclude that, because of the danger of rebellion from his three bastard sons, King Peter dares not leave his kingdom either to woo or to marry. Is that correct?"

Nicholas disliked her phrasing, but deemed it unwise to correct her. "Your Majesty summarizes rather brutally the situation."

"Marriage, Lord Nicholas, as you will never know, is a brutal business. King Peter has confessed his scandalous past and has promised a reform which his advancing years incline us to believe."

His Lordship refrained from uttering the "Ouch!" of his mind.

"Considering the deception and corruption of our own court, we cannot vouch for the value of a treaty with Arragor, though to our knowledge our sons Grimbolt and William are innocent. If you will ally with Grimbolt despite this duplicity of his advisors, we are willing to accept marriage with his Majesty on the terms which he proposes. Since it is appropriate that we should be married from our own home, we stipulate that we shall marry King Peter's sword in the hands of his representative Lord Nicholas, in whose honor and good will we have come to trust. Lord Nicholas and appropriate guard shall then escort us to Zharkovia where, if his Majesty wishes, the marriage ceremony may be repeated *in propria persona*."

"I have received and will faithfully communicate your majesty's message to my Master."

"Do you need written confirmation?"

"Your Majesty's words are burned in my memory. I shall deliver them exactly." He turned and bowed to Grimbolt. "Does your Majesty authorize the marriage of Queen-Dowager Elsa to my master King Peter? Is your Majesty in accord with the proposed alliance between Arragor and Zharkovia?"

Grimbolt suppressed the temptation to laugh. "We are pleased to authorize our mother's marriage to King Peter, and we are delighted to agree to the alliance King Peter proposes, it being understood that the details of the treaty shall be negotiated in the near future"

"Have I your Majesty's permission to withdraw?"

Grimbolt grasped Lord Nicholas' shoulders and hugged him. "Nikky, lad, I don't know how you do it. You're as good at diplomacy as you are at singing and sleuthing."

Lord Nicholas knelt to Elsa. "Have I your majesty's permission to withdraw?"

Queen Elsa nodded and, glaring at her son, turned her back on Duke Septimus, and stalked out in Lord Nicholas' wake."

"Poor Nikky!" Grimbolt laughed. "He struggles so to keep our titles straight. What is he going to call Mother when I'm crowned?'"

"Probably he'll still use 'Majesty,' since she is Queen-elect of Zharkovia," Septimus responded.

Grimbolt took the ornate chair and gazed steadily at the duke. "Now, what is Mother up to? She's furious with you for something, and she isn't exactly affectionate to me."

"I would surmise that she has just discovered an old scandal."

"Well?"

"I fear she has discovered some things about your late father."

"Father? I always found him pretty stuffy. What on earth did he get mixed up in."

"As far as I can unravel the gossip, King Humber took a mistress some time before Prince William's birth. It is generally suspected that she was associated with the Hegemony of the Pythoness, though I never found proof. She was young, very beautiful, and very knowledgeable. The King was besotted, and we had great difficulty avoiding an open scandal. When the boar gored his leg while the Queen was carrying Prince William, he and his mistress circulated the story that his genitals were damaged so that he no longer needed to share her Majesty's bed. But even before that, he scheduled frequent night meetings of the High Council which he did not attend. There were also week-long hunting excursions in which his participation stopped at her cottage on the edge of the orchard."

"And Mother never found out?"

"Under his mistress' tutelage your father became a very accomplished dissembler. Of course all the servants knew. You cannot keep anything from servants, but he always maintained the pose of formal incompetence which covered all irregularities of behavior."

"And you didn't tell Mother?"

"My loyalty was to the King. Furthermore I needed to keep watch on the mistress to make sure she did no harm to the realm. So long as she remained only a royal indiscretion, I thought it unwise to upset the court with open scandal."

"But it did make Mother look foolish—the only one who didn't know."

The Harpers and General Bludger were determined to keep it a secret. All I could do was keep a watchful eye. Apparently King Humber wasn't completely infatuated. After all, the Priestesses wouldn't have killed him if they could have controlled him."

"You think Father might have outsmarted the Pythoness' crew?"

"They never got control of his magic. I believe they killed him because he wouldn't give up secret of the royal magic. They had to kill him before they could steal his ring."

"And even with the ring they still couldn't get into the private treasure room," Grimbolt agreed. "Incidentally we still haven't gotten Father's ring back."

"Which means you will not have access to his magic." Duke Septimus went to the door and sent the messenger for fresh tea. I suppose it's going to cost heavily to get it back. Did your father ever tell you the exact nature of the magic?"

"We were never very close. He did mention a fabulous suit of magical armor. He wore it once when he led the army against the Pigborn horde. Normally he let the generals do the fighting, but he told me took the field himself in that campaign."

"And distinguished himself among the kings," Duke Septimus added. "In his younger days your father was almost dashing. It was that campaign that persuaded the Draecian Empress-Dowager to offer him your mother's hand."

Refreshment arrived and Duke Septimus poured. "Did he say anything about the powers of the scepter?"

"He said the instructions are in the Treasury. Of course the Scepter tells me everything I need to know about its powers. I think there's also a magic cloak and a book, but as you know, Father paid little attention to me. He left me to the tutors."

Duke Septimus sighed. "Unfortunately his Majesty expected to live to old age. He kept a great deal of information about the realm in his head. Your mother and I had great difficulty finding out what secret agreements he had made with our neighbors, including the Hegemony."

"Was Father's mistress an Arch Priestess?"

"I think not. But she undoubtedly reported regularly to her superiors. I suspect she was a low-level priestess used as bait. All she did was keep him favorable and milk him of information."

"And since they decided to murder him, I would guess he wasn't confiding much. Maybe he was shrewd enough to trick them."

Septimus tapped a front tooth with his fingernail. "They still don't realize how closely the magic is connected with the royal blood. When at your birth your father carried you off to introduce you to the scepter and the ring, that ritual was essential to link the magic to your blood. Your mother deeply resented the ritual, but without it you would have been excluded from the succession."

"But I still need the ring."

"And until you introduce your heir to the ring and the scepter, no one but you can use the ring to open the Royal Treasury."

Grimbolt got up and began pacing the floor. "The priestesses must have figured it out by now. They must realize that they have to control both the ring and the king." He stopped in mid stride and glared into space. "And that means we can expect an ambassador from the Hegemony at my coronation."

"And she will have to bring the ring with her and try to ensorcel you." The duke leaped up and joined Grimbolt's pacing. "We must get Farsyte to load you with protective spells." He stopped and turned back toward the king. "You need to consult with your scepter. I'll wager it has some means of communicating with the ring. There must be some magical connection between the two artifacts."

The two men slurped tea and paced and plotted for an hour more. Finally Duke Septimus hurried out to supervise preparations for the coronation, and the king flung himself into a comfortable chair and struggled to extort more information from his scepter.

Despite the short notice a surprising number of neighboring kingdoms sent representatives to King Grimbolt's coronation. Even Draecian Emperor sent a ferret-faced courtier whom Alsenius recognized as Lord Sokos.

"How is Alexis?" he asked as they munched fish-roe on crusty bread squares.

"His Sublimity is in good health," Sokos replied, sounding as if he were divulging a state secret."

"And you, as father-in law are running things?"

"One affords counsel when asked."

"And the harem?"

"One no longer speaks of it. The Empress is most solicitous. One gradually finds appropriate appointments for everyone."

"And you come as an envoy of peace?"

"One comforts the Queen-Dowager. There are rumors of remarriage."

"Perhaps you're investigating her new alliance?"

"One observes."

"Queen Elsa was a Draecian princess. If she goes to Zharkovia, will she carry ties with the Empire?"

"One observes." and Lord Sokos vanished into the crowd.

Grimbolt's coronation was simple and brief. He shocked his mother by wearing nothing above his waist except a massive gold chain, and his kilt was relatively unadorned. The ceremony had been severely abbreviated. He marched along the aisle through the guests bearing the scepter in his right hand. He mounted the steps to the throne, placed the scepter on the seat and took from the table beside the throne a circlet of golden oak leaves surmounted by a single huge ruby. Holding the crown in both hands he faced the spectators, lifted the crown and placed it upon his head. Then he picked up the scepter, raised it in both hands above his head and stood motionless. There was a long hush while the audience gazed at the unadorned, athletic figure of their king. Suddenly a single adolescent baritone voice cried, "Hail King Grimbolt," and Prince William leaped into the center of the aisle. The crowd echoed with a roar, "Hail King Grimbolt!" The voice of Lord Nicholas rose above the shout in a rendition of *The King Reigneth*, and the crowd joined in the chorus.

King Grimbolt remained motionless as they sang. As he stood, a deep voice spoke in his mind. "Your are Arragor's rightful crowned king; the magic of the realm is open before you."

"Who speaks?" he thought in reply.

"The memories of your forbears speak through your scepter. After the coronation, you must go to the King's Treasury and anoint your body with the holy oil."

"Can I enter the Treasury without the Royal Signet?"

"Now you are crowned, we can summon the signet."

The anthem ended, and Grimbolt's address from the throne lasted only four minutes. For her coronation Catherine, unlike her husband, outshone even her mother-in-law with her gold embroidered silk gown and her tapestry cloak which required nine footmen to bear its train. Lord Nicholas sang an elaborate oratorio while she stood on the dais waiting fo her husband to descend two steps to place the jeweled crown carefully upon her elaborate coiffeur. Her lord and spouse descended to her level for the five minutes she was allotted to swear allegiance. Her throne chair was only one step below his and far outshone it in elegance, so that she held the attention of the spectators while the nobility mounted the steps to swear fealty to the new king.

Queen Elsa in gold lamé and diamonds knelt and pronounced her oath clearly. When King Grimbolt extended his hand to be kissed, it was adorned only with his personal signet. There was a perceptible pause before she applied her lips carefully to the ring. It was noticeable that she declined his gesture to assist her in rising. Prince William, resplendent in forest green and gold, swore the oath with gusto, grabbed the extended hand and kissed it, then sprang up and embraced his brother in defiance of all precedent. Grimbolt responded by clasping him to his chest and murmuring "Bless you!"

After the peers of the realm—beginning with Duke Septimus—had sworn fealty, the ambassadors followed, each offering congratulations after the manner of his own country. When the Priestess from the Hegemony of the Pythoness mounted the steps, Lord Farsyte knelt in a prayer for protection, and Njal surreptitiously cast a **DISPEL MAGIC**, but she made no hostile gesture. "Let us begin your reign in amity," she said as she curtseyed. Grimbolt noticed her intensity as her eyes strove to capture his gaze. At first he refused to meet her eyes; then, feeling strength from his scepter reinforcing his will, he returned her stare defiantly.

"Very alert amity," he replied. "I assume that your mistresses are observing everything through you. For the moment, you or they are withholding something that belongs to me. I should be grateful for its return."

"All things belong to the Pythoness."

"The Royal Signet of Arragor belongs to the king." Grimbolt reached out mentally to the scepter. "She has it?"

The scepter answered, "Yes."

"Can you summon it?"

"Speak the words I put in your mind."

Grimbolt surrendered himself to the scepter and heard himself pronounce, "I, Grimbolt, King of Arragor, crowned with the sacred oak leaves, armed with the Scepter of Destiny, summon the Royal Signet of Arragor." He stretched his left fist toward the Priestess and extended his ring finger. There was a loud sound of ripping cloth, and the Priestess cried out as the heavy gold ring tore the bosom of her elaborate gown, snapped the heavy gold chain which held it around her neck, and slid itself firmly upon the extended finger.

The Priestess shrieked in fury as she clutched the tatters of her dress and felt the blood flow from the back of her neck.

Grimbolt lowered his hand for her to kiss his ring as he said, "Amity is now restored between the Hegemony of the Pythoness and the Kingdom of Arragor."

She did not kiss the ring. She backed away from him, preparing to cast a spell. Njal started the gestures for another **Dispel Magic,** but the Priestess had misjudged the size of the throne dais and toppled backward down the steps to the auditorium floor. Two guardsmen helped her to her feet and rushed her from the hall where a temple priest ministered to her bleeding neck and one of the ladies in waiting ministered to her gown. The Priestess was conspicuously absent from subsequent celebrations.

While everyone was preparing for the coronation ball, King Grimbolt hastened to his chambers. He opened the secret door in his bedroom and strode along the hidden corridor to the massive golden door of the King's Treasury. He adjusted the crown upon his brow, extended the scepter in his right hand to touch the center of a jeweled crest in the center and pressed the seal of his ring against the impression near the right-hand edge. The door immediately opened and light filled the room. In one of the wall cupboards he found a vial of perfumed oil. He stripped off his gold chain and kilt and rubbed himself with the oil until his fur glistened.

"You are now crowned and anointed king," the scepter announced. "You will find a similar vial of oil for your queen. When the time comes, you will discover the oil for anointing your Crown Prince."

Grimbolt looked around the secret chamber with its comfortable chairs, its reading desk, and its cupboards. There was even a chaise longue which tempted him to stretch out and take a nap. In the wardrobe he found elaborate forest green robe.

"This robe functions as a highly magical suit of full plate armor which will protect your entire body without encumbering you. It also makes it more difficult for hostile spells to harm you." He slid his arms into the robe and found that it adjusted itself perfectly to his body. Using the scepter as a staff, he went through the motions of combat and felt the robe adjust to every action as if it were his own skin. He attempted the steps of one of the few dances he knew and once again the robe cooperated with every move. Presently he realized it was time to bathe and prepare himself for the evening's festivities.

King Grimbolt opened the coronation ball by dancing rather stiffly with his wife and then with the Queen Dowager. He made no mistakes, but he danced no more. Queen Catherine danced with everybody and eclipsed even Queen Elsa, who shone brilliantly on the floor. The next day began late, but King Grimbolt managed to accomplish a full day's work before evening.

The chapel had to be readied for Queen Elsa's marriage to King Peter's sword. Prince William began preparations for his state journey to Draecia to view eligible princesses. Alsenius, Njal, and Emma began their packing for the long voyage to rejoin Lord Ambloq. Queen Catherine put aside the festive wardrobe which would soon be too confining and began to prepare herself for the rigors of a winter pregnancy. When she learned that Lady Mabel was in fact her husband's half sister, she decided to plague Queen Elsa by appointing Dame Mabel Morley her Senior Matron in Waiting.

Grimbolt bowed his shoulders to the yoke of kingship: the interminable meetings, the inevitable state appearances, the labors of keeping up both his studies in the library and the exercise of his fighting skills.

When Lord Nicholas finally escorted Queen Elsa of Zharkovia to join and remarry her royal husband, Grimbolt embraced him as a friend and sighed with relief as the rival for his wife's affections finally departed.

When his mother finally stepped into her sedan chair for the long journey north and east, he could not quell a little song of gratitude that her long supervision of his life had ended.

That evening, as he sat in his study drinking scalding tea with Duke Septimus—bitter and earthy, without cream or honey—and gazed with satisfaction at the genuine Royal Seal on the wall and the old bronze and marble busts on the stands—he relaxed in his chair and observed, "One queen is definitely enough."

THE END

People in Grimbolt

Aethelstan—Moonflower's son, Sub-Chief and Shaman of Southmark
Alsenius F14—Companion of Grimbolt and Njal
Aspasia—liberated Pythoness Priestess 2nd
Athalie—Slave mistress who educated King Peter
Benbow—Sergeant-Major in the army of Quatch
Bengalus and Bengalia,—Tigers attendant on Great Druid Leander
Bengt, son of Evenstar—Follower of Sven, fetches the cache of star metal. Bludger, General—Army of Arragor
Blyte, Captain—Quatch Army
Blyte, General—Quatch Army
Bodvarka—High Priestess of the Pythoness and Ambassador to Arragor
Bottomly Ensign—Recreation Officer, Quatch
Briggs, Lieutenant—Quatch army officer charmed by a priestess.
Carla—Liberated Amazon. Mage 2nd, accompanied Bengt
Catherine—Princess of Quatch, promised to Crown Prince Humber
Chowter, Jon—First Amphibian, Tribe of the Liberated
Crabhook, Lord—Arragor courtier
Constance, Lady—Lord Septimus' wife
Dothokles—Prince William's tutor
Drusus, Mark—Senior Page in court of Arragor
Eccles—Ranger, guide to Lady Mabel's elopement party
Elsa—Queen Regent of Arragor, mother of Crown Prince Humber and Prince William
Emma Thorwaldsdatter—Njal's Amazon slave—later henchman
Farsyte—High Priest of Arragor
Father Ambrose—King Peter's chaplain
Feltran, Lord—Quatch ambassador to Arragor
Fiers, Captain—Prince William's military tutor
Flora—Aethelstan's betrothed
Gorchov, General—Commands the Markovian invasion force

Grendal, Sir—Court Physician, Arragor

Grimbolt—Amnesiac companion to Alsenius and Njal.

Handyman Greenthumb—Halfling Druid 5th, attendant on Great Druid

Harper, Archibald—Master of Guards, son of Lord Harper—Arragor

Harper, Lord—Seneschal *in absentia* of Arragor

Helmwege—Liberated Amazon, Jon's mate, 2nd amphibian

Humber VII—Murdered King of Arragor; husband, Queen Elsa; father, Princes Humber and William

Humber—Crown Prince of Arragor, son of Humber VII and Elsa

Igor, Prince—Eldest bastard son of King Peter and Countess Veronica

Justin, Prince—Youngest acknowledged bastard son of King Peter

Lars—Mist's son, Sven's brother

Leander—Great Druid, husband of Miranda

Mabel, Lady—Maid in Waiting to Queen Elsa

Mahla—chief of liberated Amazons

Manly—Senior Captain of the Guards—Arragor

Miranda—High Priestess of Gaea; wife of Leander

Miriamne—Amazon Liberated, converted to amphibian, apprenticed Mage

Mist—Sven's Mother

Moonflower—Sven's wife, Senior Judge of the Southmark

Morgan app Gwydd—Druid 5th, sent from Leander to assist the Liberated.

Morley, Rupert—Candidate for knighthood; promised to Mabel; expert forger and remover of seals

Nicholas, Lord (Nikky)—Castrato; Personal Representative of King Peter

Njal—Illusionist-12th; Companion of Grimbolt and Alsenius

Peter—King of Zharkovia

Peter, Prince—Acknowledged bastard son of King Peter

Phyllis—Cleric 1st, captured Amazon

Quackenthorp—Wizard 15th level and Head of the Guild of Mages

Reina—Alsenius' Amazon slave

Roger—King of Quatch

Scrubbs—Sergeant in Army of Quatch, Handkrieger

Septimus, Lord—Steward of Arragor

Smart, Kit—Senior Page in Arragor

Smedley—Guard at Arragor palace door.
Susan—Handmaid to Princess Catherine
Sven Mist's Son—Chieftain of Southmark
Tam, Brother—Acolyte under Lord Farsyte of Arragor
Therese—Queen Elsa's personal maid
Thespia—Priestess of the Pythoness, Lady Mabel's mother.
Tilda—Handmaid to Princess Catherine
Veronica, Countess—King Peter's first court mistress
Violet—Flora's mother
William, Prince—Second son of Humber VII and Elsa,

Books by Hugh Pendexter III

Poetry
    The Pantessey A mock epic on a pantie raid
    A Prosody Examples by the author
    Adventures and Venturers
    Poems of the Sacred
    Poems of Affection
    Academic Examinations
    Hail Suburbia!
    Doctor Faustus and other Poems
Children's Stories
    Tales of the Crocheted Cat
    Farhold Island
    The Crocheted Cat in Oz
    Oz and the Three Witches
    Ring Service
Novels
    Free Transport
Novels (Ambloq)
    The Fumbling Rescuer
    The Fumbling Kingmaker
    The Paladin's Rogues
    The Quince Quest
    Grimbolt